Suicide Squeeze

by Geoff Stamper

Suicide Squeeze

by Geoff Stamper

Wokabaut Publishing, Westminster, Colorado 80030

Printed in the United States of America
ISBN -13: 978-0-9791704-1-6
ISBN-10: 0-9791704-1-9
Library of Congress Control Number: 2007938451

Wokabaut Publishing
Westminster, Colorado 80030
www.wokabautpublishing.com

Suicide Squeeze
is dedicated to Dustin Stamper,
whose story I borrowed.

ACKNOWLEDGEMENTS

It takes a village to raise a book. Dustin Stamper, the mechanic, tried to fix the rattles and broken parts of drafts one through three. Kevin Stamper, the village doctor, revived drafts two and four by breathing life into Dred and Uncle Art. Ryan Stamper, our own private intellectual property attorney, correctly and consistently scrubbed drafts two through four with his left brain, even though the author's right brain stubbornly refused to budge on certain issues. Townspeople offering valuable insights included Mollie and Kristine Stamper (drafts two and four); Linda Cook and Mary Kay Bell (draft four); Mal, Mari, and Matt Stamper (parts of draft two); and Mary Lynam (one paragraph of draft four).

Finally daring to venture outside the village limits, we stumbled upon Bill Bruton. He not only read and edited draft four, but also provided inspirational counsel. More importantly, he connected us to Nino of Pero Designs who provided the technical expertise leading to production of this book.

Chapter One

Jamie was not yet thirty, not yet married, and not yet over his childhood infatuation with baseball. As his three decade milestone crept ever closer, he waited with his usual calmness, unaware of the tempest gathering on his blindside. He could not reasonably anticipate the mischief in the upcoming Seattle professional baseball season, as it was cloaked with innocent optimism like all the others before it.

Taking no notice that this particular opening day coincided with April Fool's Day, Jamie was devouring the sports page at lunch and looking for any detail he might have missed when he first read it at breakfast. His lust for April was only about all things baseball. His fidgety cousin was not content to watch Jamie eat and read. Matt waved his half eaten sandwich while he chewed, spitting out familiar words, "I had something really important to tell you but I can't remember what it is."

"Something about how you're finally working the Rob McPherson problem?" Jamie asked without looking up from the paper.

"No, Meatball, it's something a lot more important than that."

Jamie knew Matt would probably remember by the time they went to tonight's game and it would be nothing. Still it nagged in the back of Jamie's mind during the afternoon. His productivity continued to decline even as the clock granted him an illusion of extra time by dawdling through its rounds. Finally one last click of the minute hand released him to his cousins Matt and Adam and their father, his Uncle Llew. Together they headed to the ballpark that was conveniently just a short drive or long walk from their business south of downtown. The three young men were all taller, leaner, and better looking than their leader but it was Llew, the balding elder, who was clearly in command and setting the pace as they marched toward the stadium.

Mixing with the giddy mob as they poured through the streets, Jamie marveled at the cacophony of traffic, hawkers, musicians, and the boisterous few already laced with pre-game alcohol. Swept along with the throng as one nondescript pilgrim in this annual ritual, he was sheepishly eager to be stirred by the manipulations of a fancy electronic scoreboard and assorted mascots, both professional and amateur. The fans fed each other's excitement, the sum of their energy exceeding its parts. Unlike franchises that build passion to peak during September pennant races and October playoffs, Seattle was conditioned to exhaust enthusiasm at the beginning of each season when it was still possible.

Shuffling quickly toward the left field entrance, Jamie initially kept pace with his companions who would be sharing the company seats with him. They were all avid Seattle Mist supporters, generally blending in well with the home team crowd. However, this night Jamie allowed himself to be separated from the foursome when his cousin Adam began yelling at the union pickets, "You don't belong here, go raid a pension plan somewhere!"

"Sanford doesn't even have a pension worth raiding!" one of the AFW members barked back lightheartedly as he waved a sign that read, "Sanford Shoes Step on Workers."

The union barbs were aimed at the stadium sponsor, Sanford Safety Shoes. The Associated Factory Workers literature suggested in more heavy-handed language that the millions spent on naming the stadium could be better spent on improving medical and retirement benefits for the workers they would be representing in contract negotiations later in the summer. This informational picket activity, which an injunction would eliminate by game two, was a rare negative interruption in an otherwise overwhelmingly upbeat atmosphere.

Detouring around the excitement, Jamie missed an opportunity to buy a scorecard from his regular vendor positioned too closely to the commotion. Instead, a tall, thin man with a torn Chehalis High School tee shirt caught Jamie's attention by pointing directly at him and announcing, "I've got your scorecard right here."

Jamie's first instinct was to avoid any contact with this bedraggled hawker and his penetrating gaze. But he did need a scorecard and this man who resembled a Pioneer Square panhandler was waving one in his face. Forking over his two bucks, Jamie grabbed the card he was offered, glanced at it more closely than usual, and said, "Looks like I got your last one."

"Plenty more where this one came from, my friend."

Comforted by the familiar touch of the card in his hand, Jamie moved on with the flow of the crowd. Since he scored every game he attended, at least two dozen every season, he could save money by buying a big book of scoresheets. But he craved the ritual of picking up the individual game day cards. Ever since his late father, Marty, introduced him to his first glossy scorecard, Jamie loved the purity of the hieroglyphic code used to capture the entire game on one precise page. The touch of this card flooded Jamie with unexpected emotion as he realized this was his first one since his father died last October.

Jamie's earliest memories of his father were baseball memories. Marty began bringing Jamie to the ballpark when he was four years old. In those days, Seattle was struggling just to stay out of last place and they were lucky to draw 10,000 fans to a game after the opener. Once in awhile, a superstar opponent or an irresistible giveaway promotion would entice several thousand extra paying customers. But competition for parking spaces and foul balls was certainly less intense than in recent times.

Early in the very first game Jamie attended with his father, a foul ball sailed softly over their heads, struck the front wall of the mezzanine, and bounced back toward them on the ground level. His father had been perched in an aisle seat. He was a tall man, certainly he seemed like a giant to four year old Jamie. Marty used this height advantage to outreach the eager fans crowding into the aisle, plucking the prize inches above the multitude of outstretched arms. Although they came close a few times, neither Marty nor Jamie ever caught another ball at all the games that followed.

When his father turned the ball over to him amidst great fanfare and attention by all the people in the surrounding seats, Jamie knew something important had happened. A few innings later while Marty diligently worked on the scorecard, Jamie dropped the ball. Fans in the row below confirmed its value when they scurried to retrieve the trophy for him. He clung to that sphere desperately for the rest of the game, during the ride home, and indeed, slept with it for most of the following week.

Every season after the great foul ball capture, Jamie remained faithfully devoted to the Seattle Mist. He was not alone. Over the years, Seattle fans dutifully played the part of Charlie Brown, resigned to a lifetime of disappointment punctuated by false hope. Each Spring Training some new savior was touted, whether an expensive free agent, an imported shortstop from Japan, or a rookie sensation. Then Lucy would jerk that football and the free agent would slump through the season, the shortstop would limp off on his pulled hamstring, or the rookie sensation would be traded midseason for cash. Even though disaster showed up with predictable regularity, fans were shocked and outraged each and every time it arrived.

Perhaps overly blinded by preseason sun in Arizona, the Seattle sportswriters from the gray Northwest once again inflamed the diehard fans with sparks of optimism. Of course, this is a sacred baseball tradition, once perfected by Ernie Banks who loyally predicted a pennant every year for his hapless Cubs. But the Seattle writers were particularly adept at harvesting preseason enthusiasm from the players and team management, grinding it into newsprint, and serving it to Puget Sound addicts who were all too willing to consider the fantasy of a World Series in Seattle.

Although Seattle continually finished out of the money, in recent years they did so in a beautiful new stadium in heavily promoted style with endless diversions. Coupled with a runner-up finish every now and again, fans were teased into the park at double and triple the rate as in the days of Jamie's youth. On this opening night, the manufactured anticipation fueled Jamie, his seatmates, and most everyone else into vocal frenzy as early as the fourth inning.

"Can you believe that call?" Matt yelled above the din.

The anger would be better placed on Don Grant who had just grounded into a doubleplay, but it was much more satisfying to castigate the umpire who made the fairly routine call against the home team. The outrage escalated irrationally when the Seattle starter walked in a run in the fifth inning. Another umpire had joined the conspiracy.

"Make 'em earn it!" Matt screamed at the ump.

Again the complaint was better directed at the pitcher since the umpire was likely in agreement with Matt. From the arbiter's perspective, he was making the pitcher earn his strikes. But logic occupied no place in Matt's catcalls. He had the booming voice and he exercised it often. His more selective older brother, Adam, yelled only when he had something witty enough to share with the surrounding fans. Jamie, the biggest fan of the cousins, rarely did any screaming except as part of the roar of the crowd. Llew ceded the extracurricular cheering to his sons and it was hard to tell whether he enjoyed it or tolerated it.

"I just remembered what I wanted to tell you," Matt stage whispered to Jamie after his brother left for the restroom during the seventh inning stretch. "Adam sent a note to Jeffrey Anne and signed your name to it."

"What are you talking about? What did it say?"

"I don't know. But don't say anything to Ad. I don't want him to know I squealed."

As Jamie brooded for the half inning Adam was absent, Seattle players and fans exploded with frustration at still another adverse close call in an inning already burdened with two pitching changes. The fan frenzy galvanized Seattle's third base coach, Eddy "Zip" Duda. He seized the opportunity to flap his arms and emphatically tell the offending umpire, "You might've gotten that one right but some day when you do blow one, it might not be a good time for me to get ejected. Don't make me call you one of those words. Toss me now because I gotta take a leak."

The ump obliged and Zip's bladder allowed him enough leeway to take his sweet time leaving the field, savoring the attention of being a momentary local hero. Meanwhile Adam returned and was confronted by a furious Jamie.

"What's this about a note to Jeffrey Anne? You've gone way too far this time and whatever you said isn't funny."

Adam glared over at Matt, looked back at Jamie, and said, "Whoa, lover boy. I agree it's not too funny but I can't believe you are actually buying anything Matt says to you on April Fool's Day."

"Still not funny," Jamie managed to reply while barely hiding his relief.

Eventually all the accumulated outrage in the stadium gave way to the excitement of unexpected ninth inning back to back doubles by the bottom two players in the Seattle Mist lineup. Although the home team was down 5-2 entering the last half inning, many of those starting to leave early paused at the top of the exit ramps to peek back as spunky leadoff hitter Rudy Wink sauntered up to the plate representing the tying run. With one run in, a man on second, and the top of the order coming up, fans began to calculate and cling to the possibilities of victory.

"Wink hits a homer here and we're all tied up," Jamie pointed out as the opposing manager visited the mound to confer with his veteran closer.

"Yeah, he's only had like one homer in his whole career and when he hit that one, he was so shocked, he didn't know which way to run," Matt replied.

The pitcher remained in the game and with the help of his famous slider, he worked Rudy into a one ball, two strike count. Jamie and his three companions were now on their feet, ostensibly to root for Rudy but perhaps subconsciously to prepare for a quick post game shuffle out of the ballpark from their seats in row fifteen of section 139. Rudy took a mighty swing at a sinking offering and managed to barely top the ball down the first base line. The Oakland first baseman took the easy out unassisted at his bag as the runner advanced to third.

To outward appearances, shortstop Eduardo Escobar nonchalantly entered and ritualistically dug his cleats into the batter's box. But even as a veteran with twenty-nine homeruns last year, he could feel the nervous excitement of the hopefuls who were now screaming his nickname, "E2," at the exact intervals demanded by the pulsating scoreboard graphics. Well aware of the more potent danger E2 posed of tying the game, the pitcher worked too carefully and lost him with a slider that slid too far on a 3-1 pitch.

E2 rambled down to first, partly relieved and partly disappointed. The Oakland catcher made his way to the mound surrounded by the thunderous noise of stadium dwellers going berserk above and beyond the now superfluous scoreboard commands. Larry Thorne, an expensive free agent slugger acquired in the off season, stepped up to the plate and went about his own pre-pitch ritual. Despite over a dozen years of major league success, Larry was as eager as a rookie to erase the disappointment of a hitless performance so far in his inaugural game with Seattle.

The pitcher tried to keep the ball down to induce a double play but knew he could not afford another walk. So when he ran the count to two balls and one strike, his next fastball cruised in a little too high and a little too fat. Larry just missed getting all of the generous offering and drove it high into left field. As it became obvious that the ball would be caught just shy of the warning track, the initial roar of approval from the crowd was abruptly swallowed by nearly silent murmuring. In a moment, a more restrained cheer greeted the pinch runner who scored easily from third.

The Oakland lead was now cut to 5-4 but two were out. Although clean-up hitter Don Grant was still a formidable threat, long suffering Seattle fans could be excused for any wariness creeping into their enthusiastic chanting and clapping.

"Jamie," Matt said, "I'm telling you, your M's are gonna to blow it again. What did we pay ten friggin' million for, to get a washed up designated hitter, if Thorne can't put it out at times like this?"

"Hey, he got it close and over the course of a season, more than thirty of those are going out and if just ten make a difference, we could be fighting for a playoff spot. And whadya mean, *my* M's," continued Jamie, "I suppose you're an Oakland fan? I hate coming with you, you're so damn negative. Just watch, Grant's going to knock this one out and we win on a walk-off dinger."

"Oh right," Matt replied. "Are you sure he doesn't hit a 'dinker' to end this 'stinker'? I'm just so tired of these guys teasing us all the time. I wish they'd just lose 10-1, so we could relax."

"You're such a fair weather fan," Adam interjected.

"Then I guess it sucks to be me. Maybe I should move somewhere it doesn't rain every day, so I can root for a winning team once in awhile," Matt said.

"We are going to be a winning team," Jamie insisted. "Look, I'm so confident, I've already logged Grant's homerun in the book."

"Yeah, I notice you did it in pencil," Matt said as Grant prepared to address the first pitch.

Before Jamie could answer, a deafening joyous eruption rippled through the 35,000 remaining spectators as they witnessed Grant take Jamie's cue and line that first pitch just fair into the left field seats.

Chapter Two

Out of the corner of his eye, Jamie caught sight of the strange looking vendor from opening night. Jamie had just passed through the left field portal, returning both physically and mentally to the scene of last night's dramatic victory. Without thinking, he quickened his pace and scurried away toward the "toe" of a ballpark known to fans as the "Shoe."

Although the park only vaguely resembled a shoe, the three-tier grandstand stretched out behind homeplate like a high top heel. The outfield was deep to left and short to right and the stands sloped down to one level bleachers in the leftcenter field toe. The Sanford Shoe Company actually gave impetus to the nickname when they committed $60 million over twenty years for the privilege of formally naming Sanford Shoe Stadium. The investment seemed extravagant to Jamie since the Sanford name was already well known. More importantly, he didn't like paying extra for his shoes to cover this cost.

Even though Jamie cared little about stadium naming or any part of the business side of baseball, he was interested in more than just what happened between the foul lines. He was intoxicated with the sounds and smells of the ballpark. He liked to arrive at the Shoe more than an hour before game time just to savor the aroma of anticipation. He was especially eager for a new beginning as the M's warmed up for the second game of the Oakland series. Fan excitement would be high after the unusually delicious opening night win. Jamie purchased a scorecard from a more conventional vendor and sat alone, lost in the pre-game revelry, until just before the National Anthem.

"Hey, Meatball," Matt boomed from the aisle, "Since you correctly called Grant's homerun last night, I come bearing the most expensive brew you can find in all of Seattle."

Matt settled in his seat, took a swig from his beer, and announced, "There goes the first dollar down the hatch."

Before the first inning was over the two cousins were jumping to their feet to celebrate Larry Thorne's majestic three run homer. Jamie slugged Matt on the upper arm while shouting, "That's what I'm talking about, Thorne comes through big time! I told you he was going to make the difference in at least ten games. Another correct prediction I have provided for your enjoyment."

"Remember, we started two and zero last season and we ended up with another losing record," Matt said as he sat back down.

"Actually we had a winning record until we were eliminated from the playoffs and started experimenting with farm team players in the last two weeks. And we still finished with eighty wins," Jamie replied.

This was an argument Matt would love to lose but he conceded nothing, even as the M's built up a 6-1 lead by the fifth inning. While the ground crew whirled through their speed raking drill, he made a quick hot dog run. Upon his return, he nudged Jamie and said, "These bleacher seats aren't all that bad for a change. I'm kind of glad we couldn't get the company tickets today, although they are better than the seats we had last year."

"Yeah, who got them for tonight, anyway?" Jamie asked.

"Uncle Art's family has 'em, so I imagine some of the cousin posse is over there," Matt responded, adding a grimace.

"Why does that give you heartburn?" Jamie asked.

Matt directed Jamie to the real source of his concern by pointing at the mustard river dripping down the sleeve of the beige cloth coat hanging off the back of the seat directly in front of him. Matt quickly popped the last huge bite of his condiment sloppy hot dog into his mouth, wiped the incriminating evidence from his face, and glanced furtively from side to side. He leaned down with his napkin and tried to surreptitiously wipe the mustard off the coat without disturbing the owner or attracting attention but succeeded only in smearing the goo around in a bigger mess.

"What?" snarled Matt softly at Jamie who was shaking his head in genuine disapproval.

Despite his clumsy attempt at stealth, Matt attracted the notice of the elderly lady sitting next to him as well as the victim. Although the owner of the mustard flavored coat only swiveled her head part way around in response to the rustling and stage whispering, she did catch the glance of Matt's nosy neighbor and sensed something was very much amiss.

Against an extremely strong impulse to bolt for the aisle, Matt cleared his throat and leaned forward. While nodding toward Jamie's half eaten hot dog, Matt politely confessed, "Excuse me, Miss, we're very sorry but your coat brushed our hot dogs and I would like to pay for the cleaning."

The victim retrieved the coat from the back of her seat, surveyed the damage, and wrinkled her face in disgust while Matt fished a business card out of his wallet. He passed the card with sincere contrition, "We really are sorry about this. Please send the cleaner's bill to me at this address."

As the young woman studied his card, Matt was relieved that a dispute on the field was distracting most other onlookers. He was also surprised that he had not previously noticed the beauty of this woman, considering how close she was seated to him. She seemed to be with her parents and a teenage sister who was choosing to watch this interchange rather than the on field rhubarb. Suddenly the older girl broke the heavy silence, "Matt Tinkler of Tinkler Toilets? Is this some kind of joke?"

"We do light construction work and supply contractors with portable fences and toilets," Matt patiently explained with well-practiced smoothness.

Jamie and Matt were part of a large, contentious family in the portable toilet business, not a recommended career path for attracting women. Jamie knew the drill about telling people he was in the construction business. He didn't even use business cards but found that eventually he would come across as suspiciously evasive or would get a call at work where the receptionist answers the phone "Tinkler Toilets."

Many of the younger family members could excuse Grandfather Joe Tinkler for not changing his name or even for getting into the lucrative portable bathroom business. But some wondered how a man brilliant enough to build such a successful company from scratch could be so seduced by alliteration to stamp his life and the lives of his progeny with the label "Tinkler Toilets." More importantly, why didn't the next generation change the name? Sometimes the answer was the legal and practical hassle and expense of doing the paperwork and changing signs, stationery, and tradition. Sometimes the answer was the impossibility of this family coming to any agreement on a successor name. But mostly the answer was the feisty attitude of the family.

Certainly Jamie was grateful that his mother Jo had the good sense to be born Joe Tinkler's one daughter. Jamie's six cousins, descended from Joe Tinkler's two sons, were not as fortunate. They all suffered, but the boys in a male line knew they faced life sentences. The Tinkler moniker screamed for daily commentary from the witty, the unwitty, and the nitwitty.

The young lady shook her head with disdain as she shoved the business card into the right front pocket of her jeans. Matt began to wilt under the real and imagined stares of the people around him.

"Let's head over to the Home Run Café," he finally said to Jamie.

Jamie sat frozen for a moment, but wolfed down the rest of his dog and scrambled after his cousin. As they walked around searching for seats in the mezzanine bar and grill, the first two Oakland batters in the top of the sixth were busy accepting walks of their own. Finally Jamie and Matt pounced on two counter seats almost before the previous occupants escaped.

The Café was just inside the right field line. Jamie was still in a bit of a stupor when Matt put on his happy face and bubbled, "See, isn't this great? We never get all the way over here, away from our company seats. If we had binoculars, we could see who was sitting in those seats right now."

Conversation was interrupted by soft groans acknowledging the ground rule double that Oakland's cleanup hitter bounced into the stands just below the two cousins. Matt glanced at Jamie who just scowled.

"What's wrong?" Matt asked. "Are you already worried about the collapse of the M's which I believe I forecasted?"

"I'm more worried about why no one's warming up in our bullpen yet," Jamie said, "and about why you were trying to pin that hot dog mess on me."

"I told her **I** would pay for the cleaning," Matt answered.

"Yeah, after you pointed at my half eaten hot dog and proclaimed that **we** had spilled. What was that all about?"

Matt stroked his faint chin strap beard and spouted, "My dog was already deceased. I can't help it if you're such a slow eater. You are so paranoid. Don't forget she has my business card. By the way, do you think she'll call and ask me out to discuss the cleaning bill over drinks?"

"And you think I'm crazy for believing in the M's," Jamie replied.

The Mist finally escaped the sixth inning with a 6-3 lead after a sacrifice fly, another walk, and a double play. But Oakland added single runs in both the seventh and eighth while completely shutting down Seattle. So the ninth inning dawned with Seattle clinging to a one run lead and the fans collectively squirming.

"Don't blow it," Matt screamed at the top of his lungs as the Mist took the field.

Almost on cue, the leadoff Oakland hitter slapped a single to right on the first pitch. Then on a double play grounder, the normally sure-handed second baseman, Donny Kuhn, booted the ball. A sacrifice bunt and an intentional walk loaded the bases. Seattle stuck with their closer but such loyalty was clearly misplaced when he promptly unloaded those same bases with a grand slam mistake down the middle of the plate.

A once comfortable 6-1 lead had deteriorated into a 9-6 deficit. Shell-shocked Seattle players and observers went through the motions for the rest of the ninth inning as the stands began to empty. Eventually Donny Kuhn struck out with a runner on base for an official ending. The hapless M's went home as "come from ahead" losers, an art they had perfected over many years.

"What goes around, comes around," Matt lamented as he and Jamie circled over to The Shoebox for some post-game grieving at the popular pub while the traffic cleared out.

M's fans were so accustomed to losing in painful ways that they were less in shock than in chronic despair. Jamie and Matt, regulars on the pity party circuit, were prepared to bail for home on this weeknight after just one beer apiece. But then Donny Kuhn walked into the bar and headed toward the foursome at the table next to the two cousins.

"Hey guys, is this chair free?" Kuhn asked while grabbing their empty chair in anticipation of a positive response from Jamie and Matt.

Tempered by the celebrity status of the questioner, Matt resisted his usual banter about those chairs being reserved for some hot chicks and responded pleasantly, "Sure, the whole table is free. We're on our way out."

"Hey, you guys were at the game tonight, right?" Donny asked. Without waiting for an answer, he rambled on, "Just because we stunk tonight, don't run out. Let me buy you a drink for your suffering," he offered as he motioned to the server to include Matt and Jamie in the round he was buying for his table of five.

The cousins were easily swayed. It was rare indeed that they ever sighted a ballplayer, let alone got invited to his table. Donny set his chair where it bridged the two tables into one. Brief first name introductions were made all around except for Donny. He remained unidentified on the unspoken assumption that everyone knew who he was. The attractive woman with short black hair and short black skirt seemed to be paired with Donny.

Jamie summoned up his courage and bravely said, "Just win tomorrow and it will still be a great opening series."

"Something good better happen tomorrow," Donny nodded. "My parents are up for the series. So I boot the double play, go 0-4, and some ugly creep drools mustard all over one of my sisters."

"Where are they now, your family? Are they coming here?" Matt asked as the polite laughter subsided.

"No, after meeting me outside the locker room, they headed back to the hotel. It's been a long day for them and my youngest sister is only seventeen."

"Did they really say that an 'ugly creep' drooled mustard on your sister?" Jamie interjected.

"Not only that, but then the jerk hands out business cards, bragging about how he cleans urinals for a living. Must have been an Oakland fan!"

Chapter Three

"You certainly came home late last night," Jo greeted her son.

"Sorry, Ma, I didn't mean to wake you but we got to meet Donny K last night."

"You didn't wake me, Jamie, but I thought Danny Kaye was dead."

"Donny Kuhn, the second baseman for the Mist. They just call him Don K to distinguish him from Don Grant. And if I didn't wake you, how do you know I came home late?"

"Why do they have to distinguish this Grant guy from this Kuhn guy? Do they look alike? And I can tell when you come home even when I'm asleep. I can tell in my dreams."

"Okay, what time did I come home last night? And Grant and Kuhn don't look alike. They just have the same first name."

"I thought you said one was Donny and the other one was Don. By the way, it was 2:15 in the morning."

"See, you were awake."

"No I wasn't."

Jamie stopped before he got trapped in the bicker game. His mother was an expert at it as he had observed at close range when his father was alive. He wondered if they had always done the verbal bantering even when they were dating but he knew it would take an exhausting conversation to pursue that question with his mother. He did know that when his mother was JoTinkler, she possessed an escape route in the name game. Some would say she did not set the bar very high when she married Marty Mudd. Of course, a man whose name was Mudd might be the best match for a Tinkler girl.

Jo and Marty adopted Jamie at birth early in their marriage. They had no other children and eventually became famous throughout the family and neighborhood for their ability to argue constantly about everything.

When Jamie was about ten, his parents engaged in a lengthy and heated debate about what they would do if they won the Grand

Prize in a contest sponsored by an orange juice company. The contest winner could choose eleven other guests to accompany him or her for a week at Spring Training in either Florida or Arizona. Not only were Jo and Marty at odds over the lucky dozen invitees, but they couldn't even agree on which state to pick. Marty was incredulous that Jo wanted to go to Florida, where her aunt lived, instead of Arizona where the Seattle Mist trained. Jo bolstered her case with observations on the benefits of water over desert and calculations on how a trip to Florida was worth more since it was farther away.

"Did we win a trip to Spring Training?" Jamie finally interrupted while Marty was sputtering over the absurdity of Jo's logic.

The realization that they were fighting over phantom contest winnings did not at all shame Jo and Marty as they continued this lively skirmish even after acknowledging and assuring their son that they had not won anything. Since the contest odds clearly offered no realistic expectation of any big payoff for the Mudds, this exercise could only be explained as part of a longstanding marital ritual.

Marty and Jo continued to enter contests and play the lottery even though they gave proof to the adage that money won't solve everything. After thirty-five years of marriage, Jo won a lottery she didn't want to win when her husband died and left her with hefty insurance proceeds, none of which would ever be invested in a trip to visit her aunt in Florida.

The constant verbal sparring in the Mudd household did no visible damage to Jamie who lived a verifiably normal private life prior to the extraordinary events of his thirtieth year. Until then, he was the designated witness to the adventures and escapades of his wilder cousins who couldn't even walk to school without depositing a dead bird or dog excrement in a neighborhood mailbox.

Jamie was closest to his cousin Matt. They were born 26 hours apart, so were literally together since meeting in the hospital nursery. Matt's brother, Adam, was two years older and alternated between accomplice and supervisor in this inner family triad.

Although Jamie lingered out of the family spotlight, he dutifully rounded the bases of Little League (second baseman), University of Seattle (business degree), and Tinkler Toilets (sales rep). He was currently stranded on third. His mother, needing a bickering partner to replace his father, was continually frustrated at Jamie's refusal to engage on the subjects of girlfriends, activities, grooming, news events, relatives, and neighbors. Jamie learned from observing his parents that any attempt to converse on these topics would inevitably lead back to an argument.

If his mother had ever learned anything about baseball, she might have been quickly captivated since that subject lends itself so well to meaningless debate. But baseball remained well beyond Jo's radar screen and whenever Jamie could, he sought refuge at the ballpark. Now more than ever, he was drawn to the park as the closest place to visit his father. He never minded escaping alone but he always welcomed company, so he veered out of the deteriorating dialogue with his mother by inviting her to join him at Thursday's rubber game with Oakland.

"Bridge night with the ladies," Jo answered.

"Alright, well I may be late again tonight. I'll try not to wake you."

"You won't."

Jamie was tempted to say, *"yes, I will be late,"* but he knew being cute wasn't worth the verbal trap. Instead he hurried off to work.

"God bless you until you come home again," Jo called after him as she did most every day.

"And then when I'm home, the blessing is rescinded," Jamie mumbled in the garage. Although his mother was out of earshot, she had heard that line more than a few times.

Jamie expected his mother to be unavailable for the game, but once at work he was surprised at Matt's reluctance to join him. He even resorted to bribery.

"You couldn't buy me enough hot dogs to go through another loss like last night," Matt responded

"Come on, even World Series champions lose a good sixty times a season," Jamie wheedled.

"Look, Meatball, I'm not going anywhere near a stadium that contains Donny Kuhn's family. Catch me on the next homestand."

"Why? They already have your business card and you blamed the mustard on me anyway," Jamie pointed out with a laugh even though he now knew his mission was hopeless.

After work Jamie just headed over to the Shoe alone. Standing in line for a scorecard, he caught himself looking for the scraggly vendor but didn't see him even though he was watching Jamie from the mezzanine level. Jamie felt a shiver on this cool April night. So he grabbed a coffee and settled into a bleacher seat. The game on the field started slowly but it heated up in the third when the big Oakland catcher slid spikes high into second base, tearing a bloody gash down Kuhn's left leg as Donny futilely tried to turn a double play.

The feisty Kuhn popped up, positioned himself two inches under the bigger man's nose, and vulgarly expressed what he felt about the runner's tactic and character. The Oakland catcher registered his exception to the insults with a shove, escalation ensued, and eventually both players were ejected along with a few of their closest friends who joined the fray from the dugouts. Since Kuhn would need to leave the game anyway to tend his injury, Seattle gained on the transaction when he took Oakland's star catcher out with him.

The fans were now awake and loudly into the game. E2 broke the 1-1 tie when he singled, stole second, and scored on Thorne's double. Seattle's lead was short lived when Oakland scored two in the fifth. The roller coaster continued as Seattle tied the game in the sixth on a Rudy Wink triple and an Escobar sacrifice fly which barely stayed in the ballpark. Seattle loaded the bases in both the seventh and eighth but scored neither time. This torture was excruciating for any true Seattle Mist fan, already bludgeoned by decades of near misses.

Jamie, one of the forsaken, silently berated the fates. *Why can't we catch a break? What more can I do? I give my time, my mojo, my money and I get nothing but heartache in return. As a true fan,*

I deserve better. Even a victory tonight won't make this aggravation worth it.

But Jamie was denied even a victory because Oakland plated two more runs in the top of the ninth. The rubber armed Oakland closer made a third straight appearance and his two consecutive saves gave him the last vengeful laugh, at least for this series.

Larry Thorne slumped in front of his locker and mumbled, "We let another one get away from us. And to add insult to injury, I'm going to get nailed for some big bucks for leaving the dugout during our tea party in the third."

Donny Kuhn made a point of limping by Thorne in his boxers, displaying his heavily bandaged wound as a badge of courage.

"I'm donating both money and blood for the cause," he boasted.

"We need more than a little blood money," Rudy Wink said. "We need some kind of savior to lead us out of the wilderness or this season is going to be over before May."

"We're 1-2 after only three games, all of which could have gone either way," Escobar chimed in. "We've got a lot of winning left in us, so it's a little too early to get down on ourselves."

"Okay, E2, you just let me know when it is time to get down on ourselves and I'll try to be ready," Wink replied.

Escobar could not quite decide whether Wink's tone was playful or caustic, so he ignored him. But he thought to himself, *I don't need someone to lead this team out of the wilderness, if he could just lead me out of the Mist and onto a contender.*

While E2 was smirking, lost in his own thoughts, Thorne eyed him and cautiously inquired, "What's so funny?"

"The size of your ass, Larry. It is truly major league."

Even Thorne joined in the laughter. That laughter would have risen to world record levels if the players in that locker room knew who was being groomed as the answer to their prayers.

Chapter Four

Llew took off his reading glasses and ran his hands through his remaining gray hair. Jamie waited expectantly.

"I don't know why you care so much for the Mist. After that disappointing Oakland series and even more dismal road trip against their three division rivals, aren't they like three and eight now?"

"Three and nine," Jamie gently corrected.

Despite the team's lackluster record, Jamie had been continually lobbying his Uncle Llew for the company tickets to the opening game of the upcoming California series. Llew was Joe Tinkler's youngest son. He became the only one capable of running the Tinkler business after Marty Mudd died. Llew's older brother, Art, held the ceremonial position of President but spent most of his time taking pictures of bathrooms for a coffee table book he hoped to publish someday. Passing out baseball tickets would have fit nicely into Art's job description but Llew even had to handle that assignment because conflicts could arise and decisions needed to be made.

"Okay, Jamie, you can have this ticket," Llew conceded, "but you need to host the McPhersons."

"Will Rob be using one of the tickets?" Jamie asked.

"I don't know. I gave the other three to his brother Mac at a Chamber meeting yesterday. Why, is Rob causing problems for us again?"

"Nothing we can't handle," Jamie said with complete lack of conviction.

With his ticket in hand, Jamie realized it was time to exit no matter who had the adjoining seats. And the McPhersons had always been good friends. They were Tinkler's most important customer. McPherson Construction was a family business like Tinkler Toilets but on a much grander scale and with a much more auspicious name. Rob was the youngest of the third generation McPherson brothers and was actually employed by Tinkler, nominally so he could cut the umbilical cord to the family business and make it on his own. But since the hiring was a favor for a big customer, little in that regard was accomplished. Although Rob had always been a likable kid, lately his absences at work made it appear to Jamie that McPherson used its leverage to pass along a problem employee to someone else.

When Jamie returned to his office, he knew he had to do something to address the problems Rob was causing with customers. He convinced himself he was considering options but in reality he was just stalling by over analyzing the situation and subconsciously trusting that other workplace distractions would intrude and justify his inactivity for yet another day.

Jamie's joy at finally making it to the end of another workday was not unrestrained. Even as he made the familiar trek to the ballpark that evening, the unfinished business nagged at him like an overdue term paper. He was lost in thought about what he would say if he saw Rob that night when suddenly a hand reached out and grabbed his arm. Jamie was startled and instinctively recoiled as the same scruffy vendor from opening night said softly, "Got your scorecard right here."

After hesitating and although still annoyed, Jamie produced two dollars, grabbed the card, and scooted off without a word.

When the McPhersons arrived at the seats, Jamie was pleasantly surprised to see the McPherson sister, Rebecca, was attending the game in place of Rob. Although Jamie was pleased to be spared the awkwardness of Rob's presence, Rebecca caused a very different awkwardness, albeit a more exciting version. Jamie had met Rebecca several times at business and social functions and he did notice her at his father's funeral. He liked that she always appeared to be genuinely oblivious to the social hierarchy that placed her way out of his league. He remembered one time when she had engaged him in a lively conversation on the merits of picking quarterbacks first in Fantasy Football drafts. As near as he could recall, she was arguing for running backs but with Rebecca you couldn't always be sure. She seemed more interested in the arguments than the answer.

Jamie found Rebecca both approachable and intimidating. And so he was both disappointed and relieved when she was sandwiched between her other two brothers and not sitting next to him.

When Jamie would steal a glance at Rebecca, he could not pinpoint a particular extraordinary feature that made her so alluring. Her long brown hair, the lively green eyes, the highly defined cheekbone, the well-proportioned nose, and the sparkling white smile were certainly all positive attributes. But individually they don't fully prepare the viewer for the dazzling effect of the finished product. Under the old "know it when I see it" standard, Rebecca was a consensus beauty by most any measure.

However, Rebecca was not a delicate beauty. She radiated health and athleticism. Early in the game when she eschewed garlic fries in favor of a salmon salad, her pudgy brother Mac chided her, "Beck, I think you're starting to get too thin."

"Being too thin must be a compliment," Rebecca said with a smile, "since you would never be so rude as to comment on negatives, like telling someone they were too fat or too ugly."

"Sure I would," said Mac, turning to their brother. "Dano, you are getting way too fat and definitely too ugly from consuming all that barbecue beef and beer!"

Showing no sign of being insulted, Dano replied, "Mac, you reek of garlic fries! Oink for me."

Mac nuzzled his nose into his sister's arm and snorted, "Oink, oink, oink."

Rebecca could only laugh.

In the top of the seventh inning, when Cal loaded the bases with one out, both Mac and Dano headed to the restroom to drain their beer and make room for more before the concession stand cut alcohol sales off. Rebecca moved over next to Jamie. She was still nursing her first beer and making small talk about being the designated driver. The game itself was a home town bore as the M's were still down 6-1 even after turning a double play to retire Cal in the seventh.

In the bottom of the inning, Jamie was having trouble concentrating on the scorebook because he was struggling to make conversation with Rebecca. He brightened when he remembered to ask her, "Last summer you were hiking the Appalachian Trail, right?"

"Yeah, I took a leave of absence in April and hooked up with some thru-hikers and by the time we finished, the M's were already eliminated from contention!"

As Jamie desperately racked his brain for intelligent Appalachian Trail small talk, he lost his place. When Wynn doubled, Jamie inadvertently logged the double for the next hitter. When Escobar, that next batter, did in fact double, Jamie swiveled his attention back to the scorebook.

Rebecca was answering his question about the length of the Appalachian Trail, "We counted 2160 miles although you find several different versions depending on the source you use. We followed the white blaze trail religiously."

"So how many miles was that?" Jamie asked idly while preoccupied with thoughts of the homerun he correctly predicted on opening night.

"Well, 2160 miles," Rebecca said.

Jamie realized too late that he was repeating himself and not paying enough attention to the answers. Still he was fascinated with the scorebook coincidence. Quickly he logged the rarest of hits, a triple, for Thorne who was just now lumbering up to the plate.

Thorne took the first two pitches while Jamie watched impatiently. With a count of one ball and one strike, Larry took a mighty swing and popped the ball straight up in the air. It looked as if the Cal first baseman had a bead on the ball as he waved the catcher off the play. But at the last moment, the ball drifted just out of reach, three rows into the stands.

Jamie took a deep breath as Thorne took ball two. Rebecca distracted him momentarily when she commented, "He looks kind of fat for being a professional athlete."

"I think he'll take that as a compliment," Jamie observed, "as long as you don't say he looks too ugly to be a pro ballplayer."

Rebecca laughed as Thorne ran the count to full on a pitch that looked too good to take. After fouling off pitch number six, he stroked a line drive straight at the Cal right fielder. It looked like he would be able to make the catch but he momentarily froze in his tracks. Even though he quickly recovered, the ball died and skipped under his outstretched mitt as he dove too late into the turf. After he scrambled to his feet, the ball was well on its way to the wall.

While the right fielder sprinted after the elusive ball, Thorne was rounding first and heading for second. Jamie held his breath when Thorne showed no sign of slowing down as he churned into second base. Remembering the baseball instincts of his youth, Thorne's legs kept pumping their way toward third. The second baseman recognized that Thorne was the runner and unleashed a desperate relay throw from short right field. Most players would have owned a stand-up triple but Thorne finished with a slide that was partly an excuse to collapse onto the ground in a heaving heap.

The enthusiastic cheers of the crowd heightened the adrenaline rush Jamie was experiencing. Rebecca punctuated the moment with a friendly nudge and the observation, "Thorne's way too fast for a guy so fat and ugly!"

Jamie whimpered out a laugh while they settled back in their seats. He tested fate by immediately pencilling in a triple for Grant. Jamie worried that he was risking something by asking for too much but he had a driving urge to either confirm or expose the coincidences. His shaking pencil testified that he was actually entertaining the possibility that his scorebook could somehow be affecting the play on the field.

Grant did line a 2-2 pitch down the right field line. The winded right fielder moved slower this time and Grant moved faster than Thorne. It all added up to another triple.

"Back to back triples," Rebecca enthused. "How often does that happen?"

"Not very," Jamie confirmed.

Jamie abandoned the string of triples, mostly out of an irrational sense that he might somehow be exposed doing something wrong. He furtively logged less conspicuous singles for the next two hitters, continued with a homerun for Kuhn, and ended up with sweaty palms and shaking hands for himself as his predictions all came true.

During the pitching change, the McPherson brothers returned in the drunken delirium of Seattle's explosive rally. Jamie knew his forecasting success had already exceeded the normal bounds of chance. He was relatively sure he was not asleep and not dreaming. He did know that he needed to get to the restroom in a hurry as the urge to relieve himself was suddenly overpowering.

The men's room turned out to be a good place for Jamie when he suddenly discovered he was going to throw up. Unfortunately, he regurgitated into the urinal, pretty much to the disgust of those around him. However, one unruffled fellow urinator commiserated, "Hey, pal, the M's make me sick, too, but you better leave now if you don't want to see their bullpen blow this lead!"

Jamie barely heard and didn't try to respond. He splashed some water from the sink on his face, dried off with a handful of brown sandpaper towels, and rinsed out his mouth at the water fountain. He gained enough composure to pop a breath mint and walk deliberately back to his seat. He still had some serious work ahead of him.

Chapter Five

"What a day," Jamie mumbled at about three in the morning as he thrashed around the bed, muffling his voice in the pillow. He did not sleep well this night, dozing off in short bursts of exhaustion, drifting in and out of consciousness but thinking he never slept at all.

Jamie's mind raced. *Rebecca thought I was an idiot...her brothers were too drunk and full of themselves to remember much of anything and who cares about them anyway?...but the M's won a great come from behind game which would normally be cool but I caused it in my scorebook?...am I crazy?...I need to get tickets from Uncle Llew for today's game...I can't believe I weirded out in front of Rebecca...but this was a big deal...it was...*

By 4:15 a.m., Jamie was up, finally persuaded that no more meaningful sleep was left to be wrung from this night. "Damn computer is down and no newspaper, for over an hour," he lamented to himself, even as he checked the driveway, knowing the paper wouldn't be there yet, but really knowing nothing at all anymore.

Clearly Jamie was acting more like a mental patient than some powerful prognosticator. He could not now appreciate the irony of having always been the quintessential Joe Average Anybody. No one would ever expect Jamie to approach either of the extremes of lunacy or power broker. Yet now he was bouncing between them with no safe middle ground. He knew he was very crazy or very important or both.

When the Seattle Post finally hit the driveway at 5:42 a.m., Jamie scrambled out after it. He hungrily devoured the front-page teaser, "M's Win in Bizarre Finish" and quickly extracted the Sports Page. The column on the Mist was featured on page D1 above the fold with the headline, "Kuhn Keys Crazy Comeback". The opening paragraph assured Jamie that he had not been imagining things:

"Although the Mist have always been known for exciting finishes, last night's startling 14-8 thumping of California surprised even the most ardent of fans with the sudden and unusual nature of the drubbing. Down 6-1, the M's rallied for seven runs in the seventh. Donny Kuhn who hit only one homer all of last year, keyed the uprising with a three run shot just over the left field wall. But this was just the beginning. Now nursing an 8-6 lead in the eighth, Seattle scored six more with only one basehit, a grandslam by Donny, his second dinger of the game. His seven rbi's in two innings were as many as he had in all of April last season. Two errors from Cal's third baseman, two hit batsmen, an ejection of Cal's pitcher, and two walks preceded the grandslam. Kuhn attributed his newfound power to the training regimen he employed in the offseason and an adjustment to his batting grip, apparently suggested by third base coach Eddy Duda in spring training…"

Testing the outer limits of chance by submitting a combination of outcomes that surely proved he was in control of the Mist offense led Jamie to muse with massively modest understatement, *If anyone else knew, this would be the biggest sports story of the year!*

The great philosophical questions of "how" and "why" gave way to the more practical "how" as in how to get to the ballpark again today. So for the third time this morning, Jamie watched time drag. It took forever before he could get out of bed, forever before the paper came, and now forever until a respectable hour when he could pester Uncle Llew about the company tickets.

Itching to test not only the existence but also the limits of this newly discovered power, Jamie did establish last night that he only had influence on the Mist offense. He completely failed in his attempts to successfully pre-record the Cal offense in the last two innings. Although baffled, he was anxious to experiment and explore the possibilities sooner rather than later.

Jamie's mother, always an early riser, was surprised to find Jamie wandering around in his anxious state. "Have you been to bed yet?" she asked, not unaccustomed to the late hours he and his cousins sometimes kept even on weekdays.

Jamie was usually very responsive to his mother, a quality not universally found in all his friends; but this time he wasn't even hearing her. Surprised to be ignored, Jo tried the same question again louder. This time Jamie managed a distracted, "Oh, yeah, I just didn't sleep well, I don't know why."

"Well, I'll tell you why, you need to be drinking more milk and getting a nice girlfriend like that Jeffrey Anne, whatever happened to her? Milk soothes the stomach."

"Drinking more milk" and "Jeffrey Anne the girlfriend" were common campaign themes for Jo although not usually linked in the same sentence. Even so, Jamie's mother wasn't overly smothering and he was surprisingly comfortable back living at home since his father died. Sometimes he did wonder how his mother would have reacted if he and Jeffrey Anne had ever actually fallen in love. Perhaps she thought Jeffrey Anne would be a better conversationalist than he was. At any rate, he was well practiced at deflecting his mother's questions and comments disguised as questions. Today he just said, "I think Jeffrey Anne had to take a leave of absence for a calcium overdose."

"I never heard of such a thing. Maybe she needs to drink more milk, too," Jo suggested.

"She's drinking too much milk right now," Jamie insisted.

"You can never drink too much milk," Jo prattled on. "Maybe she got into some sour milk by accident. She should try drinking some fresh milk to flush out the sour milk. You should maybe take her some fresh milk."

Jamie was tempted to tell his mother about several people in Iowa who exploded when they tried to purge sour milk with fresh milk but he knew it would do no good. Today he was not in the mood for idle banter. He just wanted to be alone with his thoughts even though they were torturing him. He also desperately needed to get back to the ballpark.

Chapter Six

"I was at the M's game last night," Rebecca apologized, preemptively announcing her arrival and explaining her tardiness all at once.

Although she had not stayed out late, Rebecca knew the male dominated audience would appreciate her excuse. It might actually raise her stock in the law firm. The truth was she had forgotten that the Wednesday morning meetings were already on the 7 a.m. summer schedule, so the partners still had time to hit the golf course early. This was no incentive for associates like Rebecca who were expected to labor into the early evening, long after the partners departed.

"That was quite a game," a fellow associate remarked, "what was the final score anyway? I turned it off in the eighth to concentrate on the AFW brief."

"Fourteen to eight," Rebecca announced, "Kuhn had two homers, including a grand salami."

While resenting the test and gagging at her co-worker's self serving statement, Rebecca did appreciate the opportunity it gave her to advertise her sports acumen. Meanwhile the senior labor lawyer took the cue to review the latest on the AFW account. Rebecca was mentally preparing her own remarks on her caseload when a reference to Tinkler Toilets caught her attention.

"But haven't they failed to organize Tinkler many times in the past? Isn't it like a tightly held family company?" an associate was asking the lead attorney.

Asking questions you know the answer to is a favorite pastime of lawyers but it still irked Rebecca. Everybody in the firm seemed shamelessly preoccupied with seeking credit and approval but the fact that she readily joined the game pained her the most. At least she could enjoy any time a sycophant got his due.

"It's not *like* a tightly held family company. It *is* a tightly held family company," the lead labor lawyer emphasized. "And, of course, we get paid whether our client is successful or not. Although Llew

Tinkler is even more anti-union than his brother-in-law was, the AFW considers this an advantage. Llew is relatively new in the CEO role. The union figures he's more likely to make mistakes than Marty Mudd did when he was alive and running things. The AFW feels certain they can at least provoke some unfair labor practices and they apparently have some pro-union people on the inside."

Rebecca was happy she was in the Environmental Law group and wouldn't have to cause any problems by having to remove herself from an account. She was also relieved not to know the names of the insiders but sorry she knew there were some. *This should be interesting,* she thought, *because I know so many people on both sides of the case. I hope Rob isn't involved. That's all we'd need right now.*

"Who represents Tinkler?" an eager associate asked.

"Ah, that's another potential advantage. In house counsel is one of the Tinkler grandchildren and the HR person is a young, inexperienced woman. So Tinkler may save some money on this campaign by using rookies but you get what you pay for. Hopefully, we won't see as much of the Tronquet firm this go round or at least not until the damage is done."

Rebecca smiled to herself thinking how the associates in this room who would be working on this relatively minor case would indeed be billing at higher rates but would actually be younger than the "young, inexperienced" people the speaker demeaned.

Chapter Seven

Jamie was initially excited when he obtained a company ticket to the Wednesday game. He successfully dodged the shaggy vendor who approached with long strides, flowing red hair, and a manner Jamie interpreted as menacing. After quickly completing his transaction with a relatively reputable looking vendor, Jamie literally ran toward the entrance to section 139. He was first in his foursome to arrive and took his usual place farthest in from the aisle. He was disappointed when the ticketholder to his left turned out to be a well groomed, enormous man in a bright orange sweatshirt of tentlike proportion. Orangeman carried at least 350 pounds and spilled over into the adjacent seats. Jamie was uncomfortable and likely Orangeman was too, although neither one gave any overt sign of distress.

While Jamie pondered the etiquette of moving into one of the other company seats, Uncle Art showed up with two of his kids. Now pinned between Orangeman and Uncle Art, Jamie found it difficult even to write in his scorecard and was further disappointed when he could work no magic. At least Orangeman made several trips to the concession stand and according to today's record of ballpark consumption, he was not a victim of defective glands but was simply out of self-control. Arriving at the game with large packets of peanuts and sweetened popcorn, Orangeman later purchased large beers from hawkers in innings one, three, and five. Trips to the concourse to buy food produced a hot dog and nachos (inning two), garlic fries and barbecue beef sandwich (inning four), and cotton candy and ice cream sandwich (inning six).

During Orangeman's absence in the sixth, Uncle Art leaned over and whispered, "Why did he bother to shave, shower, and comb his hair this morning if he cares so little about his appearance to allow for its obscene expansion?"

Jamie felt a combination of disdain for Uncle Art's intolerance and a wave of guilt that he was not so different from his uncle. Since communication with Orangeman had been nonexistent, Jamie was startled from his mental self flagellation in the last of the sixth inning when his seat mate suddenly asked, "What kind of scoring system are you using?"

"Uh, I'm just doodling, not really keeping score. Just some superstitious stuff that uh….," his voice trailed off with a shrug of the shoulders as he realized the mess he was making in his scorebook by inserting so much fiction.

Jamie's father taught him how to score games and compute batting averages long before he would study fractions in school. With his natural aptitude, he quickly grasped the concept of assigning each defensive player a number. So a fly ball caught by the left fielder was logged as "7" and a groundout to the shortstop was a "6-3". Basehits were lines drawn around the diamond in the applicable box in the scorebook grid. When a runner completed his route and scored a run, the scorekeeper colored in the diamond in the book.

Frustrated with the desecration of today's scorebook, the failure of his game plan, and the confined quarters, Jamie excused himself during the top of the seventh and headed for the restroom. He chucked his scorecard in the garbage and watched an inning from a stool in the bar area. Cal broke a 2-2 tie in a game well played by both teams, an exciting contest for any purist; but Jamie was too tired and cranky to fully appreciate it. He decided to watch the last two innings from back in his seat and was surprised to see that Uncle Art, his two kids, and Orangeman had all left even though the M's were only down by two runs.

Someone had discarded an unused scorecard on Jamie's seat and he halfheartedly baptized it by predicting a walk for Escobar. As the count ran to one ball and two strikes, Jamie pondered why his predictions could be so accurate one day and so inaccurate the next. After two more balls and a couple of fouls, E2 took ball four and Jamie perked up a little even though he recognized that the law of averages would eventually make him right once in awhile.

Jamie decided to try another walk, ordering one for Thorne. As the count progressed to 3-1, Jamie wondered if maybe the Cal pitcher was just on a normal wild streak. Thorne fouled off a pitch that looked like ball four and Jamie winced. But then Larry finally accepted a walk on a pitch that almost sailed over the catcher's head.

Jamie was anxious to try a basehit but was momentarily stymied when the Cal manager took a slow stroll out to the mound. Jamie squirmed impatiently while Cal completed a pitching change. Finally the plate umpire signaled for the next batter and Grant stepped up to the dish.

The Cal catcher called for a slider and Jamie called for a single. But first the pitcher faked a pick off throw to second as Cal checked to see if Grant might be bunting. Grant did not square around to bunt so either he showed great restraint in this "cat and mouse" maneuvering or Seattle wasn't playing for the sacrifice.

The man in front of Jamie condescendingly told his companion, "No way are we going to have our clean-up hitter bunt with the tying run already on base."

"Maybe the manager wants to stay away from a double play and get in position where a single can tie the game," she suggested in reply.

"Nah, Cal would just walk the next batter to put the double play back on and we would have a weaker hitter up," came the retort with a hint of exasperation over being challenged.

"You mean they would put the winning run on base with an intentional walk?" she asked innocently.

"Sometimes," he said with a little less arrogance.

Jamie didn't like the man's pontificating style but hoped he was right that Grant wasn't bunting. It seemed like forever before the pitcher set again. Pitching from the stretch, he finally delivered his slider. The first and third basemen were not playing too deep but they were not charging the plate either, apparently assuming from the pick off test that Seattle was not playing for a sacrifice. But Grant squared around at the last moment and laid his bat out over the plate.

The rookie third sacker began charging at top speed as soon as Grant tipped his intentions. Jamie's heart fell as he realized the single he called for was going to be preempted by a sacrifice bunt. Even if Cal blew the play, the result would be an error, not a hit.

The third baseman had plenty of time to make the play but his eagerness betrayed him. His right leg slid out from under him as he attempted to adjust his stride to execute a coordinated scoop and throw to first. Instead he found himself sliding to the right of the ball. He was able to pop quickly back to his knees and reach out and grab the ball as it rolled past him. He cocked his arm to throw, but it was now too late to get off a throw with enough leverage to get Grant at first.

Meanwhile the speedy Escobar came wheeling around third base. He was eager to score if the rookie third baseman made an errant off balance throw from his knees. Indeed, the savvy third sacker followed through on a fake throw, jumped to his feet and had an over anxious E2 trapped off the bag. The shortstop had covered third as part of the "wheel" rotation when Grant first showed bunt. Escobar feinted back toward the base, hoping to draw a throw that would allow him a slim chance to head for home and beat the relay.

Unfortunately, the rookie had the poise to run E2 back toward the bag, making the toss to the shortstop only after Escobar committed himself. E2 was dead meat. The cheers turned to groans except for Jamie who realized that Grant would be credited for a single. E2 was out after rounding third and so the play was no different than one where the batter singles to the outfield and the runner from second is thrown out at the plate.

The man in front of Jamie was beside himself, "They are such idiots. That's what they get for trying a sacrifice."

"But it worked," his companion reminded him, "only E2's eagerness busted the play. And that's how he plays. His hustle has paid off a lot of times in the past."

"You're dreaming if you thought that was a good play. It was ugly. E2 wasn't even the winning run. He needs to pull his head out of his butt. The M's suck. They're going to blow it like they always do although I'll give them creativity points for finding new ways," the man said with a sneer.

Jamie, though, was encouraged. He decided to go for broke and logged a triple in his scorebook for the next hitter who took a vicious swing at a ball. However, the ball never made it to the plate in the air. It bounced in front of home and skipped by the catcher. Both runners advanced.

"See," Skeptical Man's companion intoned, "we're right back where we were if the sacrifice had worked. It all evens out."

"Cal's just going to walk this guy and set up a double play. Big deal," the skeptic retorted.

Jamie hoped Skeptic Man was wrong. Indeed, apparently Cal was encouraged by the wild swing and the 0-1 count and decided to pitch carefully to the hitter, maybe getting him to swing at another ball. And sure enough, the free swinger lunged at a low ball and golfed it off the right field wall. The right fielder tried to make the catch but the ball was just out of reach. He wasn't in position for the carom, so two runs scored easily and the hitter chugged toward third with a triple while the ball rolled back toward the infield.

"They should have walked him," Skeptic Man observed.

Next came nine more runs. Whenever possible, Jamie tried to sequence the action in ways that contradicted whatever Skeptic Man was saying. Jamie did manage a grandslam for Kuhn, one of the regulars still in the game by the end of the inning. Fortunately for Cal, Jamie had to keep an appointment with the restroom when the score reached 16-2.

Chapter Eight

"I discovered chicks dig dingers," Donny was quick to quip when the post game interviewer asked about his newfound power.

Jamie rolled his eyes at the television as he listened to Donny take credit for his outrageous success. Even before their chance encounter after the second game of the season, Jamie held a soft spot for Donny Kuhn. Both were known as "good field, no hit" second basemen who toiled in relative obscurity, although on vastly different stages. Kuhn was fast shedding the light hitter label and blossoming into a cult figure in Seattle. He had always been known for his defense and speed, but his two homers the previous night drove in six runs in one inning. Suddenly he was the M's power leader with four homeruns and fourteen rbi's.

"Call me Donny," the emerging hero said in the next soundbite. "Maybe it's time to start calling that other guy Don G."

Jamie was amused but not yet comfortable with a celebrity Donny Kuhn. He clicked off the television and headed to work early because he needed to take a long lunch hour on this Thursday. He was certain now that he had a power to influence games through his scorebook but that the magic apparently worked only in the late innings when Seattle was up to bat. Confident in his knowledge, he used the noon hour to procure a 36 game package of M's tickets that covered about half of the home games remaining in the season. Then he headed straight for Llew's office.

Although Tinkler had grown to more than 500 employees over the years, Llew was stationed in the same old cubbyhole Joe Tinkler and Marty Mudd occupied before him. With the expansion of the business, no one had taken the opportunity to upgrade the office area or to flush the "toilet" out of the company name. Llew still knew every employee and they all knew him on a first name basis. It was common for workers to go directly to Llew with issues but Jamie was aware this wasn't a good time. The outer office was crowded with people and his uncle had earlier cancelled their regular Thursday luncheon with Adam and Matt. Fortunately, Llew's office assistant knew that Jamie had special standing with her boss.

"Make it fast," she warned Jamie as she ushered him in.

Jamie wasted no time. He quickly outlined an offer to trade his newly purchased tickets for the company tickets on the same days.

"So what do you think?" Jamie asked when Llew didn't make an immediate response.

"Are you crazy, Jamie?" his uncle finally answered. "You just spent over $3,000 on M's tickets and we already have plenty to go around? What are you going to do with them all?"

"Llew, I just feel like this is going to be a special year for the M's. I love our new seats and I don't want to miss this chance."

"Are you going batty on me?"

"Look, I got you seats as good as last years. And I only need one of the tickets. I don't even want the aisle. I'll take seat four," Jamie pleaded.

"That's my point, you only need one ticket. You went out and bought four more!"

"But I need tickets to every game and I knew you want four together for customers sometimes."

"You're going to go to every game? You're turning thirty, Jamie. You need to be thinking about your future. You should be saving your money for a down payment on a house. Maybe starting a family."

"I'm not even dating anyone," Jamie protested.

"Exactly," Llew said softly. "Look, if it's that important to you, trade them out but I think you're losing perspective here. I wish you'd come to me first. Does your mother know what you're doing? I'd expect this more from my own boys than you, Jamie."

"I'm okay, Llew. I've still got plenty saved and I'm hoping to get a condo with the money my dad left me. I plan to scalp some of the extra tickets we won't need. And I'd still like to get my hands on some Tinkler tickets for the other half of the schedule where I don't have tickets to trade. So I hope you'll keep me in mind."

"All I know is you better get outa here and get back to work because I've got some union goon waiting to see me and I'm going to be getting into a very ugly mood. We'll try your tickets tonight but if we don't like 'em, I'm not guaranteeing anything for the rest of the season."

"Thanks, Llew."

Jamie arrived early at the game even after a quick stop at Crossroads Casino to put down a $200 bet on the Mist. He didn't think he really needed to share with his uncle the entire plan for recovering the big investment in tickets. Jamie did hawk two of his four Tinkler tickets for half price and that covered his parking, beer, and teriyaki chicken.

During batting practice two overly ambitious security personnel confiscated a homemade banner unfurled by two attractive young ladies, presumably because it dared to proclaim, "Will Trade Husband for a Donny Dinger!" The professional confiscators attracted enough jeers to suggest that the merits of this enforcement action would likely come under further scrutiny.

Just before the National Anthem, Matt came by on his way to the seats Jamie used as trade bait. Much to Jamie's discomfort, Matt clambered over people in the row behind Jamie, patted the back of Jamie's seat, and scurried back to the aisle while announcing loudly, "Hey, Meatball, the boys wanted me to touch your special seat to bring us good luck!"

Matt hustled off too quickly to enjoy Jamie's discomfort. But when Matt arrived at the new seats purchased by Jamie, Uncle Art seemed to be nurturing his own irritation.

"Jamie's been acting a little strange since Marty died. I still don't understand why he gets the Company tickets," Art challenged his brother. "He's not even using them all."

"What's the difference?" Llew growled. "These seats are as good as we had last year."

"Then we were getting screwed if Jamie can just walk in off the street and get tickets as good as ours when we were season ticket holders for years."

Llew took a deep breath and spoke deliberately, "You seem to forget that Jamie's dad held those tickets for years on his own and graciously allowed us to share them."

"All I know is he's sitting in better seats than we are tonight," Art said.

"So what are you trying to say?" Llew asked.

"I just think Jamie gets preferential treatment around here."

Llew just shook his head, preferring not to continue this dialogue with the big ears of Adam and Matt nearby.

When Jamie's scorebook failed to perform on cue in the first three innings, Jamie was not worried. But as the middle innings passed and the M's fell behind by six runs, he got edgier. The seventh inning provided no relief and the scorebook provided no magic in the eighth. His mood deteriorated when the M's went down in order in the ninth. All night they rejected his suggestions and looked inept in a 10-1 defeat. Jamie not only lost his $200 but his prospects for financing his ticket-spending spree were evaporating in front of his eyes.

"What have I done?" he mumbled as he finally rose from his seat after the entire section had cleared out.

Chapter Nine

Devils invaded Seattle. These Devils were from Detroit and they came for a three game weekend series, bringing with them the mushrooming controversy over their nickname and the number 66 on the back of their star catcher. Although for decades their name went unchallenged, the cute logo that looked like a pudgy youngster in a Halloween costume had in recent years given way to more creatively chilling images. Sinister devils began appearing on clothing with messages like, "Damn the Yankees."

Jamie and Matt tried to dodge the Devil Protesters but they couldn't avoid the chanting. One protester waved a poster menacingly at the boys.

"No wonder these guys suck with all the distractions, demonstrations, and counter-demonstrations everywhere they play," Jamie said.

"They've got no talent on that team anyway. They're lucky they have an excuse to stink. This is more interesting than watching them play," replied Matt.

They did stink this night but Matt didn't realize how much of that was because his cousin was back in the groove. Jamie once again reluctantly purchased a scorecard from the aggressive red headed vendor with the baggy pants and it sent Jamie's emotions on a roller coaster ride. He was exhilarated that the power was back, surprised that it worked in the early innings, and still confused about why it didn't work when he gambled. Donny Kuhn accepted his own good fortune without any qualms as he ripped three homeruns off the Devil's starting pitcher. But the mystified Devil hurler would be better remembered for his new major league record of six strikeouts in an inning, thanks to three bizarre errors in the fourth by the catcher after strike three.

After the game, the party moved from the stadium to the hip Pioneer Square watering holes and sports bars within walking distance of the Shoe. "Two light drafts, please," Jamie shouted to the back of the slim bartender as she hurried by to take an order from a more pressing customer.

Jamie tried again even louder after the barkeep finished mixing the latest order. But she was already slamming ice into a cocktail glass for a well-dressed gentleman who was leaning over the bar with an exasperating leer. Jamie turned toward Matt for a little sympathy but Matt just rolled his eyes. "Jeez, let me get them," he said, pushing Jamie aside a little less than gently.

"I hate this place after games," Jamie replied as he watched Matt get the bartender's attention with a simple wave and a smile.

"Why? Because it's full of people having fun?" Matt asked.

Jamie shrugged off the sarcasm and waited for his drink. It was hard to argue with Matt. There certainly were a lot of people and they did seem to be having fun, at least if the noise was any indication. The Shoebox nestled among the warehouses in the shadows of the stadium and was always packed on game nights. Crowds were especially big after hometown wins, and Jamie had helped fill the place on this night.

"We only came here tonight because we knew you were working," Matt told the bartender as he handed her a twenty.

"I only came here tonight because I knew I was working," she said with a perfunctory smile as she slapped his change down on the counter.

"Yeah, so we have a lot in common. We ought to ditch this place when you're off work."

Jamie cringed as Matt's response trailed after the bartender who was swiftly retreating to satiate the masses.

"What did you do that for?" Jamie asked after they had moved to a quieter section of the room.

"What do you mean? Can't a guy chat with an attractive woman any more?"

"Not if the chatting is nothing but cheesy pick-up lines from a guy who has a girlfriend, attractive or otherwise," Jamie said with a smile.

"Bite me, you know I split with Mandy months ago. And are you implying she's not attractive?"

"She's way too attractive for you. And I heard you got desperate and took her to see some artsy fartsy movie at the Seattle Film Festival this week."

"Who said that?" Matt demanded.

Jamie answered only with a smirk. Matt grew uncomfortable with the silence and finally added, "I did break it off and thought I was away clean. But you know how her phone number is only one digit away from my brother's? Well, I called her by accident when I was trying to get Ad."

"Yeah, so what?"

"Look, I didn't realize it 'till she answered the phone. I couldn't hang up. She's got caller i.d. And I couldn't say something lame like I miss-dialed, could I?" Matt asked.

"Why not?"

"Come on. She seemed so happy I called, so I said I just wanted to see if she was doing all right. She had been pretty upset when I broke things off."

"Wow, that's great stuff, Matt, if you're trying to hook up with her, but is totally wasted if you're trying to split up. I'm thinking you subconsciously miss-dialed on purpose."

"No way, Freud. But one thing led to another and we ended up going to some movie that seemed to be about a tree."

Jamie's curiosity overpowered the smirk. He hesitated, leaned back, and repeated, "a tree?"

"I'm not kidding you," Matt sputtered. "It was about animals crawling around the tree and people playing around the tree but you couldn't even see their faces. No sex, no real action, no nothing."

"So what was the point? What was so special about this tree?"

"Look, the point is, there was no point and if there was, it was a worthless point."

"So did Mandy like it? Did she say what she thought it was about?"

"No, she didn't particularly like it but you're missing the big picture here, buddy. The fact that she could even go to that movie and not walk out is why we can never be a couple."

"So there was zero plot?" Jamie asked.

"Yeah, the tree grew old and stuff happened around it. You're so damn interested, why don't you go see it? I hope I didn't spoil things for you by giving too much away!"

"Okay, fine," Jamie said. "But what about you and Mandy? Did you hit it off? Maybe hook up for old times sake?"

Matt paused for a moment and continued seriously, "No. Actually, it was weird, like our first date all over again."

"So how did you leave it?"

"Well, I told her we couldn't be a couple anymore, which is why you have to come with us to Sunday's M's game."

With all their history, Jamie was taken aback at how Matt could continue to surprise him. "What?" he said, recoiling in horror more real than mock. "You've got another date with her?"

"Look, she felt bad about the movie and all, so we're going to a baseball game to kind of make up for it."

"You have got to be kidding me," Jamie said with a grin and a shake of his head. "You're a friggin' idiot."

"No, Jamie, that's why you've got to get a date and come with us like it's just a group thing with the old gang. You've got the company tickets. We can sit there. My brother's got your tickets, so we all meet for brunch. That way it won't look like a date and then we can fade into the sunset. You could even give her a ride home since she lives by you."

"Wait a sec," Jamie said as he turned back from his beer. "You're not pushing your problem off on me."

Matt recovered his momentum, shifting quickly from defense to offense, "No you'll have your own date, so yeah, the drive home thing won't work. But go ask Rebecca McPherson over there. I know you're hot on her."

"No way. Who says I'm hot on her? Where is she?"

"She's at the pool table with her brothers. They say you were drooling over her at the Cal game."

"No, no, no…"

"Yes, yes, yes, because you don't want me over there asking her to join us. It will make you look more like the Meatball we all know you are."

It took another beer but eventually the alcohol and Jamie's emerging self confidence allowed him to approach Rebecca. After exchanging greetings, he felt surprisingly at ease when he blurted, "I was wondering if you might want to join me at a brunch before this Sunday's game. We'd be eating some of my cousins and their dates before heading over to the Shoe."

Rebecca smiled as Jamie disassembled, "Did I just say 'eating?' I meant 'meeting.' I mean we'd be meeting AND eating but we'd be meeting my cousins and eating the brunch."

Rebecca's laugh suddenly made everything pretty cool as she answered, "Sure, it sounds like fun."

Jamie wanted to hang around and revel in this warm good feeling but his ride home, cousin Matt, was being ejected from the bar, albeit to a rousing ovation. A pair of passers-by made the mistake of wearing New York baseball jackets past the front window of the Shoebox. Matt was a momentary hero to the alcohol impaired Seattle fans for mooning them.

Chapter Ten

"You're late," Matt shouted.

"I am not. I'm in time for the first pitch," Jamie insisted as he climbed over Dano and Mac McPherson only to find Matt in the seat he coveted.

"That's late for you," Matt replied.

Jamie didn't bother to reply. He was tempted to ask his cousin to switch but the game was starting and he didn't want to embarrass himself. So he bided his time. Detroit was as listless as usual on this Saturday night. And so was Jamie's scorecard. None of his predictions came true. This allowed the Devils to keep pace with Seattle at two runs apiece through five innings. Jamie was mystified.

As the M's took the field in the top of the sixth, a young lady in purple slacks slipped through a seam in the very visible ring of security, pulled off her top, and darted toward Donny Kuhn. Several startled security officers overcame their initial shock and took off in belated pursuit. Donny did not appear threatened by the topless miss and her entourage. He stood his ground. The trespasser, later identified as Topless Tess, stopped long enough to plant a big kiss and a few words on him.

Her mission accomplished, Tess was bewildered for a moment and then tried to sprint across the infield. Players and coaches have been known to tackle drunken intruders not caught quickly enough but everyone except the security posse remained frozen. Tess managed to evade the enforcement contingent for a prude's eternity but was finally surrounded before she could reach third base. Even then her captors were comically awkward about getting a security jacket draped over their moving target.

Matt excused himself to hit the restroom with the parting words, "I hate to leave now when the game's finally getting interesting."

Jamie slipped into Matt's seat and found that the Seattle offense was now willing to take instruction in the last of the sixth. Matt returned in time to see Donny Kuhn hit a grandslam and turned to Jamie and said, "Wow, I guess I should have surrendered your seat sooner!"

"I guess the magic kiss worked for Donny," Mac hollered over to the cousins. "Hopefully, the M's will make it a regular feature of each home game!"

After Kuhn hit another grandslam in the seventh, it didn't seem like the game could get any wilder. But three batters later, Rudy Wink came up with runners on second and third. He popped a "sure" base hit into short center field but the ball seemed to hang miraculously long, just off the ground. The fleet Detroit center fielder came out of nowhere to skim the ball from the top of the beckoning blades of grass. Both runners took off as soon as it was apparent the "hit" was down. But when the phantom single evaporated, the center fielder righted himself and continued forward. He ran across the second base bag that had been vacated by the runner prematurely and by the middle infielders who had been chasing the popup.

Meanwhile, the runner on third, ignorant of the catch, had crossed home plate and was heading for the first base dugout. Detroit's center fielder just kept running toward his own dugout, touching third base, and completing a rare unassisted triple play. It looked like everything was coming up threes in the eighth when Donny Kuhn hit his third grandslam in three innings.

Jamie wasn't the only person impressed that an outfielder could make an unassisted triple play with runners on second and third. But that would only be a footnote to the coverage of Topless Tess and the inspiration she provided for Kuhn's record breaking three grandslams.

Jamie could not take any direct credit for Topless Tess and he could not take any public credit for Donny's six homers in the last two games. Fortunately, Donny Kuhn himself was up to the task of grabbing the glory. Topless Tess wasn't needed to attract national attention to the unprecedented feat of three grandslams by one player in one game but it made a big story even better.

"How would you rate the kiss?" Donny was asked on the post game show.

"It was the highlight of the game for me."

"Better than three grandslams?"

"Well, it felt like a four homerun day for me, even though I didn't get past first base on that one."

"What did Topless Tess say to you out there?"

"She asked if I could get her some playoff tickets because this is the year the M's finally go to the show!"

Topless Tess never confirmed what she said to Donny although one writer claimed she told him, "The devil made me do it."

The Devil Protesters were quick to characterize the incident as an exclamation point for the very godlessness they were fighting, citing the shocking number of spectators who were loudly cheering the spectacle.

After the locker room was finally cleared of the press, Rudy Wink asked no one and everyone, "So is the Kuhn Circus still in town tomorrow? Do we even need to show up or will Donny require some help leading elephants in a parade around the infield?"

"It's not my fault the women dig hot homerun hitters," Donny yelled back. "I'll be glad to lead elephants around the infield if you want to bring your women in."

Rudy glared at Donny as laughter rolled around the room. When Rudy took a step toward Donny, Coach Duda waddled between the two men. With his bare gut hanging over his briefs and shaving cream lathered on his face, Zip shouted, "Hey, what's going on here? We just won another game. We're 4-1 on this homestand but we've got a long way to get where we're going and we need to have everyone pulling in the same direction. So let's go celebrate and come back tomorrow ready to trash Detroit again if they bother to show up."

The locker room cleared out quietly. In the morning paper, unnamed sources were quoted as saying bad blood erupted between Wink and Kuhn. The same sources claimed that Donny was using steroids.

"The only thing Rudy and I talked about was whether elephants are the ugliest circus animals," Kuhn responded on Sunday's pre-game show. "He voted for Zippy the Clown. And the only performance enhancing drug I use is a daily dose of Mist burger and chili fries!"

When asked for his version, Rudy Wink said, "I don't know what you're talking about. Who would be crazy enough to get in an argument with a man hitting three homers a night and holding our ticket to a big post season payday?"

Zip Duda, the incongruent and gabby peacemaker, touched all the bases, saying, "There was no argument, period. Nothing happened. You guys blow things all out of proportion. Rudy and Donny took care of their business in the clubhouse like we always do. They were just joking around. They resolved their differences and their argument is ancient history. I've seen lots worse."

Chapter Eleven

Jamie and Rebecca showed up for Sunday Brunch at the appointed hour and found everyone else just sitting down with platefuls of food. Jamie was first to speak, "Don't wait on us, we're going to be on time, so just go ahead and start."

"See, I told you, we should have waited," Adam's girlfriend said.

"Jamie's kidding," Matt replied. "He told us he was going on the Love Diet, so we thought we'd eat early and spare him the agony of watching us gorge ourselves."

"Jamie doesn't look like he needs to diet," Mandy observed.

"See, it's working already," Matt answered.

"What's the Love Diet?" Mandy asked.

"Well," Matt said, "that's where you cut out carbs, protein, and fat and you live on love alone."

Rebecca glanced at Matt's midsection, which was dangerously close to giving birth to a baby beer belly but only said, "I might try that diet myself."

Jamie began to wonder if this brunch was a good idea and shifted the conversation. "Who's using the other two tickets?"

"Ad insisted on sitting in the grown-up seats with Llew and Uncle Art," Matt answered.

"We're certainly willing to rotate at any time during the game," Adam said. "But first you might want to get in the buffet line before it gets any longer."

By the time Jamie and Rebecca returned with their food, Adam excused himself and headed back to the buffet. When he came back, Mandy said, "I wish I could get on your diet. You seem to eat anything you want and never get fat."

"What do you mean? He has a fat head," his brother said.

Before long the talk migrated to the celebrated antics of Topless Tess. Rebecca took the opportunity to interject, "It's good to see that women are finally on the playing field with the men in the major leagues."

"You forgot about the ballgirls," Matt reminded her. "And some of the ground crew are females, San Diego has a female trainer, and women get to sing the National Anthem sometimes."

"Whose side are you on, anyway?" Adam said with a laugh.

"What do you think will happen to Tess for that stunt?" Mandy asked.

"Why, are you thinking about trying it?" Matt inquired in his sleaziest tone.

"If she's got a clean record, she'll probably get off with probation and a slap on the wrist when everything dies down," Adam replied more directly to Mandy's question.

"What do you think should happen to her?" Rebecca asked.

"I'm fine with that," Adam said with a shrug.

"She'll probably get a spread in Playboy or some other boost in her career," Mandy added.

"Is that good or bad?" Rebecca asked.

"What do you think?" Adam said quickly.

"I'm fine with that," Rebecca said while imitating Adam's shrug.

Rebecca then turned and addressed Mandy, "You talked about a boost in her career. What does she do?"

"Oh, I have no idea," Mandy answered. "I just assume she's an exotic dancer or something like that. And it just doesn't seem right to get free publicity and make a bunch of money for taking off your top in public."

"Probably not," Rebecca agreed. "But it doesn't seem right to pay an average ballplayer several million dollars a year when a good teacher would be lucky to make two percent of that."

"As a third grade teacher, I agree that it doesn't seem right at all," Mandy said

"That's just the law of supply and demand," Adam interjected.

"But the minor leagues are full of players lined up and eager to take any of those jobs," Rebecca replied.

"Oh, but not with the skill of the players in the majors," Adam said.

"Are you including the Detroit players in that category?" Matt asked.

"Sure, you're just so used to seeing major leaguers that you don't realize how good even the worst ones are. They're like the finalists for Teacher of the Year from each state."

"And all of those all star teachers earn but a fraction of what an M's bench warmer makes," Mandy noted.

"So the universe is unfolding as it should," Matt said with a laugh.

"Not until the M's win the World Series," Jamie added.

"I second that," Matt agreed and offered his orange juice glass for a clink with Jamie's.

"I thought they had a losing record again this year," Mandy said tentatively.

"Yep, they're 7-10 but they've won four out of five and Donny Kuhn is leading the league with ten homers and 26 rbi's," Matt answered.

"You think Kuhn is going to continue to hit like that all season?" Adam said.

"No," Matt replied, "because if he continues at that pace, he'll be walked every time up."

Jamie's relief that the conversation was meandering back to baseball statistics and strategy was short-lived. The omelets and hashbrowns were spiced up with provocative questions about the fairness of front office hiring practices, the morality of environmental practices at Sanford Shoe factories, and finally, the ethics of charging triple for food and drinks inside the stadium.

"Law of supply and demand," Adam said.

"I could understand that theory if the Shoe were in the middle of nowhere," Rebecca replied. "But supply and demand should drive the price down. With one huge delivery to a centrally located stadium, the economies of scale should drive beer and hot dog prices lower than most every other place. It seems more like the law of greed and gouging."

Matt took this as his cue, stood up, and announced, "Fortunately, they can't gouge me today because I'm so stuffed, I don't know if I can waddle over to the Shoe in time for the first pitch, let alone eat or drink ever again."

All this food for thought Jamie would need to digest later. This game he was careful to concentrate on Rebecca. Seattle was down 3-2 in the sixth when she left to use the restroom. For the first time he turned his attention to the scorebook and scribbled furiously.

Jamie's impact was immediate. The first Seattle batter reached base on an error by the Detroit pitcher. The next hitter laid down a bunt and reached safely when the catcher threw the ball into right field. The first baseman booted Wink's grounder and then the second baseman threw Escobar's double play ball away. Jamie waited nervously while the relief pitcher ran out to the mound.

The new pitcher inspired no better defense as the shortstop dropped a Thorne popup and the third baseman threw Grant's grounder away. Finally Kuhn homered and Rebecca returned. Her urinary tract would not get any recognition for the role that it played in the timing of the bizarre rally that made the difference in a 9-5 hometown win. But then neither would Jamie.

Adam and his girlfriend made a cameo appearance in the ninth inning and were greeted loudly by Matt, "Hey Ad, tell us some more about how minor leaguers couldn't possibly perform to the standards of the Detroit infielders!"

"I thought Detroit was a minor league team," Adam replied without missing a beat.

Chapter Twelve

Llew glared at Jeffrey Anne Jones and wished he had never even hired a Human Resources Director. He thought she would keep the government alphabet soup of EEOC's, OFCCP's, AAP's, and ADA's off his table. His son Adam, the Tinkler lawyer, had said she would be able to help fight the union organizing as well. But all she was doing was exasperating him.

"Listen, Llew, I am trying to help you," Jeffrey Anne pleaded, "but guys like Rob just cannot use that kind of language in today's workplace. I'm only asking you to tell everyone at the next All Hands meeting to clean it up. They'll listen to you. It'll save us some grief down the road."

"I don't get it," Llew fired back, "thirty years ago on the Smothers Brothers or Laugh In, you could hardly say 'hell' or 'damn' on television but you could swear up a bluestreak in the shop. Now you can discuss oral sex in a prime time sitcom and you can't tell someone to move their fat ass in the factory?"

"Yes, that's right, I'm glad you understand," Jeffrey Anne said with traces of a smile.

Llew didn't even understand what an attractive woman like Jeffrey Anne was doing working in the construction industry. Still he plowed on, "Years ago we told the liberal 'do-gooders' that the factory was no place for a woman but they insisted on equal rights, so we put them in the factory jobs and then they start complaining about the shop language. They can't have it both ways. We told 'em they wouldn't like the shop floor and they don't. It seems like they either adapt or stay the hell out!"

Although Jeffrey Anne was a good twenty years younger than Llew, she put on her best motherly expression and calmly but firmly explained, "Much as some of this makes no sense to us, it is in our best interest to do the adapting. It doesn't compromise any of our core values. Our mission isn't to preserve the right of Rob to demean women and practice his bathroom comedy routines at work. He can do that on his own time."

"Alright, alright, I'll do it," Llew replied, quickly changing gears, "but have we found out any more about who's leaving that union literature on the desks and work benches? That should be easy enough to pin down. And don't tell me I can't fire his ass when we find him. Can I say 'ass' if I leave off the 'fat'?"

Jeffrey Anne ignored the last question but offered, "We do have sources and we think we can get some inside info on the AFW organizing meeting this Wednesday night at the union hall. We should be able to get an idea of how many people are involved and what their plan is. Adam is putting together a booklet on the do's and don'ts for our supervisors and crew chiefs, so we don't accidentally have someone committing an unfair labor practice."

"Good, I think our unfair labor practices should all be on purpose," Llew said without any indication that he was joking.

When Llew started looking at some of the papers on his desk while talking, Jeffrey Anne knew he was fast losing interest in the conversation and she took that as her cue to exit.

"Hey, before you go," Llew looked up and motioned to Jeffrey Anne, "do we need to be getting these Employment Newsletters every week? They're sending a renewal notice for $279 for six months. Do we have to pay that much just to get more spam e-mail clogging our system? Does anyone read that stuff?"

"Yes," Jeffrey Anne asserted emphatically. "Adam and I read them and we circulate them to your management team."

"So that's why my managers aren't getting their work done. I'm paying them to do all this reading."

"Better than paying them to testify in court."

"Okay, I'll pay the ransom," Llew shook his head even as he wrote "cancel" across the invoice and bet himself a steak dinner that no one would ever notice when the newsletters stopped coming.

Jeffrey Anne resumed her exit, smugly satisfied that she was in control of employment issues at Tinkler. As she returned to the Personnel Office, she bumped into Matt rounding a corner.

Matt smiled and asked, "How was Papa Llew's mood today?"

"Oh, I think he was about ready to ask me why I'm not home with a husband and having babies but he got distracted again by his favorite passion, the union. You need to get whatever info you can from anyone who attends that meeting on Wednesday."

Matt looked confused and asked, "You didn't tell Papa Llew that I had any knowledge of what's going on, did you?"

"No, I just said we had sources and we'd keep our ears to the ground. He knows I'm telling him as little as possible so he has deniability. But anything we can find out will make our jobs easier. We'll look good if we are ahead of the game. Frankly I think a union might do some good around here but our job performance is based on how well we keep them out."

Jeffrey Anne took her leave and continued the trek back to her office but ran into Jamie just outside her door. He awkwardly mumbled a greeting. Acting oblivious to their discomfort, Jeffrey Anne motioned for him to join her inside and said, "Hi, Jamie, come on in, I was just going to call you."

"I need to talk to you about Rob," Jamie began, "he's coming in late, he's been late on more deliveries, and I think he may have a drinking problem."

"I just talked to Llew about the complaints on Rob's language and your Uncle is going to address it at his next All Hand's meeting. This other stuff should be handled directly by Matt, as Rob's crew chief. Have you talked to Matt about it? Do you have any proof of the alcohol problem?"

"That's just it, I don't have any solid evidence about the booze. I have talked to Matt about the performance issues but he's blowing me off. I'm the Sales Rep, though, and Rob is killing me in the field. I was hoping you could help run some interference."

"Alright, Jamie, I'll talk to Matt discreetly and see what I can do but you're the closest to Matt. If he doesn't listen to you, he sure won't listen to me. By the way, are you noticing any union activity? You know what a hot button that is for your Uncle."

Jamie thought for a moment but couldn't recollect anything and was more interested in just gracefully exiting the office.

Chapter Thirteen

Jamie tried to stifle the elation he felt when he spotted the scraggy red headed vendor who was now his regular source of scorecards. But he did hustle over to make the transaction just minutes after the gates opened on the Tuesday following the M's six game road trip.

"Awfully anxious, aren't we?" the hawker asked with the first smile Jamie had seen from him.

The smile did not convey warmth and Jamie was caught off guard. He just shrugged and exchanged two dollars for the scorecard.

As he wandered the Shoe, Jamie was oblivious to the upbeat mood as fans began filtering into the stadium. Although the Mist still owned a losing record at 11-13, they had managed a split on the road and the memory of the successful and exciting last homestand was still fresh in everybody's mind.

I wonder if I should ask that guy, "What gives with the magic scorecard?" Jamie mused. *What would he say to that? Would he look at me like I was crazy or would he nod knowingly? Should I talk to him?*

Retracing his steps, Jamie found no sign of the vendor. He even looked on all three levels, hatching a plan to at least observe him. But the hawker who seemed ever present was nowhere to be found. Despite the detours, Jamie still beat his cousins to the seats. Matt and Adam arrived together and Matt mauled Jamie's shoulder while yelling three inches from his ear, "The M's are catching on FIRE tonight!"

Jamie backed away and Matt continued in a lower voice, "They've won eight of their last twelve. Is this the beginning of something big or what?"

"I figure we're 6-3 at the Shoe," Adam said before Jamie could respond. "If we keep up that pace and continue to split on the road, and of course those are big 'ifs,' we'd barely get 90 wins and likely miss the playoffs anyway."

"So why are you here tonight, Adam, if it's all so hopeless?" Matt asked.

"Because it's all about hanging out with the guys on an unseasonably warm Seattle night, drinking beer, eating junk food, watching heroes rise and fall, always on the lookout for a woman like Topless Tess who might be worthy enough to join the Tinkler Toilet family."

"Speaking of Tess," Matt began, "did you guys see all the letters to the sports editor in Sunday's paper? Her performance and the confiscation of the Donny Dinger signs prompted more public debate than anything the M's are doing on the field."

"I think free speech is making a comeback," Jamie said, "as long as you're not too explicit. And especially if you can make money off it. Out in the right field concourse, the Mist Burger and Chili Fry concession stand is featuring a Kuhn Combo Plate. For nine bucks, you get the burger, fries, and your choice of a 'Chicks Dig Dingers' or a 'Dinger Dude' decal."

"What jerk is going to display a 'Dinger Dude' sticker?" Adam said.

"Hey, don't embarrass Jamie, he's trying to tell you he got one for his truck. He's probably going to join the Donny Kuhn fan club that's being encouraged to hang out in the right field bleachers."

Adam took another swig of his beer and said, "It may be premature to rally around Kuhn. He cooled off on the road trip right after they moved him up in the batting order. What was he, four for nineteen?"

"He did get a homer," Jamie replied. "And he had a .400 on base average when you count the five walks and getting hit by a pitch once."

"Boy, someone has been memorizing the box scores," Adam said. "You really should be sitting out in the right field seats with Donny's fan club."

"What did I miss?" Mac McPherson asked as he joined the threesome.

"Ad's whining that Kuhn doesn't hit three homers in every game," Matt answered.

Jamie was actually surprised that Donny had managed even one homerun on the road trip. Regardless, the Kuhnies in right field soon had something to cheer about when Jamie settled down to the scorebook and spotted the M's to a 1-0 lead with Donny's solo round-tripper in the second inning.

"What are you standing and cheering for?" Matt asked Adam. "Isn't that a little hypocritical after dishing dirt on Donny?"

"I just said he cooled off on the road trip. I wasn't trashing him."

In the third, Matt made Jamie shift uneasily when he suggested, "Hey guys, Jamie and I buy the next round of beer if the M's don't score this inning. You two buy if they do."

"How come you get to bet for the M's?" Adam asked.

"We'll take the bet either way," offered Matt. "Or Ad can join me on the pro run side of the bet and Jamie and Mac can go for a shutout inning."

"Hey enough already," Mac ended the debate, "Adam and I will take the original bet. Who cares who scores when? The important thing is that beer is showing up after this inning!"

Jamie was hesitant about gambling again. After Rudy Wink grounded out to short, Adam and Mac started getting comfortable with their bet, although wise enough to not actually cheer for the out. Jamie decided to try another test and put Escobar down for a single. E2 promptly singled up the middle. Matt was the most excited fan in the section, screaming above the din, "E2 rocks!"

Jamie scheduled a single for Thorne, thinking maybe an out after that would add some drama. But before Thorne could get a pitch to hit, the crafty Kansas City lefty picked E2 off first.

"Not looking good for the M's this inning," Adam said.

Still Thorne drilled the next pitch into the leftcenter field gap. The center fielder came out of the proverbial nowhere to cut the ball off and fired a perfect strike to second base, cutting down the none too swift Thorne digging for two.

"Damn it," Mac said, "what are those clowns doing out there? Only free beer could take the sting out of that inning. I'd sure hate to suffer through that display of baserunning by those two jokers and actually have to buy a round of beer!"

"I'd say more like 'stink' of that inning," Adam mumbled. "And I don't even think free beer makes it worth having to watch that."

Matt joined Jamie in the beer line and commiserated, "At least we went down betting for the M's although I get the feeling Mac and Ad win both ways. Either the M's score or they get free beer. What do you think, Meatball, should we revise our betting strategy?"

"Huh?" Jamie snapped back from his secret world where he was trying to digest what just happened. "What did you say?"

"Oh never mind, you're obviously off drooling over Rebecca."

"No, I was just thinking how damn slow this line is," he said to himself as much as to Matt. "We're going to miss a whole inning at this rate."

Jamie was happy they made it back to the seats in time for the M's to bat in the fourth. He was relieved to find his prognostication skill intact but played a conservative game the rest of the way. He refused to bet for beers in the sixth, begging off, "Hey, I just don't want to ever jinx them again after that pitiful display of baserunning in the third."

Although the M's won 7-4, the game lacked drama. "At least it went fast," Matt noted at the conclusion. "Just over two and a half hours. Maybe I can get home at a decent time for a change."

"That doesn't sound like the Matt we know and love," Adam said. "Mac and I were planning on hitting the Shoebox for a quick one."

"How about you, Jamie?" Matt asked. "Are you going out?"

"Nah, I'm taking a rain check tonight if you want to catch a ride with me," Jamie said. "I drove down from work because I came so early."

Matt and Jamie crossed Pioneer Square on the way to Jamie's truck. As they passed an art gallery, Matt leaned down over a homeless man sleeping in the doorway. Impatiently, Jamie stage whispered, "What are you doing, man?"

"Nothing," Matt said as he quickly rejoined Jamie.

"What do you mean nothing? What were you doing to that guy?"

"Don't go blabbing this around, I just stuck some money in his shirt pocket."

"How much?"

"A ten spot."

"Why?" Jamie asked.

"He looked like he could use it," Matt said with a shrug.

"So why don't you give the money to the musicians on the street? At least they're working for the cash. Or add it to the money we give through work to the Matt Talbot Center downtown. At least we know they use the money for food, shelter, and treatment."

"Well, everyone should get a surprise and have a good day once in awhile," Matt said. "Hey, look someone broke the window on your truck!"

"Dammit!" Jamie said.

He ran over to his pickup and began a quick inventory.

"Your buddy in the doorway probably had a good laugh going through our stuff. Luckily there's not much of value to take. It looks like they got a couple bucks in change and that little cooler of mine."

"It looks like you weren't the only one hit," Matt said. He pointed down the street where one car had a broken window and shattered glass lay next to an empty parking space.

"Damn, I liked that cooler," Jamie muttered to himself.

"Oh hell, you can buy a new one for a couple bucks," Matt tried to reassure Jamie.

"Fine. Go get that ten back from your doorway buddy and we'll buy another mini cooler. C'mon, let's get out of here."

As Matt and Jamie sped away from Pioneer Square, the game's hero was moving just as quickly to get to the Square and its hotspots. Donny Kuhn dressed rapidly and called his girlfriend to tell her it was going to be a boy's night out.

"At least you were honest and told her you were letting your boys out," Rudy Wink yelled after the emerging star as Kuhn left to check out the Tuesday night groupies.

Chapter Fourteen

"Lunch, you and me?" Matt mouthed quietly.

It was 11:35 and he was standing outside Jamie's office pointing toward his cousin and then back to himself. Jamie nodded in the affirmative as he continued speaking into the phone, "Okay, thanks for the info, I'll get back to you if I need anything."

As soon as he extracted himself from the conversation, Jamie turned and said, "Hey, Matt, did you know Theresa is no longer with Interstate Insurance? I just tried to reach her to talk about my truck's broken window. I forgot I've got a $500 deductible."

"So what happened to her?" Matt asked, "she had a great personality and always seemed pretty efficient to me."

"I don't know. They were pretty evasive when I tried to reach her."

"Well, Meatball, let's hit the Whole while Papa Llew goes uptown to The Club with Chick Pitz, Mr. Assistant Vice President of Operations for the M's. We weren't invited," Matt noted with emphasis.

Llew had been looking forward to the lunch with his old classmate. Maybe talk over old times, get the inside scoop on the M's, plan a fishing trip. Chick got his name because he claimed he could talk to chickens. He was on a baseball scholarship in college but he made spending money betting in bars that he could carry on a conversation with a chicken. He had apparently trained his pet chickens to respond to some combination of verbal and non-verbal signals. No matter how he did it, his damn chickens were famous as "gamers" when the money was down.

"How do you like your new season tickets this year?" Chick asked.

"They are definitely closer to the action than our old ones. We appreciate the upgrade. How come they came available?"

"The previous owner died and his family decided not to renew," Chick answered.

"Well, thanks for thinking of us," Llew said.

"You've been real loyal customers over the good times and bad."

"When were those 'good times?' Remind me again," Llew replied.

Chick laughed politely but altered the mood when he shifted the conversation to the union. Llew visibly stiffened and his guard went up. Nevertheless, Chick plowed on.

"I'm just telling you, Llew, you're the only non-union contractor we work with and we've been taking the heat on you for a long time. But it's hurting your business worse than ours. I know for a fact that Tinkler is losing good contracts because key union sources are blackballing you. Don't get steamed at me. I'm here as a friend. I'm trying to help you get the business you deserve."

"So what are you saying, Chick?" Llew demanded. "You just want me to cut a deal and recognize the AFW and sell out our employees who don't want a union? Why? Because those leeches take you on fishing junkets? If he knew you were helping those bloodsuckers, Papa Joe would roll over in his grave."

"Now that ain't fair, Llew, I ain't part of any sucking going on but I do know it's complicated when one guy's not on the program. The AFW's got contracts where they can't cross picket lines and they ain't working with any non union outfits. They've got their principles, you've got yours. But you being on a job can shut down everything. If no one's working, it's not good for anyone, union or non-union. They ain't asking for you to just recognize them on a card check. They just want a fair election where you let the employees vote without any anti-union lawyers running a campaign. They claim they've got the votes, Llew."

"Oh, so they get to put out their lies in their bullshit handouts," Llew continued slowly, "and we just sit on our hands letting them trash the truth?"

"Llew, you know what I mean. I loved Papa Joe. You know that. But times change. Those union busting law firms are as bad as any union lies," Chick responded before trapping the last piece of salad with some bread and stuffing it in his mouth.

Llew thought quietly while Chick chewed.

"What are you thinking, Llew," Chick asked, "that maybe you'll at least think about a clean election, letting the employees make the choice?"

Llew felt like saying he was thinking about getting himself some chicken up at the buffet but thought better of it and said, "Tinkler rolling over for the union? What next? The M's winning a World Series?"

Chapter Fifteen

Llew's frustration over lunch with Chicken Pitz was mild compared to the distress of the Seattle fans at the Shoe that night. The M's loaded the bases every single inning but had not scored through the eighth frame, another unprecedented event in all the history of baseball. Down 2-0, the Mist filled the bases again in the ninth. With two out, Rudy Wink drew a walk. When the Kansas City closer hit Escobar with a pitch, the game was tied and the stadium finally breathed a collective sigh of relief.

Larry Thorne, the big slugger in the number three spot, swaggered to the dish at just the right time. He was paid big bucks to deliver with the game on the line. Larry seemed to enjoy prolonging the drama as he stared for what seemed like forever at Zip Duda, the third base coach. Thorne finally stepped slowly into the batter's box.

The three runners danced off their bases but the pitcher ignored them. He knew everything came down to him and the batter. The pitch was a little fatter than the Kansas City closer might have liked but his confidence was lagging under the weight of his most recent wildness. So he was both shocked and relieved when Thorne squared around as if to bunt. The pitcher hoped Thorne was taking this pitch, a strike headed for the meaty part of the plate.

Jamie squirmed nervously in his seat as the runners took off with the pitch. Thorne laid his bat on the ball and the bunt dribbled into the Bermuda triangle between pitcher, catcher, and third baseman. The suicide squeeze is aptly named and rarely tried with two outs because so much can go wrong. If the batter misses the ball, the vulnerable runner from third is dead. If the batter is thrown out, the inning dies. Unlike a standard sacrifice or squeeze bunt with less than two out, success is rare. And if the hitter is a burly homerun slugger like Thorne, the chances of beating out a bunt for a basehit are even slimmer.

This time Thorne had the advantage of surprise, a hitter's pitch, and a perfectly placed bunt. The pinch runner on third came barreling down the line. The catcher had to stay at the plate to take a throw. The third baseman, who had been playing deep on Thorne, was racing toward the ball, but was well behind the speedy runner in that sprint. The pitcher actually reached the ball first, but since the runner started with a big lead and was moving on the pitch, he was going to beat any throw to the plate. By the time the pitcher straightened, turned, and threw the ball to first, he was even too late to get Thorne.

A night full of fan frustration was quickly transformed to shock and then elation as the Seattle players mobbed the pinch runner and Thorne. Jamie couldn't gamble but he could make the Seattle offense gamble.

Seattle's manager was too dumb to take credit for calling the play. Zip Duda, who could be accused of botching the play, was not shy about jumping into the credit void. "I could see that the defense was playing deep on Thorne, so I knew he could burn them," Duda said. "But I couldn't draw attention to it by calling time to get the manager's approval, so I went with the call."

Zip was later fined $100 for over-riding the manager but he would have been fined for admitting he botched the real sign anyway, so he was glad to spend the token amount to look like a hero. Thorne and the pinch runner took turns maneuvering for credit but when the media cleared, Rudy Wink shouted above the locker room din, "Hey, I don't know what you all are celebrating. We stunk. We just set a record for futility. We couldn't get one clutch basehit. KC gave us that game. We won't be able to rely on walks and suicide squeeze gimmicks every game."

"Stuff it," E2 yelled. "We won! Get used to enjoying the wins."

And so the jubilation continued. Although the dramatic win was emotionally draining with so much suffering along the way, this made the celebration all the better for the fans. Jamie said his good byes to the three McPherson employees up from Olympia for the game. He was pleased that the Tinkler guests seemed thrilled with the experience.

Jamie had been so busy with the guests and the scorebook that he had failed to eat much that night. When he got home, he was starving. He greedily eyed the well-stocked refrigerator shelves and called out, "Is any of this food off limits, Ma?"

"What do you want?" Jo asked.

"It doesn't much matter to me. I just want to avoid anything you're saving for your lady's luncheon."

"Well, don't eat the chicken salad. That's what I'm serving tomorrow. You can have anything else."

"So I can eat some of this antipasto?" Jamie asked.

"Well, I really want to put that out while we're playing cards."

"Just tell me everything that's off limits," Jamie said with a slight whine.

"That's it," Jo confirmed.

"So it's safe for me to eat the chili?"

"Why do you want to eat chili at this hour?" Jo asked.

"What difference does it make?" Jamie demanded. "Can I have it?"

"Okay," Jo sighed with a heaviness that unnerved Jamie.

"Obviously you don't want me to eat it," Jamie said.

"No, you can have it. I just like to use it when we make nachos. There's some salmon and rice from the deli. Did you see that, Jamie?"

"Yeah, I saw it, Ma, but I don't want it tonight."

"I thought you liked the salmon from the deli."

"I do, Ma, just not tonight. All I want to know is what can I eat in here," Jamie pleaded.

"Anything you want, dear. Go ahead and eat the chili. I'll buy some more."

Jamie couldn't bear to continue the roll call through the chicken breasts and leftover spaghetti. Instead he grabbed some chips and salsa and headed for his room.

"I don't know why you don't eat healthier," Jo called after him. "I can make you a BLT if you like."

"No thanks, Ma," Jamie answered weakly.

Chapter Sixteen

Jamie was surprised and relieved to see his mysterious scorecard vendor still in position in the sixth inning. Jamie was late to the game, one of several afternoon contests peppered throughout the schedule on Thursdays. Once called Businessman Specials, they were really a way for teams travelling for a weekend series to get out of town early. Jamie had planned to sneak out for the entire game but was trapped on the phone with customers in Tacoma and Olympia, trying to untangle the mess Rob McPherson was making of his delivery route.

"I had almost given up on you," the hawker said.

"I couldn't let everyone down," Jamie answered coyly.

"Well, you better hustle up because the M's are down 5-1 already."

"What's the deal with these scorecards, anyway?" Jamie asked.

"Look, I've been waiting long enough for you. I've got things to do without wasting any more time chatting. I think you have things to do, too," the vendor said as he turned and stalked off.

"We need to talk," Jamie yelled after him.

But Jamie had his fix for the day and he scurried off to his seat. He had plenty of time to imagine and then witness a seven run Seattle rally over the course of the seventh and eighth innings. The M's escaped with an 8-5 win, completed a sweep of Kansas City, and vaulted to a winning season record of 14-13.

Arriving at work early the next morning, Jamie savored the sports page account of the game while he waited for Jeffrey Anne to arrive. Donny Kuhn was again the man of the hour after pounding his league leading thirteenth homer of the season, a three run eighth inning shot that provided the winning margin. Coach Duda, always hovering around the limelight, eagerly explained how he had worked extensively with Donny in spring training on a new grip to give him more power. Kuhn retorted, "Yeah, Zipper was a big help showin' me that grip on the beer bottle. It's amazing that power guzzle of his!"

Jamie was rereading the quote when he saw Jeffrey Anne maneuver her red Subaru into the parking lot. He quickly folded up the paper and headed for her office. "Hey, I was hoping to catch you early," he greeted her in the hallway.

"Great, but we'll have to make it quick, I've got a 7:30 with Llew," she said with a fake smile which silently screamed, *Great, just what I don't need when I've got a meeting with Llew to get ready for.*

"No, problem, this will just take a sec," Jamie spoke quickly. "I just wanted to know if you had a chance to talk to Matt?"

"Matt?" Jeffrey Anne asked vaguely, exposing how little attention she was paying to Jamie's issue.

"Yeah, did he crack down on Rob or not? He's missing more deliveries than he's making."

Jeffrey Anne sensed the mounting annoyance in Jamie's tone and quickly recovered, "Oh, yes, I did talk to Matt and he's going to get with Rob and if that doesn't work, we're just going to have to issue him a written warning."

"I'm not sure we've got time for that," Jamie seethed, "because I'm going to Llew and Adam on this since customers are about to cancel orders and I just wanted to be able to tell them that you'd already done everything possible with Rob from a Human Resources perspective. This is a heads up, so you don't get surprised that the problem has escalated out of control."

Jeffrey Anne called after Jamie as he headed back down the hall, "Let me get right back into this…"

Jamie took a few deep breaths in his office, made himself a cup of tea and reflected on the whole Rob mess. Jamie knew it was out of character for him to get so agitated and he didn't like it when he showed emotion. He knew Jeffrey Anne probably was wondering why he wasn't dealing more with Matt directly but he rationalized to himself, *Isn't that what we pay an HR Director for? To run interference on the sticky "people" issues.*

Jamie began doodling a plan of attack on the scratch pad in front of him. First he would talk to Matt again and give him the same heads up he gave Jeffrey Anne. Then he would talk to Rob again. He paused and reflected, *I know that the McPhersons are important to Llew and I know he likes Rob. Hell, I like Rob. I like his sister even more. But something has to be done.*

Turning back to the list, Jamie scribbled the next items rapidly without any particular regard for their order. Number three was a telephone call to Mac McPherson who runs the McPherson operation in Olympia to set up a face to face meeting where Jamie could assure him that Tinkler had a recovery plan for fixing the delivery problem. He would also be able to diplomatically convey how much of the problem belonged to Mac's brother Rob. Number four was the same call to several smaller customers in Tacoma and to set up meetings to schmooze. Number five was developing the Recovery Plan based on the item one and two conversations and taking that Plan with him to the customer meetings.

Jamie paused to reread his list. Then for good measure, he added a number six, "run by Llew."

Jamie felt better already. By the end of the day, he had meetings set up for the following Wednesday in Tacoma and Olympia. He couldn't find either Matt or Rob, precisely the same problem the customers were having. However, Jeffrey Anne left Jamie both a phone message and an e-mail saying she had talked to Matt and that they were putting together a plan of action. "About time," Jamie muttered to himself.

Now it was time to start the weekend and head for the M's game. Jamie was nervous because it was going to be a McPherson-Tinkler night. Llew and Adam were sitting in Jamie's seats with old man McPherson and his oldest son Mac, undoubtedly talking business that would include the very delivery issues Jamie was working on. Meanwhile, Matt and Jamie would be hosting two of the other siblings in the company seats. Jamie didn't even care if Rob was there as long as Rebecca had one of the tickets.

Jamie hit the jackpot. Dano arrived with Rebecca and motioned for Matt to let Rebecca slide by to the seat next to Jamie. Dano explained, "I won a coin flip with Rob to get the last ticket after Rebecca seized the other one and wouldn't surrender it. I'm sure it wasn't because she hoped to sit with me."

While suspecting the coin flip might be fiction, Jamie was thrilled with the implication nonetheless. Rebecca just laughed and said, "You don't get too many chances to see the M's when they have a winning record and the league's rbi leader at the same time. Better take advantage of those rare opportunities when they come along."

Matt turned to Rebecca with a respectful look and seconded her observation, "Yeah, can you believe Kuhn has driven in 36 already? At that rate, he'll clear 200 easy."

"Like he has any chance of keeping that pace," Dano laughed derisively. "The M's may finish with a winning record but no way is Kuhn gonna be the first person to get 200 rbi's!"

Jamie was quiet but he felt like it just might turn into a fun night. Rebecca was curious about the scoring system he was using, so he was very shy about logging in instructions. This time he wasn't going to let the scorebook distract him from conversation with her.

"Did the Appalachian Trail experience make you more of a hiker or drive you from ever hitting the trail again?" Jamie asked in the second inning.

"It did kind of cure me from wanting to camp on the trail at least for awhile but I've already been on a day hike this spring and I'm getting the itch again. You should try it sometime."

"I've always liked hiking," Jamie exaggerated since as of that moment he truly did like the idea of hiking. "It's great for getting in shape but I'm not really in the Appalachian Trail league."

"I'm back out of Appalachian Trail shape myself, except for my appetite," Rebecca said. "An individual hike on the Trail actually isn't any different than any day hikes around here. The difference is that you do it every day for months and you camp out."

"What made you decide to do it in the first place?" Jamie asked, trying to remember exactly what he had heard about that trip.

"Three of us couples from college decided it would be a great reunion transition from dead end and nonexistent jobs we all seemed to be wallowing in. Fortunately, I was just finishing a clerkship and hadn't found a law firm job yet or I never would have been able to go."

"So you are part of a couple?" Jamie asked casually, trying without success to disguise any disappointment.

"Not anymore," Rebecca corrected. "Living on the Appalachian Trail all summer brings you together or drives you apart. One of my college roommates got engaged on the top of Mount Katahdin at the finish but the other one got injured and fed up and left the trail at Harper's Ferry. I made it to the end but the relationship didn't."

"Wow, what an experience," Jamie responded, this time trying to disguise his elation.

Throughout the game, Rebecca related some of her Appalachian Trail adventures. Jamie was a little more interested in them than the game as they provided fresh insight into this captivating woman sitting next to him. The M's did prevail 5-4 behind Kuhn's three rbi's although Adam did not seem elated when he and Mac McPherson caught up with them at the Shoebox.

When Adam had a chance to corner Matt and Jamie alone, he let them know, "Papa Llew is steamed and I don't blame him. All old man McPherson wanted to talk about was bullying us into working with the union. He basically threatened us, implying our work was in jeopardy when the current contracts come up. The AFW is really tightening the noose."

"What a crock," Matt offered. "I can't believe the McPhersons are stooping to shill for the union. When did they lose their backbone?"

Jamie was glad to hear that Rob's delivery problems weren't the focus of contention but he shuddered with concern about how this union nonsense might affect Rebecca and him.

Chapter Seventeen

"Hey, Ma," Jamie shouted to his mother as he approached the kitchen.

"Save your hay, you might have a horse someday."

"No really, Ma," Jamie continued, "did you see the front page of the Local News section?"

"I haven't touched the paper at all. Did you look on the hall table?"

"No, I've got the paper. Have you heard about Topless Tess who ran out during a ball game and kissed our second baseman?"

"No, and I don't want to hear about it."

"She is suing Interstate Insurance for unlawful termination. They apparently fired her after she was arrested at the ballpark. Her real name is Theresa Helling. Wow. She was my insurance agent. I just tried to call her last Wednesday."

"Why on earth would you have a topless insurance agent. Why are you calling up such a girl? Are you trying to kill me? What's so wrong with that Jeffrey Anne girl?"

"She wasn't a topless insurance agent. We dealt with her mostly over the phone. Apparently on her own time, she went topless at the ballgame, you know like a streaker for a prank. So her company fired her."

"Well good for them. I don't think people should have to deal with topless insurance agents. If you were doing that phone sex thing with her, I don't want to hear about it. I'm serious," Jo said.

"Ma, never mind, nothing like that ever happened," Jamie wearily answered, realizing too late that he really needed to call Matt about this.

"I can't believe they allow topless women at the ballgames now. Is that why you and your cousins spend so much time at those games? I don't want to know about it."

"That's the whole point, Ma. They don't allow it. This woman was arrested and fired from her job for doing it. You should be very happy."

"I can't be happy knowing topless women are running around insurance offices and baseball games. I sure hope they don't start showing up at restaurants and grocery stores. It's just all too much for me."

"This is all too much for me, too," Jamie said quietly as he inhaled his English muffin and headed for the garage.

After re-rigging the cardboard covering up the hole in the side window of his truck, Jamie remained in the cab, reading the Sports Page and feeling guilty for hiding from his mother. Once again Donny Kuhn was the big hero. In fact he was quoted saying, "I'm my own hero. I love what I'm doing for the M's and baseball!"

Several others were quoted as well. Rudy Wink said, "You have to look at our success as a team success. Our pitching is keeping us in games, E2 is playing big on defense, someone is always coming through when we need it."

Eduardo Escobar added, "It's a long season and we all have to stick together. I really believe this can be our year as long as we all respect each person's contribution."

The columnist's own take: "Don Kuhn's heroics have become so commonplace that Donny himself has to continually remind us just how amazing he is."

After finishing the paper, Jamie decided to drive by Rob's place since he lived less than two miles away. Maybe he could catch him in a non-threatening setting and have a good conversation. Before leaving, Jamie leaned in the back door and yelled, "Hey, Ma, I'm going by the hardware store and the grocery store to see if they've gone topless yet. Do you need anything?"

"Nope," came the clipped response.

When Jamie turned onto Eastern Avenue, he saw an old battered Buick plastered with AFW union stickers driving away from what appeared to be Rob's driveway. The car accelerated quickly as Jamie made his way down the street to Rob's house and he couldn't make out who or how many people were in the car.

Jamie parked out front, walked up the steps, and banged on the open door. From the kitchen, Rob yelled, "Come on in, did you forget something?"

Jamie stepped inside tentatively and shouted back, "Rob, it's Jamie, I just came by to talk if this is a good time."

Jamie's voice trailed off as he stared blankly at a card table filled with AFW union literature and petitions. Rob came steaming out of the kitchen, did a double take when he saw Jamie, and started spouting, "What in the hell are you doing here, are you spying on me, get the hell out of my house, and off my property!"

Jamie backed out onto the porch while Rob moved toward him in a menacing way. Jamie put his hands up, palms out, and said, "Hey, calm down Rob. I just dropped by because I wanted to talk to you away from the workplace. Maybe we could grab a cup of coffee around the corner."

Rob looked like Jamie was the last person he wanted to talk to right now, but he also didn't want Jamie running off to report on what he saw. He surely didn't want Jamie in his house, so until Rob had time to think things through, he decided to accept the offer. They rode the three short blocks in Jamie's truck. Rob asked about the cardboard window and Jamie told him.

When they had their drinks, Jamie opened by saying he was concerned about the late deliveries in Olympia and Tacoma, "Surely, you must be concerned, too, Rob. You've always been one of our key employees. The customers are chewing my ear off."

"They're such whiners, especially my brother Mac. He's always trying to make me look bad. I was late because a semi tipped last week, and no one will cut me any slack," Rob spit out defiantly.

"Rob, it's not just one customer and it's not just last week and I think you know that. I'm trying to help you by not blowing this up if we can figure out what's wrong and fix it."

Rob began to wave both his hands and spew, "Nothing's wrong. You know the damn traffic. And you don't know the damn toilets. You don't see the crap, and I do mean crap, I have to deal with. You're sitting up in your fancy office, thinking of ways to harass the guys on the firing line."

Jamie lowered his voice, hoping Rob would also, as they were starting to attract attention. "Look, you know that's not fair, Rob, I worked every job through school. I did my share of the dirty work. Has the union been filling your head with all this propaganda?"

Rob paused for a moment and then responded, "The union is what we need around here for exactly the reasons we're talking about. Here you are harassing me, threatening me about my job, coming to my home. I don't have any fancy degree or relative running the company. I need someone to stick up for me and make sure I don't get screwed."

"Hey, wait a minute, Rob. You come from privilege and your relatives call a lot of the shots at Tinkler. And they're complaining the loudest about late deliveries. I'm sorry you feel like you're getting screwed but I'm just giving you the courtesy of hearing this before it gets back to your family. I always thought Tinkler had been real good to you over the years. I know Llew made sure you got paid for all that time you took off from work when you had your personal problems. It would kill him to see you involved with this union organizing drive. But I'll go back in channels and let Human Resources handle things if this is how you feel."

"Look, I like Llew," Rob softened his tone, "but I gotta protect myself. And I don't like you threatening to drag my family into this. I gotta go, I'm going to walk back. Thanks for the coffee."

Jamie made one last plea, "I'm not dragging your family into this. They're dragging me into it."

Rob just kept walking and Jamie sat quietly and sipped on his tea for awhile. He tried to digest the astounding events swirling in his life and wondered why all this was happening to him right now.

Chapter Eighteen

Matt caught his cousin's pensive mood during the Star Spangled Banner that Saturday night. He called him out as they sat down, "Hey, Jamie, are we moping about Rebecca because we've found out she's a union sympathizing pinko or because she's found out it's not an act and you really are a Meatball?"

"By the way, I almost forgot," Jamie said in nonresponse, "did you guys see that Topless Tess is really Theresa, our agent at Interstate, and that they fired her, and she's suing them?"

"Whoa, are you sure?" Adam asked.

"Yeah, it's all over the paper and news. I heard Chick Pitz on the pre-game show commenting that the M's just wanted unruly fans ejected from the park and banned from returning if the conduct is outrageous. He said law enforcement and employment decisions were up to others."

"What a wimp that Pitz is," Adam said. "I almost want the M's to go in the tank so he gets fired."

"Why do you say things like that?" Adam's girlfriend reprimanded.

"Because he's a lawyer," Matt replied.

"Don't look now, but the M's actually have a rally going," Adam said as Don Grant walked in the last of the first. Kuhn, now batting fifth in the lineup, came up with the bases drunk with M's. Escobar made the only out when the power hitting shortstop surprised everyone but Jamie by sacrificing Wink to second on a bunt. Jamie doodled in HBP for Kuhn, calling for him to get hit by a pitch. It would force in a run and maybe give Donny a little punishment for all his bragging lately.

The first pitch to Kuhn surprised even Jamie. It was a beanball, nailing him in the back of the helmet. Donny jumped up, charged the mound with his bat, and started flailing at Cleveland's left-handed pitcher, Tommy Nagle, catching him once on his pitching arm. Nagle's catcher was fast on Donny's trail and bear hugged him from behind, causing Donny to drop the bat. With his arms pinned to his sides, Donny was powerless to stop the subsequent pounding he took from Nagle, a beefy six foot five inch ex-football player, who used his right fist to bloody up Donny' face before the base coaches, infielders, and umpires could restrain the now berserk pitcher.

Grant, Thorne, and Escobar made it to the melee late and milled around more than participated. The video replay showed Rudy Wink trotting home from third, touching the plate, and heading straight for the dugout. Kuhn, Nagle, and his catcher were all ejected. Nagle couldn't continue anyway. His pitching arm was severely injured. Donny sustained a concussion and broken nose but suffered more from his teammates' lack of support during the fight. Jamie was in shock.

When order was restored and the game resumed, the next two hitters greeted the new Cleveland pitcher with a single and a double, needing no help from Jamie. The M's scored five runs in the inning and cruised to an 8-4 win. Matt noticed Jamie was no longer keeping score and chided him, "Hey, you really must be sick. So it's not Rebecca the Radical, but Theresa the Topless you're pining for?"

"I was just wondering if Kuhn and Nagle were going to be okay."

"Oh, Mister Sensitive Man," Matt needled, "save that line for a girl, otherwise it makes you sound like one. Nagle deserves what he gets for beaning Kuhn. That could end a career and Kuhn loses a lot of my sympathy for not dropping the bat before he charged the mound. And it ticks me off that he set himself up for a long suspension just when we were getting addicted to his hitting."

Matt couldn't have known he wasn't making Jamie feel any better. Jamie left the post game gathering at the Shoebox after one drink. He got home in time to find some coverage of the beaning brouhaha on the Puget Sound Sports Show but they had no new information. The local commentators were arguing about penalties.

"A player should be banned for the season when he uses a bat for a weapon."

"That's too harsh. Juan Marichal got less and he was guiltier. He wasn't beaned like Kuhn when he whacked Roseboro."

"Just because Marichal got off too lightly doesn't justify letting Kuhn off the hook."

"I wouldn't call something like a week or ten day suspension getting 'off the hook,' not to mention the big fine."

"I agree you shouldn't mention the big fine because to a ballplayer it's chump change."

"Kuhn actually doesn't make that much right now, although if he stays hot, he'll get a big boost when he negotiates a new contract at the end of the season."

Just then Jamie's mother let herself in the front door and asked, "What are you doing home so early on a Saturday night. Is anyone else over?"

"No, Ma, it's just me at home, hoping to spend quality time with my mother. But you're out who knows where, with who knows who, doing who knows what."

Masking any possible amusement, Jo prattled on, "You know perfectly well where I was. Just like every Saturday night I was at The Club with the ladies. Guess who we saw there? Rob McPherson's ex-wife was having dinner with some doctor, a different one than she left Rob for. She was just full of herself as big as life. Can you believe that?"

"Ma," Jamie couldn't resist, "was anyone topless?"

"She might as well have been with all the skin she was flaunting. She's trying to pretend she's a teenager when she's almost forty. I don't know what this world is coming to."

"She's not that old, Ma. But anyway, I'm going to hit the sack. What time are you going to Church in the morning?" Jamie asked as he flipped off the television.

"And why would you care, you never come to Mass with me anymore? And to think the nuns always thought you were going to be a priest," Jo said with a few shakes of the head for emphasis.

"Actually I was thinking of going to Church with you, Ma," Jamie said as he headed upstairs, "so get me up if you go to the 8:30. I want to make sure no one there is topless. And only Sister

Gertrude thought I was going to be a priest. Remember, she was the same loony who thought Adam was going to be President of the United States and Matt was going to be a movie star."

"I think Adam would make a fine President," Jo noted for the record.

Chapter Nineteen

On the car ride to the Church, Jamie asked his mother, "Does Father Bob still read those corny jokes before the homily? Does he come to the Coffee Hour and do those card and magic tricks after the service?"

"Now I don't want you coming to Church if you're going to cause trouble and try to be funny."

"No, Ma, I'm serious, remember how Father Bob used to do all the goofy Houdini escape tricks for us grade schoolers?"

"I don't know anything about Houdini tricks. You should ask Father Bob about it. He would like to talk to you."

"Seriously, you don't remember the Houdini magic shows? I can't believe it."

The church was just a block off the freeway in the University District. It was old and majestic with the high ceilings and look of a cathedral, although the real cathedral was downtown. Jamie was always surprised that it still inspired awe in him even in adulthood.

After Mass, Jamie accompanied his mother to the Parish Hall for the coffee and doughnut social. He left her to the ladies and scooted over to greet his cousin, "Adam, I thought that was you. What are you doing here?"

"Same thing as you. Praying for your escape from the sinful habits you have embraced for far too long, my wayward cousin."

"Amen," Jamie said and then lowered his voice, "uh oh, here comes Father Bob looking for fresh souls to save."

"Adam and Jamie, it is so good to see you," Father Bob exclaimed too enthusiastically. "What have you been up to?"

Adam extended his right hand quickly but couldn't avoid the big hug. So Jamie resigned himself to one as well. Already awkward, the hugs approached comical since both boys were over six feet tall and Father Bob was about five foot four with a protruding belly. Adam answered for them both, "Work is really keeping Jamie and me extremely busy these days."

Father Bob seemed to ignore Adam's input, scratched the top of his hairless head, and suggested, "We would really like to see the two of you in our Singles Club. We've got a great hike and picnic scheduled for a week from Saturday and we are looking for new members like you two and maybe some of your other cousins or friends."

"Well, I'm not sure Adam is going to be single that much longer," Jamie said without thinking.

"Oh really, I hadn't heard about that," Father Bob said.

"That's because there was nothing to hear, Father. What I think Jamie is trying to say is that just because I can't participate doesn't mean he can't."

"Hey, Father, do you remember when you did the Houdini magic shows?" Jamie asked.

Father Bob turned directly to face Jamie. Adam used the opportunity to slip away. While in Jamie's peripheral view, Adam couldn't be sure Jamie noticed, but he gave his trapped cousin a parting smile.

"Sure," Father Bob answered, "we haven't done it for a long time. Kids are harder to impress these days, what with all the computer graphics and movie special effects."

To Jamie's great relief, a wealthy looking parishioner approached Father Bob and interrupted freely. Jamie used the distraction to go looking for his mother but came across his cousin first. Adam backed away in mock horror, "Stay away from me, you are a Father Bob magnet."

"Hey, I took one for the team and let you escape," Jamie said with a smile. "By the way, what happened to all the kneelers?"

"Well, that shows how long it's been since lukewarm Catholic Jamie has been inside our Church. They took 'em out in the January remodel. Standing is considered more a sign of respect now. They should spend more time screening applicants for the priesthood and less time studying how to flip flop all the rituals."

"Well, whatever," Jamie shrugged and suggested, "we should get out of here and get brunch at Emil's before the game."

"Sounds good to me, even though Emil's is 'slime' spelled backwards. Go tell your mom you're coming with me. Then we'll go wake your heathen cousin Matt up and tell him the good news that I just signed us up for the Mother's Day brunch next Sunday after Mass."

"It's Mother's Day next Sunday?"

"Where is your head these days? Didn't you hear anything Father Bob said in the homily?"

"What?" Jamie asked.

"Let's get you to Emil's. Then we can pick up some Kettlekorn at the game so you have a gift for your mother next week."

"Very funny. I already ordered her gift. I just forgot when Mother's Day was."

"Well that's understandable since it's always the second Sunday of May."

"Exactly. It's never on the same day."

"Actually it's always on the same day, Sunday."

"What I can't figure out, Adam, is whether law school turned you into such a jerk or whether you went to law school because you were already a jerk."

"A classic chicken-egg question, which reminds me, let's go get that breakfast because your blood sugar is getting low."

Eventually the overfed cousins made it to the game and the talk migrated to yesterday's beaning. Apparently, the Commissioner was reviewing the tapes today and would issue a ruling by the end of the day. His office had made some statement about the integrity of the game demanding immediate resolution. But the big buzz was over the quotations in the paper.

Donny Kuhn was caught complaining, "Nagle throws at my head, they gang up on me and try to kill me, and my teammates are standing around picking their big butts. I can hardly wait for the next time one of them wants me to cover for him with the wife while he's out on a date."

Reporters, always eager to stir up trouble, ran to Rudy Wink and got an unsavory response, "We were hoping Nagle might pound some sense into Donny's skinny butt where he keeps his brains diapered up."

Jamie still considered Kuhn his favorite player. He momentarily wondered what would happen if Rudy were hit by a pitch but that outcome was no longer in his repertoire. Wink did strike out twice and grounded into two double plays despite his speed. However, Escobar, Thorne, and Grant each homered, insuring a 6-3 Seattle win. Kuhn was medically excused from being at the ballpark.

Although the players held a team meeting before the game, nobody was talking about it to the press afterwards. The team mood was subdued even though the M's had just won their 14th game out of the last 18 and moved into sole possession of second place. Seattle fans ignored the team tensions and focused instead on being a mere game and a half out of first place. Although their emerging hero, Donny Kuhn, was somewhat tarnished, he was leading the league in the triple crown categories with 15 homeruns, 40 rbi's, and a .436 batting average.

During the exodus from the ballpark, the cousins rehashed the Kuhn-Wink feud. Matt suggested, "With the bathroom humor, maybe we could get Donny and Rudy to do a Tinkler Toilet commercial. If we could get Wink to change his name to Winkler, we could create some great slogans."

Jamie had a difficult time joining in the frivolity.

Chapter Twenty

Early Tuesday morning, Adam arrived at Jamie's office reeking of distress, waving papers, and pleading, "Jamie, talk to me about this ULP we just received."

"What's a ULP?" Jamie asked innocently.

Adam could not contain his agitation as he briefly scanned the top paper and explained, "A ULP is an Unfair Labor Practice. The AFW has filed one claiming that you went to an employee's home, apparently Rob McPherson's house in Wallingford, and threatened Rob's employment with Tinkler for engaging in union protected activity!"

Jamie finally managed a startled, "What?"

Adam moved closer and softened his voice, "Jamie, please tell me this is a load of crap."

"Well, I did drop by to visit Rob. He lives in the neighborhood but I only wanted to chat about solving our Pierce County delivery problems. What's wrong with that?"

"Damn it, Jamie, you need to talk to me or Jeffrey Anne before you do anything like that during the union organizing drive. Going off the premises to his home only makes it worse."

"I've already been working with Jeffrey Anne and it hasn't been helping at all," Jamie protested. "The customers…"

"Look, did Rob say anything about the union when you met with him? I mean, do you think he has some connection with the AFW?"

"Well, yeah," Jamie shrugged, "there was union literature all over his living room and some guy with union stickers plastered on his car was leaving when I drove up."

"Jamie, why didn't you tell me about this?" Adam said as he slapped his forehead with an open palm. "Does Papa know?"

"No, he doesn't know. I didn't tell you or Llew about this because I knew Rob would be in deep trouble and he's been through too much not to give him a chance."

"Give him a chance to do what?" Adam said with growing exasperation. "Let me get this straight. Rob is killing you and Tinkler in the field, but we want to shield him from any consequences while he tries to destroy us and turn Tinkler over to the union?"

"Look, Adam," Jamie began as he searched for an explanation.

"Okay, don't worry," Adam interrupted as he sat down. "My job is to straighten out these messes. Let's go back to the beginning and you tell me everything in sequence so we can get our act together before I take on the union or Llew. He's going to feel very betrayed by Rob."

Jamie proceeded to pour out the story. Every so often his monologue was punctuated by Adam's questions which were duly answered. After about twenty minutes, Adam rose from his chair and said, "I think I've got it now. I'll go run interference with Papa and see if I can make this ULP go away."

Although Jamie dreaded having Adam filter the story to Llew, he thanked him because he wasn't anxious to meet with his uncle on this issue either. After Adam made his exit, Jamie mindlessly flipped through the newspaper on his desk as he tried to assimilate the meaning of all the events dancing through his life. He was reading words but not really comprehending them until a picture of Donny Kuhn's bloodied face snapped him to attention.

Jamie began to read in earnest how late yesterday, the Baseball Commissioner had suspended Kuhn for ten days and fined him $25,000. Early commentary from the Seattle sports community generally supported this punishment as fair. M's fans tended to express an eagerness to forgive and forget although a vocal few locals were so outraged that one columnist wondered if even dismemberment of Kuhn would satisfy them.

The column continued, "Kuhn has smartly and rightly apologized and decided not to appeal his suspension and fine. The cynics will likely point out that by waiving an appeal, Donny will serve his time during the current road trip. Since Kuhn barely hits .200 on the road and well over double that at home, his sense of timing is shrewd. Although the Seattle ball club claims he is able to play, he could also surely use this time off to help with the healing process. Of course, the same can be said for Nagle whose five day suspension will come nowhere close to covering the time he will miss with his bruised left wing."

Not surprisingly, the Cleveland community was ripe with anti-Kuhn sentiment. One letter writer noted that many an underprivileged man served more than ten days in jail for doing less than Kuhn. Donny was fortunate that Tommy Nagle, who received a $5000 fine in addition to his suspension, was not viewed as an innocent. Otherwise, Kuhn likely would have fared worse from both the baseball rulers and the court of public opinion. Nagle himself was vilified in some quarters for starting the fracas and beating up a man whose hands were restrained.

The beaning controversy and the Unfair Labor Practice weighed heavily on Jamie. By lunchtime, he was in a full-blown funk. Then Matt pranced in and announced, "Hey, Meatball, since no one around here will ever be your friend again, I'm going to do you a favor and let you buy me lunch even though it means I will be seen with you in public!"

Jamie swiveled around and replied with resignation in his voice, "So I take it the word is out about the ULP?"

"Not so much," Matt responded casually, "you still trail Rob McPherson's ex in the gossip race. She's been overly enjoying being single and scandalizing those who love to be scandalized. You need to do something sexier than generating unfair labor practices. Maybe if you and Rebecca could engage in some morally reprehensible behavior, you could move up to the big leagues like Rob's ex."

"That's enough, let's go get that lunch," Jamie said as he jumped to his feet. "This place is bringing me down. What do guys see in her anyway?"

"What do you see in Rebecca?" Matt asked.

"I'll see a lot less of her for a couple weeks. She's heading to L.A. for a couple weeks to take depositions on some big case."

"Bummer, but what about the long term? Where are we headed with Rebecca?"

"What's with all this 'we' stuff?" Jamie said with the first hint of a smile.

"It's you and me, we stick together no matter how stupid you get, right? No matter the McPherson, we'll work it out together."

"Maybe on Rob, we'll work it out together. Isn't there anything we can do to make him either service the accounts or we get someone else?"

"Unfortunately, Adam and Jeffrey Anne say this union organizing makes it more difficult. We've got to go through a few extra hoops. It's still you and me against the world. We'll kick butt as usual. Don't worry about it. But first we got to get back to figuring out our Rebecca strategy."

Jamie felt better just knowing the message Matt was sending. Against his better judgement, he confided to Matt over lunch that he was indeed falling hard for Rebecca but sometimes felt silly thinking she could be that interested in him.

While Jamie was signing the credit card slip, Matt assured him, "Yeah, I sure don't see what Rebecca could possibly see in a loser like you who mopes around with no self-confidence. I'm guessing she thinks you're rich."

Chapter Twenty-One

Jamie wasn't feeling Matt's "we" later that afternoon when he was asked to join Llew, Uncle Art, Adam, and Jeffrey Anne in the Conference Room. It was obvious the meeting had been in progress when he was summoned. He felt like he was appearing before a Grand Jury.

"Thanks for coming over, Jamie," Llew began. "We just want to clarify a few things on this ULP."

"Sure, what do you want to know?"

"First off," Uncle Art interjected, "did you actually go to Rob McPherson's house?"

"Yes. I already told Adam that."

"Yeah, we already know he went to Rob's," Adam confirmed.

"But did anyone see you or does anyone outside this room know that?" Uncle Art asked.

Jamie began to answer but Adam held up his hand in a stop gesture and said, "What are you suggesting, Art? You know we can't promote perjury."

"Oh, get off your high horse, Adam," Art replied. "I've been dealing with the union since before you were born. And when you get down in the sewer with a skunk, sometime you get some stink on you."

"I'm not sure I'm following everything," Jamie said, "but I did go to Rob's. I talked to him about late deliveries. No way did I threaten him. I didn't care anything about the union. I'm sorry if I got us into trouble but I'm not going to lie about anything."

"Nobody's asking you to," Llew said. "We're just trying to get a handle on where we are. What else do we need to know, Adam?"

"I've got what I need. Jamie had a conversation with Rob. It touched on work concerns. It had nothing to do with union organizing. There were no threats. Rob and Jamie have been friends for years outside work and it wouldn't be unusual for either one to visit the other."

"Anything else anyone needs?" Llew asked. "Jeffrey Anne?"

"Nothing from me," Jeffrey Anne replied while the others shook their heads.

"Good, let's get Jamie back to work," Llew said. "Thanks, Jamie. In fact everyone can get back to work, except Art. Can you stick around?"

After the room cleared, Llew asked him, "What were you trying to do there?"

"What do you mean? Same thing as you, brainstorming on how to keep the union out of our business."

"You don't think you're going over the line by trying to bully Jamie into lying about his visit with Rob?"

"I think you're going over the line, Llew. I was just trying to get the facts. If we don't cross-examine each other internally, you can bet the union lawyers will mop us up when they get their day in court. And what's with all this over protectiveness for Jamie? Nobody coddled us when Papa Joe died. He's a thirty something year old man. His customers are complaining. He gets the Company baseball tickets whenever he wants. He isn't even blood. It's like his father is still alive and running things."

"Is that it? Are you still pouting because Papa Joe put Marty in charge of the Company instead of you?"

"And you were happy with it? He marries our sister and gets chosen ahead of the two boys in Papa Joe's bloodline."

"What's your preoccupation with 'blood?' Marty and Jamie are 'family.' If we find out you're adopted, should we bounce you out of the Company?"

"Are we done here?" Art asked as he headed for the door.

"Jamie's twenty-nine," Llew shouted after him.

Chapter Twenty-Two

"Rebecca, are you there? Did you hear us, Rebecca?" her lead attorney repeated.

Hearing her own name shouted out a second time caused Rebecca to snap to attention. She hated that she was available for the Thursday Environmental Law staff teleconference. She had missed the firm's Wednesday morning meeting because she was conducting a deposition in California. No such luck today. At least it wasn't a videoconference call. So once she reported on her depositions, she had tuned out the preening and droning and was quietly working on her laptop until she heard her name. Finally she managed to reply, "I'm sorry, I didn't quite follow all of that. Could you repeat the question?"

"Uh, yeah, the question was whether you made it out to either of the M's games the last two nights while they were in L.A. with you."

"Oh, sorry, we had a little static on the line. No, I don't expect to catch any of the games while I'm down here."

Realizing she had been caught not listening, Rebecca turned her attention away from her laptop. After a short rehash of the big losses absorbed by Seattle the last two nights, the group's lead lawyer began describing yesterday's staff meeting for the sake of the office assistants who don't participate and for lawyers like Rebecca who were absent.

"The Labor Group reported on the Tinkler ULP and said things were going well," he noted and then skipped quickly to another topic. Rebecca was curious but didn't dare ask about it.

Her boss finally completed his report and took a few questions. Before he terminated the teleconference, he asked Rebecca to give him a call on his office line in about five minutes.

Rebecca stewed for a few minutes wondering if she could possibly be in trouble for something as petty as not paying attention on the call. But when she finally connected with him, she was relieved that the topic was the Tinkler ULP.

"We need to keep you insulated from what's going on in the Labor section," her lead attorney said. "But I thought you should know off the record that the bigwigs at Tinkler tried to get the guy who harassed your brother to lie about it but the guy refused. It looks like we have management on the run and that your brother should be vindicated."

"Harassment of my brother?" Rebecca asked.

"Yeah, don't you have a brother working at Tinkler? That's what somebody said at staff."

"Sure, my brother Rob. How was he harassed? Who hassled him?"

"I'm not sure, Rebecca. I assumed you knew more about it than me. I was even wondering if maybe you were the source for some of this information because I was going to tell you to keep me in the loop on anything you're telling to our labor lawyers."

"Sure, I would always do that," Rebecca said while hiding her annoyance that this was really a territorial issue about getting out of channels and she was being dinged for something she didn't do. "But I'm staying out of it. I'm just glad I'm not in the Labor Group. How did we find out about the management pressure anyway? I'm sure my brother wouldn't be in a position to know insider info like that."

"I don't know. I guess maybe we both should continue to lie low on this one."

After the call, Rebecca was distracted by thoughts of her brother. Her other brothers had told her that Rob wasn't doing too well at work. That wasn't so surprising but this was the first she heard about union activity and harassment. Rob had never shown any interest in unions that she could remember but they had never been that close. She tried not to resent that he was causing complications for her. She knew her lead attorney was right. She should keep her head down, stick to environmental law, and hope that her firm wouldn't have any conflict of interest problem.

But she picked up her cell phone and looked up Rob's number before she thought better of it. "Lie low," she reminded herself as she flipped the phone shut.

Chapter Twenty-Three

Adam and Matt were mysteriously unavailable. Jamie found himself alone at Thursday's lunch with Llew. Arriving a little late, Llew greeted Jamie by asking, "What's wrong with those M's when they go on the road? They're like a whole different team. What was it last night, 8-1?"

"Actually 9-1, we gave up a solo shot in the ninth."

"Well, I fell asleep long before that," Llew said, shaking his head sadly.

"The fans must make the difference at home," Jamie said with a smile.

"Yeah, but do you see how the players reward us? Kuhn was quoted on the radio this morning as saying he was looking forward to free agency."

"That would be pretty stupid of him considering how the only place he hits is at the Shoe!" Jamie said.

After some more small talk over the salad, Jamie braced himself when Llew folded his hands under his chin and changed to a more serious tone of voice, "You know, Jamie, you can come to me and talk about anything at any time."

"I know that Llew," Jamie began, "and I appreciate it. I know you're unhappy about the ULP but..."

"Jamie, I'm not upset with you over the ULP. It's the damn union that ticks me off. They're going to file ULP's no matter what the hell we do. For the AFW, it's all about smearing our name in the press. Nobody covers the story when the legal challenges are dismissed as spurious. It's just another Union 101 tactic. Don't get your shorts in a knot over that."

"Thanks Llew, I know," Jamie said as he shifted in his seat and started again, "but I feel badly. If it were anyone else but Rob, I would have stayed in more formal channels but he and his family have such a long history with Tinkler and I didn't want to be the young punk ignoring that history and getting him fired."

"That's what I'm trying to say, Jamie, I'm not going to can Rob because the union dupes him. He may need to be sent for some alcohol treatment but I wouldn't make him the scapegoat. You know, he still blames me for his wife leaving him."

Jamie was genuinely surprised since he had never heard about any bad blood between Rob and Llew and found himself asking, "How's that?"

Llew leaned back, ran his left hand through his thinning gray hair, and spoke softly, "Well, his wife figured she had married into the rich McPherson family and she expected more fancy things than Rob could ever deliver. He wanted Tinkler to pay him more than he was worth and we even did a little of that. But then he wanted us to loan him some sizable amounts of money. We couldn't do that for his own good. She was already stepping out on him. She was going to put him into financial ruin as well."

"So what happened?" Jamie asked.

"She left Rob for some doctor not long after I told Rob we couldn't help him. She would have left him either way. It was a matter of time but Rob didn't see it that way. She ruined the doctor as well but Rob has always been bitter because I didn't help him more. He probably got involved with the AFW more to get back at me than anything. He knows how much I hate unions."

Jamie felt like asking why Llew hated the union so much but decided not to risk looking more like an idiot to him. Nor did he want to provoke an antiunion lecture. Instead, Jamie just said, "What do we do now?"

Llew leaned forward in his chair and said, "First, let me tell you a story about your grandfather. When Papa Joe was running the business in the early days, there was a local drunk named Easy who sometimes did odd jobs for us. Papa Joe would let him sweep up or run errands for walking around money. One time Easy was talking about getting off the street and going home to Montana where he had family. Papa Joe says, 'I'll buy you a bus ticket. You come by tomorrow and pick it up.' Easy thanks him. But next day he's a no-show."

Llew paused while the salad plates were cleared away. Jamie didn't say anything as he correctly assumed there was more to the story.

"So, anyway, Easy doesn't show up for a couple days. Papa Joe is wondering if Easy is in jail or if he hitchhiked to Montana or what. Then he comes by the next week. He mooches some coffee and acts like he's just looking for some work as always. Papa Joe is mystified and asks him, 'What happened? Where were you? I bought you a ticket to Montana that you were supposed to pick up last week.' Easy just looks at Papa Joe and says, 'I'm an alcoholic.'"

Llew let the story sink in and then began slowly, "Everybody has a job. Easy had one. His job everyday was to figure out how to get his next drink. He was surprised Papa Joe didn't understand that. You're probably wondering what all this has to do with our union issues?"

Jamie did wonder but just nodded almost imperceptibly.

"First of all, Jamie, I want you to know, between you and me, that it won't be the end of the world if Tinkler gets unionized. I don't like any outside interference. Hell, I don't like government regulations and I fight them all the time, but I'm still patriotic. As you know, we seek all the government business we can get."

Jamie looked a little confused but before he could say anything, Llew continued, "Now, I don't want to be quoted on that because I don't want anyone to let down their guard and give up the good fight. I am a strong believer in the non-interference route and passionate about staying nonunion. That's just who I am and what I do. Easy had his job, I've got mine. You have to find your own, Jamie. Sometimes our jobs won't make sense, but we do what we have to do. For example, just because we have it on good authority that 'the poor will always be with us' doesn't mean we stop trying to help the poor. Maybe the Tinkler destiny is to be unionized but my job is to fight it. Do you get what I'm saying?"

Jamie nodded more vigorously this time.

Llew hunched forward, looked directly into Jamie's eyes, and said, "I want you to understand that I am a practical and logical person and that I can respect differences of opinions, so you can come to me anytime and discuss anything without risking our relationship. Okay?"

"Sure, Llew, and I appreciate everything you've tried to do for me," Jamie answered.

Llew leaned back in his chair and said, "I have gained a couple of insights over the years. One is not to be so quick to condemn others for faulty views of life when maybe they're stuck sitting behind a pillar. And two, I've come to realize that much as I have a negative gut reaction to certain things, like most humans, I adapt. So if someone in my family adopts a view or lifestyle that is different than mine, I'm going to be able to accept it and move on when the time is ripe. What I like to think, Jamie, is that you would know me well enough to be able to come to me even on touchy subjects where you and I might be on different sides of an issue."

Jamie relaxed slightly. He thought this talk was about the union but with Llew you could never be sure. So over dessert, he casually made some comments about dating Rebecca McPherson.

Chapter Twenty-Four

"Guess what?" Jamie greeted his mother after work on Friday. "I made an offer on a condo in the Fremont District."

"Oh, I'll be sad to see you go," Jo said as she shook her head slowly. "But I know you have your heart set on getting out of here. I don't really mind being alone anyway."

Jamie could not be deflated. He wasn't even telling his mother the best news. He received an e-mail from Rebecca today. It was short and it wasn't sweet, but it intoxicated Jamie with a severe case of the happys. Apparently the depositions were going well and she would be coming home a little early. She signed off with the message, "I hate having to be an apologist for Kuhn down here but sometimes you take one for the team, Beck."

Jamie spent almost two hours constructing his two-sentence reply to Rebecca. It took him a good half an hour just to decide to address her as "Beck", the family nickname she used to sign her e-mail. Looking at the product of all his tinkering, he was embarrassed that it took so long to compose something that still sounded cheesy. However, in a moment of fatigue, he finally hit the send button. His return message raced off: "Now that you've got the L.A. legal community on the run, let's clear our heads on Cougar Mountain when you get back. We can solve world problems, starting with why Seattle hasn't ever been in the World Series."

Jamie snapped back from his daydreams when his mother asked, "What are you doing tonight?"

"Matt and I are going to grab some grub at the Shoebox, catch the M's on the big screen T.V., and celebrate a good day."

"I never said we couldn't get a big screen T.V. in the rec room," Jo said as she put a mild pout on her face.

"I know that, Ma," Jamie smiled patiently, "but this isn't about me going out and leaving you because I know you and the ladies are going down to The Club tonight."

"I just might have to join them tonight," Jo acknowledged as Jamie headed for the door.

Matt and Jamie were surprised by the crowd at the Shoebox. As they were searching for an open table, Jamie suddenly spotted a familiar face.

"Hey, look Matt, the bartender is that vendor from the Shoe," Jamie said.

"Who?"

"The guy who sells scorecards at the Shoe. He looks like he's really cleaned up his act. I can't believe it. Let's go sit at the bar."

Matt didn't see any other better alternatives, so he followed Jamie.

"Hey, I didn't know you worked here. I almost didn't recognize you with the haircut," Jamie said to the tall, skinny barkeep.

"I just got hired. I need some income when the M's are on the road. What can I get you?"

"Me, I'll take a screwdriver and this is my cousin Matt. He'll take a bourbon and diet cola."

"I've never understood the diet drink thing. The best diet is to cut out the alcohol."

"I figure every little bit helps if I'm going to drink the alcohol anyway," Matt fired back. "It's like an entrée salad and dessert is better than a bacon burger, fries, and dessert."

"Gotcha, coming right up," the barkeep acknowledged as he slipped away to make the drinks.

"What kind of bartender rags you about ordering alcohol?" Matt asked. "That guy's a nut case. Which reminds me, did you hear about Rob's latest odd behavior at work?"

"Well, it's about time you showed an interest in Rob," Jamie said. "I can't get anyone to focus on his performance no matter how loud I squawk. What finally got your attention?"

"I guess he's been taking other people's cigarette butts out of the ashtrays in the smoking room down in the shop and then lighting them up for a few puffs."

"You're kidding me? Why? He gets paid enough to buy cigarettes," Jamie said as he picked up the drink the bartender slid over.

"That's just it, Meatball, there is no good reason. He's acting crazy. Did you know that every Friday, Rob brings a thermos of "mung" in his lunch?"

"Sure," Jamie answered. "He throws the week's leftovers from the refrigerator into a blender and it all turns brown and lumpy. Everybody knows about that. He's been doing it forever, though, even when he wasn't screwing up."

"Yeah, but I don't think he used to pour the mung over a dish of ice cream in the cafeteria, now did he?"

Jamie was a little taken aback and managed to ask, "Oh really, when did he do that?"

"Just today."

"But it's not like retrieving cigarette butts and eating Mung a la mode is against any company rule, is it?"

"That's the problem," Matt said after taking another long swig on his drink. "Ad says we have to be real careful how we treat Rob because the union will allege we are harassing him for union activity if we take any action that is remotely negative."

"But the AFW must know Rob is going off his rocker if they are working with him closely on the organizing campaign. How could they attack us if we tried to help Rob for his own good?"

"Jamie, my man, haven't you already tried to help Rob for his own good and gotten burned once?" Matt asked as he shook his head. "All the AFW knows is that when the river is high, the Tinkler fish eat the union flies. When the river is low, the flies eat the fish. The union is trying to drain the river as fast as they can right now."

"Hey, guys," the bartender interrupted, "can I get you something else?"

"Actually, can we get a menu?" Matt asked.

The boys eventually took their time eating salads, some burgers, and nursing their drinks. As things slowed down at the bar and people migrated to tables for dinner, the barkeep found time to dodge a few questions from Jamie. He did admit to being from downstate south of Chehalis where his family runs a restaurant just off exit 68 on Interstate 5.

While Matt was in the restroom, Jamie hoped to get more, starting with the bartender's name. "I'm Jamie, by the way," he began.

"I know who you are, Jamie Bytheway."

"And how do you know that?"

"You're the guy who buys a scorecard from me every home game."

"And who are you?"

"I'm the guy who sells you a scorecard every home game."

"And I need to know what's going on with those scorecards and why I'm involved," Jamie said.

"You know more what's going on with those scorecards than I do," the bartender said as he retrieved a business card from his wallet and scrawled a message on it for Jamie. "Now, quit bugging me or you're going to get me fired."

As the barkeep scrambled away to help an impatient customer, Jamie eagerly read the message, but was disappointed when he realized it just said, "Good for a free brunch." The card itself was advertising "best in the state" brunches at Puffy's 68, the family eatery. Jamie slipped the card into his wallet after reading the name the bartender signed.

Matt returned just as the M's recorded the last out of a 7-4 victory and greeted his cousin, "Hey, a two game win streak on the road. This really might be our year."

"I think the bartender's name is Dred," Jamie said.

"That's good to know. The M's are four games over .500, but I've really been wondering about the bartender's name."

Chapter Twenty-Five

The weather was so bad in Baltimore, they didn't even try to delay the Saturday game. It was 4:00 p.m. back in Seattle when Jamie realized the M's were cancelled and wouldn't be on television as he expected. He called out, "Hey, Ma, how about you and I go out to an early dinner tonight?"

"Don't you have a baseball game?" Jo asked.

"Ma, you're more important than some old baseball game," Jamie replied. "If we go early, you can still make it to The Club for cards with the Ladies."

"We don't have to go early for my sake."

"Well, just let me know when you're ready."

"What are your cousins up to tonight?" Jo asked suspiciously.

"Oh, I think Adam and Matt are out on dates."

"Maybe you should get a date and go out with them," Jo suggested. "What about calling that Jeffrey Anne girl?"

"Ma, Adam and Matt aren't together. They are at separate functions with their dates. I'm not interested in Jeffrey Anne any more."

"How come Adam and Matt aren't together? Are they fighting?" Jo asked.

"Ma, do you or don't you want to go out to dinner with your son tonight?"

"Well, of course I do. You could even bring Jeffrey Anne with you."

"Maybe you and Jeffrey Anne should go out without me."

Eventually Jamie and Jo made their way to Jamie's truck. "Where do you want to go, Ma?"

"Anywhere is fine with me," Jo assured her son.

"How about El Torpatio's?" Jamie suggested.

"I don't really feel like Mexican food tonight."

"Okay, how about some Italian food at Mama L's?"

"It's always so crowded on Saturday."

"But it's early, Ma. We can get in."

"Still it's a long way to go," Jo continued.

"Then where do you want to go, Ma?"

"Anywhere you want is alright with me, Jamie."

"No it isn't. I know you don't want to go to the Shanghai because you don't like Chinese food. And apparently you don't want Mexican or Italian food tonight. What about the Thai place down by the mall?"

"You really want to go there?" Jo asked.

"Not unless you do. How about the Beef and Bourbon?"

"That sounds great," Jo said enthusiastically.

Jamie laughed and Jo asked, "What's so funny?"

"Oh, I was just wondering what would have happened if I had come up with the Beef and Bourbon first."

During dinner, Jamie suddenly asked his mother, "I know you and Dad met at Seattle Community College but what was it like? Were you interested in him right away?"

"I'll tell you what really made me take a long second look," Jo said as she leaned back and smiled. "During my first year at SCC, a bunch of the girls I went to high school with had lunch together every day in the Cave, a campus restaurant. Boys were always buzzing around the periphery, but the core group was us girls. I knew who Marty was because some of the girls had a crush on him since he was a star on the baseball team."

"I didn't know he was a star," Jamie interrupted. "He never acted like he was that good."

"Oh, yes, he was a pretty big deal on campus which is why I actually wasn't that interested in him. I figured he was probably full of himself."

"Did you go to the games and see him play?" Jamie asked.

"Sure, after we started dating I went. Sometimes he would hit homeruns and other games he wouldn't do so well and only got to second or third base."

"You mean he hit doubles and triples?"

"Yes, sometimes he only hit doubles or triples, but everyone got really excited when he hit homeruns."

Jamie resisted the urge to explain how good doubles or triples were because he wanted to hear more about those times. He knew his parents met at the Community College and that his father played second base on a championship baseball team. But as he listened to his mother, he realized that he really didn't know much else about those times.

After pausing to take a sip of water, Jo continued, "So anyway, one day the girls had this big discussion over lunch about what we were looking for in a man. The debate raged over the relative merits of being smart, good looking, a good provider, a good father, a good conversationalist or even a good dancer. Out of nowhere, Marty interrupts and says, 'You're forgetting the most important thing.'"

Jo took a deep breath and composed herself while Jamie wondered, *Why haven't I heard this story before?*

"Anyway, we were surprised because we had covered the topic pretty thoroughly. We all turned and looked at Marty. Someone asked him what was the most important thing we had all missed. I was half expecting some wisecrack. But he just said, 'That he loves you more than anyone else does.' I hadn't really noticed Marty before then, but he really caught my attention from that moment on."

Chapter Twenty-Six

"I'm poppin' full," Jo said on the drive home from the Mother's Day brunch.

"I don't think I'm ever going to eat again," Jamie agreed.

As they entered the house, Jamie steered his mother to the family room where he had hooked up a new forty-inch television. "Happy Mother's Day," he exclaimed.

"Wow, that's big," she said.

"Yeah, now you can see everything without squinting. And it's got high definition."

"But you're going to be moving out," Jo said.

"Not right away. The condo deal fell through. And besides the television is for you and it means I'll be over here all the time," Jamie said with a laugh.

After an appropriate amount of time investigating the gift, Jo headed out to the mall to do some shopping of her own.

"God bless you until you come home again, Ma," Jamie called out from in front of the new television as he scrambled for the sports page.

The local baseball buzz in print and on the tube centered on whether Donny Kuhn was really a threat to be the first person to hit over .400 since before World War II. Jamie studied the articles and letters to the editor with great interest, rereading several items. Then he checked out the start time of today's doubleheader in Boston and realized it was time to switch to the channel with the pre-game show.

"Yesterday's rainout makes for today's doubleheader," the network announcer was saying to his sidekick. "We'll get twice as much time to see if Seattle really is a legitimate contender for the playoffs. And what about that Donny Kuhn? With those triple crown numbers, surely he should be voted onto the All Star team this year?"

"Well, it's early yet," the sidekick answered. "Can Kuhn maintain that pace over the next month when the ballots will be passed out at all the ballparks and even in Japan? I doubt it. Not because I think Kuhn is going to collapse, but nobody can keep up the pace he is on. And some voters won't take too kindly to his attack on Nagle with the bat. Besides, New York's Bryan Bonneville is immensely popular and has owned that position for six years."

"That's true," the lead announcer conceded, "but Bryan is having a sub-par season so far. And I'm sure those Seattle fans will be stuffing the ballot box like crazy."

"Maybe below average for Bonneville," sidekick replied, "but a lot of players would love to be sub-par if it meant gold glove defense and a .290 batting average."

"I think he's actually down to .277 now, but you make a good point. And like you, I doubt Kuhn can keep that average above .400 for too long. He's no Ted Williams."

"Just like Seattle is no New York," sidekick said with a laugh.

Jamie did not laugh. In fact, as he watched the sluggish M's, they seemed to be playing in slow motion. This contrasted sharply with an animated Jamie who was yelling at a television that had no ears. His tantrum was interrupted when his cell phone went off.

"You watching this crap?" Jamie answered.

"Yeah, but I'm actually calling to tell you the latest family gossip," Matt replied. "Uncle Art may have outdone your father in the gift giving department. Guess what he gave his wife for Mother's Day?"

"A divorce?"

"Even better. He gave her three framed pictures of outhouses he photographed for that book he's working on about bathrooms around the world. I guess she wasn't too happy and is bitching about it to anyone who will listen."

"It's not like she's his mother," Jamie said.

"What? Are you defending the guy who's trying to run you out of the company?" Matt asked.

"What do you mean, he's trying to run me out of the company?"

"Well, you know how he's been harassing you about the union's ULP," Matt replied weakly.

"But it sounds like you're saying there's more to it than that?" Jamie asked.

"Nah, I'm just saying the guy is a scumbag and you're a friend of a scumbag if you like him!" Matt said.

Jamie tried to laugh but he left the phone call feeling a little unsettled. He couldn't even finish watching the M's lose the second game of the doubleheader. He could hardly wait for Seattle to finish this road trip and get back in town.

Chapter Twenty-Seven

"Where the hell are the order requisitions in the system?" Matt yelled.

Jamie was jarred from his baseball thoughts with an acid release in the pit of his stomach. "Damn," he muttered under his breath.

"What?" Matt said.

"I blew it, Matt. I forgot to enter them in the computer last night."

"You've got to be kidding me. I'm reaming Rob for missing orders and they aren't even in the system."

"I'm sorry, man. I'll put 'em in right now."

"I'll see if I can catch Jeffrey Anne. I told her that Rob screwed up big time again and she may be telling Llew in her Friday review meeting."

Jamie scurried to his task. All the distractions melted away. Nothing but work mattered. The M's two losses out of three in Florida and their three and six road trip weren't important. The scorecard mysteries didn't register. Even Rebecca was far from his thoughts. He scrambled hard on his work project and before he knew it, Matt was back.

"The bad news is that Jeffrey Anne already spilled the 'screw up' to Llew," Matt began. "The worse news is that Ad and Uncle Art were in the meeting. The good news is they think Rob was the cause of the problem."

"Why is that good news?" Jamie asked.

"Because Rob has been screwing up and so what does it matter if he gets blamed for one he didn't do? It's not like we reported all his mistakes. We covered plenty up. And it's not like anyone is lying. I told the truth I knew at the time. And you can tell the truth if asked, but you don't have to go volunteering information."

"That's part of our problem," Jamie said. "We've been sweeping too much under the rug around here. We should have been addressing Rob's performance issues a long time ago."

"Don't be lecturing me," Matt said with a flash of anger. "I'm not the one who didn't enter the orders. I'm trying to help you."

"Yeah, I know," Jamie said.

After Matt left, Jamie buried himself in his work, hoping to insure no more screw-ups and also to avoid dealing with the issue of Rob. He finally left his office late and wandered slowly down the hall, staring absently at the wall with Uncle Art's pictures of bathrooms from around the world. When he passed Llew's office, he could see his uncle was gone for the day. He wasn't as relieved as he expected, but he headed for the ballpark as planned.

Jamie took the scorecard from the evasive Dred and appeared to move swiftly toward his seat. He pretended to stop and look at some memorabilia for sale, while stealing a sideways glance at the retreating Dred. Jamie immediately turned and began to follow him, screened by the milling crowd.

When Dred ducked into a restroom, Jamie positioned himself where he could watch both entrances without being noticeable. After what seemed like forever, Jamie entered the men's room and looked around but could see no Dred. He didn't seem to be in any of the stalls but Jamie couldn't tell with certainty without attracting too much attention. He exited and half-heartedly resumed his watch while he thought about all that was going on in his life.

"What are we doing? Counting restroom use per hour?" Adam asked.

Jamie was startled by the sudden appearance of his cousin.

"No, I was just thinking. I need to call Llew and tell him I screwed up on entering the orders into the computer. Rob didn't screw up the orders today. I did."

"Matt already told Llew. He said he was going to let Rob take the rap but that you were such a straight arrow, you were going to squeal on yourself. So Matt tried to hog some of the blame for being lax on the whole Rob issue and for passing along bad info."

"What did Llew say?" a surprised Jamie asked.

"He said we ought to put a tent over this circus, like he always says."

The cousins headed for their seats. Later when Matt joined them, Jamie said softly, "I think you're right. I'm not going to own up to that mess I caused. Let Rob take the blame. He deserves it."

"You can't be serious," Matt said. "He's Rebecca's brother, after all. He could be kin someday. You don't want to cause bad blood."

"So now you think I should confess because you're looking out for my relationship with Rebecca?"

"Are you jerking me around or what?" Matt asked.

"Yeah, he's jerking you around," Adam interjected. "Which is pretty cruel since you would never pull a stunt like that."

Jamie couldn't wait for the game to start. Donny Kuhn couldn't wait either. It was the last game of his ten game suspension. Jamie not only experimented with making heroes out of other players but he tried various positions while scoring. When Matt and Adam were on a beer run, he tried scoring while standing in front of his seat with the back of his legs touching the seat. Then with the back of his legs not touching the seat. Then he sat in the seat next to his and touched his seat. Then he stood two seats over and stretched over to touch his seat while scoring. The inning finally ended and his cousins bounded back down the steps with glee.

"What were you doing, playing tag with your seat?" Matt asked.

"What are you talking about?"

"The usher made us stand at the top of stairs until the half inning was over," Adam answered.

"Yeah, it looked like you were five years old, wanting to explore, but afraid to get too far away from your seat. What gives?" Matt asked.

"I was doing some new stretching exercises Rebecca taught me for hiking."

"Rebecca wouldn't be caught dead doing those exercises," Adam said.

"Yeah, I can't wait to ask her about them the next time I see her. Maybe she can demonstrate what they're supposed to look like," Matt added.

Jamie went back to scoring the game more conventionally. He sent the scribes scurrying for the record books as all nine Seattle batters hit a homerun. The M's homered once in each inning and romped to a 14-5 win, improving their record to 21-19. And Jamie knew he had to be touching his seat for the scorecard to work.

Chapter Twenty-Eight

After buying his scorecard on Saturday, Jamie tailed Dred again. Although his red hair was a little shorter and less conspicuous, Dred was easier to follow this time. Jamie watched as he approached another vendor, exchanged a few words, and then handed him some money before quickly disappearing into the crowd. Jamie headed to his seat with a false sense of satisfaction that he was making progress in his investigation. He knew he couldn't gamble with the power. He knew he only had power over the M's offense. He knew he needed a scorecard from Dred and he knew he needed to be touching his seat. He even knew Dred's name. He was getting somewhere and nowhere all at once.

The anonymous Jamie made sure everyone noticed his favorite player was back in the lineup when Kuhn hit for the cycle with a single, double, triple, and a homerun. Kuhn's second homer in the last of the eighth inning added an exclamation point to the cycle. Whereupon, Matt nudged Jamie and said, "Wow, your boy Donny is making up for ten lost games in just one night. I think he's got all ten rbi's for the M's tonight."

"He certainly does," Jamie acknowledged. "That ought to get him a few All Star votes."

It also got him picked up for triple digit speeding on the I-90 floating bridge later that night. He denied being drunk even though he apparently admitted to the officer on the scene that he had eight or ten beers at a Pioneer Square bar. Kuhn's attorney clarified for the press that what Donny actually said was that his group of four at the restaurant had a total of eight or ten beers.

On the way to Sunday's game, Jamie winced as he listened on the radio to the account of the Kuhn escapade. Donny was not in the starting lineup but wasn't needed as the M's swept the series with an easy 8-3 victory.

On Monday night, Jamie took advantage of an off day for the M's and escorted Rebecca to a lecture by a visiting triathlete who was promoting his new book on the power of positive thinking.

Jamie was fascinated by how much emphasis the speaker put on the mental side of training for Ironman events. Over coffee afterwards, Jamie asked Rebecca, "What did you think of his claim that the mind has the power to control the physical environment?"

"His mind probably does give him an edge over other triathletes with less mental discipline, but I think he gives too little credit for his achievements to his physical conditioning and his genes. And he gives too much credit to his mind control theory."

"So you think all his theories on mental control are just hype?" asked Jamie.

"I think the power of positive thinking plays a role in people's success, but this guy was a little too mystical for me. He's giving people all this spiritual stuff to practice and they're going to crash and burn when they try to win a race by wishing for it."

"Alright," Jamie suggested, "let's try an experiment. You go home tonight and practice his Seven-Step plan and we'll see if it works. You seriously concentrate on all seven steps, channeling your mental energy on making me fall in love with you. I'll let you know how you do. If it works, you buy me dinner. If it doesn't, I buy you dinner."

"So what's your homework?"

"I apply the seven steps to mentally figuring out which restaurant you want to go to and which day you want to go out. Then I call you and let you know what you chose."

Rebecca laughed and said, "I see."

All Jamie could see was that he would do anything to make her laugh like that again.

Chapter Twenty-Nine

"Anybody home?" Rebecca called from the open doorway.

"Yeah, come on in," Rob answered. "What are you doing here?"

"I came by to see my brother. What's wrong with that?"

"Nothing. But it would be better if you visited Mom. I missed Mother's Day."

"I know, I was there. But I heard you had a nice lunch with her the day before."

"I thought you were out of town."

"Well, I'm back. And besides, I talk to Mom even when I'm on the road."

"She said you never called when you were on the Appalachian Trail."

"That was different."

"Anyway, she told you to go see your loser brother," Rob said as he finally looked away from the television.

"Sorry to disappoint you, but Mom did not send me over. You watching the M's game?"

"Yeah, Kuhn has two more homers tonight to go with his two last night. They're already up 7-1."

"You want to order some pizza?" Rebecca asked.

"I thought you didn't like pizza," Rob answered as he turned back to the TV. "But the number's by the phone. The one with barbecue chicken is good."

"Oh, I like pizza. I just eat it on special occasions because it's not so good for me," Rebecca said as she headed for the kitchen phone.

Rebecca returned to the room in time to hear Rob grousing about Seattle's pitching which had just given back two runs in the fourth. She looked slowly around the room. It was a mess but she decided not to make some comment about it. Then she spotted the union literature under the card table and said, "So you're involved in the organizing campaign at Tinkler?"

"You should know that. Your firm is working with the AFW."

"I'm in the Environmental Group and don't get involved in it. Why are you so pro-union all of a sudden?"

"Didn't you always tell me to side with the 'little guy' in the fight against oppression?"

Before Rebecca could answer, Rob swiveled around and continued, "Is this about Jamie? I heard you were dating him. He's already been over here harassing me. Whose side are you on anyway?"

"You already know I'm always on the side of the little guy."

"But what about you and Jamie? What's the story?"

"We've gone out a few times."

"But would you be upset if he went out with someone else?"

"Is he going out with someone else?"

"Not that I know of, but he's not the little guy. He's the oppressor. Although I heard that he stood up to his uncles and wouldn't lie about harassing me and about me screwing up the orders when it was him."

"And what exactly was the harassment?"

"What kind of pizza did you order, anyway?" Rob asked.

"The barbecue chicken like you said. I ordered a couple salads, too. You need some veggies. There's nothing in your fridge except beer, pop, and condiments."

"That reminds me," Rob said as he headed for the kitchen, "you want a beer?"

"You got any diet cola hidden in there."

"Not since the ex left. I got some regular."

"I'll take the beer," she said.

Rob came back with the beers and they watched the game in silence until the commercial. Rebecca started again, "So, how's work going anyway?"

"What's this about? What is Jamie saying?"

"Nothing. That's why I'm asking you. I want to know if things are alright with my brother."

"No, things are not alright. My wife left me. Work is a drag. And the M's just gave up a two run homer if you didn't notice."

"If you clean up your act, you'll find someone new. Work is always a drag. I know mine is. And the M's have won ten in a row at home. What more do you want?"

"Your work may be a drag but at least you get paid the big bucks."

"Money isn't everything."

"So say the rich. Hey, when's that pizza getting here?"

Rebecca settled into some baseball small talk until the pizza arrived. The M's finally won on Kuhn's fifth homer and tenth rbi in two games. Even Rob forgot his melancholia for an instant and bubbled, "Seattle's 25 and 19 now. Donny's got 22 homers and 60 rbi's already. I think they said he was batting over .490. Can you believe it?"

"I believe I need to head home and get some sleep, but it was good seeing you."

Rob got up and hugged his sister goodbye and warned her, "You're going to get stuck in the post game traffic."

Chapter Thirty

"Six nine two," Matt said loudly.

Jamie was startled and turned quickly from his desk and squinted at the large cousin filling his doorframe.

"Did you see Kuhn is hitting .692 at home?" Matt continued. "Is that incredible or what?"

After a short pause, Jamie replied, "Yeah, but did you see, he's criticizing management about not making the trades necessary to be a contender?"

"Sure, I saw that. He says he wants to see improvement before the trading deadline or he'll have to think about playing somewhere else next year. So what? He should put pressure on those tightwads. It's good for us if he forces the M's to spend more for a better team."

"Kuhn doesn't know when he's well off," Jamie answered.

"Neither do you, Meatball. The M's are winning. We've got the latest superstar. What more do you want?"

"Don't you think Kuhn should be a little more gracious and humble?" Jamie asked.

"Yeah, I think he should be saying that he owes all his good fortune to the fans, especially Matt and Jamie, who have been there for him in good times and bad, and that he plans to give them each a new corvette. But back in the real world, I've got some company news. You can't tell anyone, but we're leaking a memo today that Tinkler might close down if it goes union."

"What do you mean, we might close down?" Jamie asked.

"We're not going to close down. Llew's going to have an office assistant type up a phony confidential memo to the family shareholders talking about our low margins, declining business, and the effect union labor rates would have on the business. Whoever types the memo will surely blab it all over. We're positive the word will get around. If it doesn't, we'll leave a copy out somewhere."

"Is that legal?"

"Of course it's legal to leave our own memo lying around. It might not be legal for our employees to be passing around confidential info, though."

"You know what I mean," Jamie said. "Is it legal to plant a phony memo?"

"Have you seen the stuff the union is passing out? They make us all sound like multi-millionaires. Where is your cash stashed? Last I heard you were still waiting on Donny Kuhn to give you a corvette. This is war, man."

"It sounds like you've been spending too much time with Llew and Adam again. Are you telling me that basically it's alright to manipulate a good result by doing some shady stuff behind the scenes?"

"Don't tell me you're going to take a 'holier than thou' position on this, Jamie."

"Not at all. I'm really hoping you can clarify for me how sometimes the end does actually justify the means because I struggle with that concept."

"This isn't even about the union, is it? Matt asked. "Are you moping about Rebecca? Are you trying to manipulate her to fall for you with some lies? How can I help?"

Jamie laughed and said, "I don't have to manipulate Rebecca."

"Oh, suddenly we're pretty confident, are we?"

"Actually, do you really think anyone could manipulate Rebecca?"

"I don't know," Matt answered. "I'm afraid to go near her. I think she devours men. When do you see her again?"

"We're going out to dinner on Saturday."

"What about the game?" Matt asked.

"You'll have to win without me."

The M's did win on Thursday and Friday and Jamie hoped they could win without him on Saturday. But while he dined with Rebecca, Donny Kuhn was going 0-3 with two walks. After the walk in the eighth, he was thrown out trying to go from first to third on a single with no one out and the M's down by a run. The rally died, as did the M's thirteen game home winning streak. Kuhn received some mild, but legitimate, criticism from Rudy Wink and coach Duda for his baserunning. He responded by calling the former a "whiner" and the latter "a jabbering idiot."

As they were leaving the restaurant, Rebecca nudged Jamie and nodded in the direction of the bar. "Do you know who that is?" she asked.

"Wow. Yeah, that's my Uncle Art. Let's get out of here before he sees us."

"I know that's your uncle. I'm talking about the woman he's with. I know her from somewhere."

"Probably someone from the Chamber or one of the other committees he serves on."

"He's married, isn't he?" Rebecca asked as she slipped out the door first.

"Yeah, he is," Jamie confirmed.

Chapter Thirty-One

"I'm thinking Escobar gets a double right here," Jamie said to Matt at Sunday's game.

"Lucky guess," Matt replied as E2 slid safely into second.

"I'm getting strong vibrations that Grant is going to single him home," Jamie said.

"Wow, you're hot," Matt said as E2 crossed the plate. "When Ad and Mac get here, we're betting for beers on your hunches. What's Thorne going to do? You tell me and I'll call it out to our section here."

"I don't know. The feeling passed," Jamie answered.

Matt continued to press and Jamie reluctantly tried a homer for Thorne. Matt stood up and yelled to the section around him, "My man here sees the future and the future says Thorne is hitting a homer!"

Jamie cringed. Then Thorne popped up to short and he started to worry. Jamie had been flirting with telling Matt about his power, partly to see if it worked when he wasn't gambling on it. But now he was starting to panic a little at getting Matt involved. Although they bet for beers later in the game, Jamie didn't provide any predictions. He was relieved when he was able to discreetly put the M's back on a new winning streak and the team headed east with a 28-20 record.

Donny Kuhn was sitting on 28 homers and 71 rbi's at the beginning of the road trip and he was still sitting on them when Seattle limped home with two wins in seven games. These precipitous ups and downs came to be known as the MoJo YoYo and provided discussion fodder at Llew's standing Thursday luncheon.

"Can you believe the difference in Kuhn on the road and at home? How can a guy go 5-27 for a week and still be hitting .452?" Adam asked.

"Yeah," Matt added, "he has only one homer away from home all year and now he has 30 at the Shoe after the two last night. What's up with that?"

"Well, he did lose nine road games to that suspension," Llew answered.

"Even so, that's one statistical anomaly that seems well beyond the boundaries of chance," Adam replied.

"Now don't go talking about your two standard deviation tests," Llew said with a wave at Adam. "Save that stuff for Jeffrey Anne and the government."

"I think what Adam is saying is that since those numbers are statistically impossible, they didn't happen. It was an optical illusion. He really hit half of them on the road," Matt said.

"What I'm saying, smart guy, is that it almost lends credence to the rumors that we're stealing signs at home. The whole team is doing so much better at the Shoe than on the road."

"The paper says the two wins the last two days puts them at 22-4 at home versus 10-21 on the road," Llew noted. "It turns out it was a pretty good idea to get the extra season tickets this year because they're playing like champions at home."

"The new upgraded seats are pretty sweet," Adam said. "Did you get preferential treatment through your Chick Pitz connection?"

"Chick did say we were loyal over the years and the seats became available because of a death but I think he was using them to grease the skids for getting us to cut a deal with the union," Llew replied

"Do we know who the guy was that died?" Jamie asked.

"Well, aren't we morbid," Adam said.

Llew looked surprised and added, "What? Did he leave gum under your seat and you want to complain to the grieving family?"

Even Jamie laughed. "No, baseball is a game of history. I just have a keen interest in all the history."

"Well your buddy Kuhn has an interesting sense of history," Matt pointed out, "Did you see the paper today? After his six hits the last two games, Kuhn's average is back up at .467. The buzz is deafening about him being the first hitter to finish over .400 since Ted Williams in 1941. When asked about being compared to Williams, Donny didn't say he was honored. No, he says, 'I don't see it because Williams wasn't all that well rounded. He didn't have my speed and he played out in left field where he didn't have the defensive challenges I do.' Kuhn's getting pretty full of himself based on a two month hot streak."

"So, the chosen few are having another secret luncheon," Art interrupted as he entered the conference room.

"You're always welcome to join us," Llew replied insincerely.

"Nah, I grabbed an early lunch at my meeting with the Mayor's Subcommittee on Housing. One of the lawyers for the AFW was there and he claimed he had heard we were pressuring Jamie to lie about his visit with Rob McPherson. I'm concerned we've got a leak somewhere. You know that McPherson girl Jamie is dating works for the union law firm."

"Well, if you're so concerned about leaks, maybe you shouldn't be talking to the enemy lawyers at your subcommittee meetings. Let's have the lawyers talk to each other in channels," Llew replied.

"Lawyers talking to lawyers is about the scariest thing I can think of," said Art. "Just be careful you don't kill the messenger. I'm trying to help us here."

"I'm sure you are," Llew said as Art exited.

"Rebecca and I have never once talked about Rob's situation," Jamie said loudly.

"I'm sure you have better things to do with Rebecca than talk about unfair labor practices," Llew replied.

"What do you expect from Uncle Art? It's not really surprising that a guy with a hobby of taking bathroom pictures is now going to be taking leaks seriously," Matt added with enough contempt to draw a grimace from his father.

Jamie wasn't even listening. He was thinking how he didn't need this hassle. He had enough on his plate already.

Chapter Thirty-Two

"We missed you yesterday."

Even with all the noise in the stadium, Jamie was startled by the voice directly behind him. He swirled around to see Dred the vendor holding out a scorecard.

"How do you know I wasn't here?" Jamie asked as he purchased the card.

"We lost."

Sure enough, Jamie did miss Saturday's game and the M's did lose for the first time on the current homestand. But Jamie was caught off guard and just said, "Hopefully, our luck will turn today."

"It takes more than luck."

Jamie was now on the defensive and he didn't try to follow Dred this day.

"Let me know if you're going to miss another game," Dred called as he moved away.

Jamie was annoyed, but he wasn't sure he should be. He did make the final three games on the homestand. On the last one, he again caught Dred exchanging money with the same scorecard vendor. After Dred escaped, Jamie approached the vendor and recognized him as a regular. Jamie had purchased many a scorecard from him over the years and felt comfortable asking, "Who is that guy you were just talking to?"

"I don't know. He buys scorecards from me and sometimes he begs for one on credit, but he always pays up, usually a half hour or so after he buys one."

"Isn't he a vendor himself?" Jamie asked.

"Nah, are you kidding?" the vendor said with a laugh. "That guy is weird. You want a scorecard or what?"

Jamie looked sheepishly at the scorecard he was holding and declined. As he wandered away, he thought better of his decision. He returned and bought a program from the now bewildered vendor.

Dred's card was the only one that worked but it was enough to send Seattle out of town on a new four game win streak. Kuhn padded his numbers for the inevitable drought on the road and Jamie again looked forward to the break so he could concentrate on Rebecca.

The first Saturday of the M's road trip, Rebecca and Jamie joined friends attending an afternoon concert on Lake Union. The lake protruded neatly into the northern part of downtown Seattle from a canal that connected Puget Sound with the much larger Lake Washington. The stage was tucked into a park between a public marina and a museum featuring Tall Sailing Ships. It was an easy walk to surrounding restaurants and the group wandered over to The Whole afterward, where the conversation provoked rave reviews of the performance. Matt wondered what future generations would think of this music.

"Someday people will laugh at us just like we laugh at the likes and beliefs of generations before us," Adam said.

"People used to believe in human sacrifice and thought the world was round," Mandy added. "What do you think people in the future will find so bizarre about us?"

"Maybe that we thought the earth was round," Rebecca volunteered.

"What do you mean?" asked Mandy.

"Well, maybe the earth really is flat," Rebecca continued. "For centuries, everyone accepted Newton's assumptions about absolute time and absolute space because his equations correctly predicted activity in the universe. Then Einstein comes along and starts challenging Newton's assumptions. We get quantum mechanics. We get the understanding that we experience time at different rates. As we understand the universe better, some future Einstein could prove some of today's basic assumptions wrong. Maybe these string theory scientists will be back telling us the world is actually flat."

"Yeah, it's just an optical illusion that our earth is round," Matt said sarcastically. "Just like the shortest distance between two points isn't always a straight line in space."

"So you think the world is flat?" Mandy asked Rebecca quizzically.

"No," Rebecca began to answer.

"But she does believe human sacrifice will be making a comeback," Matt interrupted.

"Actually it's probably still around in various forms," Rebecca said with a laugh. "I'm just saying you have to open yourself to all possibilities by challenging assumptions. We laugh at some ancients for assuming that the world is flat. We make the same mistake if we assume things too easily."

"Maybe the world was flat back then and it's round now," Matt offered.

"So you can know nothing with certainty?" Adam asked.

"I couldn't say that with certainty," Rebecca said.

Everyone laughed politely except Jamie. He just smiled.

"Have you ever watched the M's game on cable T.V. with the sound turned down and the radio coverage turned up?" Matt asked. "The radio tells you the action before it unfolds on the screen. Is that part of this experiencing time at different rates?"

Before anyone could take a stab at answering, Jamie burst in, "Could someone be like the radio, experiencing events earlier than his friends who were like television people or something and were experiencing time at a slower rate? And this could give the illusion that he was predicting or actually causing the future when he was just experiencing it first?"

"Whoa, big boy," Adam interrupted, "slow down. I'm going to predict your future. Rebecca's going to be driving you home tonight and you're going to have a big hangover tomorrow!"

Once again everyone laughed except Jamie. This time he was lost in thought.

Chapter Thirty-Three

Normally Llew enjoyed eggs and bacon, but the ones sitting in front of him were strangely unappetizing in the florescent lighting of the Matt Talbot Center's multi-purpose room. He drank the coffee and nibbled on a pastry. His son had no such reservations. Adam eagerly pounced on his meal, greedily devoured every last bite of his own food, and began spearing fruit off his father's plate. This Tuesday the two Tinklers were representing the company at a Patron Table organized by Chick Pitz of the Mist for a fundraiser to benefit the Center.

After polite applause for the first speaker subsided, a soft-spoken man in his early forties was introduced. Although not a professional speaker like some of the others, this man mesmerized the audience with his tale of addiction and street living. By the time he had detailed his rescue by the Matt Talbot Center and his current sobriety for over two years, eyes were misting up all around the room. Adam's own eyes were fixed on leftover rolls in the pastry basket. While others fumbled for their checkbooks, he stretched out of his seat and reached across the table to pass himself the basket.

Llew handed over a healthy donation to Chick Pitz, the Table Captain. Chick discreetly glimpsed at the amount before stuffing it into the envelope. He hadn't had a chance to speak with Llew before the breakfast and motioned for him to stick around while the others began filtering out of the room. Adam liberated Llew's untouched orange juice while they waited.

Chick passed the donation envelope to a runner, turned back, and said with a big smile, "Llew, Adam, thanks for coming. This is just an outstanding program, don't you think?"

Llew was murmuring his assent when Adam interjected, "We heard on the radio coming over here that Donny Kuhn is leading the All Star vote for second basemen. He deserves it, but I was still surprised to hear it."

"Yeah," Chick confirmed, "and he's got a huge lead over Bonneville. Maybe people around the country are tired of giving all the glory to New York."

"Well, New York got the last laugh last week. They swept us and won all three by big margins. And Kuhn not only fizzled on the road again, but didn't he get arrested for fighting at some strip club in New York?" Llew asked.

Chick shook his head, "No, the Kuhn thing was blown way out of proportion. He wasn't involved in the fight or charged. He was just detained for questioning. He was more a witness than anything. The tabloids exaggerate everything."

"But he was in the strip joint," Llew pointed out.

"Llew, he's a young man. Hell, you were in those joints when you were Donny's age. I know because I was with you," Chick replied with a wink.

"I think we were a little younger than Kuhn and I only remember two incidents," Llew clarified mostly for Adam's sake. "But your point is well taken."

Chick quickly shifted gears to the other issue and said, "Even though our overall record is better this year than any time I can remember, we are actually playing worse on the road than we did last year. We just went 2-7 on this last trip back East which is as bad as our first trip at the beginning of the year. It's almost like the players are coasting, expecting to make it up at home. If we ever hit a dry spell at the Shoe, we're in big trouble."

"We can hardly expect to keep up a 28-5 pace at home over a whole season," Adam agreed.

"It has certainly been a good year for season ticket holders. My nephew even purchased an extra 36 game package back in our old section so we've had plenty to go around. We certainly appreciate the upgrade to the new seats. I think you said someone died and the family turned in their tickets?" Llew asked.

"Yeah," Chick squirmed just a bit, but continued, "normally I'm not involved with the details but I knew you and several others who were interested in upgrades so I had our staff flag nonrenewals of quality seats. I remember looking at this one because the guy,

Peter Edwards, was one of our original season ticket holders. He was a former college coach. You may remember him, Llew."

Llew caught the conspiratorial emphasis Chick placed on the last sentence and he acknowledged flatly, "Yes, the name is familiar."

When Pitz and Papa Llew lapsed into an uneasy silence, Adam assured Chick, "Well, anyway, we'll be out there tonight trying to keep Kuhn and the M's on track."

"How about the union organizing campaign at Tinkler? Have you guys thought about how you're handling that?" Chick asked.

Llew's face clouded over and he shrugged, "We're going to continue to resist the union, Chick."

"Well, good luck, and I hope everything works out alright for you," Chick said as he shook hands with Llew and Adam.

On the short drive to work, Adam asked his father, "What was all that about the Peter Edwards guy who had our seats and died? Did we know him?"

"He was a colorful local coach, very superstitious. He used to coach your Uncle Marty's college baseball team," Llew said and then changed the subject. "How's Jamie doing these days, by the way?"

"Pretty good, really," Adam answered. "He's having those problems with Rob being delinquent on deliveries and he fouled up that one requisition input but he's doing okay. He made an offer on a condo but it fell through. He's in pretty good shape financially to buy his own place when he finds the right one. And he's dating the McPherson girl. She's a good catch in anybody's book, so he's likely to get his heart broken. But who cares? The M's are still only two and a half games out of first. If they win the division, Jamie will be a happy man."

Llew smiled but told his son, "Don't ever underestimate Jamie. Sometimes the quiet guy has the magic touch and gets the girl!"

Chapter Thirty-Four

"I had to disqualify the sports page from my Good News assignment this year," Mandy told the group at the pre-game meal.

"What's your Good News assignment?" Adam asked.

"I tell the third graders they have to bring in one good news article from the newspaper. But all I was getting was sports. The M's win another one or Kuhn hits two more homers."

"What's wrong with that," Matt asked. "You don't root for the M's?"

"Sure, but it would be too easy. The Mist win a lot and Kuhn hits homers all the time."

"Not on the road," Matt said.

"So what do you get when you exclude sports?" Rebecca asked.

"That's the really interesting thing, the kids have a very difficult time finding good news in the newspaper. Some of the parents have commented on this because they thought I was making that point. But that was an unintended insight from the exercise."

Jamie felt good on the short walk from the Shoebox to the game. *Kuhn homers and M's victories are the good news in a serious world,* he chuckled to himself. *What could be wrong with that? All the better to have a hand in it. Maybe today is the day Donny Kuhn becomes the first player in major league history to hit five homers in a game.*

"What are you chortling about?" Matt asked.

"I was just remembering that somebody told me you actually paid for that haircut," Jamie replied.

The festive mood continued into the fifth inning when Kuhn came up with two on and two out. Time for homerun number three. M's fan's were ecstatic when Donny lined the first pitch off the wall in rightcenter but Jamie was mystified.

However, when the center fielder and rightcenter fielder both converged on the wall in hopes of making the catch, they were out of position for the carom. The ball careened off the wall, bounced past the two outfielders, and rolled back toward the infield. As the second baseman and the two outfielders scampered toward the Bermuda Triangle where the ball landed, Donny turned on his famous speed and motored hard around second. By the time the center fielder retrieved the ball and came up throwing, Donny was cutting the bag at third, showing no intention of stopping.

The throw was a little up the line on the first base side but the catcher made a good move after the catch to lunge back across the plate. Donny came sliding under the tag but his leg ended up pinned underneath the catcher. When the catcher finally jumped up, he was joined by teammates protesting the call while Donny writhed on the ground, painfully safe.

Kuhn was eventually helped off the field and removed from the lineup. The elation of the fans was now tempered with a realization that their emerging star might be seriously hurt. Jamie was the most distressed spectator in the ballpark.

The M's salvaged the game 9-5 even as Jamie backed off on his predictions. The players were happy with the win, but anxious to learn the fate of their second baseman. Donny was taped up and icing the leg as his teammates streamed into the locker room.

"Hey, Donny, why aren't you over at the hospital, getting that checked out?" E2 bellowed.

"I've already been there, been X-rayed, and sent back here for treatment. Did you know the radio announcers are calling me a gutsy player and a symbol of what Seattle baseball is all about?"

"Are you sure they weren't saying 'gusty' player?" Rudy Wink replied. "And since when is Seattle baseball all about bragging, brawls, and bimbo's?"

"Since forever!" Don Grant yelled. "Where have you been hiding, Rudy?"

"Hey guys, shut the hell up so we can hear what the doctors are saying about the injury," E2 screamed above the bantering. Turning to Donny, he continued, "So, what did the X-rays say, anyway?"

"The X-rays said I was one good looking dude and would I like to have dinner tonight," Donny deadpanned.

"Well, they'll probably be more interesting than the dates you had on the last road trip," Rudy said.

"Will you guys zip it just for a minute?" Escobar growled.

"The preliminary X-ray was inconcol…incolus…they couldn't tell nothing yet," Coach Duda interjected as he entered the room. "Donny's getting further tests tomorrow and they're going to compare the new stuff with old stuff in his file. So let's just chill and enjoy the victory. We've just started our longest homestand of the season and we need to make these next eleven games count."

"Thank you, Dr. Duda," Rudy said. "Let us know what happens when the X-ray stuff gets mixed with the file doohickeys, so we know how to go out and do the baseball thingamajig."

Chapter Thirty-Five

Scrambling to find some old hiking boots, Jamie remembered he hadn't used them since he quit Boy Scouts after ninth grade. The summer before tenth grade, Jamie and Matt realized that they would never be Eagle scouts and that it was not cool at their high school to even be a Scout. Although Jamie would now buy boots a half size bigger, he was surprised and relieved at how well his old ones fit.

Bathed in the nervous anticipation of meeting Rebecca on her turf, Jamie dressed quickly for their July 4th hike. Thoughts of the trek occupied the front rooms of his brain, pushing baseball to a little used closet. They planned to drive to the Issaquah Alps, about 13 miles east of Seattle. Later that night they would celebrate by enjoying the fireworks at Greenlake with some of her friends.

Jamie arrived at Rebecca's place physically and mentally unsure of himself, but psychologically terrified. He intended to swing by the Sub Marina on the way to the mountain and pick up sandwiches for the trail. But she said, "Sandwiches just get too messy, I've got some trail food we can take."

"Trail food, is that going to be like bark, berries, twigs…?" Jamie asked.

"No, I've got some apples, oranges, turkey jerky, trail mix, carrots, celery, and let's see, some grapes. We'll dig our own worms for some extra protein."

Jamie laughed, reasonably confident that he wouldn't have to eat a worm, while knowing that he would probably choke one down if that's what it took to impress her.

In the ride out to the Cougar Mountain trailhead in Issaquah, Jamie inquired almost casually, "About how long is this hike going to be?"

"As long as we want it to be," Rebecca replied. "There are all sorts of trails and routes well marked to the tenth of a mile. I'd like to take you up to DeLeo's Wall to see the view of Mount Rainier."

"Well, how far is that?" Jamie asked more timidly than he intended.

Sensing his discomfort, Rebecca flashed her man-melting smile and answered with a laugh, "Well, it will be about thirty miles, so we'll have to jog most of the way!"

"I was hoping for something a little longer."

Rebecca smiled and said, "Actually, we can do the six mile roundtrip from Red Town Trailhead in less than three hours. If we want to do more, we can detour up to the Aircraft View Peak where there's a picnic table with a view of Mount Baker."

Jamie was now committed to getting to the Aircraft View Peak or die trying, but only said, "No problem. I'm in decent shape. I play a lot of basketball and jog when I can get the time."

Damn. I'm being too defensive, he thought.

"Your shape and the shape you're in are just fine," Rebecca assured him. "It's really a matter of what we feel like doing. After six months on the Appalachian Trail with a team that had a highly regimented schedule to follow, I like the freedom of being able to do whatever we feel like. That's why I picked Cougar Mountain rather that somewhere like Mount Si with a destination eight mile roundtrip hike."

Jamie didn't absorb much about the difference between Cougar Mountain and Mount Si. He was intoxicated with the sound of "we" rolling off those gorgeous lips and basking in the high of hearing her comment about his shape. He made a halfhearted attempt to sober up by cautioning himself, *Of course, she's just joking around.* But he also knew Jeffrey Anne never made him feel this.

Jamie hung on Rebecca's every word, comfortable with any indignity if it would coax a laugh from her. Baseball was so far away that he didn't even realize it was missing until they were snacking at DeLeo's Wall. Jamie suddenly thought to ask Rebecca, "If you could have a power to do one thing, what would you want it to be?"

"Isn't world peace the obvious universal answer?"

"No, I mean something else, like the power to make a free throw every time or to make any guy fall in love with you or something like that?"

"Don't I already have that power?" she said lightheartedly, turning toward Jamie and briefly making eye contact.

He could feel his body betray him by flashing red heat to his cheeks but managed to ask, "You already have the power to make every free throw?"

Rebecca only smiled, so Jamie left the rhetorical question behind and continued, "Well, let's try this. Say you could cause people to do things you wanted by just thinking about it, what obligations would you have in the exercise of that power?"

"What would be the fun in such a power? Why would you want it? What power are you seeking, Jamie?"

Although he thought he was only looking for answers to the questions raised by his baseball powers, Jamie had to restrain himself from blurting, *"The power to make you fall in love with me!"*

Instead, he answered, "What if you weren't seeking the power at all, but it was just given to you? And you didn't know why or how, what would you do?"

"Why would you have to exercise it at all? If you could make every free throw, why shoot basketballs?"

"What if you loved basketball?"

"Then the power would be a curse, not a blessing!"

"Would it make any difference to you if you could only make the baskets if you didn't tell anyone about the power? When you tell someone, you can't make the baskets."

Rebecca didn't understand what difference that made, but she didn't say that. Her eyes narrowed and she looked back at Jamie, "Do you think about this a lot?"

Jamie laughed, "No, only when I'm surrounded by natural beauty. Then repressed philosophy wells up and oozes out of my larger pores."

As if on cue, they both rose from the log at the same time and headed for Aircraft View Peak. The uphill trek at the end was tough on Jamie, but the effort was well worth it. Lake Sammamish and Mount Baker loomed spectacular to the north on such a clear, bright day. Although the view was a reward in itself, the setting was just the prompt for Jamie's true payoff. Rebecca leaned back on Jamie and let his body support her. Then she turned back, looked up at him, and he had no choice but to kiss her.

The last two miles back to the car should have added to Jamie's fatigue but he had clearly found a second wind. They never did find Rebecca's friends that night at Greenlake, but the fireworks were the best ever.

Chapter Thirty-Six

Jamie had not mentioned his itinerary to Dred the vendor. He thought about it, but had said nothing. Jamie had skipped the M's game on July 4th for the hike, dinner, and fireworks show with Rebecca. In fact, he was taking off the entire holiday weekend, not based on any patriotic feelings either for or against his country or baseball team. He was already a day late for the family party at the Tinkler compound on Lake Cavenger. He would have gladly skipped the entire weekend with his tribe for just five more minutes with Rebecca, but she was occupied with her own family.

Mid-morning Saturday, Jamie threw his gear in the truck and headed north for Cavenger. He punched the radio dial into the Spotstalk Show to catch up with the M's loss last night. Theories plausible and implausible swirled across the airwaves, while no one mentioned Jamie's absence from the ballpark. He had a great deal to think about. He had left the M's with an eight game win streak. Although Donny Kuhn had no broken bones, he had missed four games before getting a pinch hit in his first one back. Then he sizzled in the last two games Jamie attended, stretching his consecutive hit streak to a record twelve.

A female caller asked the host, "How can Donny Kuhn look so good with twelve straight hits and then look so bad going out all four times last night?'

Other callers offered numerous answers. One suggested Kuhn had been seen on the town celebrating a little too much the night before his hitless performance. Another pointed out that the record came against weaker pitching than the Oakland starter he faced yesterday. Someone else said his wife told him that Donny had a bad horoscope on Friday and shouldn't have played at all that day.

The show's host concluded the segment by reminding everyone, "Sometimes that's just baseball. Even the worst teams win over fifty games a season and even the very best teams lose over fifty. And the difference between the best and the worst hitters in the league is whether they get two hits or three hits every ten times they come to the plate. We go to the games because we don't know what's going to happen."

Jamie knew the host wasn't speaking for him. When Jamie went to games these days, outcomes were certain. If Jamie wanted uncertainty, he needed to avoid the Shoe. He felt like using his cell phone to tell the commentator that the caller talking about horoscopes was the closest one to the truth. But, of course, he didn't. And it's not like anyone would have taken him seriously.

After the commercial break, the sports show returned with more on Kuhn. An angry listener demanded, "What do we think of Donny's escapade on the team's off day last Monday when he was a 'no show' at the party he promised to attend at Children's Hospital?"

"I think Don K is living up to the name donkey," a caller replied. "We should trade him while his value is so high. Maybe we could get a top starting pitcher and a competent replacement for Kuhn at the same time."

"You want to trade a man who is leading the league in all three triple crown categories?" the host asked. "He already has year end numbers with 46 homers, 113 rbi's, and a .462 batting average! He can coast the rest of the way and still win the Most Valuable Player award this season."

Time passed quickly as Jamie listened to the debate while trying to sort out things in his own mind. But he was growing weary of the chaos in his head and just driving into the Tinkler complex perked him up.

Before Jamie even came to a stop, Matt was waving and yelling, "Hey, Meatball, I was just headed over to the Scavenger to pick up some supplies. Wanna run me over there?"

"Sure," Jamie said. "By supplies, I assume you mean beer."

"That's a good idea, but I also need to pick up more food for tomorrow's brunch," Matt answered as he slid into the truck cab.

During the three mile drive, Matt gave a rundown on yesterday's events up at the Lake. As they entered the market, Matt turned to Jamie and said, "Okay, don't keep me in suspense. How did it go with Rebecca?"

"Fine," Jamie answered.

"Fine?" Matt asked. "Fine? Fine is something Kuhn pays when he gets hauled into court for his screw-ups. Hey, hand me a couple dozen eggs. And then pass the dirt about your big make out session with Rebecca at Greenlake last night."

Jamie had just popped open the first carton of eggs when Matt's words registered. Both of them looked shocked. Matt spoke first, "You don't need to open the cartons and count the eggs. I'm sure there's twelve in there like the label says."

"I'm looking to see if any of them are cracked," Jamie said. "Haven't you ever gone shopping before?"

Matt grabbed Jamie's head in both hands and feigned a close inspection while spouting, "Let me see if you are cracked. You've been acting really strange lately. This Rebecca is one dangerous woman. I'm worried it's suicidal falling for her."

"Who says we were making out at Greenlake?" Jamie demanded.

"Mandy saw you there. She said you were going at it like a couple of teenyboppers. Hey, where do they keep the microwave bacon?" Matt added without missing a beat.

"Mandy's up here?" Jamie asked as he wheeled toward the bacon.

"No, you know we broke up, but she called to tell me. I've got spies everywhere, so don't be holding out on me."

"What do you mean you and Mandy are broken up? She was with you at the concert on Lake Union and at the game where Kuhn got hurt," Jamie said with a big smile as he pointed at the bacon.

"She wasn't with me. She was part of our group. And what are you grinning at? You think it's funny that we use microwave bacon, Mr. Professional Shopper?"

"Actually, I was just thinking about you calling me suicidal. If Rebecca is my 'suicide squeeze,' what is Mandy?"

Matt shook his head, and said, "Let's get the beer. We need to do some serious deprogramming."

Chapter Thirty-Seven

The campfire and the radio were locked in a cackling duel. When E2 tripled in the tying run, conversation softened. Cheers erupted when Thorne lofted a sacrifice fly to drive in Escobar and give the M's the lead.

When the game went to commercial break, Matt took beer orders and headed for the cooler. Adam turned to Jamie and said, "By the way, Llew did ask Pitz about who owned our seats before us. He was Peter Edwards. He died last year and, according to Llew, he used to be your dad's baseball coach in college."

"Really? That's interesting. Do you know anything more about him or his family?"

"Yeah, they want to adopt you because you seem to be more interested in them than your own family," Adam answered.

When Matt sauntered back with the beer, the group had broken into several smaller conversations. Adam was alone with Matt and Jamie and asked casually, "Hey you two, how's Rob doing these days?"

"He's still hurting us in the field," Jamie complained.

"But he doesn't seem to be taking the visible lead in the union organizing campaign like we suspected he might," Matt added. "Rob may well be working behind the scene, but none of our sources identify him as one of the ringleaders. He's kind of between the younger guys who are really pushing the union and the old timers who are resisting."

"Are we getting him any medical help?" Jamie asked.

"We're trying," Matt answered a bit defensively, "but he sure doesn't like doctors, at least since his wife ran off with one."

"Yeah, it's hard to force someone to get treatment if he doesn't want it or think he needs it," Adam added.

Suddenly a cousin called over, "Did you hear that? The Big Ugly just hit a two run homer and we're down by one again."

"How did the runner get on base?" Matt shouted back.

"A walk."

"We kill ourselves with walks," Matt growled. "It's like giving up free runs. Let 'em hit it. They might make an out."

"Well, we let the Big Ugly hit it and look what happened," Adam said.

"All I'm saying is that we walk a lot more people than the opposing pitchers walk," Matt replied. "At least according to the stats in the paper yesterday."

Jamie hadn't seen the article, but he filed away the information in his head. As the game progressed through the eighth inning, Jamie found himself excited and agitated as Seattle stranded two runners in scoring position. His right hand would twitch with each Mist hitter he couldn't influence.

In the last of the ninth, the M's still trailed by a run. Kuhn led off and reached first safely when the third baseman booted the ball and couldn't recover in time to throw him out. The next hitter tried to sacrifice Donny to second, but he hit the ball too hard right back to the pitcher who wheeled and threw to second, nipping Donny. A pinch runner was inserted at first and he scampered to third on a single and scored the tying run on a sacrifice fly. The M's couldn't score again and the game went to extra innings.

Even though Seattle did not hold a lead, they brought in their closer. He walked the first two batters he faced, vexing Seattle fans everywhere. Some of the ones sitting around the Cavenger campfire threw in creative cursing for good measure. A double play, an intentional walk, and a strikeout turned the epithets into cheers.

In the Mist half of the tenth, Rudy Wink singled with one out and stole second. E2 was walked intentionally setting up the double play possibility. Although Larry Thorne avoided the twin killing by fouling off the low pitches, one pitch floated up in the strike zone and Larry lofted it deep into right field. The fans started shrieking and the radio announcer was screaming, "Oh yes, we've got a deep, deep drive to right…"

Unfortunately the drive wasn't deep enough and the right fielder hauled it in on the warning track. Matt tightened his grip on an empty beer can, caving in the aluminum sides. He yelled, "Damn, I hate it when the announcers pump you up for nothing. That was probably a pop up in shallow right!"

Thorne's drive was actually deep enough that Wink took third on it, except now there were two outs. Don Grant made his way to the plate. A ball. A called strike. A ball. A swinging strike. Groans around the campfire. A ball. A foul ball. Another deep drive to right field. It didn't make it over the fence either. At least not on the fly, but it did bounce over. Ground rule double. Instantly all was well for Seattle fans whether they were in the stadium, in front of a television somewhere, or sitting around a Cavenger campfire.

It had been a long time since Jamie was so exhilarated by a Seattle Mist home game. He liked the feeling.

Chapter Thirty-Eight

Jamie looked at the scorecard and froze in his tracks.

Jo had come back early from the weekend party to attend Mass but the cousins had remained up at Cavenger playing basketball while listening to the M's game. Even today's loss had energized Jamie as the very uncertainty of the 6-5 defeat lasted until the final out and provided enough excitement to alternately entertain, delight, and infuriate the cousins for over three hours. The sting of defeat still carried a tingle of rejuvenation for Jamie until his mother greeted his return with the scorecard and the words that a strange man had come by the house looking for him.

"What exactly did he say?" Jamie finally asked.

"He wondered where you had been and was acting kind of weird like he was annoyed or something. He said to give you this scorecard if you were back in time for the game today. Who is he?"

"That's what I'd like to know," Jamie muttered.

"I thought maybe he was a friend of yours even though I've never seen him before. He was wearing a sweatshirt that said, 'El Salvador Futbol'"

"He sells scorecards and he's a part-time bartender. I have no idea how he knew where I lived, but I'm sure as hell going to find out."

Jamie felt agitated all evening. On the drive to work the next morning, he was momentarily distracted by the radio report on the selections for the All Star game a week from Tuesday. Kuhn would be starting at second base, a landslide winner over Bonneville. No other Seattle player was elected to be a starter although Escobar, Grant, and Thorne all finished in the top three at their positions and Wink was one of the top ten outfielders.

Various methods of All Star voting had been tried through the years, but fans currently selected the starting position players for each league by popular vote. The pitchers and the substitutes were then picked by the All Star managers who were rewarded with their own positions by virtue of managing their teams to the World Series the previous season. Fans got one last chance online to add an overlooked player to each team.

To the chagrin of Jamie and Seattle Mist loyalists, the New York manager had not selected any additional M's player to join Donny Kuhn at this year's event. Seattle was leading their division with a 49-35 record. Although the lead was only one game over Oakland, Seattle fans were indignant in their comments on the Sportstalk Show. Outrage came easily after the New York manager added four New York players to the two already elected to the team. Callers pointed out correctly that New York was actually in second place in their division. Out of fairness, the host reminded his callers that the New Yorkers did have the better record at 51-33. No matter, even the possibility that fans would vote in another Seattle player could not quell the outrage.

Although novice All Star Donny only scratched out one single at home on the weekend, he was feeling good as he headed out of town for the final six games before the break. He still owned a robust .455 batting average. He had emerged from obscurity and even survived unpopularity for the attack on Nagle. His blockbuster games were so newsworthy that even fans historically slow to recognize changes in the player hierarchy had voted for the upstart. Of course, even bad publicity can be important in elections where name recognition is important.

When asked how he felt about his teammates getting snubbed, Donny joked, "They'll really be in trouble if I get traded to New York."

That quote did nothing to endear Donny with his mates or the callers to the radio station, but he was more interested in endearing himself with the ladies anyway. He now had a week to roam on the road before his girlfriend would join him in Atlanta for the All Star festivities. That week plus the three-day All Star break also gave Jamie some breathing room to ponder his own moral dilemmas. And he definitely knew he had to track down Dred immediately.

Monday after work, Jamie headed straight to the Shoebox. It was deserted more than he expected even for a day when the M's were off and no game filled the big screen. He made his way slowly to the one bartender on duty and asked her, "Is Dred working tonight?"

"Nah, he's not working here any more. He claimed to be heading to El Salvador. I guess he's a big fan of their soccer team and the World Cup."

"When's he coming back?"

"I have no idea about that. I don't think he's coming back to this job because he left on short notice and continually annoyed customers. He was a little too scruffy and weird for the owner. And believe me, you have to be pretty strange to register on the weird-o-meter around this zoo."

"Like, how so?"

"He had all these stories which would have been kind of amusing if he were kidding around. Like his brother was some kind of shaman who put a curse on the M's and that's why they've been such losers. After his brother died, then only his son could lift the curse. But his brother was a bachelor."

"Did he say anything specific about the curse getting lifted?"

The bartender gave Jamie a funny look and said, "We kind of thought he was a little loony and didn't pay that much attention to exactly what he was saying."

Jamie wandered away with some relief that he had avoided Dred and some relief that Dred wouldn't be showing up unannounced at his home. But relief gave way to anxiety of the unknown. Jamie wondered what was going to happen to his scoring? He certainly wasn't relieved at the prospect of losing his gift. He wished he had been more aggressive in confronting the mystery of Dred.

The Seattle Mist didn't know enough to worry about Jamie's scorebook issues. They started the road trip oblivious to the likelihood that they would blow their one game lead over Oakland in the Western Division. Instead, they played like champions in an 8-1 victory on Tuesday while the Oaks lost their game. The fans were falling in love with their team all over again. Few could remember when they had ever been in first place past the halfway mark in a season. The collective mood of the city was uplifted. So when Jamie spotted a somberly distracted Adam in the hallway on Wednesday morning, he said, "You're obviously not thinking about the M's right now."

"Oh, hi," Adam reflexively replied after snapping out of his deep thought. "Yeah, unfortunately, there is more to our world than baseball."

In the face of that rebuke, Jamie asked more seriously, "So, what's up?"

"The Labor Board has certified the union card check and set an election for sixty days from now," Adam explained.

"Translation?"

"The Board found that the union presented signed cards from at least 30% of our employees who are formally requesting an election. So we are going to have that election to determine if a majority of our employees want to be represented by the AFW."

"Was that unexpected?" Jamie asked.

"Maybe not, when you figure the union can pull all sorts of intimidating tactics to get those signatures, but hopefully after our campaign and in the privacy of the voting booth, the employees will come through for us."

Jamie nodded and Adam scurried on to his next meeting. Jamie paused in the hallway for a few moments. He was staring at one of Uncle Art's framed photographs. This one featured the inside of an outhouse in Kansas but the image wasn't registering. Instead Jamie was lost in the realization that he didn't have the same negative emotional reaction to the union election as his older cousin did. He certainly wasn't pro-union, but he couldn't help but think, *Maybe there is more than baseball to our world, however baseball is sure a lot more important than all this union baloney.*

Chapter Thirty-Nine

"Okay, Zipper, high and tight," Donny shouted out to Coach Duda out on the mound.

Donny was leading the major leagues in homers so he was invited to the Homerun Derby on the evening before the All Star game. He chose the M's third base coach, Eddy Duda, to accompany him. Zip would pitch to Donny in the contest that credits a player for total homers hit before ten outs. An out is any ball you swing at that isn't hit over the fence in fair territory. When Donny stepped up to the plate, he knew the two hitters ahead of him had already pounded out eight and nine homers, respectively. After popping the first two offerings up, Donny laced a useless single to left on the third pitch, grounded to third, and popped to shallow center to quickly claim five outs. Just when he thought things couldn't get much worse, he took a big cut at pitch six and missed it cleanly.

Although he expected to be impressed by the All-Star game itself, Donny was surprised to find himself in awe of the Derby as well. After all his recent scrutiny in the public eye, he felt this would be a fun opportunity to show off. Instead, he was clearly nervous. The press wasn't even preoccupied with him, as there were many big fish in this pond. However, Seattle fans were obsessed with the Derby this year now that one of their own was a favorite. When Donny whiffed, Seattle did a collective cringe. Jamie was the least surprised of his compatriots watching at the Shoebox. Still he hoped Donny would be able to drive a few out of the park, considering Zip Duda would be grooving the pitches.

The next four pitches were vivid to the screaming fans at the Shoebox. They were a blur to Donny, but he knew they were the wrong kind of outs. Instead of out of the ballpark, they were just plain outs. Although being shut out and even missing a pitch was not unprecedented, this was clearly an embarrassing showing for Donny. He tried his best to laugh it off. He bravely told the national television audience, "Zipper was throwin' me knuckleballs because he's still mad at how badly I beat him at Gin Rummy on the plane ride out here!"

Seattle fans who dared to be proud of their first place team and their slugging second baseman took a fall once again, humiliated on the national stage by Donny's choke in the homerun contest. One television commentator used the opportunity to punish him for his earlier flippancy by pontificating, "Donny Kuhn, the 'would be' Ted Williams, proved tonight that only his mouth works. A frozen Teddy Ballgame could do better and look better doing it than Kuhn on his best day. Granted this wasn't Donny's best day, but the Splendid Splinter did not need speed and defense to come through in the clutch, no matter what ballpark he was in."

The denizens of the Shoebox jeered the commentator, while deep down even they suspected that Kuhn was a pretender to greatness. Although Donny had a lackluster 5-27 road trip before the break, he was still batting an incredible .439 and the team had won four of those six games. Seattle held a two game lead in their division and no one, except the anonymous Jamie, was more responsible for it then Donny. And still he was the subject of criticism by his detractors and doubts by his friends.

"You guys want another round," the server asked.

"Nah," Adam answered quickly for the group.

As Jamie rose to leave, the server recognized him and asked, "Hey did you ever hear anything from Dred?"

"No," Jamie answered.

"Well, he should be pretty excited. I see his El Salvador team pulled off an upset to actually get into the round of sixteen at the World Cup."

Matt eyed Jamie curiously as the cousins filed out of the bar. Then he just said, "Dred?"

"What?" Jamie replied.

"What is up with you and all your new friends?"

"You know him. He was a bartender here who sold me scorecards sometimes. I told you his name back when he gave me that business card for a free brunch at his family's restaurant."

"No, I don't know him. I know he's weird, though. And now I know you and he hang out secretly watching soccer. If you weren't dating Rebecca, I'd be worried."

Just the sound of Rebecca's name energized Jamie. He waved to Matt with a smile, but cleared out quickly as more of the Monday night crowd from the Shoebox spilled out into the street. While the party in Seattle died early, Donny Kuhn was still celebrating hard despite his power shortage and the three hour time difference. He was eye flirting with one beauty while dancing with another. His dance partner was actually a professional partygoer. She was not only a blonde bombshell, but also owned a masters degree in sociology from Columbia and was working on a Ph.D. at New York University. She could actually make a living being hired by prominent people who wanted to liven up their parties.

Ms. Blonde Party Professional extricated herself from Donny and moved on to seek out and destroy dullness. Donny was not disappointed because he was still in eye contact with her replacement. But then his girlfriend moved into his line of sight like a familiar southern storm descending on a port city in the late afternoon.

Donny was a little sorry he had brought a girlfriend with him for the three-day break. They had both been looking forward to the trip but once in Atlanta, Donny couldn't help but wish he could be a little more single, what with all the parties and glamorous ladies beckoning. His girlfriend herself was a beauty befitting a baseball star. She was as tall as Donny in her heels, had the face of a model, and a curvier figure. She had been growing out her short black hair this season but was having trouble competing with rivals who possessed the allure of the unknown.

Donny had been flirting with every woman in range while his girlfriend pouted. She was well aware of the game since she played it well enough herself to snare Donny in the first place. She stormed over within inches of him. He took no step backward, but was in retreat nonetheless, leaning away from her.

"Hey, babe," he said with forced casualness, "Is this great or what? Are you enjoying yourself?"

"Not really. I'm kind of tired. How about heading back to the hotel, so we can be together?"

"We're together, right here," Donny cajoled, "but if you like, I can get the limo to drop you at the hotel and I'll join you in an hour or so. I'm still keyed up from the Home Run Derby and need to blow off some steam."

Donny hoped for a little sympathy, but all he got was a reluctant girlfriend staying at the party for the duration, making them both miserable for the next four hours. Fortunately, tomorrow's All Star game was played at eight o'clock in the evening and Donny didn't have to get up until two in the afternoon.

By the time Donny struggled to the press briefing before the game, he amended his story a little for the reporters, announcing with artificial bravado, "I was a little off my game yesterday because I didn't get my usual pre-game Mist Burger with Chili Fries. But I had some flown in for today, so I should be back in top form."

Although Kuhn could search for top form with the likes of coach Duda, professional partygoers, or special burger platters, he had no way of knowing that his best shot was to stay home with Jamie. Although Donny couldn't be accused of redeeming himself at the All Star game itself, he caused no great embarrassment. He fielded his one chance cleanly at second. At the plate, he grounded into a force out, but beat the relay and later scored a run. He struck out in his second plate appearance before being removed for Bonneville in the fifth.

Donny had done nothing to brag about during the three day All Star hiatus, but continued to stir his teammates up with a challenge upon his return, "I hope the rest of the team is ready to step up their game for the second half of the season. I can't do it alone. We all know it's gut-check time now. And management needs to look long and hard at how to improve the team before the trading deadline at the end of the month."

"Where do you think improvement is needed?" a reporter asked innocently.

"The sports writing position could use some improvement," Donny responded.

Chapter Forty

"Have you seen that scraggly guy who buys scorecards from you," Jamie asked his former vendor.

"A lot of scraggly guys buy scorecards," the vendor said while looking Jamie over. "You want one?"

"Sure. But the tall, thin redheaded guy with the baggy pants. His name is Dred and he sometimes buys from you on credit, do you know when he's coming back?"

"Haven't seen him. Don't have a clue. And I'm not selling you a program on credit."

Jamie paid his two bucks, took the card, and headed into Thursday's game, the first one after the All Star break. Eventually Matt, Adam, and Dano McPherson joined him. Jamie was powerless with his scorecard and the M's settled into a 6-1 deficit in the fifth. Then Dano's brother Mac came down and announced, "Llew said to come get you guys. Some of the people are leaving early from the owner's suite and we can all squeeze in."

Once inside the luxury suite, Matt whispered to Jamie, "I wish I hadn't spent all that money on hot dogs and fries. Look at all this free stuff."

Matt headed to the buffet despite being full and Jamie wandered over to where Llew was talking with Chick Pitz. Llew waved Jamie into the conversation and Chick said, "I sure can't figure why we're getting our asses kicked against such a crummy Milwaukee team."

"According to a bartender at the Shoebox, his brother put a curse on the M's years ago," Jamie said without thinking.

Matt appeared with a heaping plate of food and asked, "What did I miss?"

"Kuhn just singled again and Jamie was telling us that some bartender put a curse on the M's," Llew replied.

"His brother," Jamie corrected.

Matt immediately started grousing, "The M's always get slighted. The Cubs and Red Sox get all the publicity for the curses of the Bambino or whatever. We're just as cursed in Seattle but has anyone ever heard of the Curse of the Bartender's Brother? No way. Move our team east of the Mississippi and we'd get proper respect for our wretched failures!"

"Redemption is always around the corner," Jamie sighed. "Maybe Donny will hit .400. Maybe the M's will win it all this year."

Pitz gave Jamie a thumbs up sign and a nod as he and Llew excused themselves.

"And maybe Rebecca will marry you, have your babies, and get elected President of the United States," Matt said softly to Jamie.

After the 8-1 loss, Matt bummed a ride with Jamie. As they headed for the truck, Matt said, " I want you to listen, this is important. If I die, I know what my last words are going to be: 'I wish I spent more time at the office.' Got that?"

"Why do you think you're going to die? And hasn't somebody already said those words?"

"Jamie, Jamie, pay attention, this is the point, everyone since Shakepeare says they wish they had spent *less* time at the office. I wish I had spent *more* time at the office!"

"Why are you telling me this? Why are those going to be your last words? And most importantly, you don't have an office. You share a cubicle when you're not in the field."

"Look, Meatball, I'm telling you this in case I die in an accident and don't get a chance to say the words. You tell people I said them. Then no one can ever say again, 'No one ever said they wished they had spent more time at the office.' They just have to stop saying it or say, 'Except for Matt Tinkler, no one else ever said they wished they had spent more time at the office.' Make sure that message is inscribed on my tombstone."

"How do I know that no one else has said those words? And if you die in a plane crash, how am I going to say those are your last words? Your mother isn't going to appreciate morbid humor at a time like that."

"Jamie, if you're not going to do this for me, I'll get someone else to do it. But I trust you the most to follow through on something like this. So, whadya say, are we together on this?"

"Uh, yeah, sure, I'll take care of it. But wait, you don't even believe your own last words."

"Let me know when you find your sense of humor," Matt said. "Actually my real regret will be if I never write my novel."

"What novel?" Jamie asked. "You never told me you were going to write a novel."

"You think I tell you everything? Look, you can't ever discuss this idea of mine because once it gets out in the cosmos, someone else is likely to write it."

"That good, huh?"

"Get this. You have a civilization where the people are round. They have no legs or arms. They roll everywhere," Matt said proudly.

"Have you started writing it yet?" Jamie asked.

"No, but if I die, you gotta write it and dedicate it to me."

"Write what? What happens to these round people?" Jamie asked.

"I'm working on it." Matt answered.

"I don't even know why I'm asking. I'm not writing any damn novel about round people." Jamie said.

"Even if I die?" Matt asked.

"Especially if you die. And what is this whole preoccupation with death and dying words? You're creeping me out. There isn't something I don't know, is there?"

"I'm creeping you out? What about your fascination with the Dred man's curse of the M's? One Seattle loss and you're getting all creeped out by me?"

"Well, things are already starting to look up because no one broke into my truck tonight," Jamie replied.

Chapter Forty-One

Donny entered the locker room and started yelling at no one in particular. "I get three hits and the rest of you can only manage two total against a last place team. What gives?"

If he was joking around, he didn't get a laugh. Worse yet, he didn't even get a response. He did get some press, though, as a reporter dutifully recorded every word. Jamie was disheartened at the words, but knew that at least this time Donny had earned his three hits without Jamie's help.

More out of habit than anything else, Jamie made his way to the ballpark on Friday. He thought about the possibility that Donny could hit .400 without any more help. He thought about how he made his favorite player a hero and the guy turned into a jerk before his eyes.

While lost in thought of all the possibilities for the rest of the season, he was startled to see Dred standing in his path. "I thought you were at the World Cup," Jamie managed to say.

"It looked like I was needed back here."

"They say you don't even work here," Jamie replied.

"Do they say that you work here."

"Of course not but what's going on?"

"A pennant race. Look, do you want the scorecard or not? I went through a lot to get here and get this to you."

"Yes," Jamie said as he eagerly grabbed for the card. "But I've got some questions I need answers to."

"Welcome to the club, but I gotta run," Dred said as he beat a hasty retreat.

"Will you be here tomorrow?" Jamie called after him.

The silence of the noisy stadium crowd was all Jamie heard. But he immediately turned his attention to the precious scorecard. He embraced it with the pleasure of an addict and raced to his seat. He all but ignored the customers he was seated with as he experienced the thrill of seeing his predictions come alive. The home team came away with a 13-3 win despite Donny Kuhn's five strikeouts.

The newspaper was forced to delete a couple of expletives from Donny's post game tirade, but it was explosive enough in print: "It's about time some of the others pulled their weight like I suggested. I really wanted to see what would happen if I tanked it. Would my mates step up to the challenge?"

Sensing he was treading on dangerous ground, Donny added hastily, "And to their credit, they did. It will make us a better team."

Donny's addendum didn't make as many stories as his original quote. By the time he struck out four more times in Saturday's 8-2 win, his agent had shut him up. The Commissioner was investigating the possibility that Kuhn was striking out on purpose based on his comments about "tanking it".

Kuhn finally issued the following clarification statement, presumably written by his agent, "I have never intentionally ever given less than my best. I said that when I went into the tank, as all players do when they hit dry spells, I really wanted to see how my teammates would respond. And as I noted, they stepped up and picked me up, just as I have done for them many times. The press completely misconstrued any suggestion that I would ever perform at less than my best. I am too competitive and too interested in bringing a World Championship to Seattle."

Despite the statement, many people wondered out loud how a .400 hitter could suddenly strike out nine straight times. The manager considered giving Kuhn Sunday's game off, since he often rested regulars when a day game followed a night game. But Donny insisted on getting a chance to clear his name. He did break out of his strikeout binge, but sent the statisticians scurrying for the record books when he hit into three double plays and a triple play. He refused to talk to the press while his teammates celebrated their three game win streak.

Kuhn did not have to play in Monday's win because he was in jail for throwing a plate of spaghetti at his girlfriend and cutting her face, requiring a hospital visit for the stitches.

Chapter Forty-Two

Jamie was one of the first fans to arrive at the ballpark on Tuesday night. He was determined to catch up with Dred. Sure enough, shortly after the gates opened, Dred wandered in and headed for the guy selling scorecards. He took the card and headed for the mezzanine level that overlooked the entrance Jamie usually used. Jamie followed him at a safe distance because the early crowd was fairly sparse.

Dred tucked into a corner, pulled a small round container out of his pocket, and looked as if he were rubbing something from the container on the scorecard. Jamie watched for awhile, but when Dred did nothing more, he circled back out of the stadium at another exit. Jamie re-entered the stadium at the left field entrance and ran right into Dred. He gave Dred a five-dollar bill and told him to keep the change. As soon as he got to his seat, Jamie studied the card. He could barely detect a faint smudge on the back.

The scorecard satisfied Jamie's craving for predictions as Seattle romped to a 12-7 slugfest victory. Donny made bail and was back in the lineup, but Jamie left him on his own. He managed a single in five appearances.

The post game revelry was unusually raucous after a weeknight win. After all, Seattle had now won five of six games since the break, improved their record to 58-38, and extended their lead to three and a half games in the Western Division. Coming up big with six runs in the last two innings was invigorating for everyone but Jamie. He felt detached from the celebration going on around him at the Shoebox. Just a year ago, he would have exulted in such electrifying drama. Now he had the power to make it happen, while the certainty of victory made the attainment strangely empty. Everything that was fun about the post game victory scene a year ago, left him uneasy now.

As he drove home early, Jamie pondered why he had the baseball power. He wondered how many powers go undiscovered. He might never have stumbled on his if he hadn't pre-recorded outcomes in his scorebook. How many others had a power but never found it? His mind boggled. What if someone had the power to make himself desirable to any woman, but never found out he had it? Jamie wouldn't mind finding that power and testing it on Rebecca. He always hated Philosophy class but now wondered if he should have paid more attention to it in school.

Jamie woke up on Wednesday with determination that today he would learn more about the scorecard mystery. He dressed quickly, but paused on the landing and took a long look at the familiar picture of his father in the Seattle Community College baseball team picture. Everyone was waving trophies from the league championship. The photographer must have had trouble getting them to stand still for the photo because people were looking every which way. The coach obviously wasn't helping get everyone organized because he seemed just as lost in the joy of the moment as his players were. They all looked as happy as if they had just won the World Series.

It was a little early for profundity but Jamie thought to himself that perhaps too many people get sidetracked dreaming about what is out of reach when joys just as big are all around them. Why wonder about the pleasure of winning a World Series, marrying a celebrity, or hitting the lottery jackpot when you can experience as much happiness in your everyday life? Surely the Seattle Community College champions in this picture were as happy in this moment as any World Series winner could ever be. They were already bursting at the seams with joy.

Eventually Jamie snapped out of his daydream and made it down to the breakfast table where his mother was sipping her coffee and reading a magazine. He mustered a muffled, "Morning, Ma."

Jo continued to flip through the magazine without looking up or acknowledging Jamie in any way. Just this subtle difference in her normal response forced Jamie to ask, "What's wrong, Ma?"

"Nothing," Jo answered curtly.

"Come on, Ma, I can tell something's wrong. What is it?"

"I had a dream last night," Jo stated flatly.

"Yeah, and…?" Jamie prompted gently.

"You got married and moved back to the East Coast and would never call or visit," Jo spit out accusatorily.

Jamie smiled, relieved that nothing serious was amiss. "So what were you upset about: me moving back East, me getting married, me not calling, or me not visiting?" he teased.

"You know perfectly well that it is plain mean to ignore me," Jo said angrily.

Jamie was a little taken aback and proceeded with more caution, "Ma, it was just a dream. You don't think I've been ignoring you, do you?"

"You were just so mean, some of the things you were saying to me," Jo continued.

"But, Ma, it was all a dream. I didn't say any of those things."

Jo just glared. Jamie waited a second and then asked, "What? Do you want me to apologize for things I never said? I don't even know what they were. Jeez, it was a dream, Ma!"

Jo just shook her head. Jamie didn't know what that meant but he gulped some orange juice and said, "Look, Ma, I'm running late but I love you. Don't listen to my evil twin in your dreams. I'm not moving to the East Coast. I'm not getting married. Jeffrey Anne and I are moving to Chicago and plan to live in sin. But we will call and visit you regularly."

Satisfied with just the beginning of a smile from his mother, Jamie headed for the door. When he arrived at his office, he found Matt sitting in the desk chair with his feet up on Jamie's desk. Not the least defensive about his trespass, Matt looked up from the page he was reading and asked nonchalantly, "Where you been, Meatball? You even went home early last night, so you have no hangover excuse."

Jamie wanted to say he had been interpreting dreams but asked instead, "What's going on?"

Matt jumped out of the chair and waved a document under Jamie's nose, "The union filed some more unfair labor practices and we haven't even gotten to our dirtiest campaign tactics yet!"

Jamie looked straight at Matt and pleaded, "Please tell me these ULP's have nothing to do with me."

"Everything always has to be about you, doesn't it?" Matt mocked. "Yeah, the union is upset that you're dating Rebecca. They don't think management should get all the hot chicks. They want their fair share."

"No, really, what is it this time?" Jamie asked less urgently.

"Remember that memo we planted threatening to shut down the plant if we become unionized?"

"Yeah," Jamie answered.

"No you don't and neither do I," Matt said slowly.

"I'm just glad it's not about me," Jamie sighed. "I've got enough problems."

"Like what?" Matt asked incredulously. "The M's are in first place. You're dating the best woman you will ever get near in your whole life. You have a job, health, and me for a best friend. What exactly are your problems?"

Jamie thought back to his dad's baseball picture on the hall landing and thought, *I don't even take my own advice about finding joy all around us!*

For Matt's sake, Jamie laughed. He couldn't talk about his baseball power and he didn't want to talk about Rebecca. So he groped for something plausible, "I guess you're right but I meant here at work. I'm worried about Rob and what he's doing to our clients. What can you do for a guy like that? We can't force him to get professional help but he needs it."

"You need to let Jeffrey Anne and Adam worry about Rob, especially with a union organizing campaign going on. Stay far away from Rob after your last fiasco. I know I do."

"That's part of the problem, Matt. You're his team leader," Jamie said too seriously.

"So you think I'm the problem? I've done everything I can. What more do you want from me? How about we change jobs?"

"You know I would suck at your job," Jamie offered in a spirit of conciliation.

"Maybe Rob is a curse from Dred's brother," Matt responded. "Ever notice how people want to take credit for both the good and the bad? Dred's brother wants credit for all the failures the M's have had over the years."

"Dred's brother is dead, Matt. I don't think he is seeking credit for anything."

"See, that even proves my point more. People seek credit for both the bad and the good even if they have to ride the coattails of a relative or friend!"

"Well, I'll give Dred some grief on this very subject when I see him," Jamie said.

Matt thought his cousin was being sarcastic and just said, "I can't wait."

Chapter Forty-Three

"Where the hell have you been?" Matt demanded when Jamie showed up in the middle of the first inning.

"I had some errands to run," Jamie lied. He had actually been in the ballpark for over two hours looking for Dred who never appeared.

"Where's your scorecard?" Matt asked. "Did you give that vendor so much grief he wouldn't sell you one?"

"Nah, I was just in a hurry. I'll get one on the first beer run."

"I like the sound of that," Matt said. "But not the sound of that," he continued as Kuhn popped up to end the first.

Jamie made the beer run but spent a great deal of time looking for Dred. Finally he returned and dodged some barbs from his impatient cousin until some Tinkler customers arrived and Matt had to behave. The game actually turned out to be fairly enjoyable as the M's pulled out a 6-5 win. They were not so lucky the following night. Dred was again nowhere to be found and the Mist went down 7-2 and promptly left town.

By Saturday the M's had lost their first game on the road trip, but Jamie and Rebecca were back in the Issaquah Alps east of Seattle, this time on Squawk Mountain. Jamie was remarkably comfortable with the silence they shared for most of their hike. When time came to stop and eat, Rebecca said, "All of this natural beauty around makes me want to believe in a higher power."

"I used to not know whether God existed and not care too much one way or the other, making me an agnostic, I guess," Jamie said. "But lately I've been finding that I do care and I really want to know if God is out there."

"Why the change? Why is it important to you now, Jamie?"

Jamie hated not being able to share everything about his life with Rebecca. But he couldn't really explain the baseball power, especially since he seemed to risk its existence the few times he tried to show it off. Jamie mumbled, "This theological stuff just seemed to get more important to me after my dad died."

"Look, a bald eagle," Rebecca said.

Jamie was pleased to be rescued from the conversation but Rebecca didn't know that and she felt badly about her interruption. So she asked, "Well, do you go to church now?"

"Not really. Sometimes I go with my mom."

Although he rarely attended Mass anymore except for big family occasions like Easter or Christmas, Jamie suddenly thought about talking to Father Bob. Although this conversation died, he resolved to visit Father Bob the following Monday after work.

On the way back down the mountain, Rebecca turned to tell Jamie, "You know that woman we saw with your Uncle Art. I remembered who she was. She's married to one of our senior partners."

"What does she do?" Jamie asked.

"I don't know. I just remembered that I had seen her before at a Christmas party."

This reminded Jamie that he could invite Rebecca to Uncle Llew's 55th birthday party tomorrow, but he chickened out. He didn't want to press his luck. It was just too early for a family function. He didn't regret his decision when the conversation during the cocktail hour turned on whether or not Matt and Mandy were really and truly broken up. Jamie didn't need to add any of his own fuel to those kinds of discussions.

"What is with Kuhn, anyway?" Matt asked to change the direction of the conversation.

"He got too big for his britches," Adam said.

"But how did he get so good so fast this season?" Adam's girlfriend asked.

"Some kind of steroids, I'll guarantee you. Then the negative side effects caught up to him and he's paying the price," Matt replied.

"It seems like more than steroids can explain," Adam suggested.

It was frustrating for Jamie to listen to people talking about things they were so wrong about and not be able to correct them. He sipped his drink slowly and drifted toward thoughts of Rebecca.

"Hey Jamie," Matt said as he slapped at his cousin's knee. "You've been awfully quiet even for you. You're the baseball nut. What do you think will happen to Kuhn now?"

When Jamie shrugged and hesitated before answering, Matt plowed ahead, "I thought he might have that one big season like when Norm Cash hit over .360 or when Brady Anderson hit 50 homers. Maybe he would just be an anomaly for one year but I don't think he's even going to make one year. He's in a deep dive."

"He got a hit today," Adam said.

"That makes only two in his last seven games," Matt countered.

"He's still got 46 homeruns and 118 rbi's and it's only July 27th," Adam said.

Before anyone else could offer further insights, Jamie's mother interrupted the chain of conversation. She peeked out from the door to the deck and politely suggested that it was time for the young people to join the dinner party in the private room they had reserved.

As he worked his way through the buffet line, Jamie wondered why he hadn't spread the glory around more evenly. Maybe let everyone enjoy a few more hits. He thought he was doing Kuhn a favor by allowing him to be a hero, but had seemingly put him on a road to misery and controversy instead. Meanwhile, the rest of the team reaped the benefits of being in first place by two and a half games without experiencing the agony Kuhn was going through. Jamie knew he had to be prepared if Dred resurfaced as he so often did. Jamie would need to decide whether to run from the whole morbid mess or try righting the negatives he inadvertently spawned. Perhaps talking with Father Bob tomorrow would help him sort things out, except right now he had some roast beef and mashed potatoes to attack.

When the dinner toasts for Llew were winding down, Jamie's one married cousin announced that his wife was expecting a baby in March. Llew was perfectly happy to have his birthday upstaged. This new revelation touched off much celebration and merriment as it marked the beginning of the next generation. Even Jamie was snapped out of his melancholy meditations as the happy couple received unsolicited advice on names.

"How about Donny for a boy or Tess for a girl to mark the extraordinary events of this year?" Adam suggested.

"No matter how great a first name you get, little cousin, you will still be stuck with 'Tinkler' on the end of it!" Matt reminded the gathering.

Chapter Forty-Four

Jamie's normal aversion to Father Bob was dissipating under the weight of desperation. He headed over to the rectory on Monday night and rang for him. As the portly padre bounded into the waiting room in his unfashionable jeans and white polo shirt, Jamie couldn't help but think how unpriestly he looked. He had seen Father Bob out of uniform many times over the years but never got used to it. Jamie didn't even try to dodge the welcoming hug this time as Father Bob greeted him, "Jamie I'm so glad you stopped by to chat. Let's go into the den."

Father Bob ushered Jamie through the big double doors and offered, "Can I fix you a drink? I've got both hard and soft drinks. You know the old Catholic axiom: whenever three or four are gathered in His name, there's always a fifth!"

Jamie laughed in spite of himself. He wasn't thirsty but asked, "You got something like a diet cola?"

"Sure do," Father Bob responded cheerily as he reached into the mini-fridge and pulled one out. But he did seem a little disappointed when Jamie declined his invitation to mix the cola with something harder.

However, Father Bob also grabbed a soda pop, snapped his fingers, pointed at Jamie, and spoke briskly, "Say, I wanted to thank you for reminding me about those magic tricks after Mass the other day. I've decided to get back into that hobby. I've signed up for a week long class in Ashland, Oregon in October."

Although his thoughts were elsewhere, Jamie managed to answer, "Oh really?"

"Yeah, I'm going to take my vacation down there and see some plays at the Shakespeare festival. I signed up for one that's a dramedy, which apparently means it's part drama and part comedy. I never heard that term before. I can't keep up with everything these days. I don't remember the name of the play. Something with 'disappearance' in it. Or maybe it was 'hippopotamus.' I can't rightly recall. I never heard of it but they told me it was quite famous.

And then there's one you might like about computerized baseball taking over from the real thing in the future."

"Shakespeare wrote about computerized baseball?" Jamie asked.

"No, not all the plays are Shakespeare. They have modern ones, too. You and your cousins used to be in the CYO plays," Father Bob rambled on. "Did you keep up with drama at all?"

Jamie barely remembered the bit parts, but did recall how much of his time was spent in Catholic Youth Organization activities. He answered, "Mostly it was Matt who was into drama. I was more behind the scenes."

"But you were really into the scouting program," Father Bob persisted.

Jamie shifted uncomfortably in his seat, hoping Father Bob didn't think he was part of the prank at the Boy Scout Jamboree Father Bob attended. Cousins Matt and Adam had rearranged the red flags and rerouted the nature hike into the latrine. Then they had taken the latrine sign and posted it on Father Bob's tent and thrown straw and muddy toilet paper inside for good measure.

"Yes, those scouting days were good times," Jamie said. "Sometimes the kids went a little crazy, but I think we learned a lot."

Father Bob nodded and asked, "How is your family doing, Jamie? Your mother seems very healthy."

"Yes, everyone is doing fairly well, all things considered," Jamie conceded.

"Well," Father Bob paused and then asked, "what's on your mind these days?"

"Father, what I was wondering about is like if God gave you a tremendous gift, a special power, He would expect you to use it, right?"

"Yes, yes, Jamie, He would," Father Bob nodded.

"So it would be wrong not to use the gift, wouldn't it?" Jamie pleaded earnestly.

"Yes-s-s," Father Bob agreed a little more deliberately this time. "Jamie, when God calls to us, we need to heed that call. It means we are blessed to be chosen."

"So why would God suddenly out of the blue decide to gift some anonymous soul?" Jamie asked

Father Bob leaned forward and assured Jamie, "No soul is anonymous to God, Jamie."

"What I mean is, why would He pick out a sinner? I can understand why a believer like Mother Therese gets chosen. And how do you know what to do with what you've been given?"

Father Bob raised his palms and said, "Let's take this slowly, Jamie. First, we are all sinners. But I must caution you that while the Church is desperate to welcome young men who believe they have the gift of a vocation, the screening process tries very hard to weed out men who are overly fond of other men."

Jamie was taken aback. Father Bob could see that he had startled Jamie and continued in a soothing voice, "Now like I said, we are all sinners and God is always loving us. And as long as we make a sincere commitment to remain free of our sin, with the help of the Almighty, it can still be possible to follow the call."

Jamie stood up, grimaced, and said hurriedly, "You have been a big help, Father. Thank you for talking with me. I need to get going now."

On the way out, Jamie resolved to himself that he must remember to avoid Father Bob at all costs, even if it meant moving to another state.

Chapter Forty-Five

Jamie's reflection in the mirror was somber as it parroted the message, "If I get another chance, I'm going to do less meddling. I will let the M's play on their own. Miracles will be reserved for times when absolutely needed after all other natural options are exhausted."

He felt better already after a restless night of half-sleep. The M's finished their road trip 3-3 after taking the last series. Jamie continued to jabber, reminding himself that they were competitive without him. When he finally made it downstairs for a quick breakfast, his mother asked, "Were you talking to me? I couldn't hear what you were saying upstairs."

"Uh, yes, you were behaving quite badly in my dream. You were refusing to go to Church or allow milk in the house. So I was telling you that I loved you, but that you should see a doctor."

Jo looked blankly at Jamie and then asked, "Are you going to your cousin's birthday dinner tonight?"

"Damn, I forgot about it. I've got tickets to the M's game tonight."

"You have tickets to every game. You can skip baseball one night for your cousin's birthday. She's turning sixteen."

Jamie pondered this and then said, "Yeah, but in my dream, you told me to go to the game and skip the dinner."

"Okay, funnyman, I'm just going to have to tell everyone you couldn't be bothered with family and would rather be doing baseball."

"Won't that reflect poorly on you as my mother?" asked Jamie. "Like you didn't raise me with the right values?"

"Lord knows, I did my best to raise you right…."

"Ma, I will definitely make an appearance at the dinner," Jamie said with regret that he had gone there. "Do you have a card and something in your re-gifting box that I can give her?"

"Actually, you can take the blouse I bought her and I'll pick up something else up while you're at work. Here, let me show you."

"I'll just buy a CD for her at lunch," Jamie said as he eyed the blouse and wondered where his cousin would wear it. "Thanks, Ma, you're the best!"

Jamie and Matt ended up CD shopping together. They still had time for some teriyaki take-out on the patch of park just north of the open-air portion of Pike Place Market. The pleasant weather summoned the noon time crowds to the Market's colorful booths and the festivities spilled over into the small park. The cousins found a small section of ledge where they could soak up the waterfront view on Puget Sound while they ate. Matt dribbled food down his shirt without noticing. He was busy expressing disapproval that Jamie was going to attend the M's game during the birthday party.

"Just for part of it," Jamie emphasized. "Between you and my mother, you'd think I'd never done one right thing my whole life."

"And you're trying to turn the blame on us for doing the right thing and telling the truth?" Matt replied.

Even though Matt was just pulling Jamie's chain out of habit, Jamie could barely resist getting irritated. So he quickly switched direction and said, "Hey, did you see the World Cup final?"

"Yeah, I watched part of it. El Salvador pulled off quite the upset," Matt answered.

"Well, you know, Dred goes to the qualifying round and his El Salvador team miraculously gets into the round of sixteen. He comes home and they get killed in the first game. Now he's gone again and they pull off four straight upsets. What do you make of that?"

"You're talking about that weird bartender who puts curses on the M's?"

"His brother," Jamie corrected.

"Now he puts curses on soccer games and his brother?"

"No, I keep telling you it's his brother who put a curse on the M's. Now when Dred's around, funny things happen with the M's. When he's in the soccer world, his team starts winning."

"First off, we're all around when funny things happen with the M's. Second of all, the M's don't seem very cursed right now and El

Salvador soccer certainly isn't cursed. And third, I can't believe I'm actually discussing this with you."

"It just seemed like a coincidence to me," Jamie said.

Matt ignored Jamie's attempt to end this dialogue and continued, "What coincidence? I don't even see the coincidence you're talking about. And if there is some coincidence, then look up the word in the dictionary. It's a common occurrence. Coincidences happen all the time without Dred or his brother causing them."

"I didn't really expect you to understand," Jamie muttered.

"Oh, so it's my fault? I'm too stupid to understand that Dred and his brother are running around cursing sports teams and influencing championships? And that you have to blow off your cousin's birthday party because you're on a mission to investigate and expose these curses? And apparently I'm too dumb to realize that your investigation entails watching lots of ballgames to the exclusion of living a normal life?"

"Yes, you are too dumb. Way too dumb, you stupid face," Jamie replied with a very slight smile.

"I'm so stupid, I'm going to join you at the game, so you don't have to be alone when we show up late for the birthday party."

Early that evening, Jamie trudged to the ballgame. He was thinking how hard it was to find anyone close to him that could handle a conversation about magic scorecards even if he were willing to risk jeopardizing the power by talking about it. He was so lost in thought that he was startled to see Dred suddenly standing in front of him, waving a scorecard.

"Hey, El Salvador won the World Cup," Jamie said off the top of his head.

"Yeah, they did. M's turn today."

"I gotta talk to you," Jamie said.

"I'm a busy man, but I'll be around the Shoebox when the M's leave town."

Jamie was anxious to possess Dred's scorecard. He let him escape and checked to see that there did seem to be a faint smudge on the back of the card. He then waited in his seat until Matt showed up. Jamie couldn't keep his promise to avoid making predictions until other options were exhausted. He just had to order a first inning walk for Wink. And just in case Rudy's subsequent base on balls was coincidence, a walk was ordered for Escobar. Thorne got one for good measure. The next three walks were for Matt's benefit.

While the new pitcher warmed up, Jamie could resist no longer and leaned over to his cousin and challenged him, "So the M's walk more people than our opponents?"

"I never said that," Matt stated emphatically.

"Sure you did, up at Lake Cavenger over July 4th weekend," Jamie insisted.

"I said our pitchers walk too many people and they do," Matt argued. "It's the sports columnist I quoted who claims our guys aren't patient enough to draw walks. I personally don't like walks even when they are in our favor. You can't tell me you find this parade around the bases exciting."

Getting less satisfaction from the walks than he expected, Jamie concentrated on pounding the relief pitcher. When the lead reached 11-0, the cousins made an early exit and headed for the birthday party. Matt stopped at The Club's restroom and Jamie thought he slid in unobtrusively, but Uncle Art came right over and said loudly, "Nice you could make it. Sorry we didn't think to change the party to a day the M's were out of town."

Chapter Forty-Six

The first scorecard was propped up on his front porch. Some came later by Federal Express. The return address varied. Sometimes it was the Shoe, other times the Shoebox. Once it was from a mental institution on Capitol Hill. But each time on the remainder of the homestand, the card worked. Jamie used them sparingly, reverting to his minimalist approach. He even missed two games. One game, he didn't even have a conflict. But he and Rebecca were now a couple and even when they were apart, she knew his whereabouts. So his absence at that game was part of the fight to disguise his baseball obsession.

Two victories temporarily satisfied Jamie's addiction and delighted the fans when he provided dramatic ninth inning rallies. Rudy Wink and Eduardo Escobar took turns being the hero in those wins. Donny Kuhn was left on his own and managed a 9-41 showing, slipping to a normally spectacular .379 average.

Jamie was able to step back a little, not only because he was busy with Rebecca, but also by the logic of Seattle's hold on first place. He combined pleasures by taking her to the last game of the homestand on the second Sunday of August. The M's win put their record at 70-43, five games in front of Oakland. Such a lead was certainly not insurmountable, especially considering the vagaries of Dred's life, but Jamie resolved to worry about one thing at a time.

The happy couple wandered down the waterfront after the game, detouring into the Ye Olde Curiousity Shop, ordering shrimp cocktails at the takeout window of a seafood restaurant, and finally arriving at the Sculpture Park. They completed the trifecta of sappiness by holding hands, laughing over nothing, and celebrating each sculpture with a kiss. Jamie's head was certainly full of Rebecca right now. Although he was sexually timid, this had for once worked to his advantage since Rebecca had grown weary of overly aggressive males.

Although not entirely inexperienced or repressed, early in life Jamie had fallen behind some of his braver peers and entered a downward spiral. His relative lack of experience caused him anxiety when he thought women might find him lacking sexual savvy. This inhibition slowed him even more. So a boy who started out fairly normal was going backwards while in his mind at least, his cousins and friends were gaining momentum. He was now so deliriously in love with Rebecca, though, that both his anxiety and his ability to overcome anxiety expanded.

On the way back out of the park, Rebecca said, "You know my friend from the Appalachian Trail that I told you about. She's getting married in Portland on the first of November and I'm a bridesmaid. I was thinking you might like to join me as my date for that weekend."

"You were thinking pretty clearly," Jamie responded casually. "I would like to join you even though I'll have to cancel many previous engagements."

Jamie projected enough delight that Rebecca knew he was pleased with the invitation. Even so, he had successfully repressed his true reaction, controlling the instinct to shout out "yes" multiple times while dancing around and shaking his fist in the air.

"We would have to drive down on Thursday unless you wanted to come down later. You would be invited to the Rehearsal Halloween Dinner on Friday and the wedding on Saturday. We could probably drive back on Sunday."

"Halloween Dinner?"

"Yeah, the Rehearsal Dinner falls on Halloween, so we're all going in costume." Rebecca explained.

"Well, Thursday's no problem for me. I've got plenty of vacation saved," Jamie responded, neglecting to add that he would quit his job and move to Borneo if it suited her.

"Maybe we could share the cost of the motel room?" Rebecca suggested offhandedly, introducing the elephant in the park before it got too big.

Jamie would gladly pay the entire expense, but he was smooth enough to confirm, "Sounds like we got ourselves a deal."

When he floated home that evening, his mom asked Jamie, "What are you so happy about?"

"I'm always happy, you know that, Ma," Jamie laughed and then quickly thought to add, "The M's won today and any day with a Seattle win is a good day."

"No, you're not always happy and I'm not too happy when my sister-in-law tells me you got a new girlfriend I haven't heard anything about. Is this how you treat your mother?"

"There's nothing to tell, Ma, we've had a few dates is all."

"Well, that's something to tell right there. Why haven't I met her yet? Already your aunt knows this girl and I don't."

Jamie couldn't even be exasperated. Nobody could ruin his good mood except Rebecca. Patiently he explained, "Ma, my aunt only knows Rebecca from some work functions a couple of years ago and you don't work at Tinkler. That's the only reason she's met her and you haven't."

"So you think I should still be working in the family business after all the years I put in down there? Is that the only way I get to meet your friends? Is that what you're telling me?" Jo asked sternly.

"No, Ma, you know perfectly well that I'm not saying that. I absolutely do not think you should be back working for Tinkler," Jamie said with a little too much emphasis.

"What, you don't think I could handle the work? Before you were born I did hard work, not all this fun stuff where you play games on the computer and go watch baseball with customers."

Jamie was happy the conversation was swerving away from Rebecca but not happy enough to continue in the passenger seat. "Look, Ma, I already ate. I've gotta catch up on some work in my room."

Jo answered only with a pout but Jamie just laughed and said, "I love you, Ma."

As Jamie scampered up the stairs, Jo suddenly regained her focus and shouted after him, "So I'm not going to hear anything about this Rebecca?"

Jamie turned and said, "Your sister-in-law can tell you all about her. We take her on all our dates."

When he was alone in his room, he jumped on the bed, spread his arms out wide, and relished the satisfaction of a relationship with Rebecca that seemed to be gaining permanency as it careened in all the right directions.

But wait. The anxieties started creeping back. Was he just a safe date for Rebecca? Someone she could count on. Someone who was fun, but wouldn't get too serious. The out of town weekend two months in the future was a clear signal she was planning on the relationship lasting longer than tomorrow. But what does it all really mean? As easy as it was for Jamie to talk with Rebecca, discussion of their relationship was currently stranded in the land of innuendo along with the subject of supernatural baseball powers.

Chapter Forty-Seven

Quickly scanning the Shoebox, Jamie was almost relieved that Dred did not appear to be working. He didn't think a meaningful conversation with Dred was going to be possible with Matt tagging along. Jamie was here because the last time they met, Dred told him he would be working at the Shoebox when the M's went back on the road. Seattle was playing a Monday game in Chicago and with the time difference, the cousins could watch some of the action while they ate. As they settled in their seats, the home team grabbed a 1-0 first inning lead on a ground rule double. "A bad sign," Matt said.

"Yeah, but we've already won seventy games and some years, we haven't won that many in a whole season," Jamie replied.

"With that five game lead over Oakland, we could sure use a good road trip right now," Matt said. "If we could hold our lead on the road and then start padding it at home, we could actually make the playoffs this season. I hope Kuhn doesn't get derailed by those assault charges because we're going to need him at full throttle."

"I think we could still win without Kuhn, but I read his girlfriend wasn't cooperating with the prosecution anyway," Jamie said.

"Doesn't matter," Matt said, "because they prosecute domestic violence cases hard these days regardless of the victim's cooperation."

"Yeah, but I also read, the case won't make it through the legal process for at least three or four months, so if he has to go to jail, he'll be doing time in the off season."

The sight of Seattle grounding into a double play to end the second inning diverted Matt's attention. "Ouch," he winced.

Later as they labored over their meal, Matt asked Jamie, "Have you seen the latest union campaign flyers?"

"Well, I saw the cartoon where they show Llew emptying a Tinkler Toilet and offering the contents to the employees with a caption that says, 'And here's your fair share....'"

"Can you believe that crap, pun intended?" Matt asked.

"Well, what about the stuff we put out?"

"That's different," Matt replied.

"Is this going to be another lecture on the ends justifying the means?" Jamie asked.

"Oh, oh, oh," Matt said, suddenly absorbed by Escobar's double off the left field wall in the third. "Here we go."

The M's managed one run after E2's hit to knot the game at one, but later Chicago would score four unanswered runs and leave the Mist holding the loss. When Matt headed for the restroom, Jamie asked the bartender if Dred was back working at the Shoebox.

"Hell no," she replied. "He came back looking for work, but the owner threw him out. I guess he hired him originally because he knows his family. They're also in the restaurant business. But Dred kept screwing up. He wasn't reliable and he never called in when he was supposed to. And then he sometimes got weird with the customers. I liked him but he needs to find a gig where he fits in better."

"Okay, thanks," Jamie said. He was going to say he liked him, too, but let the silence hang in the air.

Matt emerged from the head, took note of Jamie's pensive expression, and asked, "What's wrong, Meatball? Did Rebecca text you and cut you loose for being undersized or what?"

Jamie couldn't even muster scorn for Matt but he did snap back to the present. "No, we're fine. Can't I be down after an M's loss?" he managed to reply.

"Then how come you're spending so much time hanging out with me if everything is so fine with Rebecca? What gives? Is she the real deal or is she just using you to get close to me?" Matt prodded.

Jamie ignored the humor of Matt's inquiry and answered solemnly, "You know, Matt, I just don't understand women."

"Women are like lottery tickets," Matt volunteered. "There are very few winners but you gotta keep investing in them, hoping for the big payoff."

"Yeah," Jamie said with a smile.

"So come on. What is going on with you and Rebecca? I tell you everything," Matt said.

"Right," Jamie replied. "You tell me you and Mandy broke up when you haven't. You tell me all sorts of stuff, but it's usually laced with more fiction than campaign literature."

"Mandy and I did break up. Can I help it if she's in denial?"

The bartender returned with the change and said, "If you guys see Dred, say 'hi' for me."

As they headed for the door, Matt squinted at Jamie and emitted a baffled, "So?"

"Oh, I just asked where Dred was. You know I buy my scorecards from him," Jamie replied before he could swallow his words back.

"Well, I got news for you, Meatball. They have other vendors at the Shoe who will be more than happy to sell you a scorecard. What does Rebecca see in a nutcase like you, anyway?"

Matt was interrupted by patrons cheering an Oakland loss on the television while Jamie said, "I really don't know."

Matt looked back from the T.V. and responded, "Don't know what?"

"You asked what Rebecca saw in me. And I don't know," Jamie said with a shrug. "She seemed excited to ask me to this wedding months from now, but sounded busy this week all through the weekend. It's like I'm on hold for awhile. What does that mean?"

Matt slapped Jamie on the back and exclaimed, "It means we party hard all week long and let the chicks fall where they may!"

Chapter Forty-Eight

"They should have a system where the people who are late get the closest parking," Matt grumbled. "The early people have plenty of time to park far away."

"So do you think that really is a better system?" Jamie teased. "You would vote for that and think it would really work?"

"I would vote for Matt learning how to make a U-turn and we could have gotten that spot next to the Shoebox," Jeffrey Anne said.

"I didn't hear you saying you were paying the ticket," Matt replied. "The cops were all over that intersection."

"Jeffrey Anne can't be paying your tickets," Adam interjected. "She's got to save every penny for World Series tickets."

"Well, you didn't miss anything," Jamie assured the threesome.

The M's were back in town after escaping a Midwest trip with a 5-5 split. Jamie hadn't partied hard as Matt suggested, except for agonizing in front of the tube over a couple extra inning games and another couple of one run losses. Although Seattle's hold on first place was back down to four games, the magic of this year's homefield advantage fed a growing local confidence that the M's would begin to pull away from Oakland. Jamie was immune to the optimism because he was painfully aware that the M's fortunes were jeopardized today by a missing Fed Ex delivery. Worse yet, he couldn't figure out what possessed his cousins to bring Jeffrey Anne to the game.

The M's were so caught up in their own lives, they took no notice that Jamie's off the rack scorecard held no magic. Unaware that they were doomed, Seattle splurged with three runs in the second. When Donny turned a spectacular double play to hold the opponents to three runs in the sixth, Matt shouted at Jamie, "Did you see that? I'm buying this round."

Jamie took this opportunity to tag along after Matt as he headed up the stairs to buy beer. When they reached the concourse, Jamie caught up and said, "What in the hell is Jeffrey Anne doing here?"

"She's an employee who uses the tickets sometimes. Ryan's girlfriend wasn't available. Jeffrey Anne has been asking about tickets. What did you want me to do? Ask Uncle Art instead?"

"Don't get cute with me. You know what I mean. Did she know I was going to be here?"

"I don't know," Matt replied thoughtfully. "I can't remember if we mentioned it."

"Well, did you ever think it could be uncomfortable for her?"

"Not really, but maybe I'll ask her when we get back to our seats. Why would she be uncomfortable, anyway? She dumps you, you've got a new girlfriend. Everybody's happy."

"I'm not happy right now."

"Why did you guys break up anyhow? You never did make any sense explaining that."

"I think she kind of liked dating the CEO's son. After Dad died, that was gone. Don't be surprised if you're suddenly more attractive to her now," Jamie replied.

The cousins returned to the seats in plenty of time to see Seattle scratch out an eighth inning run for a 4-3 lead. When Seattle's closer walked the first batter in the ninth, Matt suggested, "Hey, maybe we're going to go ten innings to make up for the one we missed."

"Don't be so pessimistic," Adam admonished.

When the next hitter bunted and the pitcher threw the ball in the dirt at first, Matt pointed out, "See, I was being optimistic about a tenth inning. With the tying and lead run on base and nobody out, we may end up being very happy to get to the tenth!"

"We always have our bats in the ninth," Jeffrey Anne reminded everyone.

"Yeah, but we're at the bottom of the order," Matt said.

The groans escalated when Seattle walked the ninth hitter in the lineup to load the bases. Now Seattle had to contend with the top of the order. The batter in the lead off spot took a ball, a strike, and then blooped a pop up into shallow right field. The ball looked like it would drop in, but Donny Kuhn made a perfectly timed leap and just missed doubling the runner off first. The cheers drowned out the sighs.

The next hitter worked the count to 2-2 and then hit a bouncer toward the pitcher. He grabbed the ball and lobbed it home. The catcher rifled the relay to first, but the throw was too late and once again a double play was barely averted. The bases remained loaded, except now two were out. A lazy fly ball to left field completed the tortuous escape for the Mist.

The foursome began the exodus from the stadium in joyous spirits, surrounded by thousands of others in a similar state. Jamie was lost in the moment of camaraderie as Matt ducked into the restroom. Then he heard the booming voice of Dano McPherson.

"What a game, huh?" Dano said as he eyed Adam, Jamie, and Jeffrey Anne.

"It does look like our year," Adam confirmed as Dano was swept away with his group.

When Jamie finally returned home, he found the missing Fed Ex delivery that a neighbor brought over while he was at the game. On Saturday the scorecard showed up on time, but Jamie was committed to a birthday party honoring Uncle Art's wife. He decided he better not be late for this one, even though the extended family produced more birthdays than anyone should be reasonably expected to attend.

The M's game began not long after everyone was seated for dinner and several people, especially the male cousins, contrived excuses to sneak in the lounge to get updates. Early reports of a 4-1 deficit made it easy for the restless baseball addicts to remain at dinner.

After some time had elapsed from the last report, Matt got up and announced, "I need to powder my nose. Jamie, would you care to join me?"

Jamie laughed, while declining with a shake of the head. Some scowls followed Matt's exit, but the birthday aunt smiled and asked, "What makes all the boys so crazy about baseball?"

Jamie cringed when his mother took the opportunity to describe Jamie's first game at the ballpark. She accurately captured the details of the foul ball catch made by Jamie's father as she wrote herself into the story.

"Ma, you weren't there," Jamie protested.

"What do you mean I wasn't there?" Jo shot back, taking her turn to be annoyed.

"It was just me and Pops. You came to games with us, but you weren't at that one," Jamie pointed out firmly.

"I definitely was at that game," Jo insisted.

Jamie was not about to continue this debate publicly, but he was shocked that his mother had inserted herself in such a memory for no apparent reason. The incident was clearly about Marty catching the ball and Jamie's reaction to it. He was incredulous and wondered to himself if the retelling over the years was so vivid that his mother might actually have stored the memory as one of her own. Indeed, the mind was capable of some amazing tricks.

Matt and a younger cousin soon returned with the latter passing on the somber news, "8-1 in the fifth."

The score had a chilling effect on further defections for baseball updates. The party began to spin around the memories of birthdays past for the honorees. Someone recalled the one where Matt proved that water balloons thrown from the roof of a three-story house could crack a car windshield.

"Matt should have done better in physics," his mother said with a laugh.

"You're laughing now," Llew reminded her, "but you definitely weren't laughing then."

"I just remember Matt was barreling down the stairs between the second and first floor when he met my parents charging up from below," Adam reminisced. "Matt blurts out, 'I almost caught them. I think they jumped out a second floor window!'"

Jamie remembered the incident well. He was cowering in a third floor closet, while Matt took the blame. Only Matt knew that part of the story and it never has come out. *Maybe next year,* thought Jamie.

The M's finally lost 13-3 even after Jamie surreptitiously proposed outcomes in today's scorecard. His predictions would not work from the lounge's restroom as he knew they wouldn't. He would take no chances tomorrow. He headed to Sunday's game with his precious scorecard. Rebecca joined him. What could be better than that?

The scorecard worked, although Jamie used it sparingly. He was too absorbed in Rebecca's universe to obsess about baseball prognostication. The Mist eventually prevailed 7-5, taking the series along with the game. Seattle sportswriters labeled Don Grant (two run homer) and Larry Thorne (three run double) as the heroes. Jamie didn't quibble about that. Instead he invested his energy in working up the courage to ask Rebecca, "Would you like to join me at the Tinkler Labor Day weekend party up at Lake Cavenger?"

"Sounds cool," Rebecca assented. "I'd love to meet the rest of your family. Will your mother be there?"

As Rebecca answered, Jamie wondered if she could possibly be as excited inside as he was when she invited him hiking or to her friend's wedding. *Yeah, right,* he thought but said out loud, "If my mother hears you're coming up to Cavenger with me, she'll postpone her own funeral to make that event!"

Later that evening when he returned home, he resisted telling his mother that he had invited Rebecca to the Labor Day bash. He would deal with that later. She surprised him by asking, "How did that Denny Kuhn do today?"

It sounded almost like a test. When he was younger, she might ask, "What was the sermon about?" to see if he went to Mass. Surely she wasn't checking up on him to see if he was sneaking around with some girl instead of going to the baseball game! But he answered cautiously, "It's 'Donny,' Ma. He was one for four but how do you know about Donny Kuhn?"

"Is one for four any good?" Jo asked.

"Not particularly," Jamie acknowledged, "but he did make some great defensive plays in the field. Why are you suddenly interested in Donny Kuhn?"

"He came to 8:30 Mass this morning," Jo said casually.

"What? He was at our church this morning before the game?"

"Yes, he was," Jo confirmed smugly.

"How did you know it was him?" Jamie asked.

"It was the talk of the congregation at the coffee hour afterwards," Jo answered.

"Was he at the coffee hour?"

"No, of course not," Jo replied with a dismissive tone, "he had a ballgame to play."

"I know that, Ma, but what was he doing there at all?" Jamie asked impatiently.

"Well, I expect he was there praying like everyone else and maybe asking God to enlighten those who weren't at Church," Jo responded.

Jamie changed tack slightly, "What were people saying?"

Jo thought for a moment, "They talked about what a big baseball star he was and how he was at Church with his girlfriend that he had thrown a plate of spaghetti at. But he is a good man. He was dressed in a tie and sport jacket."

"If he's so good, how come he stole a base this afternoon?" Jamie teased.

Jo took no notice and kept reading her magazine. After all, she had the advantage on her son this time. Rare indeed when the subject was baseball.

Chapter Forty-Nine

"You didn't tell me you went to a game with Jeffrey Anne last week," Rebecca said.

"I didn't," Jamie responded too quickly.

"My brother said he saw you there."

"Yeah, with Matt and Adam."

"She wasn't with you?"

"She was with us as a group."

"Kind of like how Mandy isn't with Matt, but is just with the group?" Rebecca asked.

"The three of them came together. I had no idea she would be there," Jamie protested.

"It's not as if it's a problem you were at the game with Jeffrey Anne. I just was surprised you hadn't mentioned it when we went the next night."

"That's how inconsequential it was," Jamie replied.

It didn't feel inconsequential when Rebecca called it a night earlier than usual. She said she had a 7:00 conference call in the morning with some people on the East Coast and left Jamie wondering if it had been such a good idea to skip the M's game for this date.

As soon as he was alone in the car, Jamie quickly punched the radio dial back to the M's station. The post game show was bubbling about how Seattle scored 15 runs in a big victory. Rudy Wink's four hits won a woman free groceries for a year. The supermarket chain running the promotion was probably relieved that the M's were at home and that Escobar, Grant, and Thorne didn't get to bat in the ninth, sitting on three hits each. Jamie half expected the show's host to announce, "A young Seattle lad found one of Dred's scorecards in a back room, took it to Jamie's seat, and began pounding out extra base hits with it!"

Jamie's mood worsened the next morning when customer complaints started rolling in. Matt came by asking about lunch and Jamie said, "First can you try to locate Rob on his cell phone?

He doesn't seem to be making his deliveries in Pierce County. I'm getting calls from Tacoma every ten minutes and although I haven't heard from Olympia yet, I'm guessing we're going to be late there, too."

"I'm sure it's just traffic. Let's head over to the Whole and worry about it after lunch. We can discuss playoff ticket strategy. Did you get your package? Llew got the one for the Company. They sure ain't cheap."

Jamie just glared at Matt and so finally Matt picked up his cell phone, sighed with exaggerated annoyance, and left an SOS message with Rob. "Satisfied?" he asked.

"All right, I might as well dodge customer phone calls for awhile, at least until Rob surfaces somewhere. Let's go and you can tell me what's up with him. I heard we were going to pull his work packages. What happened?"

"We didn't quite pull the trigger, but this disappearance is going to be the bullet that finally kills the camel. We're basically ready to tell him he has to go into treatment or lose his job," Matt answered as he drove them to the restaurant. "I know Jeffrey Anne and Adam met with him on Friday and he balked at any suggestion of requesting treatment voluntarily. We were letting him think about it over the weekend. When he came in early this morning, he seemed fine and I let him take the truck out as usual without talking any more about this whole issue. It really is sad because Rob is a decent guy and he used to be great to be around. But, anyway, check out the playoff ticket package."

Jamie began to glance over the package, then suddenly exclaimed, "Hey, Matt!"

"Hey, Jamie!" Matt responded, mocking his cadence.

Jamie ignored the retort and explained, "I just remembered. Did you hear Donny Kuhn was at Mass yesterday before the game?"

"Yeah, Ad told me."

"I didn't know he was Catholic," Jamie said.

"Adam's always been Catholic," Matt deadpanned. Getting no response, he finally said, "Maybe Donny isn't Catholic. Maybe his girlfriend is. Did you see the newspaper column today where he in essence apologized for some of his actions this season?"

"Yeah," Jamie acknowledged while continuing to scan the playoff schedule. "He said that all the bad boy stuff wasn't the real Donny Kuhn."

Suddenly Jamie sat back, gasped, and uttered a string of profanity he reserved for rare special occasions.

This snapped Matt to attention, "What is it?" he asked apprehensively.

"I just realized that Game 6 and 7 of the World Series conflict with the Portland wedding I'm going to with Rebecca," Jamie said to himself as much as to Matt.

"Glad I'm not invited," Matt offered. "Hey, can I have your rights to any tickets for those games?"

"Don't make light of this, Matt. I can't believe I didn't see this coming. The die hard M's fan screws up."

"What do you mean you screwed up? I suppose you should have said to the love of your life, 'Sorry I can't attend the wedding and spend the weekend falling in love with you. Why? Because Seattle, which by the way, has a demonstrated record of failing to ever make it to a World Series, could theoretically be in one around the time of the wedding. Or the Series could be over by then, even if by some miracle the M's get in it, but I better not make any commitments until Thanksgiving because of possible rainouts and the fact that I'm a big fat LOSER!'"

Although still feeling like he'd been kicked in the gut, Jamie couldn't help but smile at Matt's rant and noted, "Actually rainouts could be a good thing. At any rate, nothing can be done today. I need time to think about this. If Seattle wins in five games, no problem…"

"Or if they lose in five," Matt mimicked, "no problem except Jamie the Loser would need to go on anti-depressants."

Jamie ignored Matt and continued to ruminate, "If Seattle gets up 3-2, I could skip Saturday's game and get back in time for the last one if the M's lose game six. Rebecca might even want to do that if I could get a second ticket. How are we working the tickets?"

"We're going to have a draft on Labor Day weekend at our anti-union picnic, so bring the paperwork for your tickets and we'll throw them in the hopper with the Company tickets. You can probably avoid the games with the Portland conflict and use your picks for the other games. And hey, I remind you once again that the M's haven't even qualified for the playoffs yet. And nothing in their history suggests they're likely to!"

Jamie couldn't argue with Matt's logic, especially since he couldn't assume anything involving Dred or the playoffs. He laughed out loud, "Yeah, what am I worrying about anyway? What are the chances Seattle ends up in the World Series?"

Chapter Fifty

"Hey, Meatball, are we writing an encyclopedia or are we watching a baseball game?" Matt asked as he watched Jamie juggling several scorecards.

"You do the watching and I'll take care of the scoring," Jamie mumbled as he erased entries on yesterday's card and attempted to reuse it. He had even tried using a new one from a regular vendor and once changed seats between batters. He knew those things wouldn't work, but his craving for control was getting the best of him.

"Okay," Matt said, "What's the score now? Oh wait, there it is, up on the big scoreboard. I wish we had noticed that scoreboard before. Then you wouldn't have to work so hard! You might as well be listening on the radio if you're not even going to watch the game. You should at least be getting paid for all that work."

"We are getting paid," Jamie reminded Matt.

"Oh yeah, I forgot we cut out of work early today. But I worked past 7:30 last night delivering those units that Rob screwed up. And I was in early today."

"Yeah, in early reading the sports page," Jamie said with a smirk.

"Whose side are you on? I'm the one cleaning up Rob's messes so your life goes easy. You'll be laughing out your other hole when the union puts out an election bulletin saying management goes to the ballpark during working hours while the worker bees struggle under the weight of inadequate sick leave and vacation policies."

"I did charge the afternoon to vacation," Jamie pointed out.

"Well, sure," Matt stuttered, "but the union will misrepresent that."

"They won't be able to misrepresent *that*," Jamie said as he pointed at Thorne hitting into a double play to end the first inning.

During the break between innings, the Tinkler guests arrived. Jamie made polite salutations and then excused himself. Once on the concourse, he phoned home and asked his mother, "Did my Fed Ex package come yet?"

As soon as he heard the package had arrived, Jamie sprinted down the ramp and headed home. He was back by the fifth inning and Matt greeted him by remarking, "That must have been one long line at the restroom."

Jamie offered no explanation. After the victory, when they were finally alone, Matt said, "Where in the hell were you? That wasn't cool leaving me to make with all the small talk."

"Some work stuff came up," Jamie answered.

"What? What's going on? Is it about Rob?"

"No, not this time."

"About the union?"

"It's nothing. Forget it."

"Forget that you left me alone with our customers for a couple hours with no explanation?"

"It was barely an hour," Jamie countered.

"This is about Rebecca isn't it? Let's celebrate the victory with dinner over at the Shoebox. We can talk."

"Actually I can't. Speaking of Rebecca, we're going to the Symphony tonight."

"So that's what you were doing, arguing about the symphony. She's making you go. Please don't tell me any more about it. I don't want to gag."

"I want to go," Jamie said.

"It's worse than I thought," Matt, said. "Just remember, there's a big 'phony' in symphony."

Jamie wasn't a big fan of the arts, yet Seattle attracted an impressive array of cultural events and he occasionally could be found attending one. He didn't even notice the traffic on this night since he and Rebecca were trapped together in the conga line slowly snaking it's way toward the Mercer Street parking garage. He was absorbed in the conversation where ordinary events of the day assumed a surprising sense of importance just by touching Rebecca's world. The pleasure of being alive in such moments rubbed against a vague wariness he felt about the Jeffrey Anne misunderstanding.

Jamie didn't even remember parking or walking across the bridge to the symphony hall when suddenly he was exchanging his ticket for a program. As he absently flipped through the pages, Rebecca said, "There's no scorecard in there if that's what you're looking for."

Jamie laughed and wondered if the program held any special properties for anyone in this audience. Although he had expected to merely endure the Symphony, he settled into his seat and quickly relaxed as the music rolled over the two of them. Not such bad duty after all.

After the performance, the couple retired for drinks and dessert at a waterfront restaurant. Jamie tried to tell her how much he enjoyed the music, to which Rebecca just smiled and said, "Sure, because the M's won today, everything is good."

Jamie was amused and decided not to protest too much. Rebecca waited a moment and then turned more serious, "This is going to sound silly to you, but my grandmother used to be a musician and she took me to the Symphony all the time."

When Rebecca paused, Jamie protested sincerely, "What's silly about that?"

Rebecca smiled wanly and Jamie decided he should shut up for awhile. She continued, "Gram often told me to be sure and take time for the music and that I would always be able to hear her long after she was gone. After Gram died, it was a long while before I could even return to the Symphony. But when I did, I swear I could hear her talking to me through the music. That's pretty crazy coming from a cynic like me, right?"

Jamie decided against a direct answer and instead asked, "Like how exactly do you mean that she talks to you?"

"I can shut my eyes and actually hear her talking to me, telling me things like, 'Follow your heart.'"

"Were these things she said to you when she was alive?" Jamie asked.

"Sure, sometimes."

Jamie had several thoughts, but just said, "That's pretty cool." That turned out to be the right answer for this evening.

Chapter Fifty-One

When Jamie retrieved the Sunday paper at the crack of dawn, it seemed like an eternity until he could pick up Rebecca at her Fremont condominium. Now they were heading north to Lake Cavenger and time couldn't go slow enough for him. He wasn't even doing the speed limit in the right lane. The longer he could spend time alone with Rebecca the better. And yet, he was straining to hear the radio playing softly in the background.

Every so often, an announcer's voice would rise into a conversational lull and provide some wisp of information. The M's were in Cleveland and facing Nagle who was pitching for the second time since coming off the disabled list and his suspension. And, of course, it would be the first time he faced the Mist and Don Kuhn since the notorious beaning incident.

Before the Cleveland series, a subdued Donny Kuhn was quoted in the paper as saying, "I've talked to Tommy Nagle. He says he wasn't throwing at me. I believe him. I have apologized for going after him. We've buried the hatchet."

The article went on to report, "Although only the hatchet was officially reported as buried, we trust the baseball bat and spaghetti plate weapons are in the ground as well. For Kuhn, what goes around, comes around. His alleged girlfriend, rumored to be a victim of a Kuhn pasta assault, has refused to press charges."

The annual Tinkler Toilet picnic was always held on the Sunday of Labor Day weekend out at Lake Cavenger. Joe Tinkler bought 40 acres of land long before decent roads and astronomical prices made their way that far out in the middle of nowhere. Located northeast of Seattle, nowhere was now accessible from the city in less than ninety minutes. Although the company had grown to over 500 employees, plenty of room still existed for everyone to spread out. Much of the site across the road from the water had been cleared off for parking and camping, complete with a ballfield and restrooms. Most of the long tenured employees made the annual pilgrimage with their families, while many of the newer ones found the drive too long, their lives too busy, and the Tinkler bond too loose to warrant the long roundtrip.

The official beginning of the picnic was noon on Sunday although family and some of the inner circle came up Friday night or Saturday. Anyone who didn't want to drive home on Sunday night was encouraged to camp over. Jamie begged off from being part of the party set-up crew on Saturday because he had invited Rebecca to join him. To keep his options open if they decided to stay over, he had thrown a tent and sleeping bags in the trunk even though his mother's cabin had plenty of room.

As they slowed in a traffic jam approaching Everett, Rebecca said, "Tell me a little about your family before I meet them today."

"Well," Jamie began, "you've already met Uncle Llew and his wife and you know their sons, Adam and Matt. And you know, let's see…"

"But what about your mom? Tell me about her," Rebecca interrupted.

Jamie laughed lightly, "I'm sure she'll like you although you may have to get used to how she likes people!"

"Is she taking your dad's death hard? Do you ever talk about that with your mom?"

"No, that stuff doesn't come up much. We usually talk about whether I'm drinking enough milk or flossing my teeth," Jamie said.

"I'm sorry to bring it up if it makes you uncomfortable."

"No, not at all," Jamie exaggerated defensively. "There just isn't that much to talk about. We both miss Pops and that comes up from time to time, but there is nothing we can do about it."

"Were they very much in love?"

"Yes, I think they really were in love in their own way," Jamie said.

He looked like he was going to say more, so Rebecca waited and Jamie continued, "The one thing that was a little sad to me was Christmas when I was about nine. For several weeks before the holiday break, when I would get home from school, I would always run to see what miniatures Ma put into the Christmas scene she made each year. She would bring out a few more each day and maybe even add some new ones we didn't have the year before. We would sit and play with them and admire the Christmas tree and talk a little about Christmas or what happened at school."

Jamie paused again. Whether he was just straining to hear what the M's were doing in the radio background or whether he was straining to articulate a long ago memory, Rebecca knew to wait.

After a few moments, Jamie took a deep breath and resumed, "During this particular Christmas season, Pops had very nicely wrapped up a present that was about the size of three extra large pizza boxes stacked on top of each other. When we were sitting in our own little Christmas wonderland, Ma liked to pick up the gift addressed to her and shake it. She would say, 'I wonder what your father got me in such a pretty box. Do you hear that rattle? Maybe it's a game.'"

Jamie let out a whimsical soft laugh, "Well, this ritual continued every afternoon until the big day arrived. You can probably well imagine the let down my mother experienced when she opened the gift on Christmas morning and it was a toilet seat. Oh, it was a fine custom-made heated toilet seat, something Ma really wanted for the master bedroom. But Pops just didn't get it. As a nine-year-old, even I knew this was not a good thing for a Christmas gift."

"Ma was polite enough about it, but she couldn't resist telling the story on Pops at all the holiday gatherings. Her telling wasn't malicious. It was a great story if it's not about you. Pops never fully understood what he'd done wrong. He was a good sport and all. But the sad part wasn't that Ma got a toilet seat for Christmas. The sad thing was how this incident defined my father in the family. The glorious telling and retelling over the years made him into sort of a buffoon, just because his gene pool left him with this one blind spot. And he deserved better."

Although this story was one designed for laughs, Rebecca was touched by Jamie's rendition. He broke the mood with a lunge for the volume knob on the radio, "Hey, here it is, Kuhn is coming up to bat against Nagle for the first time since the beaning."

As it turned out, Kuhn weakly struck out. Since he was still one of the leaders for the batting title, speculation swirled around baseball land that Kuhn may have intended to whiff as a form of apology to Nagle for taking the bat to his arm. All suspicious strikeouts were not created equal. Despite the rumors, this one was not investigated like the ones in Kuhn's strikeout streak.

Kuhn singled sharply to center in the fourth when he faced Nagle for the second time. Perhaps the hanging curve was Tommy's return apology for the beaning. Or perhaps it was just the beginning of Nagle's demise. He was knocked from the box in the fifth and he and Kuhn would not face each other again this season. More importantly, the M's won a series on the road, guaranteed a winning season with their 82nd win, and opened a six game lead on Oakland. Jamie wondered if he would even need to use a Dred scorecard for the last month of the season.

Chapter Fifty-Two

"I'm so pleased to finally meet you, Rebecca. I've heard so little about you," Jo cooed.

Only the demands of his mother's pinochle game allowed Jamie to escape with Rebecca after the introduction he had been dreading with good reason. As they skimmed through some of the catered food, Jamie was only slightly surprised to find Matt with Mandy. After exchanging greetings all around, Jamie asked, "Where is everybody?"

In subdued style, Matt noted, "Adam and the younger cousins are out in the boat together."

When Matt finally maneuvered Jamie out of earshot from the ladies, he confided, "I should warn you, Jeffrey Anne is up here with Rebecca's brother.

"Not Rob?" Jamie asked.

"No, of course not. Mac."

At that moment, a commotion down by the waterfront caused everyone to turn toward the noise. More and more eyes and fingers pointed skyward as the wave of awareness rolled through the complex. A small plane was circling the lake with a banner proclaiming, "AFW Supports Tinkler Workers-Vote Union!"

Jamie laughed, Matt scowled, and the plane turned low over the playing field and began excreting parachutes. Partygoers, especially children, began running for the chutes as they landed. Squeals of delight reverberated as the earliest scavengers began opening the parachute bags to find candy, gum, toy puzzles, super balls, playing cards, and mini flashlights with the union logo.

The union leaders would surely be disappointed when insiders later reported that the Tinkler family did not seem overly distressed by the union drop at their picnic. Of course, the Tinkler public face differed significantly from some private ranting in Llew's cabin. When probed for public reaction, Llew calmly made comments about the inappropriateness of disrupting the Company function, noting that Tinkler would respect a union picnic by not intruding. This disapproval soundbite was calculated to counter any impression that the Company was comfortable with the union just because the Tinkler clan was maintaining a professional demeanor.

As dusk drifted in, the young adults began to congregate around the campfire closest to the beach. Jamie was still uncomfortable around Jeffrey Anne. It was a bit unnerving that her date was Rebecca's brother but the key detail was that she had a date. This made things better for him with Rebecca.

Mac McPherson remained quietly on the perimeter until the turn of the conversation prompted him to direct a question to Adam. "You're an attorney, right?" Mac asked.

"Yeah," Matt quipped, "but we try not to embarrass him in public by mentioning it!"

Adam just smiled and nodded as Mac continued, "Well, I've got this idea I want to get a patent on and could use some advice on how to go about it."

"What's the idea?" Matt asked.

"It's called a Dine and Dash kit," Mac answered without hesitation. "It's a phony wallet with keys and fake sunglasses attached. You leave them on the table at a restaurant while you make an exit without paying."

"So, because you left a wallet with keys and stuff at the table, nobody suspects you're skipping on the bill until it's too late?" Matt confirmed.

"Yeah," Mac grinned.

"But couldn't you just pay for the dinner for what it costs to make these Dine and Dash kits?" Matt probed with genuine curiosity.

"Actually, it's quite cheap. A couple bucks. Remember it's not a real wallet. It just looks like one with half of the sunglasses peeking out of a pouch. So for a few bucks, you save forty, fifty, or more," Mac replied proudly.

"You're not troubled about marketing a product to be used by people to skip out on their bills?" Rebecca asked her brother.

"Well, you'd only use it when you were in a jam or when you were getting poor service or something," Mac countered.

"Yeah, you could put a disclaimer on it," Matt said. "Something like 'only to be used for gags and in emergencies.' That would work, right, Ad?"

"Wouldn't restaurants get wise fast to the kits?" Mandy asked. "Whenever someone sees wallets, keys, and sunglasses being left on a table, wouldn't that raise an immediate red flag?"

"So what you do is leave nothing on the table when you're skipping. Then you're above suspicion!" Rebecca said.

Adam laughed and said, "This whole discussion reminds me of a time when my law school roommate and I were coming back from a bike ride in the islands. We were ordering a big meal in the ferry restaurant. We got separate tickets and each one had a couple sandwiches on them because we were ravenous. So we thought maybe we could save some money if we just paid one ticket. But while we were waiting in line to pay at the door, we saw that everyone, even married couples, had separate tickets. Luckily we figured out the system before we got caught trying to pass one ticket for two people!"

Before anyone else could offer to top Adam's story, Jamie's aunt came running over calling for her sons, "Adam, Matt, your father needs your help right away."

The urgency in her voice made the boys run toward their mother quickly. Jamie followed more slowly. He could see an animated conversation as they slowed to a fast walk when they reached their mother. By the time Jamie got to Papa Llew's place, he found several people trying to calm down an agitated and barefoot Rob McPherson.

Rob kept lunging forward as Llew and Adam held on to him from each side. Rob kept repeating, "I need to see my wife. Where is she? I found the earrings. We need to catch the plane to Hawaii."

Llew motioned to Matt and whispered to him, "Bring my car around. We're going to take him to the hospital in Mt. Vernon. How he drove up here is beyond a miracle."

Jamie was watching the drama unfold and wondering how he could help when Rebecca tapped him softly and said, "Jamie, Matt doesn't need to bring the car around. My brother and I are going to take care of Rob. Mac's getting his car and I'm driving the three of us. Hopefully you can see that Jeffrey Anne gets home and maybe get someone to bring Rob's car back tomorrow. I don't want you to have to leave your family right now."

"I'd be glad to drive you and Rob back tonight and Mac could stay here with Jeffrey Anne. Or I could come down with you and… well, whatever works best for you," Jamie trailed off.

"Thanks, Jamie, but I think it's best if Mac and I take Rob and get him some help. And I've only been drinking water tonight, so I think it's good for me to drive. Tell your family how sorry we are to have caused such trouble at their party."

Chapter Fifty-Three

Early on Labor Day, Jamie was thankful when Jeffrey Anne volunteered to drive Rob's car back to the city. But then his mother suggested, "Jamie, you can take your friend home and I can bring your car down later because I came up with your aunt."

"Ma, you can't drive my truck."

"Sure I can," Jo insisted.

Jeffrey Anne put on her Human Resources hat and assured everyone that it was best for her to drive Rob's car back and she headed for the parking lot before Jamie could strangle his mother.

Jamie was not far behind Jeffrey Anne. As soon as he was gone, Art cornered Llew and said, "I'm telling you that Jamie is bringing us nothing but trouble. Those McPhersons are killing us."

"The McPhersons are our biggest customer," Llew reminded his brother.

"Better Jamie should go work for them than having Rob working for us. What about a trade like that?" Art suggested, realizing that might actually be a good idea.

"I got a lot to do," Llew said as he walked off.

"Think about it," Art shouted after him.

Jamie himself was doing a lot of thinking as he caught up on the mundane in his life. He did his laundry while watching the M's lose 8-5 in St. Louis. He called Rebecca. She said Rob was fine and that she would be tied up with family for awhile. Matt called and reported more information than Jamie had extracted, "They pretty much knocked Rob out with a heavy dose of drugs. Apparently the doctors think he is bipolar and eventually want to stabilize him with something like lithium."

On Tuesday, Matt came by Jamie's office to see if he wanted to grab a bite downtown, "I've got to drop some paperwork off at the permit office. Then we can eat at the Shoebox."

As they were walking into the restaurant, the cousins were chatting about tomorrow's union election. Suddenly Matt snapped his fingers and said, "I forgot to tell you about the latest eruption.

Apparently Chick Pitz called Llew and wanted to trade him different playoff tickets because the season ticketholder for seats five and six in our row has some pull and wanted six tickets together."

Before Jamie could react to this news, he spotted Dred working the tables. Jamie waved and screamed, "Hey, Dred!"

Dred sauntered over and greeted the cousins, "You guys playing hooky today?"

"Nah, just on lunch break," Jamie assured him, "but what are you doing here?"

"I work here, remember? I told you to come see me when the M's were out of town."

"But that was a month ago. And they told me you didn't work here any more."

"Yeah they tried to dump me, but I'm filing a complaint."

"What kind of complaint."

"A big one."

"Well, where were you?" Jamie asked when Dred refused to elaborate.

"El Salvador," Dred said as he walked over toward a group motioning to him at the bar.

Jamie and Matt sat down and watched as two of the men escorted Dred out of the bar. When the server came by, Jamie asked, "What was that all about?"

"Oh, Dred came in here today like he was an employee and started working. We had to call the people from the group home where he's staying to come get him."

"What's wrong with him?"

"He's got some strange delusions near as we can tell."

"Where is he staying?" Jamie asked.

"I think it's called 'El's Safe Door' up on Capitol Hill."

After the server left, Matt asked, "What? Are you going to go visit him?"

"Yeah, I think I might."

Chapter Fifty-Four

"You want the good news first or the bad news second," Matt greeted Jamie when he arrived for work.

"Out with it," Jamie demanded.

"We don't have to worry any more about all those unfair labor practices the union filed."

"How come?" Jamie asked.

"Well, that was the good news. The bad news is that we don't have to worry about them because the AFW won the election last night."

To Jamie, the M's winning their game in St. Louis yesterday and losing the union election the same day was like splitting a doubleheader. But he knew that to Llew and Adam, the loss to the AFW dwarfed everything else. To escape from getting sucked into any emergency meetings on the union situation, Jamie slipped out of work before lunch and headed up to Capitol Hill.

The intake officer at El's Safe Door was very pleasant and confirmed that Dred was staying at El's. When he then requested a visit, she asked, "Are you a relative?"

"No, but I'm a very close friend."

"Well I'm sorry. Right now he has been restricted to relatives and can no longer leave the grounds until he gets better."

"Is this because you think he has delusions?"

"We can't discuss a patient's condition."

"But what if his delusions are real? What if I could verify some of his delusions?" Jamie asked.

"You mean, like if you were having some of the same delusions?"

"Not exactly. But what if they weren't delusions at all?"

"Why don't I get El to come talk to you?" the intake officer said as she eyed Jamie intensely.

Before she returned, Jamie was gone. He headed back to the office and found that only Matt had missed him.

"Where were you?" Matt demanded.

"I think we should activate our own union avoidance plan and go watch the game at my place," Jamie said.

Matt didn't even notice the change in subject and was right behind Jamie as they fled to pick up some takeout Italian food. Jamie called his mother from the car and warned her. When he and Matt triumphantly carried in the food, she said, "I could have fixed you dinner."

"You fixed us enough dinners over the years, Aunt Jo. It's our turn," Matt replied.

"What, you don't like my cooking anymore?" Jo teased.

"Yeah, but we don't deserve it today. This is the day we let the union into our business," Matt explained.

"It took them long enough," Jo stated flatly.

After laying out the food and saying grace, Matt turned to Jo and said in an innocent voice, "Don't you think Jamie and his girlfriend, Rebecca, make a wonderful couple?"

Jamie scowled as Jo politely asked Matt, "I see you and Mandy are still a couple. Will we be finally having another family wedding anytime soon?"

"We're waiting on Adam so we can go in order," Matt responded with a grin.

"So does he have any prospects?" Jo asked.

"Yeah, he has the prospect of being Uncle Adam to Jamie's kids."

"Am I missing something?" Jo asked the two boys.

"Yeah Ma," Jamie interjected, "you're missing that Matt hasn't changed a bit since preschool."

"No he hasn't," Jo said pleasantly.

As much fun as they were having, Jo declined the invitation from the boys to watch the third St.Louis game with them. Just as well, since Seattle was losing big and the boys weren't pleasant to be around.

"Maybe we would have been better off in the union meetings," Jamie lamented.

"No, we wouldn't," Matt contradicted. "I think the official Tinkler plan is to make it as difficult as possible for the union to negotiate a contract. You and I do not want to be at that negotiating table."

"Who's going to do the bargaining?" Jamie asked.

"I think Adam is planning to be our spokesperson with Llew staying in the backroom. Adam will probably put Jeffrey Anne and someone from the line on the team. Hopefully not me. I'm guessing one of the respected oldtimers, who won't mind jerking around the union. Our mission is to use the Company baseball tickets while everyone else is fighting at the negotiating table!"

Chapter Fifty-Five

No Fed Ex scorecard at home, no Dred at the ballpark, and Oakland is in town for a four game series. Thorne injured his toe in St. Louis and is out of the lineup. Rebecca invited Jamie to a co-ed bridal shower that would conflict with the fourth game on Sunday. He was a little edgy. An Oakland sweep could severely diminish the five game lead that seemed so comfortable. Conversely, a Seattle sweep could just about guarantee a playoff spot for Seattle.

Jamie was bemoaning that Rebecca thought this particular weekend would be a good time to meet the rest of the bridal party when the bride was up from Portland for a wedding gown fitting. Matt could mount little sympathy and chastised his cousin, "Don't be greedy, Meatball. You get to go to three of the four games and we are getting a lot of pressure in the family to spread the tickets around. The fair weather fans are out in force!"

Adam joined his cousins at their seats. Matt greeted him with the news that a radio bulletin said contract negotiations between Sanford Shoes and the AFW had broken off and that a federal mediator was being called in to try to prevent a strike.

"Good," Adam replied. "Maybe this will keep the union out of our hair for awhile or make our employees realize what a mistake they made."

"Enough shop talk," Jamie interrupted. "Who is using the other tickets tonight?"

"My parents and Uncle Art and his wife are sitting in Jamie's seats," Adam said.

"Yeah, Ad doesn't get to be in the grown-up section," Matt added.

"Okay funnyman, why don't you tell him who else is joining you?" Adam prompted his brother.

"Mandy is coming, but it's not what you think. Last New Year's Eve when we were still together, we made a resolution that if the M's were in first place on Labor Day, we would go to the first Oakland game of September," Matt explained.

"So, I suppose you also had a pact with Mandy to attend the Tinkler Labor Day picnics for the rest of your natural born lives," Jamie said.

"Come on, you know she knows everyone there from way back and it's pretty much an open party. Quit mouthing off or next time, we'll invite Jeffrey Anne again," Matt threatened.

Right on cue, Mandy joined the threesome in time to watch the M's give up two runs in the first inning. It only got worse as Oakland spanked the Mist 8-1. Jamie called Rebecca after the game and discovered she was going to visit her brother Rob. "Where's he at?" Jamie asked.

"Some place up on Capitol Hill."

"It's not El's Safe Door by any chance?" Jamie asked.

"Yeah, that's it. How did you know?"

"Maybe I heard something about it from somebody at work," Jamie replied. Then he quickly added, "Hey, how about I come with you to see Rob when you visit?"

"Are you sure you can get off work tomorrow in the morning?"

"Sure, Rob's our employee."

When they arrived at El's, Jamie was a little less sure he should be there. He doubted Rob would appreciate seeing him under the circumstances. At least the intake officer wasn't the same one, however she did want to verify that Rebecca and Jamie were relatives. Rebecca identified herself as Rob's sister and represented Jamie as her fiancé.

"Sorry to get you engaged so suddenly, but we had to cut through the red tape as quickly as we could," Rebecca said with a laugh as they headed up to the second floor.

"It's always good to travel with a lawyer," Jamie said.

Rob seemed a little groggy at first. Then he appeared genuinely excited to have visitors. He was surprisingly lucid and abruptly asked, "What's he doing here?"

"I'm going to find a restroom and will meet you downstairs, Beck," Jamie said as he excused himself. "Take care," he called after Rob.

Once in the hall, Jamie started searching the name cards in the holders next to each door. He was startled when an orderly said, "Can I help you?" in a loud and suspicious voice.

"Yeah, I guess I mixed up the directions. I'm looking for Dred's room."

"Dred Edwards?"

"Yeah," Jamie replied hopefully.

"Take a right down there," the orderly pointed. "Third door on the left."

Jamie scurried away with a quick "thanks" and knocked quietly on Dred's door. No answer. He knocked a little louder and cautiously opened the door a few inches. Dred was alone in the room, standing by the window. He looked over at the door, waved Jamie in, and said casually, "Your scorecard is on the table."

Jamie was startled and said, "How are you?"

"I'm fine, but this place is full of crazy people. You gotta get me out of here."

Jamie didn't know what to say. It was the second time he could remember seeing Dred smile. Jamie smiled back and finally said, "Where did you get this scorecard?"

"Over at the Shoe."

"Aren't you on restriction in here."

"Yeah, it's easier when you're free to come and go. But they make up the set for each homestand well in advance, so…," Dred said as his voice trailed off. "What was I talking about?"

Jamie fumbled for two dollars and put them down on the table. He looked Dred in the eyes and said, "You were about to tell me what this is all about? What's with these scorecards? Why do they let me predict outcomes? Why me? Who are you?"

"I know how you feel, Jamie. I have some of the same questions. When my brother was dying, he said he had to make his peace and break the curse. He told me how to find you and said I needed to get you a scorecard before each game."

"Why did your brother pick me?" Jamie asked.

"He said you were the one."

"The one what?" Jamie asked.

Before Dred could even think of answering, Jamie continued his rapid fire interrogation, "How do I get the scorecards while you're in here?"

"It's easier when I get off restriction. Otherwise I have to get one of the staff to bring me one and help me mail it."

"Can I bring them to you?"

"I don't know. We can try it."

Before Dred could finish, Jamie caught a glimpse from the window of Rebecca looking around outside. "Uh oh, I gotta go," he said as he moved to the door. "How can I get back in to see you?" he suddenly remembered to ask.

"Tell them you're my nephew. I'll put you on the list. How did you get in today?"

"It's a long story," Jamie called back as he started running down the hall toward the exit.

By the time Jamie hit the first floor, Rebecca was engaged in conversation with an orderly. She turned, saw him, and said, "Oh, there he is."

"The orderly said he thought you were the guy who was here to see some patient named Dred. What was that all about?"

"Wow, yeah. What a coincidence. This guy I know is in here too," Jamie replied.

"So when did you find that out?"

"Well I just found out his last name today when I was talking to the orderly."

"I don't get it. How did you know to be talking to the orderly about this guy?"

"It was freaky. He asked me if I was here to see Dred. How many guys are named Dred, so I figured it was the same guy. The orderly must have thought I was somebody else. He was kind of screwed up."

"Yeah, he thought you asked him about Dred," Rebecca said. She knew Jamie was being evasive, but continued, "Did you get to see him?"

"Dred? Yeah, I did."

"Where did you get that scorecard?" Rebecca asked.

"He gave it to me. Said he couldn't use it in this place."

"Don't they let him watch the games on television?"

"Man, I don't know," Jamie said. "The people in here are loony. Who knows what crazy stuff they do? If they made any sense, they wouldn't be in here," Jamie said with a little too much disdain.

Rebecca gave him a hard look. Before she could say anything, he said, "I mean, not everyone in here is loony, but this guy Dred is very strange. You can ask Matt."

Jamie stopped speaking and silently amended his earlier comment about travelling with a lawyer: *The downside is that they're trained to cross-examine.*

Chapter Fifty-Six

Art Tinkler's mistress couldn't tell her suspicious husband she had been with Art at a downtown hotel, so she said she had been playing bridge with some of the ladies at The Club. Before he could start asking some hard questions, she distracted him by saying, "I heard today that the McPherson boy who works for Tinkler has gone bonkers and is in a mental institution. He's the brother of that Rebecca girl that works in your firm."

"I know who he is," her husband acknowledged.

She rattled on with more news, relieved that her husband could so easily be sidetracked by news that could give him any edge in his law practice. Oblivious to their role in the infidelity gossip, Uncle Art and Jamie were part of the Tinkler foursome at game two of the Oakland series. Matt had begged off, but Jamie couldn't afford to miss the game, so he joined Matt's parents and eventually Art.

When Don Grant led off the bottom of the ninth with a double, Jamie didn't want to spoil the M's opportunity with any interference. The game was tied 6-6, but they squandered the chance for a dramatic win, leaving two men on base.

"Looks like they're going extra innings to make up for the ones you missed by being late," Llew kidded his brother.

"Yeah, thanks a lot," Jamie's aunt said sarcastically without a trace of humor.

When Oakland couldn't score in the top of the tenth, Jamie continued to sit on his hands as the M's went out meekly. In the eleventh, Oakland finally took the lead 7-6 on a solo homerun.

In the bottom of the eleventh, Rudy Wink reawakened hope by reaching base on an error. The M's put on the hit and run for Escobar, partly so they wouldn't have to make a power hitter like E2 bunt. Escobar was out on the grounder to third, but with Wink running on the play, a doubleplay was averted. Even though the play was partially successful and the tying run was in scoring position with less than two out, Jamie was forced into action.

He could not now risk a doubleplay, no matter how unlikely. He thought momentarily about tying the game with an extra base hit and then withdrawing again to let fate take its course. But once the interference was introduced, Jamie decided to put the crowd out of its misery with Larry Thorne's winning two run homer.

Resigned to his destiny, Jamie made his way to El's on Saturday with a scorecard in hand for good measure. When he approached the intake officer, she recognized him from the day before and said, "Hi, you're back to see Mr. McPherson, I see."

"Yes, I am," Jamie answered as he seized the opportunity for entrance. He moved quickly toward the stairs without bothering to find out whether he was eligible to visit Dred as a purported nephew.

Jamie watched carefully as Dred took the card and removed something from the nightstand drawer while shielding his actions from Jamie. Dred returned the something to the drawer and the scorecard to Jamie.

"Why did your uncle identify me and how did you find me," Jamie asked.

"He said you were the one and gave me your address."

"How did he know my address?"

"How would I know?" Dred said.

As Jamie and Dred bantered, Rob McPherson's parents made their way to the front desk. "Oh, hello, your daughter's fiancé is already upstairs with your son."

"Fiancé?" Mrs. McPherson asked.

"Yes, Jamie Tinkler," the intake officer confirmed.

The McPhersons looked at each other and started upstairs without a word. When they arrived at Rob's room, they found no fiancé and Rob confirmed that they were his first visitors. While the McPhersons talked, Jamie left the building for the game with no great satisfaction from the answers Dred could provide.

Before Mac McPherson even sat down next to Jamie, he asked, "Did I miss something? Are you and Beck engaged or something?"

"How did you hear about that?" Jamie asked.

"My parents just called and asked me what's going on."

"So it's true?" Matt interrupted.

"No, it's not true," Jamie said almost too vehemently. "Beck just said that, so I could get in to see Rob," he continued.

"I better go call my mom, in case she hasn't tracked Beck down," Mac said as he headed out to the concourse with his cell phone.

"That's interesting," Matt began, "Beck said you were engaged."

"Yeah, because only family was allowed to see Rob."

"Why did you want to see Rob?" Adam asked.

"He's our employee and he's Rebecca's brother for pete's sake," Jamie answered.

"You didn't talk about the union or harass him again?" Adam asked.

"I never harassed him in the first place," Jamie said.

"Wait a minute, I think we're missing the bigger picture, Meatball," Matt interjected. "Rebecca can visualize you as a fiancé. You would tell me first if anything like that was going to happen, right?"

"I would definitely not tell you first." Jamie said. "She's actually a little ticked at me right now."

"How come?"

Jamie thought about how he had botched things with her by visiting Dred, but just said, "Who knows? You know how women are."

"You got that right," Matt said as Mac returned.

"Boy were they relieved," Mac noted as he sat down.

Jamie was surprised how disappointed he was that his "engagement" didn't last and that the McPhersons were so relieved. Matt decided to let the opportunity to comment pass and instead said, "Look, the M's are already down 2-0 while we're horsing around and not paying attention."

"I was paying attention. They gave up a two run double after two walks," Adam said.

Jamie was almost paralyzed by his own thoughts and was easily seduced into trying once again to take a night off and just enjoy a Seattle win without his aid. Early on the Oaks looked like they would oblige. The pennant race pressure appeared to be getting to them when they committed two errors and walked three M's in the first inning, yet only two runners scored. Oakland settled down, scoring a run in the fifth and holding Seattle to just three scattered hits until the eighth, when Wink and Escobar both singled with nobody out.

"Finally," Jamie nudged Matt, "we're going to beat Oakland, right here, right now."

"What do you mean 'finally'?" Matt answered. "We just beat 'em yesterday."

The dialogue was cut short when Larry Thorne ripped the first pitch to deep rightcenter. Wink thought it might be caught and as the potential tying run, he tagged up at second. E2 read the ball correctly and took off at the crack of the bat, planning to score the go ahead run on a 'sure' extra base hit. The ball bounced off the wall and right into the glove of Oakland's right fielder. He wheeled and launched a rocket toward home plate. With nobody out, the base coach held Wink at third. Unfortunately, E2 came roaring toward the overly popular third base.

The only thing uglier to a baserunner than being passed by a thrown ball on the race to base, is the gut wrenching sighting of a teammate camped on that same base. Over 40,000 fans experienced right along with Escobar the disheartening panic of being trapped.

So now Wink is standing on third while E2 puts on the brakes short of the same third base bag and reverses field heading back toward second. Meanwhile, the hitter, Larry Thorne, rounded first and was motoring hard for second. Thorne would later explain, "I was just hoping to draw the throw, so the more important runs could score."

Unfortunately, Thorne, like E2, had miscalculated the conservative approach taken by Wink and third base coach Zip Duda that conspired to keep Rudy on third. So Escobar was denied even the slim chance a trapped runner has to get back to safety because compatriots had claimed both the bag in front and behind him.

The Oakland pitcher was confused by all the movement after cutting off the throw, but recovered quickly and started running toward Escobar, who was feinting between the two occupied bases. Both Wink and Thorne simultaneously decided to help their trapped teammate out. Wink broke for home and Thorne headed back toward first. The Oakland shortstop signaled to the pitcher who whirled and threw home, nabbing the sliding Wink easily.

Escobar wanted to leave Wink a safe haven at third in case he got in a pickle to avoid being tagged out at home, so he retreated to second. Thorne seeing Wink trying to score, reversed his route to first and headed back toward second, apparently presuming that E2 would take over third. Thorne quickly experienced the previously described horror of finding a teammate on the destination base. He quickly retreated once again, yet not in time to avoid being picked off at first by the catcher's quick throw.

Escobar remained rooted on second and did not try to advance on the throw to first. Perhaps he was tired. Perhaps he was not about to risk running three straight hits into a triple play. Ironically the once popular third base now housed no one. Jamie could restrain himself no longer and was the only person in the stadium not surprised when E2 stole third and then home on the next two pitches.

Since the game was now tied, Jamie relaxed momentarily. Grant struck out, the M's held Oakland scoreless in the ninth, and Jamie resumed his help. Kuhn singled, stole second, stole third, and then stole home on the rattled Oakland defense.

Escobar and Kuhn had all sorts of rationales for their daring base running in the last inning and they expounded long and hard on the subject for the media. Wink should have been happier to be off the hook for his own running gaffe, but he would only say, "The only thing we forgot was to paint our clown faces on before the game."

Chapter Fifty-Seven

When Jamie showed up in his regular seat on Sunday, Matt did a double take and said, "I thought you were giving your ticket to one of the younger cousins."

"I changed my mind," Jamie answered tersely.

"You are the man, Meatball," Matt said as he jabbed Jamie on the shoulder. "Rebecca needs to know baseball is first priority."

"Yeah, right," Jamie muttered.

Jamie fidgeted with the scorecard he had cycled through Dred. The first half inning seemed to take forever with two walks, a basehit, and numerous foul balls. Down 1-0, the M's came to bat in their half of the first and they came out swinging. The first ten hitters all scored with no one out. During the second pitching change, Jamie excused himself and bolted for the exit.

Although Jamie and Rebecca were late to the shower, they deftly blamed their tardiness on the M's traffic. Jamie easily bonded with the other males as they all plotted ways to sneak into the rec room and catch as much of the M's game as possible.

"You missed an amazing first inning," the groom-elect informed Jamie. "The M's scored ten runs before anyone made an out. It was awesome. They're up 13-2 in the fourth."

Jamie thought to himself, *I didn't miss the ten runs; I caused them.* But out loud, he said, "Yeah, we caught some of it on the car radio."

Since the game ended up a 14-5 blowout, undivided attention was not necessary from the men at the party. They were in good spirits and able to endure a few obligatory games, passing oranges neck to neck and taking quizzes that might have been funnier if they were drunker. After the "groom to be" good-naturedly opened his gifts which included a screwdriver, vaseline, and other items that were undoubtedly hilarious in another time and place, the sexes were both relieved to separate to their own corners.

After exiting the party, Rebecca took a call from her mom on the cell phone as she and Jamie walked to the car. "Yes, he's right here, I'll ask him," she said turning toward Jamie.

"Ask me what?"

"She wants to know if you want to join our family for dinner next Sunday?" Rebecca asked with her hand cupped over the phone.

"Uh, oh," Jamie answered softly.

Rebecca looked at him expectantly and finally returned to the call and confirmed, "Okay, Mom, he'll be there."

When Rebecca eyed him one more time, Jamie froze and was unable to seize his last opportunity to object. He did need to get back in her good graces. *Sunday is a week away,* he thought, *maybe something will come up.*

"Who will be at this dinner?" Jamie asked after Rebecca hung up.

"My parents, my three brothers, and my sister-in-law. My parents have a tradition of a family dinner every other Sunday night whenever possible," Rebecca explained.

"Well, I hate to butt in," Jamie said.

"Too late, you're already committed," Rebecca said.

Sensing Jamie's discomfort, Rebecca added, "Look, it's no big thing. My brothers bring guests and family friends all the time. For all I know, there may be others there."

"Yeah, but I was just thinking about this whole '*fiancé*' thing. It's embarrassing."

"Why would it be embarrassing," Rebecca asked.

"I meant awkward," Jamie amended.

"I'm just teasing," Rebecca answered with a laugh. "You're screwed!"

"What about Rob?" Jamie asked. "Does he usually come to these dinners?"

"Yeah, a lot of the time. I don't know if he'll be out by Sunday. We really bullied him to admit himself to El's. With all the laws designed to protect patients from involuntary commitment, Rob may not realize, he could leave if he wanted to."

"How's he doing?" Jamie asked.

"He's got some medicine that is supposed to stabilize his bipolar condition. We hope he can get back to normal, but the big fear is that he will keep drinking. Alcohol is bad enough for his condition and I expect it would be a disaster with the drugs he's supposed to take."

"What do you suppose causes something like that, Beck? I mean, did Rob always have problems and this is a flare up or was he pretty normal before this hits out of the blue?"

"I think Rob went off track after his wife left him," Rebecca speculated. "He started hitting the bottle and deteriorated rapidly. But who knows? Perhaps some things were always there and we didn't really notice. Maybe his wife experienced some of his disease and for all we know, his condition could have helped cause the divorce in the first place."

"So," Jamie probed, "you never saw any signs of any problems until the divorce?"

Rebecca thought for a moment and continued, "Nope, nothing out of the ordinary. Sure, Rob had idiosyncrasies. Everybody does. But the divorce clearly sent him over the edge. Some people probably don't need a crisis to break down, but traumas like war, death, divorce, and stuff like that can't help. Did you notice anything at work? Is his job stressful?"

"I never noticed anything odd until recently and no, I don't think of his job as overly stressful. But maybe I don't have a good vantage point," Jamie answered.

"It makes you wonder about your own breaking point," Rebecca said.

"I don't know why some people are lucky enough not to be tested with breaking points," Jamie said. "However, I do know that my own stress at work has gone way down with Rob out on leave. All the Pierce County deliveries are going smoothly now. I'm glad he can be treated and if he comes back to work, which I kind of dread, I hope he's really stabilized for everyone's sake. I mean, a big part of his job is driving all over the Puget Sound area."

"Speaking of driving all over Puget Sound, you're about to miss my exit," Rebecca interjected.

Jamie made a quick recovery and noted for the record, "I just hope this Sunday dinner doesn't trigger my own psychotic episode."

"Hey, I went to your family's Labor Day party. Things couldn't go any worse than that! Besides, I figure your threshold could only be triggered by a baseball game," Rebecca said.

Jamie laughed because it wasn't a joke. He said nothing but was thinking, *If you knew I spent an inning at the ballpark this evening, you would think I was crazier than Rob.*

Chapter Fifty-Eight

Jamie breathed a little easier when he was able once again to get by the intake desk. He knocked on Dred's door and entered slowly when he got no answer. He looked around and headed for the nightstand drawer. Inside he found a chewing tobacco tin. He was about to open it, when he heard Dred at the door and quickly moved away.

"Here's your scorecard," Jamie said.

"No, here's your scorecard," Dred said after quickly performing his ritual at the table by his bed.

"You know, I think you can leave here if you want," Jamie said in a heavy whisper. "I did some research and found out they can't involuntarily keep you past 72 hours unless they get some court order."

Dred looked at Jamie blankly and finally said, "I gotta take my shower now. I just finished my exercises."

Jamie was happy enough to take his scorecard and get out. Seattle held a seven game lead and with this card, they weren't going to lose any ground today. They didn't. But on Wednesday when Jamie returned, he was told that Dred had signed himself out. He couldn't get any forwarding address, but confidently expected to see him at the evening game.

When Llew, Adam, Matt, and Jamie met for their standing Thursday lunch, everyone was rehashing the reasons for the M's loss the night before. Jamie wished he could explain it was simply because Dred hadn't shown up, that Jamie may have erred in prompting him to leave El's. But instead, Jamie had to listen to every theory from Thorne's gimpy foot to Kuhn's second half slump.

When lunch arrived, Adam turned a little more serious and asked Llew, "Do you want me to get a hold of Chick Pitz and see if I can negotiate some better playoff tickets if we give ours up? Or maybe I can get rights to some extra ones."

With all of his preoccupation with Dred, Jamie had completely forgotten about the playoff ticket problem. Horror crept over the pit of his stomach and he blurted out, "What? We can't give those seats up!"

Llew stroked his chin and asked Adam, "What about this idea that the union is behind all this? Do we know if the sister of the regional VP for the AFW has the seats next to us? Because if that's true, we should fight this with every ounce of your legal poison."

Adam said, "I wish it were true. I would love to take that issue on, but I checked it out. I think the sister of the union muckety-muck was actually a guest of the people who sit next to us. So that rumor was blown out of proportion."

"Could we negotiate away two or three of the seats and still save one?" Jamie asked pensively.

The other three stared at Jamie. Matt spoke first, "You are so attached to your seat, you would sit there alone?"

"No," Jamie stammered, "I was thinking more like splitting into two sets of two."

"You didn't even last past the first inning of last Sunday's game. What was up with that?" Matt asked.

"It was already 10-1," Jamie replied.

Llew regained some control of the conversation by telling his elder son, "Adam, you go ahead and work it out, but let's try to keep our seats. Split them if the two we give up can be moved next to the four tickets that Jamie got us. That way we can have six together and Jamie can have some privacy with his girlfriend."

Only Matt laughed. Jamie was lost in his own thoughts as he finished his soup and salad. *It's not enough I have to worry about Dred going AWOL or missing key games for bridal showers, but now I've got to worry about losing my seat for the playoffs.*

Late that same afternoon, Matt swung by to pick up Jamie and said, "I meant to ask Papa if Adam could negotiate some free playoff hotdogs for us while he was at it. But Ad is Llew's right hand man because he doesn't smart off with the old man. So I decided to try that strategy."

"So when will we know?" Jamie pressed his cousin.

"Know what?"

"Know about the playoffs seats," Jamie clarified.

"Beats me," Matt shrugged and added in an exaggerated voice, "I guess I'm glad I didn't go to law school and become the right hand man because I don't have to do the confrontational wrangling Adam loves so much. Remember when he wouldn't get his haircut in eighth grade?"

"You mean when Father Bob cut it?" Jamie asked.

"Yeah," Matt confirmed, "it was too long and shaggy for the dress code and the principal brought in Father Bob when Ad wouldn't cut it. Father Bob thought he would teach him a lesson by cutting swatches out of it so that he'd have to get a haircut after school. But he came home with it in patches. I think he thought Father Bob was going to be in big trouble."

"It made Adam kind of a school hero, but what did your parents do?"

"Papa just said, 'I used to think Father Bob was kind of wimpy. Now I'm starting to like him more and more.' And that was the end of that episode."

Jamie laughed and Matt said, "Speaking of dinner tables, it's a great night to park down on the waterfront, get some sandwiches at the Sub Marina, and walk up to the game."

"Good plan. So what do you actually think of this union conspiracy theory on our playoff tickets?" Jamie asked.

"It's absurd. But we're all so jumpy, especially after the flyby at our picnic, which was actually pretty cool when you think about it. We've got a case of the big ego if we think we're the center of the AFW radar screen with everything going on. I mean, Sanford has over 50,000 employees. We have about one percent of that. I'm guessing the union doesn't even care whether their regional VP gets playoff tickets. And I'm sure he has no idea who his sister sits next to and doesn't give a rat's rump."

"So did you ever dump this opinion on Llew and Adam?" Jamie said as they disembarked from Matt's sedan.

"And spoil their fun investigating the conspiracy?" Matt replied as he held open the door to the Sub Marina for Jamie. "No way!"

"My turn to buy," Matt said. "You want a Turkey Sub with cheese, right?"

"Yeah, on wheat," Jamie said.

"Make mine a Meatball Sub on sourdough," Matt added.

"Do you want cheese with that Meatball?" the order taker asked.

"Did you just call me a Meatball?" Matt challenged the startled worker.

"I asked if you wanted cheese with your Meatball Sub," the young man replied evenly.

"Oh, sorry, no cheese," Matt muttered meekly, while Jamie tried vainly to suppress his laughter.

Chapter Fifty-Nine

Rob listened as the Group Leader outlined the exercise. Each patient was asked to write down their worst memories, their worst fears, and anything negative that was going on in their heads. Rob scribbled down a message describing his urge for revenge against his ex-wife and her doctor boyfriend. He laced his epistle with anger directed at his family and his work.

Although it actually felt good to express his rage on the printed page, Rob balked when the psychologist asked the patients to come forward and toss the papers in the fireplace. The leader explained that they would now destroy their demons once and for all by burning all of their negative baggage.

Rob looked around at the other patients. He knew many of them pretty well by now and he felt certain that burning a piece of paper wasn't going to be a miracle cure. Still they eagerly paraded to the fireplace and tossed the papers in the fire.

"This is a bunch of crap," Rob muttered to himself as he slipped the paper into his pocket and headed to the lobby to get a newspaper.

"Hey, you looking for me?" Rob asked when he spotted Jamie at the intake desk.

"Yeah, there you are," Jamie replied without betraying his real purpose which was inquiring if anyone had heard from Dred.

Jamie quickly moved away from the desk and sat down on the couch with Rob. They made some small talk and Jamie assured him they were keeping a spot open for him at work. Rob surprised himself when he answered, "I've finally turned the corner and I'm coming back soon."

Although he had mocked the burning exercise, Rob did feel he was beginning the slow ascent from the abyss. Jamie couldn't tell if that were true. He was just relieved when an orderly came looking for Rob because this unplanned visit put Jamie way behind schedule. He moved at a decidedly faster pace, sprinting for his car when he was finally free. He shuddered to think what the repercussions of this impromptu meeting might bring, considering that recent encounters with Rob had precipitated unfair labor practices and complications with Rebecca.

Jamie bounded up to Matt's door and banged loudly.

"Somebody's sure anxious to get to this game," Matt greeted his breathless cousin.

"It's just that we're late," Jamie said.

"Late only by the standards of someone who likes to be at the ballpark two hours early so he can leave after the first inning," Matt countered.

"I keep reminding you that game was 10-1," Jamie replied, wondering if he was ever going to live that down.

"All the more reason to stay. Besides, I've never seen you leave a game early before, not once, not ever."

"You knew I had the party with Rebecca that afternoon," Jamie explained. "I got to see the exciting part of the game and take in a shower. Haven't you heard of having your cake and eating it too?"

"I understand the part about you needing a shower and craving wedding cake, but what if the game was 1-1 after the first inning, what do you do then?"

Jamie was taken aback by a question he knew he never had to consider, but managed to answer, "What do you think?"

"I honestly don't know anymore. Rebecca's got some spell on you. You're acting crazy!"

"I've always wanted to be just like you," Jamie said. "You should be flattered."

When they arrived at the ballpark, Jamie's fears were confirmed. Dred was missing in action for the fifth straight game. Seattle managed to win two of those and still held a six game lead over Oakland, yet Jamie was worried. When Dred didn't show up on Sunday either, Jamie didn't even stick around for the game. He decided to be plenty early to pick up Rebecca for the McPherson dinner.

Rebecca's parents lived in a gated suburban community along the northeast shore of Lake Washington. Their stately white mini-mansion had sweeping views of the water, the Olympic mountain range, and downtown Seattle. Rebecca's mom and sister-in-law greeted Rebecca and Jamie at the door. Although he already knew Beck's father and brothers, he was anything but comfortable.

Rebecca's mother was quite attractive. It was easy to imagine her as a raving beauty in her youth. She likely would have aged gracefully under normal circumstances, but it looked like she took no chances and worked hard maintaining her now elegant good looks. Jamie could tell by her very polite and solicitous interest in him that she did not like him.

"Hey, Jamie," Dano bellowed, "did you get a chance to catch the M's game? Escobar and Thorne each jacked one. The Oaks lost again today. They are never going to catch us now."

"I caught a little of the game on the radio," Jamie started to answer.

"The Oak's are not dead yet," his brother Mac interjected. "Mark my words. It's all going to come down to the last three games of the season against Oakland in California."

"Not if we're up by four games going into that series," Dano countered. "Oakland is folding up their tent after that whupping we gave them up here last weekend."

"You say 'we' like you are part of the team," Rebecca said with a laugh.

"We all live in Seattle, Beck," Dano replied. "The team is the Seattle Mist and I know you root for them. I'm betting you've called them 'we' many times. So don't be playing lawyer with me."

"So when the Seattle Police Department beats the unruly crowd silly on Fat Tuesday, you as a native are inclined to say, 'We whupped them punk rioteers good.' And when the Seattle Ferry System rams a dock, you shake your head and say, 'we probably should stop drinking on duty.'"

"You're going to scare your *fiance* off if you keep talking like that," Dano said with a smile.

Rebecca's mother raised her voice higher than necessary and called for Mac to get Jamie a drink and show him into the family room. Mac brought Jamie a beer and asked, "Did you ever get your playoff tickets straightened out?"

Jamie was caught off guard and asked cautiously, "What do you mean?"

"Jeffrey Anne told me the M's were trying to move you for the playoffs and that you weren't about to give up your lucky seats," Mac explained in a cheery voice that didn't seem so friendly to Jamie.

"I don't know too much about that," Jamie lied nonchalantly, "but I expect we will end up with our same seats for the playoffs, that is if we get into the playoffs. I hope I'm using the term 'we' correctly."

Everyone laughed and Jamie suddenly felt more comfortable in the family room. He noticed Rob was nowhere about. So when he got a chance, he privately asked Rebecca how Rob was doing.

"He's been released," Rebecca said. "We were over at his place yesterday, but he says he doesn't do parties anymore. I expect you'll see him at work soon enough. He plans to get medically cleared to return," she whispered.

Jamie was just settling in at dinner when Mac asked, "Do Beck and Jamie have anything they want to announce?"

"Yeah," Dano seconded his brother loudly.

Mrs. McPherson was deftly trying to change the subject when Rebecca loudly proclaimed, "Yes, we would like to announce that my brothers are still jerks."

Chapter Sixty

Matt just stood in the office doorway smirking, so Jamie was finally forced to say, "What's up?"

"Well, I'm up for watching the game on the tube tonight. Llew is going to have to be up for meeting with an International VP of the union on Wednesday. Jeffrey Anne and Adam are riled up because Rob is getting medically cleared to return to work, and I'm guessing Rebecca is up for getting married as soon as you make amends by popping the question."

"Don't even joke about that," Jamie said.

"I'm not joking," Matt insisted. "The AFW Vice President for the Western States is flying in on Wednesday to meet with Papa Llew on these very premises."

"You know what I mean," Jamie replied.

"I know what you mean. I know just what you mean," Matt mimicked. "You mean you are one serious dude now that you've grown up and joined the adult world. But for old times sake, before you shed your childish ways, let's head over to the Shoebox and watch the game on the big screen."

"I think I can handle that," Jamie conceded.

Yet he didn't handle it that well. Seattle lost, while Oakland was winning its game. Seattle's magic number remained at eleven. The Seattle media had to educate a population not familiar with magic numbers that "eleven" meant that any combination of Seattle wins or Oakland losses totaling eleven would clinch the division championship for the M's. The odds certainly favored Seattle since there were still sixteen games to go for both teams.

But Jamie feared that Mac McPherson was correct in predicting that Oakland wasn't just going to roll over. After all, Seattle still had ten games on the road. The Oaks had only six road games and three of those were in their home state of California. More importantly, they would host Seattle in the season ending series. When Tuesday became a repeat of Monday with both a Mist loss and an Oakland win, a few more people joined Jamie in squirming.

Since Wednesday's Texas game was televised at 5:15 p.m. Seattle time, Matt and Jamie scooted out of the office a few minutes before five, while Papa Llew was still in his meeting with the union vice president. Matt turned down the pre-game show on the car radio and said to Jamie, "I feel a little guilty sneaking out while the big meeting is going on. I wonder what's happening?"

"I'm sure we'll find out at tomorrow's lunch," Jamie assured Matt. "Besides, who has his priorities mixed up now? We have a ballgame to watch."

"You're right about that! It's not like we were invited to the meeting or dinner."

The Shoebox proved surprisingly crowded this night. The boys took a table in the corner just as the opening pitch was thrown. It was a called strike. The Texas ace followed with eight more that inning, striking out the side. "That hurt," Matt said during the commercial.

Things did not improve much for the M's over the first five innings. They were down 2-0 in the top of the sixth when they finally squeezed a run out of a bloop single, stolen base, infield out, and a sacrifice fly. Seattle's flickering optimism faded in the bottom of the inning when the opposition sandwiched a three run homer in the middle of a five run uprising.

When the M's went down meekly in the seventh, many dinner patrons started an exodus. The bartender wandered over and greeted Jamie, "Say, I saw your friend Edwards at the airport last week. He said he was trying out for some reality show."

The name didn't register at first, but then Jamie remembered Dred's last name and said, "You've got to be kidding! Did he say where he was going or when he would be back?"

"Nah, he said he couldn't talk about it. He had to sign a zillion pages of confidentiality agreements which he thought he might have already violated except he never read them before signing."

The bartender scurried away when an older gentleman who appeared to be his boss summoned him to help a customer by barking, "We got any more quadruple ex-large sweat shirts left?"

"Wow," Jamie said softly while thinking that Dred was full of surprises.

"Wow, you have a new best friend who left town without telling you; or wow, you didn't know they made sweatshirts for guys that big?" Matt asked.

"Yeah, I'm sure he appreciated having his size broadcast to the whole place," Jamie responded while he watched the large man choose an orange sweatshirt from the meager selection the bartender presented.

"I've seen that guy at the ballpark before," Jamie noted idly.

"He would be hard to miss," Matt observed. "But who is this Edwards buddy you now have? I can't keep up with all your new friends?"

"Dred, the scorecard vendor, who used to work here. You know him."

"No, *you* know him," Matt corrected. "I know who he is. It sounds like he got his first and last name mixed up. Dred Edwards, is that alliteration or something like that? I can never remember what's a homonym and what's an antonym."

"I think we always have to be very careful not to be making fun of anyone's name, what with Tinkler Toilets being alliteration and onomatopoeia at the same time," Jamie answered.

Matt knew just enough to laugh.

Chapter Sixty-One

"So what happened with the big AFW Grand Poohbah yesterday?" Matt said with a glance at Adam.

"You'll have to ask Llew when we get to lunch," Adam shrugged. "They went one on one and kicked everyone else out, including all the local union officials."

Without even some baseball small talk, Llew gave a dismissive wave in greeting and began slowly, "Nothing special happened. No secret deals or threats. Nothing like that. He made it clear that he had proudly worked for union causes for over thirty years and that he considered it an honorable profession to represent American workers. He acknowledged that honest differences can exist between reasonable people, but he intended for his local people to treat us with respect."

"Did you ask him how respectful their campaign literature was?" Adam asked.

"No, and he didn't take potshots at our campaign either," Llew responded evenly. "He emphasized that any type of election campaign can get nasty but that once the people speak, it's time to turn toward doing what's best for the Tinkler employees."

"You're not buying any of this load of crap, are you?" Adam asked. "What's best for our employees is not getting run out of business by giving in to unreasonable demands!"

"Let me finish, Adam," Llew said sternly. "We both acknowledged that we didn't have to like each other and that we were free to fight tooth and nail over our disagreements. But he expected we could work together on things we agree on."

"Like what?" Adam asked defiantly.

"Like getting our fair share of business with the state," Llew began.

"Which we haven't been getting because of the union," Adam interrupted.

"Exactly," Llew agreed. "He also planned to be putting some private and public pressure on the city to stop crippling businesses like us with the absurd paperwork burdens required to show compliance with the regulations passed at last month's City Council."

"So he did some homework," Adam acknowledged.

"And no surprise, the union intends to push us hard for better retirement and to resist health plan increases," Llew continued. "He said if negotiations get to a breaking point, I should call him direct to discuss the sticking point man to man. He said he intended to do the same with me."

"I still think it's all snake oil," Adam said.

"We can never let our guard down," Llew agreed. "But just between us, the election is over. We do need to bring peace to our workplace and not put our own employees in the middle of a war."

"I can't believe I'm hearing this from my own father," Adam said, shaking his head. "Whatever happened to the Tinkler motto of 'Never Give an Inch?'"

"When I was about your age," Llew began while glancing at all three cousins, "I once ran my car out of oil because I wrongly believed the oil warning light was defective. I had some reason to think that but I won't embarrass myself by going into the details. By never giving an inch, sometimes we miss obvious signs."

"How come I never heard this story before?" Matt chortled. "How come I took such grief when I ran the sailboat aground because the depth indicator was stuck at twenty feet?"

"Another good example," Llew said with a laugh. "You took grief because it had to be obvious you were running the boat up on the shore no matter what the depth finder said. I couldn't see the actual oil."

"I don't see any difference," Adam said curtly. "You're both crazy."

Jamie remained silent as he was thinking, *No one can accuse me of doing nothing when faced with warning signs that I could affect baseball games, but my signs sure didn't contain obvious answers like 'add oil' or 'head for deeper water.'*

Chapter Sixty-Two

"It's a little early for you to be leaving work, isn't it Ad?" his brother asked as they headed for Adam's place to watch the game.

"Hey, if Llew is just going to hand over the company to the union, why should I be down there burning the midnight oil?"

"No shop talk," Matt replied. "Let's do baseball, beer, and pizza. I'm ordering a large pepperoni and a big M's victory unless you want to add something."

"Why don't you add an Oakland loss for dessert?" Jamie interjected, but he was thinking, *I wish Matt could order up road victories the way I used to deliver wins at home games.*

The pizza and the Mist victory tasted great, but the dessert left a bad taste as Oakland won big in the later game. At least the M's finally moved the magic number to ten. Don Grant, who had the winning hit for the Mist in the ninth, was quoted on the post game show saying, "We have control of our own destiny."

Asked if the team looked ahead to the season ending Oakland series as ultimately deciding who would win the division, Grant said, "No, we're really only taking one game at a time. If we can keep playing our type of baseball, the wins will take care of themselves."

When the press dispersed, looking for juicier material, a smiling Rudy Wink told Grant, "I think you really captured the thoughts of all of us, but you articulate them in ways that are so original."

"I'll articulate your scrawny neck if any more crap comes out of it," Grant growled.

Donny Kuhn was just happy to see others coping with the limelight. Life was a lot easier that way. It would get harder. M's players needed to enjoy this victory because the next one would be awhile coming. They were swept in their three game weekend series. Oakland finally lost, but only once. The seven game lead was down to two games in the blink of a week. Seattle's magic number was nine, with only ten games remaining.

"We knew it was too good to be true," a Seattle sportswriter trumpeted in his column. The doomsayers were now out in force. People were checking the great collapses in history to see if Seattle could rival the Cubs or Phillies as if that type of fame was almost as exciting as winning the division.

"What about the wild card?" Matt asked Jamie on the Monday off day for both teams. "If we can't win the division, maybe we can get in the playoffs as the wild card?"

"Won't happen," Jamie assured Matt. "Boston and New York are in the same division. One has 94 wins, the other 95. The one that finishes second gets the Wild Card. We've known that all year."

"But we have 90 wins with ten left. Technically we still have a chance at the Wild Card, right?" Matt insisted.

"But if we start winning, especially against Oakland, we win our division," Jamie explained. "And if we lose enough to lose the division, we'll never catch the wild card."

"But mathematically, it's still possible," Matt said.

"Sure, and it's mathematically possible for you to be President of the United States, but it's not going to happen," Jamie replied.

"Don't be such a pessimist."

"You're the pessimist. You're trying to get the M's a Wild Card berth while I'm still planning on a division title," Jamie said.

In truth, Jamie was consumed with pessimism. Dred was gone, the M's last three games would be on the road in Oakland, and Rebecca couldn't see him tonight. He liked to go out with her when the M's weren't playing to store up credits for the times he needed to be at the ballpark or watching the games. Things just weren't going well at all.

Jamie took some of his night off to fool around on the Internet. He decided to look more seriously for information on the former owner of his seat. He had previously discovered that Peter Edwards was a very common name. But he had learned from Adam that this Peter Edwards used to coach baseball teams, including the one his father played on. Jamie had to admit that the name certainly had a familiar ring to it. He wasn't sure what he was looking for anyway. A deceased man was unlikely to tell him anything even if he closed his eyes at the Symphony. Suddenly Jamie realized why the ring was so familiar. "Dred Edwards. Peter Edwards," he said aloud.

Chapter Sixty-Three

Dred startled Jamie even though he was in the one place he could most hope to see him. "You're back," Jamie said. "I have some more questions for you."

"This is the only answer I have," Dred said as he handed over the scorecard.

"What about the reality show?"

"Who said anything about a reality show?"

"I don't know," Jamie said cautiously. "Maybe they told me about it at El's when I went to look for you. What's the difference? What happened?"

"I can't talk about that. I don't even know if I made the cut. And I don't get paid until after the show airs and only if I don't violate the confidentiality agreement."

"Well, how about Peter Edwards? Are you related?" Jamie asked.

"Yeah, you know he's my brother. I told you about him."

"You never told me his name. I'm sitting in his seats," Jamie said.

"Yeah, so what? I sat in them many times over the years. Section 139. Row fifteen. Seats one through four."

"Well, I'm trying to make sense of this scorecard thing," Jamie replied.

"Jamie, you can't make sense of it. You'll go crazy trying."

"Can't you tell me anything?" Jamie pleaded.

"Okay, Listen," Dred said softly as he leaned in close to Jamie. "The Reality Show is about a bachelorette who is choosing a man, but she doesn't know that one is a criminal, one is gay, one is a mental case, and so on. She can't really win because I understand that the only normal guy is going to be the nerd."

"I thought you couldn't talk about that. And anyway, I'm talking about the scorecards."

"I can't talk about it. But let them try to sue the mental case they had sign a contract."

"Look, Dred, are you going to be around for our next five home games?"

"Yeah, the show starts November 3rd if I get picked. I think I was auditioning to portray an eccentric older rich guy, but they're pretty evasive about it all."

"What about the chewing tobacco? Can you tell me about it?"

"It's bad for you. I quit awhile back. I'll see you tomorrow," he said as he disappeared down the stadium ramp.

Jamie wasn't all that satisfied, yet he had his precious scorecard. After winning the last road game on Monday, the M's managed to hold on to their two game lead. Their magic number was eight and Jamie figured he could take care of six by himself. If Oakland lost two games or Seattle beat them once in their last series, the Oaks were eliminated.

"Donny Kuhn seems to be taking the brunt of the criticism for the M's collapse," Matt said as the first inning opened.

"They haven't collapsed yet. They still have a two game lead. And Kuhn still has a batting average over .300, 48 homers, and over 140 rbi's, way above his career numbers. He's more responsible for the M's being in first than anyone else," Jamie replied.

"Yeah, but he's been in a free fall since July. Only two of those homers came in the last two months."

"So even though Donny leads the team in homers and rbi's, he's the most to blame?" Jamie asked.

"Sure, have you been reading the paper?" Adam asked as he joined the conversation. "It's what have you done for me lately. You know expectations are always higher on the superstars. Remember A-Rod? And it didn't help that Donny was acting like such a jerk when he was riding high."

Jamie wanted to protest that Kuhn was no A-Rod. He only had half a season of glory. But he knew his cousins were basically right. Although, he didn't want to meddle unless he was needed, Jamie was anxious to test the scorecard and granted a single to Kuhn in Donny's first at bat. When the M's were down 2-0 in the fourth, Jamie couldn't resist a homer for Kuhn, but by the top of the sixth, the M's were down 4-2.

"I've got some real bad feelings about this. I can see us blowing everything in the last week of the season," Matt said.

"Relax," Jamie said more in annoyance than reassurance.

Matt pointed to the section of the scoreboard showing scores of the other games, "How can I relax? Oakland already has a three to one lead in the fifth. We're going to be down to a game lead after tonight. I knew it was all another cruel joke."

"We haven't lost tonight," Jamie reminded Matt. "Have a little faith."

"So you are suddenly the optimist," Adam said. "Next thing you'll be predicting that Mandy will finally get Matt to the altar."

"I'm stuck in the comedy hour for dreamers," Matt replied, "and just for the record, I've got a date with Leslie for a week from Friday."

"Leslie the lush, the cocktail waitress at Crossroads Casino?" Adam gasped in mock horror.

"Now why do you call her a lush?" Matt demanded.

"Maybe because of that time she was barfing and passed out at the waterfront concert," Adam answered.

"Oh, and you've never gotten sick drinking, I suppose," Matt said with a sneer.

"Okay, Bro, who am I to put down a potential sister-in-law? Where are you taking her?" Adam asked.

"She wants to go to the opening of Octoberfest down at the Garden," Matt replied.

Adam rolled his eyes.

"Tell me you aren't going to Octoberfest this year," Matt shot back with some edge in his voice.

If only for the sake of family unity, Jamie had Kuhn pop a homer in the sixth. For good measure, Jamie provided the margin of victory for the M's when Donny hit his third dinger of the game in the eighth. Although Oakland also won, the M's held on to their two game lead. The mood of the media circus that followed Kuhn was upbeat for the first time in a long time, but Donny just said, "I got lucky tonight."

Chapter Sixty-Four

"I'm serious, Llew. We need to shake things up around here." Art said. "Things are going to hell. Papa Joe must be spinning in his grave. Costs are up. Business is down. The union's in our knickers. There's no more loyalty. We got Jamie leaking info to the enemy. You heard about that financial data the union has on us, didn't you? You can't just ignore all this."

"And what exactly are you proposing?" Llew asked.

"Well, you know my son, your nephew, is getting his M.B.A from G.W. next spring. Maybe we bring in some fresh blood, start him in Jamie's job, and after six months…"

"And what happens to Jamie?" Llew interrupted.

"Like I said on Labor Day, maybe we trade him to McPhersons. We've got Rob, so they get the better end of the deal. And that way, Jamie's working on the same side of the fence as his girlfriend. Hell, maybe he can feed us some information."

"And then suddenly costs will go down, business will go up, and the union will go away?"

"I'm telling you, we gotta start somewhere. Change is good. I'm sure my son will have a lot of good ideas for us to implement."

"I'm sure he would. And we can probably find a place for him if he really wants to work here, although he has never seemed that interested before," Llew said.

"That's because you never gave him anything important to do."

"One thing you're right about, Art, is that change can be good. This is confidential and you can't tell anyone including your family. This is insider stuff. McPhersons wants to buy us out. This could make us all very rich and key people will be offered five year contracts to stay on."

"You're kidding? When's this all supposed to happen? Are we sure it's in the best interests of the family to go along with it? Who are the key people?"

"The negotiations will begin soon and you'll be a key person in any big decision, but you can't say anything until we get the formal offer, okay?"

"Sure, Llew."

As Art headed back to his office, Llew made his way down the hall to see Jeffrey Anne. "Look," he began, "as our HR person, I need to give you a head's up on something extremely confidential. You can't discuss it with anyone."

A few hours later, Jamie was having his own crisis that he couldn't tell anyone else about. Dred was missing in action. He was nowhere to be found in and around the ballpark. Reluctantly, Jamie proceeded to his seat for the National Anthem. As soon as the singing ended, Matt began chattering, "Did you see the group bidding for an expansion team in Portland is floating the idea of letting a sponsor pick the nickname?"

"What do you mean?" Adam asked and then proceeded to answer his own question, "Like, Portland could be the Portland Pontiacs and General Motors pays for the naming rights?"

"Yeah," Matt confirmed, "and Seattle could change to the Seattle Starbucks. What do you think, Jamie?"

"I think we're in big trouble," Jamie said as the Seattle pitcher gave up a lead off homerun.

Jamie was correct. The M's were thrashed 7-2. Oakland won their game and the noose tightened. Seattle's lead had dwindled to one game. Art Tinkler was just as glad he hadn't gotten the company tickets to the game. But he would still use the game as an alibi for his family while he was holed up in a fancy downtown hotel.

"Where is your husband this time?" Art asked his partner in marital infidelity.

"In California. Something big is going on down there."

Well, something big is going on up here," Art said. "And it's going to be good for us."

Chapter Sixty-Five

"Where the hell were you yesterday?" Jamie yelled at Dred after suppressing the initial leap of joy he felt when he spotted him.

"I had an interview to tape for the TV show. But I don't have to account to you, anyway," Dred said calmly.

"Well," Jamie said as he paused for a second to collect his thoughts. "What about your brother? Isn't he counting on you to break this curse on the M's?"

"That's between him and me, don't you think? But I expect he's counting on you to break the curse."

"But I can't do it without you."

"That's why I'm here. Get to work."

"Will you be back tomorrow?" Jamie asked

"Will you be here?" Dred replied.

"Of course," Jamie answered.

"Because you haven't always shown up," Dred said. "Now you know what it feels like to be stood up."

Jamie didn't have time for a reply before Dred walked away. For now, he was content to watch the M's produce a victory mostly without his help. He did drop a few hits on Donny Kuhn. *I should at least test the card,* he mused to himself as the Mist romped 9-3.

While he and Matt made their way to the Shoebox, Jamie retrieved a text message from Rebecca. He studied it somberly until Matt said, "What? Did Rebecca break up with you by text message?"

"Worse. She's got tickets to the Symphony on Saturday."

"That's perfect," Matt said.

"What's so perfect about that? The M's are playing that night," Jamie replied.

"Yeah, I could use an extra ticket. Can I have yours?"

Jamie was lost in thought and didn't answer. After entering the Shoebox, Matt headed for the restroom and Jamie took the opportunity to call Rebecca. He started the conversation by suggesting they meet at the Symphony.

"You're not trying to go to the game first, are you?" Rebecca asked. "Because the Symphony will be over by the time the game ends. I can get my mom to go if you don't want to, but I figure we're going to the last home game together this Sunday and I know you're going to the others this week. I was thinking you could skip one."

"Yeah, I plan to be on time for the Symphony. It starts at 8:00 p.m., right? I just have a late meeting, which I can cut out of it in time to meet you at the Mercer Street entrance before eight. Then we can use your car to go out for drinks and dessert afterwards," Jamie suggested.

Rebecca knew she would be working that Saturday herself. So it was a fairly convenient plan for her, but she projected subtle disappointment for Jamie's sake. She was a trained negotiator after all.

Friday's game went as planned. Dred appeared. Jamie helped Donny Kuhn recapture his hitting touch, and the M's did the rest. Just as importantly, Oakland lost and dropped three games behind Seattle with only five to go. Two more wins at home and the Mist could do no worse than tie for the division title. And a pre-determined coin flip had already awarded any potential playoff game to Seattle. Everything for Jamie hinged on getting to the stadium on Saturday for the 7:05 start time, pounding out some first inning insurance runs, and catching a cab over to the Seattle Center for the Symphony.

Dred was waiting when Jamie arrived. If he hadn't been, Jamie knew the upside was that he would be plenty early for the Symphony. The downside would be that Matt would be very annoyed that he wasted a valuable ticket.

"So you did skip the Symphony," Matt said when Jamie arrived at the seats. "I was worried when I saw you weren't here yet."

"Oh, I've been here for awhile. I just made a beer run," Jamie replied as he passed one to his cousin.

"You are the man," Matt said as he eagerly accepted the plastic bottle.

"Actually I do have to bug out early," Jamie confided, hoping the beer bribe would temper Matt's reaction.

"What do you mean early? Isn't the Symphony like right now?"

"Yeah, Rebecca and I are going out for drinks and dessert afterwards, though."

"Where are you going? Maybe I'll join you," Matt said.

"I'm not sure. Maybe, I'll call you," Jamie replied, knowing that phone call would not be made. *Not tonight,* he thought as he fidgeted with his watch. Out loud, he said, "What's going on, anyway? Why isn't the game starting?"

"It's fan appreciation night. You ought to know. You're Seattle's biggest fan."

Jamie's heart jumped off a cliff. He knew it would take at least fifteen minutes to get through some speeches and give-aways. It would take at least ten more minutes before the home team could even get up to bat. "Damn. I gotta go," he said as he bolted for the exit.

The good news for Jamie was that he was now able to catch a cab in plenty of time and arrive early at the Seattle Center. He also didn't leave Dred in the lurch. The bad news was he left Matt in that lurch. And as he found out later, the M's lost.

Chapter Sixty-Six

"What happened?" Dred asked with the first real concern Jamie had seen from him.

"What do you mean?" Jamie answered.

"The scorecard I gave you yesterday. It didn't work?"

"No, I'm sure it worked fine. I just wasn't able to use it."

Dred's mood changed. He looked like he was going to ask another question when he suddenly became aware that a woman had joined Jamie. So he just offered him the card.

"Don't worry, everything will be fine," Jamie said as he forked over the two dollars.

Rebecca handed Jamie his tea and blew softly on her coffee while they walked to their seats. "What will be fine?" she asked.

"The M's are still a game ahead of Oakland. We're going to win this thing," Jamie replied.

So often in year's past, the last home game of the season was meaningless for the Mist, but not this year. The local fans were on the edge of their seats throughout the game, while Jamie was relatively relaxed, enjoying the weather and the pleasure of Rebecca's company. Even though the couple's flirting remained low key, by the seventh inning it drove Adam and Matt to the Home Run Café on the mezzanine level. Jamie celebrated their departure with a superfluous Kuhn single.

Although time seemed to be moving very slowly, Jamie wished it would stop altogether. The M's eventually coasted to a 6-3 win. As the crowd started to exit, an announcement was made that Oakland had lost again. The roar from the fans sent a shiver through Jamie. Things were just getting better and better. Seattle was now two games ahead with three to play. They headed to Oakland with 95 victories. Although the magic number was two, the M's needed just one win to clinch the division title because any Seattle win was an automatic loss for the Oaks. Oakland could only win the title by sweeping the series. There could be no tie. Boston and New York were tied in their division with 96 wins each, so the Wild Card wouldn't be a factor.

Cautious optimism surrounded many a television in Seattle when the Oakland series opened on Tuesday night. Early on, it became apparent that win or lose, Seattle was going to put their fans through agony first. They stranded eight runners in the first five innings of a 1-1 ballgame.

In the seventh, Larry Thorne broke the tie with a homerun. The M's nursed the 2-1 lead into the bottom of the ninth. Three outs from the playoffs. A fly ball. Two outs away. A walk. A strikeout. One out away. A single. Puget Sound viewers held their collective breath.

Seattle fans began cheering the moment the batter popped a ball high in the air just to the right of second base. Donny Kuhn circled under it and just as the ball was about to settle in his cavernous mitt, a small movement sent it glancing off the side. By the time the first baseman retrieved the delinquent sphere and threw home, the runner on second had scampered across the plate.

The demoralized Seattle pitcher was able to induce the next hitter to ground out to third. So the game marched into the tenth inning. Seattle left two more runners on base when Donny Kuhn struck out. Oakland went down quietly. In the eleventh, the M's only stranded one, but it was the fifteenth of the game. Oakland stranded nobody in the eleventh because their first hitter homered.

Baseball can turn fortunes so quickly. After game 159 on Sunday, Seattle was in command and Oakland was in despair. On Tuesday, one game later, the roles were reversed. Seattle still held a one game lead but suddenly they felt like underdogs trapped on foreign ground.

Most of the players gave Donny wide berth. A few offered a pat on the back or a soft word of encouragement. Rudy Wink, ever the extrovert, stretched out his hands and said loudly to Donny, "What happened?"

"Shit happens," Donny said with a shrug.

"Yeah, but you make your own diarrhea," Rudy retorted.

Donny was too lost in his own thoughts to process the comment. But Escobar stepped in and addressed the team, "Let's keep our spirits up. We're still in control of this opera and we're going to make that fat lady sing tomorrow night."

The fat lady was not even warming up in the first inning of Wednesday's game. Before too many fans had even settled on their barstools, Seattle was rocked for five runs.

Jamie was watching the game at Matt's condo on Queen Anne Hill with a half dozen friends and family. He turned to Matt and moaned in the second inning, "I have very bad vibes about what is going to happen. Oakland's got all the momentum tomorrow."

"Hey, wait a minute, Meatball," Matt said, "aren't you the one always nagging at us for tossing in the towel too early? It's only the second inning. Remember earlier this week at the Shoe when we came back and won 9-8? You were the one predicting a rally."

"But that was a home game," Jamie lamented.

"So what?" Matt demanded.

"Well, we just play so much better at home," Jamie offered weakly.

As the boys set up for a game of Texas Hold 'Em, Adam shouted. "Let's play some cards since this game sucks!"

"If only we had won one more game sometime at home during the season. We needed that game Saturday night," Jamie muttered mostly to himself while he thought what his trip to the Symphony had cost.

Matt was close enough to catch the gist of what Jamie was mumbling and said, "No, we needed to win one more on the road. We only have 31 'away' game victories all season. And what do you care? You'd rather go to the Symphony than a big home game. I think we're going to win this thing tomorrow if we don't do it tonight. It's not like the M's haven't played their heart out this year."

When the deflated M's gave up three more runs in the third, even die-hard fans knew Seattle was down to one last chance. Jamie left the poker game before the 13-1 laugher ended. Even on his best days, he donated too much to Adam at the card table, but tonight

Jamie was especially distracted. He possessed all this power, but with the weight of impending doom, he could sense that the M's would fall one game short. After so much worry that using his power was an abuse, Jamie was now faced with the thought that not using the power may have been the abuse.

Chapter Sixty-Seven

"Who won?" Jo asked cheerily as Jamie struggled down to the breakfast table.

Who won? How can anyone ask such a question? he wanted to scream before he sourly muttered, "Probably Adam, but I left the card game early."

"No I mean the baseball game," Jo said.

Jamie needed no clarification, but felt like his mother should be punished for her cheeriness and obliviousness. He managed to spit out tersely, "Not Seattle."

"That's too bad. Is the season over now?" Jo asked.

"Jeez, do you pay attention to anything going on?" Jamie ranted. "If Seattle loses again tonight, then you can be happy the season is over."

"Can I make you some eggs?" was Jo's only response.

Thankfully she was off the topic of baseball, but Jamie remained annoyed. He said "no" to the eggs, but it was actually a generic "no" to everything in the universe.

Jamie suffered through the day, happily distracted by daily mundane tasks at work. Lunch with Llew was cancelled so he made a noontime call to Rebecca and arranged to meet her at Greenlake at 6:30 that night. The popular park just north of Jamie's Wallingford neighborhood was also convenient for Rebecca who would be coming from her aerobics class.

He and Rebecca met in the parking lot, just west of the par three golf course. She greeted him with the question of the day, "Are you sure you don't want to watch the game?"

"I told you I'd rather walk Greenlake with you," Jamie said with a smile.

"I'm flattered, however I know you are the all time M's fanatic and this is the biggest game of the season. What gives?"

"I guess I'm such a serious fan, I can hardly stand to watch, but maybe we can catch some of it over dinner," he answered as they began the three mile walk around the Lake.

"Well, I take back the designation of number one fan if you aren't watching because you think the M's are going to lose," Rebecca chided.

"It's not that I think they're going to lose. It's more like I'm so into it that I can't stand the tension. The stress is incredible. And, yeah, maybe I do sense impending doom. You know how sometimes you can feel something bad coming and it's even more annoying that the other side thinks they're in trouble and you know they're soon going to be celebrating your doom? There's a certain momentum. You can just see how things are going to unfold even before they happen."

"So, this sixth sense you have, can you tell me anything about what is going to happen in the world outside of baseball?" Rebecca teased.

"You know what I mean. I'm talking about the premonitions that everyone gets."

"Well, I don't get them," Rebecca said while shaking her head. "But maybe I understand what you're driving at. Do you know how sometimes when you are up somewhere high, like downloading on a ski lift or on the roof of a building and you feel a 'jump' impulse even though you absolutely have no interest in jumping? It's like the fear you have is sending a signal that just adds to the terror."

Jamie looked puzzled and said, "Actually, no, I don't know about that particular impulse. So you have a fear of heights?"

Rebecca was a little flustered, "No, not a phobia. You've been hiking with me. I can hike or ski high in the mountains. I don't mind flying. But I don't like being on the edge of cliffs. I'm not overly comfortable with heights. I don't want to rock climb, for example. You're looking at me funny, Jamie, like I'm confessing that I'm some suicidal freak or something."

"I'm not looking at you funny at all. Being in love with a suicidal freak is very serious to me. In fact, it's downright scary," Jamie said with a big smile.

When they were just over halfway around the Lake, Jamie realized the game was starting. He was a little surprised that he didn't see or hear radios everywhere, but apparently members of the baseball subculture were all inside somewhere watching the game on the tube. The bigger surprise to Jamie was how big the non-baseball universe was. There were dog walkers, there were joggers, there were in-line skaters, there were picnickers, there were basketball players, there were soccer players, there were frisbee fanatics, there were people fishing and rowing boats. None of them seemed too concerned that Seattle was playing its biggest game of the season, actually the biggest in their history.

Three miles passed quickly for the couple and they started a second loop, heading for the restaurants that were located in a business cluster at the northwest edge of the lake. One old guy fishing off the bank seemed to be listening to the game with some radio headphones, but Jamie decided not to go over and disturb him about the score.

Neither Rebecca nor Jamie was opposed to eating in the sports bars that would have the game on television, but those establishments looked crowded. Finally they settled on Real Toes, a small and simple Italian eatery a couple of blocks off the lake. While sipping wine and snacking on bruscetta, Jamie and Rebecca were suddenly startled by loud groans and screaming emanating from the kitchen.

Moments later, their waiter explained sheepishly without being asked, "The M's just blew a 2-1 lead in the fourth. Oakland's big catcher jacked a three run homer after Escobar booted a double play ball. The cook is a fanatic Mist fan, but he's real good about keeping his tears out of the pasta."

"Well, I guess I'm glad I'm not watching this game," Jamie said for the benefit of the waiter and Rebecca both.

After finishing their salads, Jamie and Rebecca were treated to exclamations of joy now reverberating from the kitchen. When the waiter returned to retrieve the salad plates, the couple waited eagerly for the good news. Without being asked, the server obliged with a report that Thorne's two run dinger had just tied the game 4-4 in the fifth.

Jamie demonstrated enough excitement at the news to encourage more reports, but to Rebecca he said with a smile, "I still have a vague premonition that the M's are going to jump off the chairlift."

Rebecca didn't appear as amused with Jamie's wit as he hoped, but she seemed pleased with her pasta vongole. Jamie was equally impressed with his veal marsala except that it was served with a bulletin of a run scored by Oakland in the sixth. Spumoni ice cream came with the chilling news that the Oaks had scored again in the seventh. As he computed the tip, Jamie was distressed by the two run lead Oakland still held in the eighth, although apparently Wink was on base. "How's Kuhn doing?" Jamie asked the waiter.

"I think he's 0-3, so it looks like he's going to lose the batting title on the last day because that guy in Boston apparently went 3-4 in his game back east and the announcers said he passed Kuhn. Donny's only chance now is for an extra inning game because he needs two more hits," the server reported as if this calculation were more important than his tip.

It was now past 9:30 p.m. and the sated couple decided to work off the early dinner by walking the long way back to the car. "Well, the absence of a doggy bag means we ate way too much, but it sure was worth it," Rebecca said.

"At least we're getting in a six mile hike," Jamie noted.

"It's pretty flat to be called a hike."

"All the better to keep you away from heights, my dear," Jamie said with an exaggerated flourish.

"This is going to get real old, real fast," Rebecca replied.

Jamie figured they would catch the end of the game when they got back to the car radio, but a sudden flurry of horn honking when they were almost there gave him a sense of hope. Sure enough a three run eighth inning rally by the M's held up according to the overly exuberant post game commentators. The Mist won 7-6. They were in the playoffs. Possibilities were everywhere.

Chapter Sixty-Eight

Matt couldn't wait for lunch on Friday to burst in on Jamie, "Did you see that game? Or more importantly, where did you see that game?"

"Actually I didn't see the game, but I can't believe how good that win feels!"

"What do you mean you didn't see the game, Meatball?"

"I walked Greenlake instead. I guess we get to play Boston which at least means we get homefield advantage. Hey, when do we divvy up the playoff tickets anyway?"

"Wait a minute, wait a minute," Matt stretched out the words the second time and held up both hands with palms facing out.

"What?" Jamie asked with feigned innocence.

"You know what. You walked Greenlake. The biggest M's fan in history. The biggest M's game ever. What is going on?"

"Well," Jamie began slowly, "Rebecca and I…"

"I knew it," Matt exploded, "I can't believe Rebecca wouldn't let you watch that game. I've held my tongue Jamie, but that girl is trouble."

Now it was Jamie's turn to interrupt, "Slow down, Matt. It wasn't Rebecca's idea. I called her and suggested it. You're barking up the wrong tree."

"Someone must have pissed on your tree because the bark is starting to peel and underneath I'm starting to see pussy whipped willows," Matt said with a hint of a smile.

"Think what you like, Matt, but I was overloaded. The walk around Greenlake was just what I needed and now I'm ready to attack the playoffs."

Matt shook his head and said, "Sometimes I just don't get you. But anyway, we're all planning on meeting at the Shoebox to watch the opener on Monday night. The playoff tickets have been split up and you can get yours on Sunday at Adam's. We're watching football and playing some cards, if you're not out walking Greenlake!"

"I'll be there, smart ass," Jamie said with a big grin, "but you better get used to trouble because I'm bringing Rebecca on Monday night."

"Hey, I never said trouble was bad. I've been looking for trouble all my life. By the way, you were a genius buying those extra four seats this year. We get more playoff tickets that way. Good call. See you at lunch," Matt said with a mocking salute of simulated six guns as he withdrew from Jamie's office.

Jamie was having a hard time concentrating on his work. Eventually he took out the sports page and started reading in detail all the baseball articles he had skimmed when he picked up the paper at home.

Even in victory, a Seattle columnist tweaked Donny Kuhn: "In 1941, Ted Williams put his .401 average in jeopardy by playing in a meaningless doubleheader on the last day of the season and was rewarded for his courage with five more points. Pundits suggested that Donny Kuhn was more likely to request sitting out a meaningful game if it would protect his batting title. However, all accounts confirm Donny was eager to play. Although he went 0-4 and lost the batting crown, his speed likely contributed to Oakland's fatal throwing error in the eighth. That led directly to the winning run and this time Donny, his teammates, and thousands of his closest friends all reaped the reward together."

The playoff schedule in the newspaper footnoted the reasoning of why Seattle drew Boston, the Wild Card opponent. New York had the best record in the League which would normally entitle them to play the Wild Card team, but no one is allowed play an opponent from their own division in the first round. Seattle had a better record than Central Division champ Minnesota, so Boston was matched with the M's. And although Boston actually won more games than Seattle, their Wild Card status assured Seattle of home field advantage in the opening best of five game series. Giddy to actually be in the playoffs, the M's would have likely been happy to play an All-Star team and so Boston was just fine, thank you.

The nature of cross continent travel put the first two games in Boston with the remaining contests as needed in Seattle. In the well-played opener, the M's took a tough 5-4 loss in ten innings. Spirits remained high because the Mist had performed well in defeat under the national limelight and Seattle fans and players were still somewhat in awe of just being in the playoffs.

The Tuesday night loss hit harder. Seattle was shellacked 8-1 on a three hitter and now they were suddenly facing elimination after six months of hard work. The season was escaping too fast although the flight back to Seattle seemed to the M's like it would go on forever.

Everyone knew the Mist would have to start hitting at home like they had all year long. Media analysts were making a big deal that Seattle had ten hits in the series and Donny Kuhn, a notoriously weak hitter on the road, had half of them. Donny was 5-7 (.714) with two walks while the rest of the team was batting .109 (5-46). No other player had more than one hit. The commentators postulated that Donny was fresh from the pressure of chasing a batting title in the middle of a tight pennant race. With all his other controversies and legal problems, perhaps he had learned to cope with pressure better than his teammates. More likely the ball just bounced his way for a couple of games, but the experts were paid big bucks to analyze something and they did it ad nauseam.

Jamie flirted with the urge of producing a Seattle win with everyone except Donny hitting. But a Kuhn tailspin wouldn't faze the media as they are rarely embarrassed by yesterday's comments. He would really only be punishing Donny. Certainly Kuhn wasn't provoking any backlash. He just said, "Where were those hits when I needed them for the batting title? I'd rather be hitless and up two games to zip than be in the hole we're in, but I'm confident we've got the horses to turn this around starting Thursday."

Although the other players were chirping in publicly with the mandatory sports cliches, the mood in Seattle was a collective hope for one win to look respectable and at least avoid a sweep. The idea of advancing to the next round seemed far away. Jamie wanted to chastise others for this wimpy thinking whenever he encountered it, but he was surprisingly restrained in his public comments. After all, he couldn't afford the luxury of too much confidence in the home field advantage unless Dred came through.

In fact, Jamie found plenty to worry about. He worried whether Dred was still upset and whether he would bring him a scorecard. He worried whether the playoff cards held any magic. He worried that he would have an emergency appendectomy and be unable to attend. He worried that an earthquake would untie the Shoe and that the series would move to another stadium. He could worry with the best of the them.

Chapter Sixty-Nine

"We need to redraw for the playoff tickets," Art demanded.

"And why is that?" Llew asked.

"The M's could be eliminated tomorrow and then some of us won't get to see a game. We need to distribute them more evenly. I've got four tickets to game five, but I should probably get two to game three and two to game five."

"You knew that risk when you bid to take your whole family to the potential deciding game," Llew replied. "Now when it looks like there might not be a game five, suddenly you want to change the rules. You can't have it both ways."

"It just seems like the kids are getting the better deal. We should have priority. After all…"

Before Art could finish, Llew's office assistant burst in with an announcement of an important phone call.

"Look, I'm sure the M's will win the next two and then everyone will be jealous that you've got four tickets to the final," Llew said as he waved his brother out the door.

After Art was out of earshot, Llew thanked his assistant for following the standard protocol of the five minute interruption anytime Art wandered into the office alone. But his assistant insisted, "No, you really do have an important call. The Regional V.P. for the union is on the line."

Llew took the call and listened carefully as the AFP Vice President suggested that Llew work closely with the union to make the merger with McPhersons go smoothly for all parties. "This is a real opportunity for a win-win for two fine companies, the union, and the employees," the union leader emphasized.

"I don't know anything about a merger," Llew responded.

"I know this is highly confidential at this point, but I'm sure at the appropriate time, you will want to protect the transfer of all rights and vestings of your employees to any new entity. As a sign of good faith, I'm going to pass on some information that would be better for me left unsaid, but which you should find extremely useful."

Llew listened thoughtfully as the union leader offered his barter. Although Llew learned nothing new at this point, he just thanked his counterpart for the input. After cradling the phone, Llew removed his glasses and rubbed his eyes with his fingertips. His assistant re-entered the office and asked, "Art said you might want to call a meeting about the baseball tickets?"

"Absolutely not," Llew said with a laugh.

Undeterred by Llew, Art visited Jamie on his own and suggested Jamie trade his ticket for tomorrow's game for an additional one to game five.

"No thanks," Jamie said.

"It doesn't seem right, you have tickets to all three games and I get tickets to only one game for my whole family," Art continued.

"I have a total of four tickets for the series and you have four. I bought four season tickets with my own money and I think I'm sharing pretty generously. Besides, we already had a draft where everyone agreed to the rules."

Jamie had never spoken so harshly to his uncle before and Art didn't like it. In parting he told Jamie, "You may have won the battle of the tickets, but you have a lot to learn. You're hurting your career, my friend."

Jamie wasn't sure he needed too many friends like Uncle Art. Meanwhile, he had bigger issues to worry about. The biggest was solved when Dred showed up at the game waving a scorecard. No matter what Seattle thought of their chances, the novelty and energy of a playoff game in Seattle had galvanized the city. Politicians from the states of Washington and Massachusetts had elbowed into the limelight by making public bets of local delicacies. Tickets were a hot property with rumors of scalping at obscene levels. Jamie now had his precious card and after testing it on Rudy Wink, he luxuriated in the ambience of Seattle playoff baseball.

Wink's homerun leading off the bottom of the first gave the M's the first lead of the series. The crowd, so desperate for something good to happen, went wild. Matt pummeled Jamie while shouting, "Did you see that, Meatball? Is that a good sign or what?"

A very good sign, indeed, thought Jamie with a wry smile.

The game went well without further interference from Jamie, while providing enough tension to put the fans through an emotional ringer before Seattle prevailed 6-4. Jamie was pleased to take the rest of the night off and enjoy the natural rhythm of the contest. He almost regretted the Wink homerun although he couldn't be sure what impact it had on the game beyond the one run it added. That one at bat changes everything that follows from the emotional lift for the M's to the pitch selection from the opposition.

On Friday, Jamie made Rebecca get to the ballpark early. After all, it was the playoffs. A high point of any day at the Shoe was seeing Dred with his scorecard. This time Jamie experienced an extra click at the sight and asked him, "You want to join us after the game?"

Dred seemed surprised at the extra-curricular banter, but replied, "I'm not allowed to hang out at the Shoebox. I'm heading to the Whole."

"Good, we'll see you there," Jamie said with an air of certainty.

"I thought we were going to the Shoebox," Rebecca noted curiously as they made their way to their seats.

"You want to go to the Shoebox?" Jamie asked.

"No. I don't care, but I thought you told Adam to meet us there," Rebecca reminded him.

"Yeah, except it's going to be so crowded," Jamie said. "I'll just tell Matt to let Adam know we're heading to the Whole. Maybe they'll join us."

"How come you know Dred so well and why isn't he allowed in the Shoebox?" Rebecca asked. "Wasn't he the guy you visited at El's?"

"Yeah. I know him from selling programs and he used to work at the Shoebox," Jamie answered sheepishly.

Rebecca nodded, but couldn't help feeling that it was out of character for Jamie to be altering social plans based on making friends with a ballpark vendor who looked too raggedy even for a hawker.

Matt and a younger cousin joined Jamie and Rebecca as a result of the draft for playoff tickets. Adam and some other relatives were assigned the other seats. One little victory last night had dramatically transformed the hopes of Seattle fans from dreams of respectability to a real expectation that today would lead to a tied series and ultimately to the next round of the playoffs.

The game was just what national television producers wanted: an exciting contest with many lead changes. During the seventh inning stretch with Seattle clinging to a 5-4 lead, Matt gagged at the singing antics of Jamie and Rebecca. So he turned his attention to teasing his other cousin about his experience with the opposite sex. His youthful victim attempted to validate his prowess by boasting, "Last weekend a couple of really hot girls started hustling my buddy and me at Dirk's drive in. They wanted to trade a bottle of vodka for a bottle of bourbon, because they didn't like vodka. So we swung by my buddy's place and made the trade. He got their number and is setting up something for tomorrow night."

"What are you doing with liquor? You're not twenty-one yet. And how come they didn't want to hang out that night you made the trade?" Matt asked.

"They had to go to some all-girl's bachelorette party," the underage cousin said as he felt his stock rising with Matt.

"Have you tasted the vodka yet?" Rebecca interjected, having overheard the exchange.

"No, why?"

"Just curious," Rebecca said.

"Oh no," Matt groaned as the eighth inning opened with a Boston double off the center field wall.

The double led to a two run outburst. Tension mounted as Boston protected their 6-5 lead through the eighth; but the fans never lost faith, loudly cheering each time the M's retired an opponent. They even celebrated foul balls. The loudest cheers were reserved for Seattle's hitters. Jamie felt happy to lend his hand to the excitement. He ignited a ninth inning M's rally, keeping his trigger finger from getting rusty. Thorne singled home two runs, the Mist prevailed 7-6, the series was knotted at two games apiece, and exhilaration reigned.

On the drive over to the Whole, Rebecca quizzed Jamie again. "How are you going to work the wedding weekend if Seattle makes the World Series?"

"I'm planning to skip the Saturday game because being your date is more important to me," he said with a smile as he inched forward in the traffic gridlock.

"You're just saying that because you know the M's only have a 25% chance to be in the World Series," she chided.

"Actually, I do believe Seattle will beat Boston tomorrow and when they do, you'll at least have to change those odds to fifty percent," Jamie stated emphatically.

No matter what he said, Jamie would get more credit for his confident loyalty than he deserved. He knew better than anyone that the M's were likely to beat Boston. However, Seattle was unlikely to secure homefield advantage in the next series because the heavily favored New Yorkers had the best regular season record and were already leading Minnesota two games to one in their playoff series. Jamie knew too well the power of the homefield and how potentially damaging his absence from any home game could be. So Rebecca could not fully appreciate the significance of Jamie even entertaining the possibility of skipping a World Series game. Jamie wasn't all that sure he could actually skip one even under the best circumstances. And consequently, he couldn't be absolutely sure where Rebecca fit in his life. But first things first.

Chapter Seventy

"And you thought the Shoebox would be crowded," Rebecca said.

"Wow," Jamie answered while wondering if he might miss Dred even if he was part of the mob.

Rebecca maneuvered to a bar seat, while Jamie stood right behind her. As they waited for their drinks, he leaned down and said, "So you think my cousin was scammed by those girls with the vodka bottle."

Rebecca nodded, "Yeah, I think his friend is going to be telling him that phone number was a take-out teriyaki place and that the vodka tastes like water."

"So why didn't you warn him?"

"How would that help him in front of his older cousins? And why would I want to look like I know anything about a trick like that?" Rebecca added with a laugh.

"So did you ever do that kind of stuff?" Jamie probed.

"I'm sure I did things I wouldn't want to be reminded about."

Before Jamie decided whether to explore the topic further, he spotted Dred yelling and signaling from a table in the corner off to the side of the bar. Jamie did a double take because Adam and Matt were sitting at the table as well. Jamie and Rebecca scooted over and asked how everyone got over here so fast.

"The Shoebox was so crowded there was a line at the door, so we headed straight here," Matt acknowledged.

"Yeah, Dred here must have some great connections because he somehow got a table in this mess," Adam added.

After introductions of some people Jamie didn't know, he finally cornered Dred while everyone else was engaged in conversation and asked softly, "Do you really think it's right for us to be using these scorecards to affect all these ballgames?"

"Why not?" Dred responded.

"Somehow I still feel guilty all the time," Jamie said.

"I think the M's should feel more guilty about how they treated my brother than he should ever feel guilty about how he treated them."

"What do you mean?"

"He was a coach, but they blackballed him after he got the daughter of the owner pregnant. He wanted to get married, except they kept him away from her and she didn't survive childbirth. The M's dumped him and made sure he couldn't get another coaching job. So he used his power to get even. If you think using such power is wrong, you can think of your role as reversing the wrong."

"What would your brother think of the M's success this year?"

"I think he would be pleased. The owner he hated is long gone and I think he really wanted to make his peace. He was actually into positive thinking, the whole psycho-cybernetics thing," Dred replied.

"Is that where you believe you can positively affect performance by visualizing success?" Jamie asked. "You know, like shooting free throws in your mind."

"Yeah, something like that."

"What about death? Is that what breaks the curse?" Jamie continued.

"Death doesn't end such a curse. If the instigator doesn't end it, his direct descendant has to," Dred replied.

"Hey, what are you guys talking about so seriously over there?" Matt asked loudly. "Are you solving world hunger or something because Rebecca's feeling ignored and is getting bored over here."

"As boring as Matt is, I don't feel ignored," Rebecca clarified.

Nevertheless, Jamie moved back over next to Rebecca. Matt was squeezed out and migrated over by Dred, where he took the opportunity to ask, "So what's all this stuff about a curse on the M's?"

"What has Jamie been telling you?" Dred asked defensively.

"Nothing," Matt said cautiously. "I think some bartender at the Shoebox was saying your brother put a curse on the Mist."

"I know you think this is all crazy, but my great grandfather once cursed the Chehalis basketball team and they had a losing record until my father removed the curse fifteen years later. I think that's a matter of public record," Dred asserted.

"So these curses are just on sports teams?" Matt asked sarcastically.

"No, man, but this is why we don't talk about it," Dred replied and excused himself.

"What happened?" Jamie said when he saw Dred exit. "Is he coming back?"

"I don't know. The guy's a nut case," Matt answered.

Jamie caught Dred outside and said, "Were you getting hassled? I want to tell you I appreciate everything you have to say."

"Thanks. I'm cool. It's just time for me to get going."

"Before you go, I was wondering, did your brother ever use a scorecard?"

"Sure."

Jamie paused as if he expected a longer answer and then asked, "Did he ever gamble on the M's?"

"Some people thought he lost money gambling on the Mist and that was why he put the curse on, but my mom says it was all about getting screwed out of working as a coach.

"Maybe it was a combination of factors," Jamie offered.

Dred shrugged, "Maybe. He did like to gamble. His anti-M's bias was not one-dimensional. It was also a way to tease his nieces and nephews and be the devil's advocate with family, friends, and customers at the restaurant. My sister always thought he was a secret M's fan. But not me. He just seemed so satisfied when we were at the ballpark and they lost."

"Did that upset you?" Jamie wondered out loud.

"Sure," Dred confirmed, "but he was a great brother. He was twelve years older than me and coached all our teams. We won a lot because he was a good coach, but he was especially good with his players when we lost. I didn't fit in so well with the other kids and he looked out for me. When he was sick at the end, I think he was trying to make his peace and one way was putting me on this mission."

Matt poked his head out the door and yelled, "Everything okay out here?"

"I really do have to run," Dred said, but he only walked away.

Chapter Seventy-One

Llew pounded furiously on his son's door at five in the morning, repeatedly yelling at him to "open up" until finally a very irritated Adam appeared and softly said, "Keep it down. Do you want the neighbors to call the police?"

"Art's in jail. You gotta go get him bailed out," Llew said as he brushed by Adam.

"For what?"

"He was taking pictures in a restroom late last night and somebody who was in a stall called the police on his cell phone. They thought he was some kind of pervert."

"We ought to be able to clear that up. It's just his hobby," Adam reminded Llew.

"You and I know that, but it gets worse. Art was a little intoxicated and supposedly resisted arrest. The officer says he was assaulted."

"Oh, jeez," Adam said. "Let me get dressed and I'll see what I can do."

Adam disappeared into his bedroom and Llew kept talking in the hallway, "I should also fill you in on something else about Art. He's been the one leaking info."

"How do you know?" Adam shouted back.

"I planted a false rumor that we were merging with McPhersons and it already bounced back from the union V.P."

Adam reappeared in the hall with just his pants on and repeated, "But how do you know it was Art?"

"He was the only one I told. I planted a different rumor with Jeffrey Anne. I told her we were moving out of state. You, Art, and Jeffrey Anne were really the only ones with access to some of the details that were getting leaked. Art's having an affair with that woman from the Chamber who's married to a lawyer in that union firm. Even the AFW vice president knew that. And Jeffrey Anne's been dating Mac McPherson, so they both had potential."

"Wow, you know a lot of what's going on. So you knew I couldn't be the leak?" Adam said partly as a statement and partly as a question.

"No, for all I knew you could have been telling stuff to Jamie that was getting back to Rebecca and her firm. If neither rumor bounced back to me, I'd know it was you," Llew said.

Adam thought maybe his father was teasing him, but he sure didn't want to pursue it and he ducked back inside and finished dressing. Since it was the weekend, he couldn't get Art out in time for Saturday's game. Art did get to watch it on the jail television, where he was the least enthusiastic of the prisoners when Escobar hit a first inning homerun.

Jamie didn't need to help Seattle this day. E2's second dinger of the day powered a 7-2 Seattle win. The M's looked good even on the low definition prison television. The victory was almost anti-climactic for Jamie, but he went wild right along with Seattle Mist fans and players. The bandwagon picked up speed. Jumping on board were fair weather friends and even the cynics burned so many times in the past. The collective mental health of the region was surely at an all time high.

Jamie's own mental state was still confused. He thought, *Why not revel in this? I'm not doing anything illegal. I can write whatever I want in my own scorecard. I didn't ask for this power. I'm just like a coach asking his players to execute. I'm not going to feel guilty if my mental telepathy is working!*

But, of course, he was just trying hard to rationalize his nagging doubts that lingered somewhere in the murky area between "illegal" and "immoral." He had a difficult time getting advice from anyone, although earlier in the season he tried obliquely with Rebecca and Father Bob. He could do little research on the subject. Dred had been the most helpful so far, although the family history on curses made Jamie suspect it wasn't an unprecedented power. He began to wonder if some Minnesota sympathizer had a similar form of the power, considering how easily their Cinderella team tied up the series with New York after four games.

Chapter Seventy-Two

"I hope Papa Llew and the Tinkler employees who voted for the AFW see just what happens when you get a union," Adam caustically greeted the television report that the AFW was on strike against Sanford Shoes after the federal mediator failed to broker an agreement before the midnight deadline. "You get strikes and everybody loses."

Mandy took strong exception to Adam's comments since her father was a union steward at Sanford. Jamie couldn't help but think, *Why can't we just stick to the topic of baseball where we can all agree to love the M's and root against New York?*

Fortunately Jamie was close to getting his wish because the deciding game in the series between Minnesota and New York was about to begin. Adam had invited a big group of friends to his townhouse to watch the game on his high definition television.

Minnesota got down quickly. By the third inning they were trailing 4-1.

As disappointment over Minnesota's performance mingled with the lingering tension of the earlier debate about unions, Jamie took a long swig of his drink and blurted out, "Hey, I've got a riddle for you. Let's say you were granted the supernatural power to affect the outcome of major league baseball games. You didn't ask for it, you didn't know how or why you had the power, but say you could influence the outcome of this game just by giving instructions to the television set. What do you think?"

"I think that once again you better let Rebecca drive you home tonight," Matt responded.

"What do you mean, what do we think?" Adam said. "Are you asking if we think it's possible? Or are you asking if we think this would be a cool power? Or are you just asking if we all know you are loony?"

"I'm just asking if we think it would be ethical to exercise the power," Jamie clarified.

"Well sure," Matt said, "all the super heroes like Superman and Batman exercise the power."

"Yeah, but they exercise their powers within a strict ethical framework," Rebecca said. "Superwoman and Batwoman only use their powers to save the world from evil. They don't use the power for personal gain. I think Jamie is asking what the ethical framework would be for exercising the baseball power."

Jamie nodded, but Matt said, "Yeah, Jamie uses terms like 'ethical framework' all the time."

"Look, do you think it's right for Michael Jordan or Tiger Woods to use their extraordinary powers to affect games?" Adam asked.

"But that's different. Those are their own talents that they have worked hard to perfect," Jamie countered.

"Do you think you and I were gifted with the same potential as Michael Jordan and that if we had just practiced harder, we could be as good as him?" Adam continued. "Give me a break. Everyone wasn't created equal. Maybe they should have equal rights. But somebody who grows to six foot ten is going to have an advantage in some sports. Someone gifted with extraordinary vision and reflexes may be able to hit a curve ball. All these things influence games. So if I were gifted with special powers or skills, why would it be wrong to exercise them?"

"Yeah, but Jordan and Woods, well, they have such public powers," Jamie replied.

"So, you can make your power public, too," Matt said. "Go ahead and give instructions to the television set."

"I wish I could. But so you think if I had the power, I would have to use it?" Jamie asked.

"No," Adam answered. "Tiger Woods doesn't have to golf. Michael Jordan doesn't have to play basketball. He can play baseball or be an accountant if he wants. But he's as free as you or me to play basketball if he wants to."

"But wouldn't there be some ethical limitations, like not being able to gamble on the outcome?" Mandy asked.

"Well, sure," Matt said. "Sports stars aren't supposed to gamble on their sports."

"Aren't superheroes only allowed to use their powers to fight evil?" Mandy asked."

"But when could you ever use the baseball power if it could only be used to fight evil?" Adam asked.

"Well, aren't the New Yorkers evil?" Matt asked, prompting a round of laughter.

"One could argue that a superhero shouldn't even use her power to fight evil let alone alter a baseball game," Rebecca said.

"So you're saying it would never be ethical to exercise the baseball power," Jamie asked with heightened interest.

"Yeah, isn't there some prime directive on Star Trek where you're not supposed to affect other civilizations even when you could help them?" Mandy said.

"You guys better hurry up and resolve whether you're going to use the power," Matt interrupted, "because New York just got another homer to make it 5-1. So we need to decide if we can ethically use the power or if we have to leave it up to some comic book characters."

After being diverted by the game, conversation eventually resumed in a different direction. The group was debating the propriety of the latest local craze, naked sky diving, when Matt said, "Hey, has anyone seen that local commercial where some car dealer has Topless Tess hawking convertibles?"

"Is she topless?" Mandy asked.

"No, they just blot out her chest with one of those black censorship strips to give the impression she's topless," Matt replied.

"Yeah, I saw it," Adam said. "She doesn't even have any lines. The announcer makes some cracks about driving topless is the only way to go."

Baseball interrupted again as Minnesota mounted a two run rally in the sixth. Interest stirred around the room. When Minnesota scored two in the ninth and continued to shut down New York, all attention in the room focused on the game.

In the tenth inning, Minnesota took a one run lead on a controversial two out balk call with men on first and third. Then the Minnesota sympathizers agonized as New York loaded the bases with one out in their turn at the plate. After almost four hours of weary watching, the gathering at Adam's house was rewarded when New York was erased on a quick double play. The party exploded in celebration, partly because it was fun to root against New York, partly because Minnesota was a weaker opponent for the M's, and mostly because it gave Seattle homefield advantage in the next series.

Chapter Seventy-Three

After assuring Art that Adam would connect him with a good criminal lawyer to fight his peeping Tom and assault charges, Llew said, "I have more bad news. The McPherson merger is off. News leaked out. You're right that we need to deal with the loyalty issue. That woman from the Chamber who is married to one of the union lawyers spilled the beans. What's her name?"

"Yeah, I know who you mean. I can't remember her name. How do you know she was the one?"

"I've got a source inside the union. I'm going to hire an investigator to track down our leak. This has cost you and me some big bucks."

"But why does the leak scuttle the deal?" Art asked.

"I think the McPhersons got goosey when confidentiality got breached. Trust was a big issue to them." Llew replied.

"Well, do you really think a big investigation is the way to go? Maybe we should lie low and hope we can resurrect the deal when this blows over," Art suggested.

"Lie low on this? I don't know. Let me think on it."

Llew didn't have much real thinking to do, but Jamie did. So he skipped Monday Night Football with his cousins and headed north on Aurora Avenue. When he got to the cemetery, he turned left and slowly made his way to his father's gravesite. He found an old concrete bench where he could sit and still see the gravestone.

Jamie thought for awhile about once again broaching the issue of his baseball power with Rebecca. He worried that raising this topic one more time would signal to her that he was obsessed with it which, of course, he was. And no matter how often he discussed it, no definitive answer ever emerged anyway. Most importantly, he was afraid of what he might hear.

Away from the noise of his everyday, hectic life, Jamie's thoughts drifted to recent conversations and particularly to what Dred and Adam had said. He began to experience a new clarity of thought. A sensation of peace filled his body. His gift of making baseball predictions had limitations and it wouldn't necessarily have been his choice. He had not been gifted with a naturally perfect golf swing, musical genius, or a brain of Einstein proportions. But neither was his gift more frivolous like being double jointed. The exercise of his power was just part of balance in the universe. No matter how much one speculates on the how and why of it all, the world is always full of some mystery.

Regardless of how he came to his conclusions, Jamie left the cemetery comfortable that he was just part of nature's balancing power. Whatever curse Dred's brother may or may not have inflicted on the Mist, Jamie felt less compelled to resolve the rightness or wrongness of it. It was enough to know that it was apparently being lifted, even if only temporarily, through channels established by the originator, but with Jamie center screen. The redemption of the Seattle Mist could possibly be the redemption of Peter Edwards. Or it could be an illusion with the curse ominously lurking for an opportunity to strike at a more painful point. What bigger disappointment could there be for the Seattle franchise than to finally make it deep into the playoffs and have some bizarre twist of fate cripple the new found hope? Even then, if you're going to be cursed, perhaps the M's deserved the notoriety of making it into the Curse Hall of Fame along with the Bambino and the Cubs.

Jamie awoke on Tuesday with his contentment still firmly in place and a genuine excitement for the first game of the championship series with Minnesota. Work was a blur and he left before three o'clock, not so much to insure arrival for the 5:05 start time, but because he was accomplishing nothing useful down at Tinkler anyway. He didn't accomplish much at the ballpark either. He wasn't needed. The underdog Minnies, winners of only 89 games in the regular season, seemed flat after their improbable victory over New York. They committed two costly errors and gave in easily, losing 7-3 to a pumped up Seattle squad.

The second game started the same way. Seattle scored two in the first to take an early lead. Minnesota came back with three in the second and three more in the fourth. By the last of the ninth, Minnesota held an 8-2 lead. Most M's fans were resigned to the idea that the series would be tied when their team headed to Minnesota for the next three games. But Jamie didn't give up easily and went quietly to work. A medley of basehits led to four quick runs interrupted only by a pitching change. With two runners on base and the potential winning run at the plate, the Minnies made a second desperate change of pitchers. By the time Thorne hit his three run walk off homer, Jamie was going just as crazy as the rest of the Mist fans.

After the game, Thorne cautiously affirmed the party line, "This series is far from over. We're heading to Minnesota and we don't intend taking the Minnies lightly. We saw what they did to New York."

Commentators were less restrained. A Seattle sportswriter mused in his column, "The devastating nature of game two's defeat may have buried the over-achieving Minnies once and for all. Seattle is unlikely to let Minnesota pry loose the infectious momentum seized in last night's magical ninth inning."

When the series resumed on Friday, Minnesota started fast again, except this time they finished even faster. After Seattle's humiliating 13-1 defeat, at least M's players didn't have to eat any words. Escobar echoed a common sentiment, "We knew it wasn't going to be easy. As we've said all along, Minnesota isn't going to give this series away. We're going to have to take it."

Others who had words to eat, went on a diet. The Seattle sportswriter who had buried Minnesota a day earlier, now forecasted with no apparent embarrassment, "This series is as close as it can be after three games. Someone has to be up 2-1 and only one bad inning kept it from being Minnesota. The Minnies have pounded M's pitching at a rate of eight runs per game and have outscored the Mist 24-17. If Mist pitchers don't find a way to get hitters out, they'll once again be watching the World Series on television. No matter who finally prevails, it looks like we're in for a good old fashioned slugfest."

Seattle pitchers did figure out how to get some outs, but so did Minnesota's ace hurler. He threw a 1-0 complete game, allowing only three hits and one walk. A paunchy middle aged man in a

Mickey Mouse costume was getting national attention for his alleged role in the recent Minnesota victories. He claimed that every game this season where he wore his Mickey Mouse ears resulted in a Minnie win.

For game five, the Minnesota front office arranged for Mickey Mouse to be stationed at the main entrance to the stadium where fans could rub his ears before entering. Talk was circulating that he would be flown out to Seattle for any remaining games. "They better bring some body guards for that guy," Matt quipped. "His ears won't last long in a hostile crowd."

Everyone around the Shoebox was enjoying the Mickey Mouse sideshow on the television but Jamie was pondering what impact a rival good luck charm might have on his own powers. As soon as the game commenced, the mouseketeer ears were forgotten. Seattle broke a scoreless tie in the fifth with their first run in eighteen innings. It was important because Seattle ended up winning 2-1 in eleven innings. Denizens of the Shoebox celebrated as if the M's had just won the World Series.

Nothing more was heard from Mickey Mouse. Jamie wondered if Mickey made a mistake going public.

Chapter Seventy-Four

The thought briefly crossed Jamie's mind. Maybe he should help the M's lose game six against Minnesota, so there could be a game seven. Things were going too well and too fast. After decades of waiting, suddenly Seattle was winning a game that could put them into the World Series. It was almost anti-climactic.

Already leading 4-2, the Mist put the first two hitters on base in the sixth. While the Minnesota manager made a visit to the mound, Matt asked his cousin, "Did you see the article in the paper about that prospect the M's are chasing down in Taiwan?"

"The one that pitches left and right handed?" Jamie replied.

"Yeah, wouldn't it be cool if you could change from a righty or lefty depending on who was batting?"

"Or maybe you're a starter that can go on only two days rest by changing which arm you pitch with," Jamie added.

It was a day for dreaming. And even though Minnesota wiggled out of their fifth inning jam, they never caught up and eventually lost 6-3. Seattle fans remained standing throughout the ninth inning, chanting with each pitch. When the last hitter popped out to short, the stadium remained packed. No one wanted to leave. Players took curtain calls. The city partied like they had won the World Series.

Uncle Art was subdued as he watched the celebration unfold on his home television. The news of his arrest was finally getting to be public knowledge. He had a big fight with his mistress when she wouldn't agree to finger Jamie as the leak in the investigation that Llew threatened. And he wouldn't get to use his ticket to the non-existent game seven.

While driving over to Adam's house the following day, Matt couldn't help but chuckle about Art's ticket although Jamie reminded him that those tickets were automatically good for the first game of the World Series. Jamie hoped that Pittsburgh defeated Atlanta for the right to play Seattle in that game.

"Why do you care?" Matt asked. "We get homefield advantage either way."

Jamie had studied the record of the two teams and noticed that Atlanta had a much better record at home than Pittsburgh did. He decided to root against them and just said, "Atlanta consistently wins a lot of games year in and year out. They scare me a little."

True enough, but Jamie was really worried over any signs of other gods in the baseball universe. Perhaps another tribe member resides in the land of Atlanta. And although the M's could play as many as four games in the Shoe, he needed the Mist to win at least one game on the road to allow his attendance at the wedding during game six.

"Yeah, but they never win big games on the road," Matt countered. "And we're a hard team to beat at home."

When I'm at home, Jamie thought, but said, "Well, the home team has won all six games in the series, so Atlanta certainly looks like the favorite now. But I'm picking the M's in seven against either of them."

Seattle fans were so giddy with their own entry in the World Series that most didn't really care which team advanced. They just hoped the winner's pitching staff would get as worn down as possible.

"Now all we have to do is find the key," Matt said as they pulled up to Adam's place.

"How come? Where's Adam?" Jamie asked.

"He's having a grumpfest with Papa Llew, so I said I'd go on ahead. Ad told me to try the key under that rock," Matt said, pointing to the dirt to the right of the front door.

Jamie reached down flipped the rock over and looked back at Matt. "No key. What do we do now?"

"Let's try the back-up key on the patio," Matt responded with no hint of surprise.

"Ad has a back-up key for his back-up key?" Jamie asked while following Matt to the other side of the house.

"Sure. You know Ad. He has a back-up in case someone uses the key and forgets to put it back. Yep, here it is," Matt exclaimed triumphantly.

"Well, you better make sure and put it back," Jamie advised. "Especially since the first back-up is missing."

"Don't worry, I'm sure he has a third back-up that only he knows about," Matt said with a laugh.

"So, what do Llew and Adam have to be grumpy about?" Jamie said as they let themselves in.

"Oh, the union leadership made a big stink with the city about us being screwed out of our fair share of business and amazingly, the city has agreed. They're going to upgrade our eligibility status and it looks like we're going to get a new million dollar contract."

"Why is that bad?"

"It's not, but Llew can't stand that the AFW is actually helping us. And Adam is ticked because now he thinks Llew will go soft on the union," Matt said with a shrug. "Some people refuse to be happy. If we passed out free $100 bills as a surprise, some employees would grumble they didn't get more. Some would gripe that we didn't use more convenient twenty-dollar bills to hand out the money. Others would bitch that we didn't give it to them by direct deposit in their bank account. Somebody else would complain, 'About time!' You absolutely can't win, so I usually refuse to try."

Jamie laughed and settled in on Adam's couch to watch the two teams battle for the right to play Seattle. A dramatic late game two run homer sealed Pittsburgh's fate and touched off a mild celebration in Atlanta. This contrasted dramatically with Seattle's boisterous clinching party that was still going on. Having been to the Series several times in recent years, Atlanta could only get truly excited if they won it all.

After a two-day break, the Atlanta entourage descended upon the Shoe on Saturday, October 25th. They threatened to bury Seattle in the very first inning when they loaded the bases with nobody out, courtesy of two walks from the obviously nervous Seattle pitcher. After a group meeting on the mound, the clean-up hitter lined a shot right at the third baseman for the first out.

The next hitter ripped the ball past the mound, but E2 made a great scoop running to his left, touched second and fired to first for the doubleplay. The cheering practically drowned out the national broadcaster who was remarking how Seattle had settled down to get out of the jam.

Jamie's reaction was closer to the truth. "Wow, we got lucky, there," he said to Matt.

A combination of luck and skill eventually produced a 4-1 Seattle lead after eight innings. The M's drew only two walks all game, however both preceded homeruns. Atlanta had out hit Seattle eight to three, but still trailed by three runs heading into the ninth. Jamie had so far restrained himself from helping and when the first two Atlanta hitters reached base safely, he wished he had power over the Seattle defense. He couldn't stand the tension and longed for a victory as quickly as possible.

Nothing came quickly. The Seattle manager wandered out to the mound. The next batter hit a sacrifice fly, scoring one run. Then came a walk. The manager returned and replaced his pitcher. Time was slowing down. The relief pitcher loaded the bases when his first four pitches were balls. More conferences. Another sacrifice fly. Finally an actual strikeout and the M's win their first World Series game. Jamie felt exhausted.

Celebration was confined to less than twenty-one hours as game two relentlessly followed. Dred prepared with his usual ritual. He arrived early and entered the park with the "standing room only" season's pass his brother had left him. He bought a scorecard and then removed a pinch of ash from the chewing tobacco container. He carefully rubbed this portion of his brother's remains on the back corner of the card.

Jamie arrived for the game nagged by lack of knowledge over whether his power of prognostication was still intact. He didn't tell Dred he hadn't even used yesterday's card. Instead, he asked, "Did you find out yet if you made the cut for the reality show?"

"Don't know what you're talking about, man," Dred said with one of his rare smiles and a wink.

Jamie smiled back and moved on. He was almost rooting for the M's to require his help so he could verify the power. But as the M's sprinted out to a 2-0 lead, the purist in Jamie resisted the impulse. He knew he had Dred's scorebook, he knew he was in the right seat, and he guessed the power was available as usual. Yet he didn't know for sure. He would bide his time.

The game itself was electric with excitement: Escobar out trying to stretch a double into a triple, the Atlanta center fielder robbing Grant of a homerun, Kuhn turning an amazing double play. The M's mothered a 5-4 lead into the bottom of the eighth. Still Jamie hesitated to touch the power. He was having fun and he knew he could save the magic for the last of the ninth. The Mist went down in order. When Atlanta led off the next inning with a line drive single to right, it looked like another last inning nail biter was coming. But the next hitter grounded weakly into a double play and the last batter popped out to the catcher. The M's now had five chances to win two games and clinch a World Series title.

Jamie still didn't know for sure how the power was holding up, but Seattle did just fine on its own. In all of the post game celebratory excitement, he only had momentary twinges where he missed being the unsung hero.

Chapter Seventy-Five

Escobar's wife was explaining that her husband's increase in batting average this season was due to dietary changes she had made at home. She claimed to have severely reduced junk food and starch in his diet, totally eliminating it after 4:00 in the afternoon. Jamie listened in rapt attention to the interview. Even though they were the ones sitting on the up end of a 2-0 series lead, the Monday travel day seemed to drag on forever for M's fans and players alike. Now even the fluffy pre-game coverage on the wives of the players was drawing big audiences.

The interviewer from the local channel was very protective of his relationship with the players, so he neglected to point out how many bacon cheeseburgers with fries he had watched E2 devour late into the evenings. The interviewer just cut quickly to a segment where Natalie Wink described her own elaborate game day rituals.

When Natalie began outlining the connection between her cell phone calls to her husband and the M's success, Jamie headed for the kitchen and mumbled in disgust, "False prophets."

"Get me a brew, will you?" Matt shouted out after Jamie. "And what are you grumbling about now?"

Jamie returned with two beers, handed one to Matt and responded, "Oh, I just can't believe all the people taking credit for the M's being in the World Series."

"You gotta lighten up, Meatball," Matt said.

Before he could muster any rebuttal, Jamie was distracted by Don Grant's wife who was assuring the announcer that she could tell how the M's were going to do by reading the signs in her pet pig's daily poop. The announcer feigned shock and made a hasty cut to commercial in the taped segment.

Matt laughed and pointed toward the screen, "See, they're just spoofing. You're too serious. Is everything okay with you and Rebecca?"

"Yeah, she's just all tied up with this wedding," Jamie acknowledged.

"Just don't let her tie you up in a wedding," Matt warned.

By game time Tuesday, an epidemic of anxious anticipation had spread throughout the local population. Fortunately, the Seattle ballplayers were less nervous than their loyal supporters. The starch deficient Escobar ripped a two run homer to jump start the M's in the first inning. Charged up by cell phone, Wink added a two run single in the second to propel the M's to a 4-1 lead.

"I'm thinking sweep," Matt whooped.

"I don't need a sweep," Jamie said. "But being up three games to nothing would be awfully sweet."

Unfortunately, the Mist smelled worse than Grant's pig as they started stinking up the joint while stumbling to a 9-5 loss. The Seattle players maintained their composure. They still held the Series lead and home field advantage. Just one win in Atlanta would put them in a commanding position.

While Donny Kuhn was dressing for game four in the relatively relaxed confines of their clubhouse, he shouted out, "Hey, I just heard they're sending Grant's wife down here to read E2's droppings because the airline wouldn't let her pig on the plane."

Rudy Wink pointed at Don Grant and announced, "False rumor. They did let her pig on the plane. He's right here!"

The comedy carried over into the game. The M's committed three errors, executed a major baserunning blunder, and broke a post season record for spitting and crotch scratching on national television. Not surprisingly, they also lost the laugh riot 10-3.

"I knew our two game lead wasn't going to hold up," Jamie moaned as he settled in on Adam's couch for game five.

"So we're back to Mr. Pessimist man again," Matt observed.

"No, I just meant the first two games came so easily," Jamie explained, "that I was lulled into a false sense that we were gaining momentum. We barely edged Boston, but took Minnesota with a game to spare. Then we jump on Atlanta."

"Two one run wins isn't exactly 'jumping on' Atlanta," Adam objected.

"But we still have two home games even if we don't win this one," Matt added, "so we are still in the driver's seat."

Jamie wanted to say that he was only planning on attending one of those home games so they didn't have as big an advantage as they thought. Instead he decided to change the subject and said, "I heard Rob was doing a lot better now that he's got some medication."

"Well, he doesn't seem to be twirling in his seat and glaring at people these days, but I keep waiting for the other shoe to drop," Adam said.

The thoughts of the trio quickly returned to baseball as Rudy Wink stepped to the plate. Rudy didn't get on base, but later that inning Larry Thorne hit a solo homerun for a 1-0 Seattle lead. "I told you at the beginning of the season that he would come up big for us this year," Jamie reminded his cousin.

Much silly debate over who said what to whom ensued until Atlanta came back with two runs of their own in the bottom of the second. Seattle tied the game in the top of the fourth, Atlanta scored one in the sixth, and Seattle knocked the Atlanta starter out of the box in the seventh by loading the bases with nobody out. Thorne was up and there was nowhere to put him.

"Just a sacrifice fly to tie it up," Jamie pleaded.

Matt trumped that with his plea, "How about a basehit to take the lead?"

"As long as we're wishing," Adam suggested, "then how about a grand salami to put the game out of reach?"

Ball one. Thorne fouled a pitch off his left foot and hopped around in agony for a minute. Ball two. And then Thorne was late on a fastball and sliced a sinking liner into the gap in rightcenter. Even though he was a slow runner, he had an easy double. However, he decided to slide a little too late and jammed his left foot against the bag. Try as he might to walk it off, he had to be removed from the game.

The pinch runner later scored and the M's 6-3 lead looked big. They nursed it through the seventh, but surrendered two runs in the eighth. Seattle fans began to sweat blood in the ninth when the leadoff Atlanta hitter singled. A walk put two on with nobody out. A sacrifice bunt was followed by an intentional walk. Suddenly the bases were loaded. At least in the previous two losses, the Seattle faithful were spared the pain of agonizing defeats.

The Seattle manager visited the mound. The middle infielders were set at double play depth. On the corners, the defense crept in for a play at the plate. All the strategy was moot as the next hitter fanned on a ball out of the strike zone.

The defense went into a normal alignment. Ball one. Ball two. In Seattle, literally tens of thousands of people were screaming at their television sets, cursing their own closer. The words varied little. They conveyed the idea that the pitcher, modified by vile adjectives, should not walk in the tying run, but rather throw strikes and take a chance the hitter can't capitalize on it. Some mentioned that he was getting paid six million dollars this year and emphasized the point with vulgar descriptors.

Whether the collective sound of the message carried all the way from Seattle to the mound in Atlanta has not been suggested, but a strike was thrown and taken. Sighs of relief in Seattle were quickly erased by ball three. The ranting following ball two was repeated wherever Seattle fans gathered. Foul ball for strike two. Runners are moving on the full count. Another foul ball on the strike two "do over". One more fastball. Crack of the bat. White speck lofted deep to center field. Caught on the warning track. All is forgiven. Seattle loves their closer once again.

Chapter Seventy-Six

Even before game five ended, Chick Pitz tracked down Sanford's General Manager in Portland to get him working on a special shoe for Larry Thorne. Sanford Shoes was on strike in Seattle, but fortunately some of the best high tech shoe engineers in the company were located at the Oregon plants.

The General Manager explained patiently, "Look I'm as a big a fan as anyone, however there's nothing we can do until tomorrow. We'll need Thorne to come down to the Lab or someone to send us a cast of his foot. We can probably get something to fit over any swelling or taping, but we can't work medical miracles and heal injuries overnight."

"The weight of the World Series is hanging in the balance," Pitz bullied, "and think of the publicity you'll get for Sanford."

"We are extremely eager to help," the General Manager assured Chick. "But just call me at the plant tomorrow morning so we can make arrangements to fit Larry's foot. I'll round up my best people. You got the number, right?"

The General Manager was a little exasperated and tempted to wait for the morning to do anything more. But he was also intoxicated with the idea of playing a role in the World Series drama, so he did make a call to the Lead Scientist in the Lab. As soon as he hung up, he received three more calls from Sanford officials who had been roused and were all independently overkilling the same problem.

Thorne himself was largely oblivious to the firestorm whirling around his big toe. He was boarding a chartered flight for Seattle, secure in the knowledge that he would be reading a lot about himself in the papers tomorrow. He had called his wife and told her to tape every sports and news show she could. His foot was swollen, but he felt good under the influence of a few drinks, a 3-2 lead in the World Series, and a day off to recover.

The charter flight would arrive in Seattle around five o'clock on Friday morning although the time their bodies had been on since Monday would make it seem like 8:00. A few of the players caught some decent sleep on the plane and they would stay up. Most would nap during the day, especially the ones partying on the plane. Thorne had celebrated for awhile, fallen asleep for a couple hours, and awoke to find he was limping badly just to get to the plane's restroom.

As they de-planed, Chick Pitz babbled at Thorne that he needed to have a mold made of his foot. Larry just waved him off and said, "Call me after I get some sleep."

Although Larry Thorne's toe was now the center of the universe for so many, Father Bob didn't even know who had won last night's game by the time his magic class ended the next day in Ashland, Oregon. He packed up the new Houdini escape devices he had bought for the class and drove up to Salem, where he had grown up. He had planned to drive home the next day, but an old schoolhood chum he was staying with convinced him to stay an extra day.

Father Bob and Jamie both moved around freely in their worlds without a thought that anyone controlled their actions. And yet, so too, the Seattle ballplayers and Chick Pitz moved about oblivious to Jamie's existence. Jamie himself was amused at all the attention Thorne's toe was receiving. He knew that Dred's scorecards were far more important. Still Jamie was particularly excited that he had not used his power once in the World Series. The M's led three games to two with two chances at home to win it all. He could attend the wedding, knowing he was available for the deciding game if necessary.

Matt watched Jamie's happy revelry throughout lunch. Finally he said, "After all the games you've attended over the years, and especially this year, the irony is that the M's are going to finally win a World Series on Saturday and you're not even going to be there!"

Jamie hadn't really thought about that before. Although it made him briefly consider and reject rooting against the M's in game six, he just smiled and replied, "It's no different than if the Mist had won the series in five games, finishing on the road."

"Keep telling yourself that, Jamie, because we have the momentum now and I think Atlanta is going down on Saturday," Matt predicted, joyously thrusting his right arm in the air.

Jamie wondered why he was going to the wedding. He wasn't in it. Rebecca was a baseball fan. She would understand. If only the invitation had come up when everyone knew about the World Series. But he was just too exhausted to try and unravel his decision now. He was lucky to get all the tickets he had wangled for the playoffs. He had taken some grief over that. No one was about to give him a ticket to a possible clinching game now. The M's were either going to win early or win with him on Sunday. The important thing was they were going to win and he was going to be in solid with Rebecca.

Chapter Seventy-Seven

With some time to kill before he had to leave for the wedding, Jamie struggled with the idea of opening this particular conversation with his mother. Finally he began abruptly at the breakfast table, "Ma, I'm adopted."

Jo turned slowly to look directly at him and replied, "I had no idea. Why did you wait so long to tell me?"

"That's very funny, Ma. Very good. But seriously, I need to know more about my adoption."

"Why," Jo asked, "what brings this on?"

"You and Pops are my parents, I know that, but I want to understand a little more about where I came from."

"Is this about your trip to Portland with Rebecca? Is something about to happen that you should be telling me about?"

"No, really, I think it would be more strange if I were never curious about it," Jamie answered.

"That makes me wonder why you bring it up out of the blue. But what do you need to know?" Jo asked brusquely.

"I'm hoping this subject isn't hurtful to you."

"On the contrary," Jo said in a softer tone. "Your adoption was one of the happiest days of my life with Marty. We were so excited to have a baby. After not being blessed, you were suddenly available."

"So, where did I come from?"

"Our lawyer arranged for us to adopt you straight from the hospital when a young woman wasn't able to keep her baby. That was not so uncommon back then."

"Did you know who my, uh, who the father and the mother were?"

"Marty and the man weren't close friends as such but they did know each other from the college baseball team. They worked through our lawyer to make all the arrangements with the girl's family."

Jamie struggled through a few more questions and all his mother could or would tell him was that his two fathers did not keep in contact with each other after the private adoption. Jo said neither she nor Marty knew the pregnant girl, but that she was from a prominent family and that she had died a long time ago.

Jamie wasn't sure what all this meant to him and whether he would mine for more information on another day. But he knew he needed to head for Portland and he had enough to ponder for now.

On the long ride down Interstate 5, Jamie realized he was finally comfortable with his scorebook powers and serious enough about Rebecca to share with her. He began by asking, "What would you think if someone told you they had the power to control the outcome of certain ballgames unbeknownst to the general public or the officials?"

Rebecca thought for a moment and replied, "I would think that maybe this someone was a mobster who bribed players to fix games or point shave. Or maybe he was not altogether right in the head. Or maybe a higher power is at work. I might think a lot of things, but why are so fixated on this topic?"

"Why do you say I'm fixated?" Jamie asked.

"Because you always talk about this, like on our Cougar Mountain hike and at the party at Adam's."

"Okay, if you don't like talking about it, we won't," Jamie said.

"I didn't say that," Rebecca corrected. "I just asked why you were so interested in a hypothetical that most people would drop after being amused by it in a parlor game."

"What's a parlor game?" Jamie asked absent-mindedly.

"You know, a party game, like charades, played in the parlor back in the day."

"Well, if people play charades over and over again," Jamie asked slowly, "why would it be odd to continue discussing this hypothetical parlor game as you called it?"

Rebecca showed a slight annoyance in her tone as she spoke, "I did not say it was a parlor game. I said it was a hypothetical in a parlor game. You can play charades many times, but no one wants to play the same charade over and over. So, if you're playing the game, 'what if,' why would you want to play the same hypothetical over and over?"

"You'd have to be a moron to want to do that," Jamie assented so quickly that Rebecca laughed in spite of herself.

"I didn't mean to cut you off," Rebecca reset to a softer tone. "I didn't think being a bridesmaid would add that much stress to my life, except with work and lack of sleep, I'm in a cranky mood. I'm especially not good at hypotheticals because I'm blunt and I deal with them too much in my job."

"I have the power to cause outcomes at the Shoe by logging them in my scorecard before they happen," Jamie blurted out.

Rebecca laughed out loud. Jamie turned to her briefly and confirmed in as serious a face as he could, "No, I really mean it."

Rebecca wasn't sure yet if he really meant it, but she replied, "I liked it better when I thought you were joking or obsessed."

"You don't believe me," Jamie stated flatly. "The woman who can hear her grandmother through the Symphony assumes I'm crazy because I can predict some baseball outcomes."

"I don't assume you're crazy, I know you're crazy," Rebecca said with a laugh. "So does that mean you believe I hear my grandmother speaking to me?"

"Sure," Jamie answered quickly before deciding what he actually believed.

"Look, what do you expect? You know I'm a doubting Thomas from Missouri," Rebecca continued. "I think that UFO's and other supernatural phenomenon are possible, but I don't believe in them based on what I know now."

"So you need concrete evidence of the supernatural before you can believe in it and yet by its nature, the supernatural defies the brick and mortar world," Jamie said.

"I don't have to see something physically to believe in it. I believe that Christ was a historical figure who existed. I don't have any evidence to believe the same about Adam and Eve. I believe men have walked on the moon, but I don't have any reason to believe that you're controlling major league baseball games with your scorecard."

"I guess me telling you wouldn't be reason enough," Jamie said. "But I don't have any hard evidence and I'm not sure I could get it because the power can be unpredictable when it is exposed. If the M's win on Saturday, I would have to wait until next April to even try to prove it to you. And it may be gone by then. But if the M's lose tomorrow, I want to try to show you the power even though it's risky."

"You really are serious," Rebecca said slowly as she shook her head. "You haven't told anyone else about this power? Not even Matt?"

"Who would believe me? Who wouldn't think I was a nut case?"

"Why did you tell me?" Rebecca asked.

Jamie paused and said, "I'm starting to wonder that myself! But like I said, when you told me that you believed the world was flat because your grandmother confirmed it to you in a visit from the hereafter, I just figured…"

"Very funny," Rebecca interrupted. "Just exactly how did you use this supposed power?"

"Mostly after I realized I had it and after some initial experimenting, I just waited until the last inning. Then if Seattle was losing, I would create a game winning rally," Jamie answered.

"So you're claiming that you were personally responsible for like how many wins?"

"More than a dozen, even if you don't count the dozens I influenced where the M's might have won anyway," Jamie said with a shrug.

"You're actually saying the M's wouldn't be in the playoffs except for you?" Rebecca pressed.

"As crazy as it sounds when you verbalize it, that is the plain truth," Jamie replied with resignation heavy in his voice.

Neither Jamie nor Rebecca was too happy with this unusual revelation. Jamie knew now that it was a mistake. Rebecca wondered who Jamie really was. In an unspoken pact sealed with an awkward tension, they both decided to change the subject. They busied themselves in talk about tonight's Halloween rehearsal dinner. Jamie was going as Donny Kuhn. Rebecca was still debating over tee shirts, one that said "Topless Tess" and another with spaghetti stains.

No matter how poorly Jamie's Halloween was going, Uncle Art's went worse. At the party he attended, someone came as Art, the bathroom photographer. And his mistress would no longer take his calls after the last one, where he again babbled about blaming someone named Jamie if investigators contacted her.

Chapter Seventy-Eight

"Whadya mean it won't be ready for today's game?" Chick Pitz yelled into the phone.

The top lab workers came into the Bluestreak shop on Saturday to work on a special shoe for Larry Thorne. Using the mold they received on Friday night, they were proud of the progress they made so far, but it wasn't good enough for Chick Pitz.

"The gel is going to have to set around the new steel plate. We can do this overnight and get it up to you Sunday morning in plenty of time for the seventh game," the General Manager explained calmly.

"There might not be a seventh game!" Pitz shouted back.

"But that would be good, right?" the genuinely puzzled manager asked without any hint of sarcasm.

"Can't you do a speed setting of some kind?" Pitz barked.

"We did vent one of Thorne's shoes we had on hand and already sent it up to you by hot truck. If he uses it, you've got to understand that it's only temporary. He would risk re-injuring the toe worse if anything hits it."

Pitz changed his tone slightly to a begging whine, "Look, if it's a matter of money, we are willing to pay a premium."

"I assure you, we are busting our butts on this. A normal set would take two nights. You have the risky fix on the way and we've got a better solution that we'll get to you in plenty of time for any game on Sunday. That's the best we can do."

Pitz forgot to thank the General Manager and his crew for all the extraordinary hard work and overtime they were putting in on this project. Later on the pre-game show, he would at least acknowledge the great effort the Sanford team in Oregon was devoting to engineering an emergency shoe.

As Jamie listened to that pre-game show, he suddenly realized he had forgotten about Dred. He called Matt on his cell phone and said, "Listen, you gotta do me a big favor. Before the game, look for Dred at the left field entrance. Tell him I tried to contact him but couldn't track him down. I forgot to tell him I'm at a wedding and won't be at the game, but I'll be back tomorrow if there's a seventh game."

"Are you trying to be funny?" Matt finally said.

"No, I really don't have time to explain right now. Just find Dred and tell him that, will you?"

"What is it with you and this Dred guy anyway? Look, I can't guarantee anything. It's a zoo here. The logistics today are crazy. And so is Dred by the way. The chances of me seeing him are slim."

"He'll be at the left field entrance looking for me," Jamie repeated, knowing that Matt would take care of it despite his protests.

The wedding reception was just a blur to Jamie. He wandered and danced through the evening as if he were a zombie groom. Rebecca was in her element, flitting amongst her friends, people that Jamie didn't really know. He was certainly proud to be her escort, as she looked absolutely stunning in the bridesmaid dress she had disparaged as being so ugly. Jamie followed the game by sporadically joining some other sports addicts who were huddled around a television in the back bar.

As it turned out, the M's were happy enough not to start Thorne in Saturday's game. It would give him an extra day to heal. He would be available to pinch hit if necessary, especially if the M's could knock Atlanta's ace out of the box. According to baseball's righty/lefty convention, the right-handed Thorne should feast on Atlanta's left-handed starting pitcher. But instead, he was 9-61 (.148) with no homeruns lifetime against him. This statistical anomaly appeared to defy explanation, but the media explained it anyway with some half-baked and unbaked theories. Thorne never did get a chance to pinch hit. The Atlanta ace threw a five hitter over eight innings and by then, the M's were down 8-2 and in need of much more than one Thorne hit.

Jamie didn't know whether to be depressed over the loss or excited that he would get to see game seven. Both Friday and Saturday evenings were so hectic and laced with alcohol that the weekend came nowhere near resembling a romantic getaway he had fantasized about. He knew he should have kept the baseball scorecard prediction business to himself, but still he gave Rebecca a sealed envelope with the words "Seventh Game Predictions" scrawled across the front. She slipped it into her purse.

Chapter Seventy-Nine

After a fitful sleep, Jamie quietly packed his suitcase while Rebecca pretended she was asleep. She didn't have to get up for the bridesmaids' hike for at least another hour, so Jamie decided to leave her a note. When he went to write it, he noticed his prediction envelope sitting in the wastebasket unopened. His heart sank as he hastily scrawled, "Have a great hike. Headed to the game."

He quickly fled the room for Interstate Five and consoled himself that he wouldn't have to worry about whether his written predictions would work or not. He could concentrate his efforts on any last inning heroics if needed.

Rebecca tried, but couldn't get back to sleep. While dressing for the hike in slow motion, she noticed Jamie's envelope had fallen out of the purse that she had haphazardly tossed on the table the night before. She retrieved the envelope from the basket and opened it with a nail file. She quickly scanned the message inside which read, "Let's celebrate the World Championship when you get back to Seattle. The first four Seattle batters in the second inning will hit a single, double, triple, and homerun in that order."

Rebecca shook her head as she folded the paper and put it into her purse. She wondered what Jamie would try to say about this after the game. By the time she left for her hike, Jamie was approaching Exit 68 on I-5. A sign for Puffy's caught his attention and he swerved to make the exit. After pulling into the restaurant parking lot, he searched his wallet and found the Puffy's business card Dred had given him that day he was working at the Shoebox. It clearly stated, "Good for a free brunch" and was signed "Dred."

Jamie hadn't expected to eat on the drive home, but the "Best in the State" brunch slogan on the sign reminded him of the business card. He was surprised he hadn't thought of it before since he was hungry for any information at all on Dred and the Edwards family. He knew he had plenty of time to eat, drive home, nap, and shower before the 5:00 p.m. game. So he sheepishly presented the business card to the hostess.

"Mama, we got another one of Uncle Dred's cards," the hostess yelled over to the heavyset woman behind the counter.

Mama motioned Jamie over to the counter and asked if he was alone. Jamie nodded affirmatively and she pointed him toward the seat at the end of the counter while she poured him some coffee. Although Jamie hadn't asked for any coffee, he was willing to drink it this morning.

While waving to some customers at the front door, Mama said, "Now you just let me know if you need anything. The brunch is laid out over there in the Lewis and Clark Room. Juice and other drinks are included and you'll find them all set up. So help yourself."

Mama scurried off and Jamie went exploring in the Lewis and Clark Room. The walls were painted in large murals depicting what Jamie presumed to be scenes from the Lewis and Clark Expedition. He grabbed an orange juice and filled his plate with scrambled eggs, bacon, hash browns, and blueberry pancakes.

As he walked back down the hallway with his food, Jamie glanced idly at the photographs on the wall, wishing Peter Edwards were alive. *He might be better able to explain things than Dred could,* Jamie speculated to himself.

Suddenly he stopped abruptly and almost dropped his plate right in the hallway. Some juice sloshed out of his glass as he swiveled his body closer to a familiar photograph. Hanging in Puffy's hallway was the same championship picture Jamie passed every day on the landing at home. He squinted at the inscription to Coach Puffy Edwards and remembered that Peter Edwards was the coach of the Seattle Community College baseball team when Jamie's father was playing.

As he slowly made his way back to his seat, the connections overwhelmed Jamie. Peter Edwards getting blackballed over a pregnancy. Jamie being adopted from someone on Marty's baseball team. The Dred connection started to make some sense, but Jamie ached for more information. Immersed in thought, he dawdled over his food. Mama came by and asked suspiciously, "Is everything all right with your meal?"

Jamie stopped playing with his food, and assured her, "Oh yeah, thanks, the food's great. By the way, where does the name Puffy come from?"

"Oh, it's just my brother's nickname. Came from his initials. PFE sounded a little like Puffy and he was always bragging about one thing or another. He didn't use the name Peter after he came back here and opened the restaurant. Now, are you one of Dred's friends from El Salvador?"

"No, I'm from Seattle."

"I mean from that place we call El Salvador, up on Capitol Hill in Seattle?"

"You mean, El's Safe Door?" Jamie asked.

"Yeah, that place. Dred's given his card to a few people from there. Real nice people," Mama said.

"When I came in here, I heard the hostess call him Uncle Dred," Jamie said as his mind raced with the idea of taking a chance and testing a suspicion. So he continued quickly with a lie, "But Dred told me that his brother only had a son and that the boy was put up for adoption a long time ago."

"That's my daughter and I'm sister to Puffy and Dred. And Dred shouldn't be airing that private family business to strangers," Mama scolded.

"Oh, I'm not a stranger. Dred and I are really close and have been for quite awhile," Jamie said as he reeled with the significance of Mama's confirmation.

Mama eyed Jamie carefully and said, "How come I've never heard of you? Where is Dred and exactly how close are you?"

Before Jamie could answer, his cell phone went off, generating a mixture of embarrassment and annoyance. He checked and saw the call was coming from Adam. He apologized and walked toward the door to take the conversation outside. He answered tersely, "This better be important."

"Very important, Jamie," Adam began in his most officious lawyer voice, "Jeffrey Anne just called me from the plant. She says she found a long, rambling note from Rob. She happened to come in today to stuff the envelopes with the pay rate changes and she took a tour of the plant to see if the union was posting anything illegally. She saw the note on Rob's desk and called me because among other things it said something about tying up his ex-wife and her boyfriend and strapping them inside a Tinkler Toilet at the Olympia worksite."

"What?" Jamie shouted into the phone.

"Now, don't panic. He's the guy who once said that the President of the United States sent him a coded message through his television set, telling him that it was vital for the defense of the country that he bring the union into the Tinkler workplace. But we haven't found Rob yet, so we're not sure of anything. Now, you're driving up from Portland today, right?"

"Yeah, I'm in Chehalis right now," Jamie answered.

"Good, could you buzz by the McPherson site in Olympia and make sure everything is okay? It will help us track Rob down and know if we need to call the police or anything. Meanwhile, I'll see if I can locate Rob's ex-wife and/or her boyfriend."

"Sure, sure," Jamie numbly replied.

"Call me if you learn anything and I'll do the same for you," Adam said curtly as he hung up.

Jamie stared at his phone for a second or two, glanced at Puffy's, and headed straight for his car. It was 8:52 a.m. Chick Pitz was already on his seventh phone call of the morning.

Chapter Eighty

By the time Father Bob hit the road a little before ten, Jamie had already pulled up to the McPherson Construction site in Olympia, found it locked up tight and decided on a course of action out of character for him. He didn't see an emergency phone number posted and wasn't about to call the McPhersons on Sunday morning anyway. He tried to call Adam's cell phone, but the line was busy. Jamie saw no sign of dogs, so he parked his truck near the fence, got up on the cab, and climbed over the fence, letting himself down on top of a big trash container.

Jamie detected no sign of Rob or any disturbance whatsoever, but to be safe, he began to methodically open and check out the inside of each Tinkler Toilet unit. After searching the two near the gate, he began to circulate throughout the site to make sure he covered each unit. By the time he experienced the relief of finding nothing amiss, he confronted a new anxiety.

A policeman had pulled up to Jamie's truck and was standing next to his squad car with his hands on his hips. Jamie froze in terror when he spotted the officer staring at him intently. The policeman motioned for Jamie to join him and Jamie scrambled back over the fence in reverse of how he originally scaled it.

"And what do you think you're doing, sir?" asked the officer in an accusatory manner.

"It's not what it looks like," Jamie assured the policeman.

"That's good, because it looks like maybe you're getting ready to load your truck with construction supplies that don't belong to you."

Jamie stammered, "Not at all, I'm with Tinkler Toilets and, uh, I was just inspecting them for, uh, any irregularities."

"Why don't we start with some identification?" the officer suggested sternly.

Jamie fumbled for his wallet and produced his driver's license.

The officer studied the license and asked, "So you're Jamie Mudd? Do you have anything that says you work with Tinkler Toilets?"

"No," Jamie answered, "the normal delivery guy carries a key to this site, but I'm doing a special check."

"A special check on Sunday morning?" the officer asked.

"Yeah, see the regular guy on this route has gone a little wacko and was making some threats about stuffing his ex-wife and her boyfriend in the toilets on this site. And since I happened to be driving up from my wedding in Portland anyway…"

The officer interrupted gently, "So you just came from your wedding?"

"Not 'my' wedding," Jamie corrected, "but the wedding I went to with my girlfriend."

"And where is she?" the officer inquired.

"She's back in the hotel in Portland or actually by now she is probably out on a hike with the bridesmaids."

"So your girlfriend got married without you?" the officer asked with just a tinge of sarcasm.

"No, no, no, she was one of the bridesmaids. The wedding was yesterday and I headed back early for the World Series game. Then I got this bizarre call from our lawyer to check out this site to see if anybody was locked in our toilets. We thought it was a hoax and it looks like it was," Jamie exclaimed with a certain smugness that came from finally giving an explanation that made sense.

"So you're playing in the World Series today?" the officer asked smartly.

"Just watching today," Jamie smiled.

"Have you been drinking today?" the officer asked.

"No," Jamie responded with an annoyance wrought from his surprise that things weren't going as well as he thought. He became acutely aware that he hadn't showered and was in rumpled clothes he had thrown on in his haste to leave the motel quietly.

As the policeman continued to eye him, Jamie made the common mistake of filling the silence with too much information,

"Well, I've had nothing to drink since I got up this morning. I did have some drinks after midnight so technically I had some today."

"Why don't you join me down at the station and we can straighten all this out, sir?" the officer asked politely.

"Can't we just straighten it out here?" Jamie pleaded. "I've really got to get back to Seattle."

"I think it would be better to do it at the station," the officer suggested firmly.

While Jamie was riding in the squad car to the station, Chick Pitz was going even crazier because the Thorne shoe was not yet on the road. The Sanford officials had assured Pitz all along that the shoe was going to be leaving by 11:00 a.m. Sunday and everything was still right on schedule. But until the shoe actually arrived, Chick was destined by nature and occupation to churn as if his incessant frenzied activity was necessary to the successful completion of the mission.

Chapter Eighty-One

"Sorry about the false alarm," Adam said as he assured the officer that he had sent Jamie to check on the McPherson site.

"But is this Rob fellow still at large?" the officer pressed.

"No, he's actually at a convention for supporters who want to reinstate Pluto as a planet," Adam said.

It took a couple more exchanges and the McPherson phone number before the officer decided to wash his hands of a very sober Jamie and drive him back to his truck. Jamie started to shake as he headed back to the Interstate and suddenly realized he needed to make an emergency pit stop. After a quick bodily evacuation and a few very deep breaths, Jamie was back on the road that was now slick from a light rain. Finally he got Adam on the phone and demanded, "What was all that about?"

"Look, Jeffrey Anne overreacted to a note Rob wrote a long time ago in a therapy session. The note was supposed to be burned as part of the exercise, but Rob kept it and it's been buried on his desk for awhile. No one was ever supposed to see it. Jeffrey Anne must have been rummaging through his desk, trying to get dirt on the union," Adam explained defensively.

"Not good enough," Jamie said.

"Some day you'll laugh about this, Jamie. Part of the problem is Rob's ex-wife went missing under suspicious circumstances. But after a few emergency calls, we found out that she left to be the star bachelorette on some reality show. It's all supposed to be a secret until the show airs. Oh yeah, and Matt wanted me to tell you something about, let's see, what was it?"

"Look I gotta go," Jamie said as he hung up. He was slick from his own sweat, driving now in a rainstorm, and too frustrated to talk or play any cute verbal games his cousins may have concocted this time.

As much as Jamie was sweating, Chick Pitz was winning the perspiration race. It was a little over four hours until game time and the Thorne shoe was now on Interstate 5 around Olympia, according to the latest check-in from Pitz. "Where are you now?" he would ask the exasperated driver every ten minutes or so.

At 1:10 p.m., Jamie was about five miles north of Olympia and he didn't think his weekend could get any worse. But then Chick Pitz made one call too many. The Sanford Safety Shoe driver reached for the cell phone, but knocked his coffee backward from the cup holder into his lap. He yelled, "Hot damn," as he jerked the steering wheel, causing the van to fishtail from the left lane into the middle one where Jamie was driving fairly conservatively. He was not speeding and he was not tailgating, but he could not avoid nicking the back right bumper of the swerving Sanford van.

Even though the two vehicles intersected ever so slightly, the physics of speed, direction, and wet pavement sent them both into orbits that could no longer be controlled by the drivers. In fact, the instinctive driver reactions on brake and wheel compounded the dangers. Eventually Jamie's truck came to rest upside down on the grass median. The mangled cab was crumpled down into the dirt so far that it looked physically impossible for a man Jamie's size to be in one piece. The Sanford van came to rest pointed south in the northbound passing lane with five other cars connected to one long train of metal.

Father Bob was driving one of the first cars to avoid the rear end party, possibly due to the luck of his spin more than anything. After he caught his breath, he ran on to the median, where he was surprised to hear a live person moaning in the upside down truck. A big old battered sedan with AFW union stickers on the bumpers pulled around the chain of cars. After parking on the left, a large man in an orange sweatshirt emerged with his cell phone. Father Bob shouted to him, "Call 911, there's a guy alive in here."

The moaning stopped. Father Bob sensed it would not be good to wait until the emergency aid arrived. The window frame had caved in, but the door lock wouldn't open. Father Bob ran to his car and returned with his magic bag. He quickly worked the lock with his pick and was able to wedge the door open slightly. He applied some grease around Jamie's shoulders, clipped off a thin piece of metal with his mini shears and called for help from the large man in the orange sweatshirt.

"Are you sure we should be moving him?" the man said as he slipped his cell phone into his pocket.

"I think he's stopped breathing. We gotta get him outa there," Father Bob replied.

The strength of the large man against the seat was all that Father Bob needed to work his magic. He wiggled Jamie free of the window in just a few deft maneuvers. Jamie's exit was gentle since the top of the cab was only a couple of inches from the ground. The large man in orange confirmed that Jamie was not breathing and immediately began mouth to mouth resuscitation.

The scorecard for Jamie's life took a turn for the good when he started breathing again. The man in orange became the next player on center stage when he recognized Jamie's left pant leg was soaking up blood at an alarming rate. He was able to cut open the pants with a jack knife he extracted from his front pocket. Ripping off his own shirt for the tourniquet, he quickly stopped the bleeding.

While it seemed like forever, emergency vehicles were on the scene in a matter of minutes after the extraction. Jamie was removed in the first ambulance. The driver of the Sanford van sustained head injuries and he was taken in another aid car. Fortunately there were no fatalities in any of the affected vehicles. Away from the scene, Chick Pitz was trying to have a heart attack. Convinced that the Sanford van driver was now ignoring his calls, Pitz began ringing up any top Sanford officials he could get on the line.

The hyperactivity by Pitz stirred up enough intelligence that he actually found out about the crash before Jamie's family. It was almost three in the afternoon when Sanford was finally able to dispatch a team to the scene to try to recover the Thorne shoe. On Monday, they would send someone around to the hospital to check on the driver.

Chapter Eighty-Two

Matt was mildly surprised that Jamie wasn't back from the wedding when he showed up at his house at the appointed hour. He couldn't get an answer on Jamie's cell phone, but left a message, "Hey, Meatball, where are you? It's after two. Did Adam give you my message that Dred said he wasn't going to be at today's game? He said to tell you he got the part and was flying out of town and that you'd know what he meant. My guess is he meant he wanted to sponsor you for membership in the Crazy Club. Uh, oh, gotta go, your mom needs something. Call me."

"Jamie's been in an accident. He's in the hospital!" Jo screamed as she waved the directions that Father Bob had just given her over the phone.

Father Bob had not even recognized Jamie when he pulled him from the car, but had retrieved his wallet when it fell out of a pocket during the extrication.

"Is he going to be okay?" Matt asked.

"Father Bob doesn't know yet, but he'll call us from the hospital if you call him at this number and give him your cellphone number," Jo said with remarkable presence of mind.

Matt drove the two of them to Olympia, leaving messages for Llew and Adam on the way. Father Bob was not able to provide much information by the time Matt and Jo arrived at the hospital. A young, curly haired doctor finally joined them in the reception area and said, "Jamie has been through a lot. We think he's going to be all right. We're optimistic that he won't have any lasting problems. However, he has been delirious. He keeps repeating, 'I wish I had spent more time at the office.'"

Matt let out a laugh, but quickly sobered up under the somber stares of the two women. He tried to mutter something about a private joke with Jamie as the doctor talked over him, "Jamie's heavily sedated right now, but you can see him if you like."

While Matt and Jo waited patiently with Jamie, game seven of the World Series began. At the same time, the recovery team for Sanford exited from the wrecking yard where they had finally found the Thorne shoe in the damaged van. They were rushing to the very game they were listening to on the radio. The navigator's job was to stay in constant phone contact with the now hysterically incoherent Chick Pitz.

Jamie had been moved to a room with a television over his bed. It didn't take long for Matt to suggest, "Maybe we should turn on the game. It might help Jamie come back to consciousness because he loves baseball so much."

Jo was dubious and didn't want to interrupt Jamie's rest, but after a time when the doctor returned, Matt received everyone's permission to turn on the game with a low volume. Happily for Matt, the M's were ahead 5-1 in the top of the fourth. But Atlanta had the bases loaded with only one out. Matt grimaced and stifled his groan when Atlanta's third baseman singled sharply to left, driving in two runs. Matt had an even tougher time restraining his enthusiasm when the Mist turned a double play to end the threat.

Matt was surprised to see that Thorne wasn't playing as predicted, but the missing shoe may have actually helped the M's. When Thorne's replacement batted in the fifth inning, the graphic showed he was two for two with two runs, a triple, homer, and three rbi's. Unfortunately, Seattle was unable to mount any further offense through the eighth inning. Atlanta tacked on a run in the seventh and the M's clung to a 5-4 lead heading into the ninth.

Only three outs away from their first World Series championship, the Mist closer gave up a leadoff homerun. Matt could not contain his disgust. "Dammit, no," he exclaimed as the ball nestled into the right field seats. Matt quickly softened his voice and turned to apologize to Jamie's mother. But Jo was absorbed with the awakening of Jamie.

Jamie was fairly groggy at first. By the time Jo fetched the doctor, Atlanta had men on first and third with one out and Jamie was now aware of the unfolding baseball drama. The Atlanta hitter popped out and Jamie whispered, "Could we please turn the volume up?"

The doctor took Jamie's pulse and replied flatly, "We'll see."

As the commercial came on, Jamie looked around and asked, "What happened to me?"

"You were in a car accident," The doctor answered. "But you should recover if you take it easy. Do you remember anything about the accident?"

"I remember being at the police station," Jamie said.

"The police station?" Jo interrupted.

"Yeah, something about…I don't know. My head hurts. Could I have some water, please?"

"Sure," the doctor replied as she passed him the cup of water on the tray. "Then we just need you to get your rest. We can talk about all this tomorrow."

"But, can you move, so I can see the game?" Jamie pleaded.

"Certainly," the doctor said with a laugh. "But don't get too excited," she continued while looking at Jo.

"Won't the game excite him too much?" Jo asked.

"Not seeing this game is what would excite and agitate him," Matt said impatiently.

The doctor turned back to Jamie, "Okay, I'll check back in an hour or so to see how you're doing."

The doctor took her leave at the same time the commercial ended. Jamie turned his attention to the Seattle hitters. Atlanta brought in their closer even though the game was only tied. It was after all, the bottom of the ninth in the seventh game of the World Series.

Chapter Eighty-Three

The mood of the Seattle fans brightened when Rudy Wink walked to lead off the inning. But the stadium collectively sighed when Escobar fouled off two bunt attempts. Redemption was greeted with a loud roar as E2 singled to left. Mist supporters tingled with the excitement of unprecedented possibilities.

The Atlanta infield huddled on the mound with their manager, outnumbered in a hostile crowd. Under the circumstances, the home plate umpire gave them more time than usual before breaking up the conference. The Atlanta outfielders were waved in a little so that there would at least be a chance of throwing out the speedy Wink at the plate on a single. This whetted the appetite of Donny Kuhn, batting third in a lineup juggled for Thorne's absence. Donny knew that a deep fly could now get over the heads of the outfielders and that a line drive could more easily find an outfield gap.

Donny turned to catch the sign from the third base coach and couldn't believe he was being told to bunt. He lingered a little too long and then settled back in the batter's box. Although Donny was surprised that he was bunting in the number three spot, it came as no surprise to the Atlanta infield that was fully expecting it. Donny had been an excellent bunter long before he became a slugger. Unfortunately, he popped out to the catcher in foul territory.

The deflation of Donny's failure was countered with a walk to Grant. The bases were now loaded with only one out. Even a reasonably deep fly ball would score the winning run. The yo-yo continued with an excruciating called third strike on a full count pitch to the next batter. The bases remained loaded, but now there were two outs. Thorne's replacement and surprise hero was due back up at the plate. Seattle decided not to go to that well one more time. Thorne was finally going to get a chance to test out his freshly delivered new shoe against a closer he hit better than most.

The infield played deep because they knew they would have extra time to get Thorne at first. With two outs, the runners would be off with the crack of the bat, but the force was on at any base. Thorne took a mighty swing at the first pitch and looked foolish, missing by a baseball mile. Jamie groaned with groaners everywhere in the Puget Sound. His mother was startled and asked with anxiety, "What's wrong?"

"Thorne's timing is off. He hasn't played for a few days and came into the game cold," Jamie answered.

Jo did not fully appreciate the significance of Jamie's alert response and assumed he was ignoring her. She went back to reading her magazine.

Thorne took a ball, although it looked too good to take under the circumstances. He stepped out of the box, laid the bat against his body, rubbed his hands on his pants, and took a deep breath. He stepped back in the box, tugged at his cap, and slowly took a couple of half swings. The catcher set up on the outside of the plate. The pitcher shook off one sign, nodded, and went into his wind-up from the stretch.

The ball was going to catch the plate more than the pitcher wanted. As fast as the pitch was coming, the next few moments seemed to be unfolding in slow motion. Thorne squared around to bunt to the amazement of everyone in the stands, everyone in either dugout, everyone watching on television, and especially the three baserunners.

The ball bounced slowly down the third base line. As surprised as they were, all three runners were off on contact. Rudy Wink was barreling down the third base line ahead of the third baseman who was caught playing very deep. The catcher stayed home because he judged he couldn't get to the ball before Wink was by him and thought the pitcher might have a play at the plate. The pitcher was startled, yet finally made it all the way over to the third base line, but too late to make a play on the sliding Wink. So he turned and fired hard to first in an attempt to nail the thundering Thorne and save the game. Under the pressure of a World Series at stake, the pitcher made a throw right on target.

The play was close at first, yet not close enough to cause any second-guessing when the umpire called Thorne safe. Seattle Mist players and fans erupted in spasms of joy. In the hospital room, Matt jumped to his feet, turned to Jamie and yelled, "Can you believe it? A suicide squeeze to win the World Series!"

But Jamie just kept screaming over and over, "I taught him that, I taught him that!"

Chapter Eighty-Four

When Matt stopped jumping up and down long enough to register what Jamie was saying, he didn't ask what it meant but chalked it up to delirium. As happy as the hospital staff was with the M's victory, they kicked Matt out of the room and tried to settle Jamie down.

Two hours later, Llew and Adam showed up at the hospital and Matt wangled his way back into the room with them. Jo took a break when the three of them entered, but not before admonishing in stern tones, "Don't get Jamie excited or you'll all be kicked out."

Llew hugged Jo and asked Jamie if he caught any of the game. After the exchange of triumphant baseball jargon and an inquisition about the accident, Matt asked, "How did the wedding go this weekend?"

"Not so good," Jamie said. Weakly attempting a smile, he added in true baseball lexicon, "but wait 'till next year."

No one in the room knew exactly what Jamie meant, as he was thinking of Rebecca. Little did he know that she had been thinking of him. Earlier that day, Rebecca made the other bridesmaids listen to the first two innings of the game as they drove back from the hike. "I can't believe you even care about this game," one of her friends teased, "or is it Jamie you're interested in?"

When the M's led off the bottom of the second with a single and a double, Rebecca had gotten nervous. When Thorne's replacement then tripled and scored on the homerun that followed, she had groped for her cell phone.

Rebecca recorded a short message on Jamie's phone, "You are the luckiest man in the world."

And he was.

ABOUT THE AUTHOR

Geoff Stamper was born in New York where his parents and grandparents made him feel like he was the center of the universe and he has never been able to shake that feeling. He grew up on baseball in Michigan and Wisconsin, playing right field when he wasn't sitting on the bench. Managing to graduate from Seattle University and George Washington University Law School without "laudes" of any kind, he began working on a Ph.D. at the University of Washington. But when his father discovered Geoff had voted for McGovern, educational funding suddenly dried up.

Forced into gainful employment, Geoff spent four years in Alumni Relations and Development at Seattle University and 28 years in Human Resources at The Boeing Company, where thankfully he was never ever allowed anywhere near an actual airplane part. His wife and three sons find it ironic that he made a living delivering "people services" while regularly alienating family members with his own lack of people skills.

Geoff has been a member of the Washington State Bar Association since 1973. Although historically self centered, he anticipated that the day for this page might come. So he has served on the Boards of the Foodbank Warehouse in Wichita (1993-1997) and the Matt Talbot Center (a ministry of healing for the addicted and homeless) since 1998. Running for state representative in Washington in 2004, he received 30% of the vote and was surprised and disappointed not to be declared the winner. Unfortunately, it was his bad timing to pick an opponent who was actually named on almost 70% of the ballots.

The sum of all these experiences clearly qualified Geoff to write a novel. Having accomplished that goal, he has moved on to his next project of raising moles as pets. Since they are easily trained to live outside and construct their own housing, he expects a huge market. Later if he has the time, Geoff plans to win a Nobel Peace Prize.